THE ULTIM...
THE C...
WILL...

A computer renegade ... system for billions and throws the country into chaos—in a breathtaking act of electronic terrorism.

GEORGE ANDERS

His job: keep tabs on the erratic Willard, in the name of the shadowy organization that commands his blind loyalty.

MARLIE

She has the key to Willard's control—satisfy his kinky, high-tech sexual tastes.

THE COPS:
PAUL SAGER

The computer scientist in uneasy alliance with the National Security Agency, directing a supersecret campaign of electronic counterwarfare.

OTIS WHEELING

Paul's dedicated shield in the battle between cooler heads in government and fanatical White House operatives.

NATASHA ELLSWORTH

Her private war: seducing Paul to sell his talents to her electronic think tank.

THE BIG BYTE

Peter J. Ognibene

BALLANTINE BOOKS • **NEW YORK**

Library of Congress Catalog Card Number: 84-90863

ISBN 0-345-31418-2

Manufactured in the United States of America

First Edition: July 1984

For Brigid

ACKNOWLEDGMENTS

Several people were generous with their time and gave me valuable advice during my research and the writing of this book. I would like to give special thanks to: Len Adleman, for sharing his knowledge of computers and public-key cryptography; Doris Grumbach, for her encouragement; Bob Halleck, for helping to demystify the banking system; Sybil Pike, for her insight into computer language.

PART I

CHAPTER 1

The room was cold, airless; the only sound, the steady hum of the machines; the only light, the eerie green glow of cathode ray tubes.

"Look, George, you can do whatever you want. It's your metal; you own the chips. But I run this machine. Me and no one else. We agreed to that. *You* agreed to that."

"I did indeed agree to that. What I did not agree to were your irresponsible stunts."

A nervous grin flickered briefly across the wan face of Willard Zack. "Stunts? What stunts?"

"You know precisely to which I refer."

"No, I don't."

"I am speaking," said George Anders, the lines in his round, ruddy face tightening, "of your reprogramming the traffic lights in downtown Cleveland."

"Hell, what's wrong with having a little fun?"

"You call that *fun*?" said George, striving to contain his anger, the blood vessels of his forehead engorged. "I fail to see the humor of turning all the traffic lights green during rush hour."

Willard began to laugh, his lanky frame doubled over.

The muscles around George's small blue eyes tightened. "There were one hundred and thirty-seven collisions. People could have been killed. This is no laughing matter."

"Come off it, George. Nobody cares what happens to Cleveland."

"You think so. Then, let me inform you: all three networks carried it on the evening news."

"They did?"

"They most certainly did."

"Where?"

"What do you mean 'where'?"

"I mean, was it the first item? Somewhere in the middle? Or at the end?"

"I fail to see the point of your question."

"Answer me. Was it the closing item?"

George hesitated.

"Yeah, it *was* the sign-off, wasn't it?"

George nodded imperceptibly.

"That last cutesy touch to give the folks out there a little chuckle before the game shows come on."

"I fail to see the point," said George.

"Like I said: nobody cares about Cleveland."

"I care. And more important, the director cares. If you are unwilling to accept the organization's mission—"

Willard cut him off. "Look, I never would've gotten involved in this whole damn thing if I'd thought you were going to back out."

"I am not abrogating our agreement, Willard."

"Don't call me that."

"Sorry. It was a slip of the tongue."

"That's the name my old man gave me. He's the only asshole that ever called me that. Except for a couple of asshole teachers."

"Be reasonable, Whiz. The organization has given you excellent equipment and technical support. You know that. And I know that."

George paused, seeking affirmation. None was given. "Correct me if I am mistaken," he continued, "but we have provided you with excellent equipment, have we not?"

4

"You didn't get me that Josephson-junction device."

"Was that a reasonable request?"

Willard shrugged.

"I will acknowledge that I am no expert in computer science, but your request was examined. I was informed that a Josephson junction requires liquid helium so that it may operate at extremely low temperatures."

"Four-point-two Kelvin," Willard proclaimed with authority.

"Precisely," said George, "and that is the problem. The organization does have limitations due to logistics. That rules out a facility for liquid helium. Equally important is the need for absolute security. That means we must remain small in size and number of personnel. The director has been explicit on this point. We have to take *no* risks that could compromise the operation. That rules out a permanent location. We must continue to remain elite and mobile."

"I know all that shit."

"I am aware that you do. In light of recent events, however, I am equally aware of the necessity of reiterating certain points of reference."

"Meaning Cleveland?"

"That is correct. As a result of your irresponsibility, the Ohio operation has been ordered terminated."

Willard shrugged. "After the Kansas job, it's almost no challenge. Most of the banks use the same crufty old software. All I've got to do is get on line, superzap the program, and substitute my own." He paused, a wry smile on his lips. "What I really want to go after is the Switch."

"In time, Whiz. In time."

Enthusiasm ignited his voice. "The Fed's got some mean, moby machines. That J-j would make a difference." He sighed. "I suppose you didn't get the gallium arsenide either."

"As you no doubt know, gallium arsenide chips were recently put on the restricted list. They are rather hard to obtain."

"So you didn't get them?"

George allowed himself the hint of a smile.

"You did?"

George nodded.

His anger gone, Willard could barely contain his excitement: "You got them? You really got them?"

"The chips will be flown in next Tuesday morning," said George.

"I can't believe it!"

"It is all set. We leave here Friday at twenty-one hundred hours and drive straight through to Wisconsin. We have a follower there with a large farm south of Rhinelander. The weather is expected to clear Saturday evening. Tom will put up the solar array on Sunday and recharge the power units. You will have Monday to realign the machines."

Willard nodded.

"How much time will you need with the new chips?"

"I'm not sure. Two, maybe three days to knock the crocks out."

"Would you be able to run a test Friday?"

"Possibly. What's the target?"

"A small bank near Wausau."

"No sweat," said Willard. "With the new chips for a cache, we'll win big."

"For once, time is not of the essence. We plan to stay at the farm for two, maybe three weeks."

The look of ecstasy slowly faded from Willard's face.

"I thought you would be pleased," said George. "It has been your regular complaint that you never have more than a few days in any one place."

"It isn't that," said Willard.

"What is it, then?"

"It's just that it gets so damn lonely. Working on the machines eighteen, sometimes twenty hours. A sleeping bag on the floor. No windows. Can't tell if it's sunny or if we're in the middle of a fucking snowstorm."

"I know it has been difficult," said George, his voice conciliatory. "So, I am happy to inform you that you will not have to sleep in the trailer. You will share a small house with Tom and Zed about three hundred yards from the main house. You will have a bedroom to yourself. The refrigerator will be stocked with fresh meat, fruit, and vegetables." George brought his hands together with feigned ebullience. "Well, then, what do you say to that?"

Willard glanced to the side and then back again. "It beats this shit."

"Is that all you have to say?"

Willard sighed. "It gets pretty lonely here, George. Real lonely."

"I know it does. And the director is personally aware of the sacrifice you are making."

"He is?"

"He most definitely is."

"Then why won't he let Marlie come here? We could find something for her to do. She could, uh, help Tom with the solar array, like she did that day in Kansas."

"She was just a courier. All she did was bring us the new solar cells."

"She did more than that," said Willard, voice rising. "She helped us check out the system."

"We discussed this before," said George, his voice tightening. "Marlie has her own work to perform for the director at headquarters."

"Like what!" exploded Willard. "Sucking him off?"

"Do not ever refer to the director in such a contemptuous manner again!"

Silence.

"Is that understood?"

More silence.

George audibly drew a breath. The voice was restrained. "I have tolerated your abusive language when it has been directed at me because I am willing to put the mission above any personal feelings I might have. But I shall not permit you to speak of the director in so coarse a manner. If you persist, you will do so at the risk of untoward circumstance. Is that clear?"

"Nothing you ever say is clear, George."

"Then perhaps I should be more plain. Speak disparagingly of the director or compromise the mission, and you may be summarily terminated."

"What the fuck do you mean 'terminated'? Like a credit card?"

The voice was cool, even. "It means dead."

With that, George turned on his heel and opened the trailer door. A widening rectangle of sunlight entered the room, forcing them to squint.

Willard followed him down the shaky metal steps, reaching him as he neared the door of the warehouse where the trailer was hidden. The words tumbled out. "Look, George, I'm sorry. I've had the machine up since about three this morning. I can't sleep. I'm lonely as hell. And all that junk food is turning my insides into cement."

Short and muscular, George had to raise his head to see Willard's face; disgust made him turn away. Willard, with his scraggly growth of beard, unkempt hair, sallow face, and sunken eyes, seemed more an apparition than a man.

"I said I'm sorry, George," said Willard.

George drew a breath. "I accept your apology, Whiz. And I sincerely trust we shall never have to speak so harshly again."

He turned and opened the warehouse door. Willard stood in the doorway and watched him get into the back seat of the idling Mercedes. As the car began to pull away, Willard raised his hand, but the lone passenger continued to gaze straight ahead, withholding any sign of recognition.

CHAPTER 2

"Damn it, I'm mad."

Paul Sager looked up from the report he was reading and saw his wife framed in the front doorway.

"That damn computer at the bank! They lost my check. *Again*!" said Helen.

"They'll find it, they always do."

"Hmph." She closed the door.

Something on the television caught his attention; he turned to watch the newscast.

"...and while no one at the bank is willing to go beyond the bank president's statement that it is only a 'down' which has caused the bank to close its doors, people in this small Ohio town are clearly worried."

Helen walked across the room to Paul's chair and sat on the matching ottoman. The camera cut from the correspondent to a tiny gray-haired woman. "I don't know what-all's wrong," she said. "It's them durn old computers. They're nothing but trouble. They got my Social Security check in there and swallowed it up."

"Yeah," murmured Helen, "I know the feeling."

"Federal banking officials arrived this afternoon," the correspondent continued. "And while they declined to appear on camera, one of them told NBC News that the problem here is only a down—that is, a computer malfunction. But as you can see"—the camera cut to the crowd milling outside the bank—"the people in this small Ohio town don't know what to believe. They're worried about what's happened to their money. For some of them . . . their life's savings." A portentous pause. "Barry Blanchard. NBC News. Strongsville. O-Hi-O."

Paul lowered the volume with the remote control. "What's with these guys?"

"Who, dear?"

"TV types. Like Barry Blow-Dry there. They breeze into a little town that's had a tragedy. It doesn't matter what it is. A fire. Explosion. Some loony picking off motorists with a rifle. No matter what happens, it's all the same. It even *sounds* the same. Our man on the scene. The unctuous voice. The pitiful victims bayoneted before the camera.

"But what really gets to me is the way they sign off. Very dramatic. Staccato. 'Barry Blow-Dry. NBC News. Strongsville.' And then he can't even say Ohio in a normal voice. It's got to be 'O-Hi-O.'" He paused. "You know what he reminds me of? Those old Miss America contests where you'd have all these gorgeous but stupid broads whose talent was 'dramatic recitation.'"

Helen brushed back a wayward wisp of ash blond hair and slipped the round tortoise-shell glasses from her oval face, the hint of a smile at the corners of her blue gray eyes. "What was that word, dear?"

"Huh? What word?"

"I do believe you said 'broads.'"

"Sorry. I meant 'gorgeous but stupid members of the female persuasion.' There. That better?"

"For now."

She leaned back until she was resting against his legs. "What's for dinner?"

"You mean you're not interested in my socially relevant observations about media in the post-industrial age?"

"After dinner. Maybe."

Dinner was, as usual, the cooperative endeavor of a modern American couple. Helen made a salad of bibb and romaine with a yogurt-dill dressing while Paul frenetically whisked cream, tarragon, mustard—Dijon, of course—and hot vermouth into a sauce for the boneless chicken breasts.

It was the hour of day Paul liked best. A time when he could forget about his students and computers and savor the presence of the woman he had been fortunate enough to marry. And he indeed felt fortunate. A skiing trip with two other teaching assistants from MIT. A chance encounter on the chairlift at Stowe. The icy roads between Middlebury and Cambridge during the two winters that followed. Chance. What philosophers call *fortuna*. He had been lucky. Blessed. It was at moments such as this, as he watched Helen's animated gestures, listened with amusement to her Yankee accent, and savored her presence, her love, that he realized the fragility of it all. A drunk swerving across the median. A malignancy. In an instant, it might all be destroyed.

"Paul?"

No reply.

"Darling?"

"Oh, I'm sorry. What?"

Helen shook her head, smiling. "Sometimes, I get the feeling you don't hear a word I say. Even when you're looking straight at me."

"I'm sorry, dear. I *was* listening."

"I could have sworn I saw a glaze covering those big brown eyes of yours."

Paul looked across the table. "The wine. The candles. A beautiful woman. How could I not be mesmerized?"

"You *would* mention the wine first."

"Really, I was paying attention." He smiled sheepishly. "Well, maybe not completely."

"I know. You're just a bit preoccupied."

He shrugged. "I guess."

Helen nodded. "Well, to get back to what I was saying, I think a lot of people are afraid of computers. They've been told time and time again by authority figures that computers are the servants of humankind. And for the most part, I guess they are."

"As well they should be."

"But when they hear about these banks closing because of

a down, people don't understand. They've been conditioned for years to believe that cash is obsolete, that all they need are plastic cards with magnetic strips on the back. Then a computer goes haywire, and their money vanishes as suddenly as a bolt of lightning."

"Computers don't go haywire. Sure, a microchip blows now and then; parts break down on all sorts of machines. But ninety-nine out of a hundred times, the problem is human, not mechanical."

"That's all very rational. But it's hard to keep something like that in mind when it's your money."

"Did you sound off at the teller?"

She shook her head. "What good would it do? It's not his fault." She paused. "I went through our checkbook and credit card receipts the other day, after that little bank in Kansas went down, just to see how much of our money we actually, physically handle. Do you know what I found?"

Paul shook his head.

"Less than ten percent."

"You're kidding."

"No, I'm not. And I'd be willing to bet most other people are in pretty much the same boat."

"I never thought about that."

"And you're a computer expert?"

"I'm still something of an anomaly on campus. More a theoretical mathematician than a nuts-and-bolts type."

"Still," said Helen. "Your field *is* computers. Imagine what it's like for me, and people like me, who have no understanding of them." She sipped her wine. "When I was a girl, my father used to pay his workers at the farm every Friday afternoon. He'd go to the bank in the morning, and after I came home from school, I'd sometimes help him count out the bills and coins. After he'd figured out the payroll, he'd put the money in little brown envelopes and personally hand them out to each of his workers.

"Watching the news, I thought about how all that's changed. In the past, a man or woman could see, feel, hold what they had earned. All most people get for their work today is a slip of paper telling them that a few electronic blips have been transferred from one computer to another."

Paul shrugged. "But what's the alternative? You want to get paid in a brown envelope?"

"Of course not. It's just that people no longer have control of their money. It's controlled by computers, and they can't get their money out if the machines misbehave."

"It's not machines that misbehave. It's people."

"Okay, but try to put yourself in the place of that woman on the news tonight. All of a sudden someone's told her she can't have something she in fact owns. You won't convince her that computers are her servants. As far as she's concerned, the machines are the masters."

"The old 'powerlessness syndrome'?"

"Don't laugh. You may not see it with your students, and you're sure not going to see it in your machines, but with the people I see every day, it's the principal fact of their lives."

"But aren't your patients, by definition, troubled people?"

There was an edge in her voice. "First of all, as you well know, Paul, a therapist has clients. Psychiatrists have patients."

"Sorry," said Paul.

"And it's not so much their feelings of powerlessness that make them different from other people—we all get those feelings now and then—it's the degree to which they feel overwhelmed by those feelings."

Paul nodded. "You're right."

A truce was declared, and they turned to more immediate matters. A few minutes later, the phone rang. Paul took the call in the kitchen and rejoined Helen at the table a minute or so later.

"That was odd," he said.

"Who was it?"

"Otis Wheeler. *Colonel* Otis Wheeler. Remember him?"

Helen shook her head.

"He's the fellow that had the *Journal* pull my paper on algorithmic encryption."

"Oh, yes. I do remember him. He's the one who said your theories would make it easier for the Russians to decipher military communications. 'A violation of national security,' he called it."

"He's the one."

"But that was three years ago. What does he want now?"

"He didn't say. He just said he was going to be in Cambridge next week and would like to stop by my office."

"What do you suppose he wants?"

"Maybe he wants to apologize," he replied with a laugh.

Paul was reluctant to leave the warmth of their bed the next morning but forced himself to get up, carefully lifting himself from the mattress so as not to waken his wife. Padding barefoot, first to the bathroom and then to the basement, he slipped off his robe, put on a jock strap, and looked in the mirror.

Two inches shy of six feet, Paul Sager was of medium height with a disposition to match. He had thinning brown hair, clear brown eyes, and a rugged, slightly crooked nose. Only the strong lines of his jaw suggested there might be steel within. He flexed a bicep and grinned at his reflection in the mirror. Hail, Mercury, winged messenger of the gods.

Though his shoulders were wide and well proportioned, time and gravity were conducting a relentless siege on his midsection. He raised his arms over his head to do the stretching exercises that began his daily battle of the bulge. Sit-ups and push-ups followed. His forehead was beaded with sweat as he put on an ancient gray sweat suit, laced up his running shoes, and pulled a knitted wool cap over his head. March slapped him in the face as he went out the door.

God, how he hated to run. It wasn't that he disliked exercise. One of the things he most enjoyed about their weekend trips to Vermont was the opportunity to walk. It didn't matter where they went or how long it took, as long as the pace was their own. But the daily routine in Cambridge left little time for long, leisurely strolls with Helen. So, he ran. Not very far and not very long. His was no search for a metaphysical high. No, damn it, he ran for just one reason: to delay his inevitable surrender to gravity and time.

Cool and moist, the air brought tears to his eyes and seemed to frost the hair in his nose. He forced himself into a rhythm, inhaling every other time his left foot hit the ground, exhaling on the other beats. A lone sculler was methodically rowing up the Charles as Paul turned onto the well-worn path beside the river and joined the narrow stream of runners. His legs and lungs strained at first but then found their natural cadence. Thoughts seemed to float toward him as if suspended in air. Helen's eyes. Her arms locked tightly around his back as she pulled him into her. The aroma of their mingled juices. A momentary smile came to his lips and then evaporated. A new thought hove into view.

What the hell does Wheeler want?

CHAPTER 3

A dappled Guernsey, her udders swaying heavily with milk, moved with quick, almost dainty steps toward the milking shed. A northerly brought the moist chill of distant Lake Superior against the back of Willard's neck; reflexively, he raised the collar of the red down-filled parka to shield himself. A light convection fog hovered above the stream like wisps of a gray diaphanous veil. The sodden earth squished beneath his work boots as he walked across the meadow toward the shed. How strange it all seemed. It was as if he were in a dream on a beautiful but alien planet.

Moving from one wasted mill town to another in New England, head always in a book, hands constantly tinkering with electronic gadgets, all remaining energy focused on escaping the irrational wrath of his alcoholic father, Willard had been oblivious to those green and fertile places between the cities of his childhood. At MIT and the other universities where he had briefly been a student, reality was encapsulated by a green, glowing screen. By gently stroking the keyboard, he could create dynasties of letters, numbers, symbols. The pulsing numerics of the light-emitting diodes, the sighs and undulations of the high-speed printer, the surge of paper when it all came perfectly together; such was his world. He became the absolute patriarch in a realm of his own creation.

Only now was he beginning to discover, and appreciate, the physical world in which he had been living for the past twenty-three years. How strange it had been to awaken with the sun this morning. The small cottage, its walls freshly painted in yellows, blues, and whites, gleamed brightly in the steeply slanting light. Willard had enjoyed his first full night's sleep in months, the sheets crisp and cool, the down comforter gently holding the warmth of his body. Savoring the moment, he had lain awake, a pillow shielding his eyes, as he slowly became aware of his new surroundings: the sun spreading its heat across his body, the birds' frenzied chirping, the wooden frame of the old cottage creaking and groaning in the breeze.

In the bathroom, he peered into the mirror, at first with detachment but then with a growing sense of revulsion at what he saw: deep gray hollows beneath dull brown eyes, sallow skin, hair hanging limply along the sides of his face, an unruly stubble on his chin. Amid so much natural beauty, he suddenly realized the physical toll he had paid in the two months since George had talked him into working for the organization.

Now, as he walked in the cool of a spring morning, he found himself breathing deeply of the fecund odors of the earth, and smiling.

"Good morning."

Startled by the voice, Willard turned and saw a burly red-bearded man emerge from the milking shed. "G'morning," he replied.

The farmer grabbed a shovel that had been leaning against the side of the shed, gave Willard a soundless nod, and returned to the narrow wooden structure.

Willard froze with indecision. It might be nice to go into the shed. He had never seen a cow being milked before. The man seemed friendly. He hesitated. But after they shook hands, what would they talk about? What would he talk about? Willard turned and began walking toward the cottage.

Tom and Zed were having their first smoke before breakfast, and the pungent marijuana fumes hit Willard full force as he opened the door. He closed it and went to his trailer, which was in an old barn not two hundred feet away.

He inserted an electronic card into the slot. When the door opened, he went immediately to the console and punched in the codes to deactivate the alarm. It had been sunny the day before, and Tom, who was responsible for the power supply, had recharged the batteries from the solar cells. Willard tapped the keyboard; a number appeared on the screen: 32.89. He now knew how many hours of self-contained power would be available for normal operation.

He began typing on the keyboard, each command punctuated by a flourish of the hand as he hit the execute key. The machine made several clicks and flashed a signal in green on the light-emitting diodes: GO. He picked up the pace, typing faster, hitting the execute key rapidly and not even waiting for the LEDs to flash, knowing the electronic innards of the computer would respond faster than the mechanical display on its face. The machine began clicking like a clutch of satisfied hens. Suddenly, there came a buzzing sound.

SHIT said the computer.

Willard retyped the command.

SHIT said the computer, its LEDs flashing red.

"Shit!" said Willard.

He stopped and drew a breath, a half-smile on his lips. After all, the machine was simply saying what he had programmed it to say whenever there was something wrong.

He slowly scanned the last line on the cathode ray tube and found the misplaced symbol. He retyped the command and received a green light and a gurgle of clicks.

Several hours had passed when the door opened. Willard squinted toward the intruding sunlight and saw a familiar stocky frame and curly blond hair.

"What is it, Tom?" asked Willard.

Tom closed the door and stepped into the trailer, a cannabis smile of eternal bliss on his face. "Hey, just thought you'd like to know that I'm going to, you know, run some of that sun stuff into the grid."

"Thanks, Tom. I'll switch to auxiliary."

The first time they used solar cells, an electric surge had blown several microchips. Since that incident, Willard had insisted he be warned any time the array was connected to the grid.

After switching to auxiliary power, he glanced at the digital time display. A few minutes past noon. Ordinarily he did not stop for lunch, but he had made several mistakes, stupid mistakes, and decided the break would do him good. He was also aware that he was hungry. He left the trailer and walked to the cottage.

Zed was in the kitchen washing dishes. Short, dark, and stocky, Zed seldom had much to say, preferring grunts and nods to words. The team's handyman, Zed kept the van and truck running and supplied the four of them with food and clean laundry. He moved slowly and silently, and at first Willard had assumed he was mildly retarded. Then, one day when George was talking to Tom, Willard observed that Zed's seemingly impassive face was merely a facade. The dark, hooded eyes missed nothing.

"What's for lunch?" called Willard.

Zed wiped his hands on a dish towel, opened the refrigerator, and pointed to the sandwiches stacked neatly in plastic bags.

Willard leaned against the refrigerator door and looked inside; moments later, he smelled something foul. Several seconds passed before he realized the odor was coming from his own armpit. Closing the door, he went straight to the bathroom, stripped, and turned on the shower. He scrubbed himself hard with a washcloth and shampooed his hair.

Then, he padded to his bedroom, opened the closet, and found shirts and pants neatly lined up on hangers. Zed had been doing laundry that morning.

Oblivious to his dripping hair, he put on his normal uniform of the day—white button-down shirt, khaki slacks, and a black belt several inches too long—and returned to the refrigerator.

"Thanks for the laundry," said Willard.

Zed responded with a nod as he left the kitchen.

Willard opened the refrigerator, took the top two sandwiches without even checking to see what they were, grabbed a can of soda, and sat at the table. He began to eat almost mechanically, alternating bites of sandwich with sips of soda but tasting neither, his mind elsewhere.

Marlie. He had never seen a woman so beautiful. No, perhaps he had. But none of them, he knew, had ever really seen him. They would stride gracefully by on the campus or on the street without the slightest flicker of acknowledgment. At night, as he stroked himself beneath the covers, he would try to imagine that a beautiful woman was actually touching him, but his mind could never conjure a face. Two large breasts with blond hair above and below—such were the perimeters of his imagination.

Now, he had a face to accompany his fantasy. Marlie's face. She was different. She had spoken to him. Though it was only a few words, she had met his eyes and seemed even to smile. No other woman, no *beautiful* woman, had ever done that. What had she said? It was only a few words, but try as he might, he could not remember. All he could see was her face; all he could imagine was her body.

Willard had been hanging around the computer center at Stanford, using a borrowed I.D. card to gain access to the machines, when he met George at a house where several fellow hackers lived. Silicon Valley had hordes of recruiters who did nothing but look for new talent. George was older and dressed far too neatly to be a hacker himself, so Willard assumed he was a corporate scout.

Then, one night while the others were out, George asked Willard if he had ever broken into a company computer. Suddenly concerned that George might be a federal agent, Willard clammed up. But when George began describing the way one of his friends had broken into the computer of a San Francisco firm, Willard began listening intently. Soon he was filling in some of the technical details George either missed or got wrong. With little additional prompting, Willard described several of the dozens of computer break-ins he had pulled off. Though he could have crashed those computers, he was content to do little more than browse through the files.

When George asked why he had done it, Willard mumbled something about the excitement and the challenge.

"So, you see it essentially as a game," George had said. "Is that right?"

"Yeah," Willard had replied, a big grin on his face. "That's what it is. That's all it is."

Several weeks later, Willard laughed when George offered to provide him with several million dollars' worth of equipment to play a game against some of the banks. The next day, when a trailer jammed with computers, receivers, and antennas appeared, Willard realized it was no joke. Hesitant at first, he took only a few seconds before deciding: What the hell, I'll do it. The banks? The Federal Reserve? Such abstractions meant nothing to him. What mattered was the game.

George hated him now, that much was certain. What was equally certain was that there would be no operation unless

George gave him what he wanted: Marlie. Though George denied it, Willard sensed that George had the power to bring Marlie to Wisconsin.

Eyes closed, smiling now, Willard leaned back in his chair. George might despise him, but he had no choice. If he wanted Willard to work the machines, he would have to meet his price. And that price was Marlie.

A bank for a woman. The thought made him grin. Now there's a fair exchange.

But suppose she does come. Suppose Marlie actually comes here. He suddenly realized that he had absolutely no idea what to say to her, how to approach her. Oh, he knew exactly what he wanted her to do. Lying alone in his sleeping bag in the trailer, he had spent hours fantasizing about her and what they would do, what she would do to him. He replayed the scene night after night since that first time he saw her nearly two months before. He had even toyed with the idea of programming his fantasy on the computer and giving her the printout so she would know what he wanted. And the more he thought about it, the more the idea took hold. He could never tell her, face to face, the wonderfully obscene things he wanted her to do with her hands, her tongue, her cunt. But a program? He was grinning broadly. Yeah, he thought, I'll do it.

CHAPTER 4

Though medals and epaulets were nowhere to be seen, Otis Wheeler's light gray, three-piece wool suit was poor camouflage: the man was unmistakably a military officer. Erect in bearing, though a bit too short for a recruiting poster, Wheeler had wavy blond hair that was graying at the fringes, a strong, straight nose, and a steady gaze. A blue-eyed eagle.

Wheeler extended his hand and a toothy smile. "Dr. Sager. How good to see you again."

"Good morning, Colonel," said Paul, as they shook hands. He unlocked the door and let Wheeler precede him into the book-cluttered office.

Paul took a stack of papers off the chair beside his desk, brushed away the chalk dust, and motioned for Wheeler to sit. A few minutes later, he returned with two Styrofoam cups of coffee.

There was an awkward silence as each man faced the other.

Wheeler spoke first. "I'm sure you're wondering why I'm calling on you."

Paul gingerly sipped his coffee and then nodded.

"Since our last, ah, encounter," Wheeler began, "I have been reassigned from the National Security Agency to the National Security Council; that body, as you may know, is responsible for giving the Agency policy guidance. I'm on Dr. Simpson's staff. You were colleagues here, if I'm not mistaken."

"So we were," said Paul. He and Wiley Simpson had indeed been colleagues on the MIT faculty, but acquaintances rather than friends. Formerly a liberal, Simpson migrated to the right soon after winning tenure and became something of a campus curiosity: a leading theoretician of the neoconservative movement and author of right-wing screeds for political journals whose audience was minuscule, loyal, and rich. He might have remained an obscure academic but for the improbable circumstances that propelled one of his most faithful readers into the White House and Simpson into the West Wing as the President's national security adviser.

Wheeler continued: "Because of your work in algorithmic encryption, Dr. Simpson suggested I speak with you. To get straight to the point, he would like you to do some consulting for the Agency."

Paul smiled and gave a slight shake of the head. "As you might imagine, members of the faculty here receive quite a few offers to consult for the government. It's permitted, if the work does not take away from teaching and lab responsibilities. In fact, it's encouraged in a subtle sort of way, so the government will, to be blunt about it, continue to pour money into the school. But my own inclinations are to decline such offers. You may be aware of that."

Wheeler sipped his coffee. "Yes, I am. In fact, Dr. Simpson and I discussed this very point just before I called you last week. However, he remained insistent that I see you." He paused. "At the risk of sounding a bit melodramatic, the government is confronted with a technological problem of considerable magnitude. At this point, I am only at liberty to say that it involves computers and the security of extremely sensitive data."

"I don't wish to be impolite, Colonel, but I have no interest whatever in consulting for the military. I can't tell you how many approaches I've received. Weapons labs, telecomm outfits, the Army, Navy, Air Force—I've been asked by just about all of them at one time or another. And my answer's always been the same: no."

"Would you under *no* circumstances consider helping your government?"

Paul pondered the question and then replied: "The government—or, as you put it, *my* government—is a rather diverse collection of departments and agencies. If you were to ask me to help Smokey the Bear prevent forest fires, I'd be more than happy to. But I rather doubt the Forest Service needs someone with my background."

Wheeler relaxed and chuckled appreciatively. "If I were here representing so esteemed a government official as Mr. Bear, they'd have sent me in uniform." He paused, looking for, and receiving, a smile. "I'm afraid my mission is a bit more difficult than that. We, meaning Dr. Simpson and the Council, would like to have you serve on a temporary basis as a consultant to the National Security Agency."

"NSA is responsible for military communications, is it not?"

"Military *and* diplomatic," Wheeler emphasized. "But yes, it does come under the Department of Defense. Its current director wears an Army uniform and three stars."

"As a matter of personal conviction, then," said Paul, "I would have to decline."

Wheeler nodded. "We anticipated as much."

"You did? If you knew I'd say no, why did you come?"

"Because," said Wheeler, his smile not wavering, "my mission is to persuade you."

"Though I bear you no personal grudge, in spite of your role in that, ah, unpleasant episode . . ." He let the words trail off.

"It was the director of the NSA, not I, who made the decision to oppose publication of your paper in the *Journal*. He was concerned that the theories and calculations in your paper touched—inadvertently, I'm sure—on highly sensitive methods of encrypting and decrypting data communications. It was his belief that the publication of your paper at that time would have been of material value to potential adversaries."

"Meaning the Russians?"

"Yes."

Paul felt the anger rising inside him and once again worked to restrain it. "Surely, Colonel, you don't believe that Russian scientists are our mental inferiors. My paper was about theories and methods. If I can develop such thoughts, they most certainly can as well. It's not as if I was trying to give them the plans to the Norden Bombsight."

"As a military officer, Dr. Sager, I have sometimes been called upon to execute policies that I do not personally agree with. It goes with the uniform. I hope you understand that my role with regard to your paper did not arise out of any personal animus."

Whenever Paul thought about the *Journal*'s bowing to the NSA's pressure and refusing to publish his paper, the outrage that had cooled over the years quickly rekindled. Yet, as Helen had often pointed out, everything had ultimately worked out for the best. Though the paper did not get published, it had given him the idea for a book that brought together his thoughts about mathematics, computers, Rothko's paintings, and Mozart's music. *Algorithmic Metamorphoses on a Theme by Alan Turing* had not only created its own cult of followers on college campuses; it had found a surprisingly large audience of readers in the general public as well. What's more, he was still receiving royalty checks from the paperback publisher.

"Dr. Sager?"

Paul realized he had been gazing into the distance and shook his head. "I'm sorry, Colonel, I was just thinking."

"That's what they pay you to do, if I'm not mistaken." He smiled. "But to get back to my reason for being here, let me address what the government would do if you would agree to consult for NSA." He paused. "Because of the rather exacting nature of the work, the rate would be substantial. To be precise about it: twelve hundred dollars . . . *a day*."

It was, Paul knew, several times the government's maximum rate, and he was initially tempted. Hell, five or six days on Uncle Sam's payroll and he could have the electricians as well as the plumbers completely redo the house in Vermont. It was too juicy an apple not to be tempting.

Paul exhaled, fighting off the temptation. "My feelings about working for the military remain the same, Colonel Wheeler. I choose not to."

"Oh, I'm sorry. Perhaps I failed to make myself clear. The work we have in mind has nothing whatever to do with the military."

"Then why are *you* here?"

"I'm liaison officer on the NSC staff for matters having to

do with computers and telecommunications. Had there been a civilian in that billet, they would have sent him instead of me."

"I'm not at all clear, then, on what it is you want from me."

Wheeler took a final sip from the Styrofoam cup. "You are considered by many to be the nation's foremost expert in algorithmic encryption. We need to tap that expertise to protect electronic transmissions of sensitive data of a nonmilitary nature. We have reason to believe that this data is in danger of being compromised."

Paul's reply was immediate. "As you may recall, one of the principal points of my paper was the paramount importance of protecting telephone lines and computerized data links; that Ma Bell's system is about as private as a ten-person party line; that if we failed to protect these sources, our right to privacy would be undermined." Paul realized he was getting carried away and abruptly stopped.

Wheeler nodded gravely. "Dr. Sager, time has proven you right and the government wrong. You have every reason to turn us down. We realize that. What we are hoping is that you will at least consider our proposal. Naturally, you will be free to terminate your consultancy at any time you choose. And, of course, you will receive twelve hundred dollars for every eight-hour day you serve as a consultant."

"But doing what?" asked Paul. "I need to know *what* I'll be doing before I can possibly consider your proposal."

"Dr. Sager, you come from the university: an environment that encourages openness, thought, argument, dissent. My world, of necessity, is much more closed. Whether you agree with particular policies or not, I think you would concede that the government has a need to protect vital information. And that need compels individuals such as myself to be highly circumspect about what I say *and* where I say it." Wheeler glanced momentarily around the room. "I doubt your office is bugged. But it could be. I doubt there is someone across the street aiming a laser beam at your window and listening to our conversation by converting the timpanic vibrations on your windowpane into digitized speech. But perhaps there is. Call it paranoia, if you wish, but I would not be here were it not a matter of the utmost urgency. Computer experts are a dime a dozen these days. But there is only one Paul Sager. There may be other scientists as potentially able in the same field, but we have no idea who they are or how to find them." He drew a breath. "But more to the point, we have no time to find them."

"But surely you can give me some idea of what it is you want me to do."

"If you agree to work for the government, you will have complete access to some of the most highly classified information we have."

"With my sort of political beliefs? I'd be amazed if I were given clearance to that sort of information."

Wheeler smiled. "You're already cleared."

"What?"

Wheeler nodded. "Joining a student-faculty committee to lobby Congress against the Vietnam War is not exactly high treason. Of course, I'm not sure what the President would *personally* think of your twenty-dollar checks to Kennedy's campaign. Not that it matters, mind you."

"How did you get that information?"

"Political contributions are a matter of public record. The same is true for many public lobbying organizations. Health records, banking records, credit-card purchases—there's a national network now. A few strokes at the keyboard, and you've got a printout. You're a computer expert. Surely this shouldn't come as a surprise."

"You mean you've got a dossier on me?"

"It would have been irresponsible in the extreme not to have inquired into your background before seeking you out."

Paul gritted his teeth.

Wheeler took a small notepad from his jacket, quickly wrote something in it, and then looked at Paul. "For reasons of security, I simply cannot *say* what the nature of the problem is. You'll just have to accept this," he said, handing him the slip of paper.

Paul took it and stared at the three words: "Banks. Computers. Terrorists."

After Otis Wheeler left the office, Paul glanced at his watch and called Helen, catching her in the ten-minute break between clients. They arranged to meet for lunch.

Paul got there first, found a table under a large asparagus fern, and sat facing the door. Helen arrived several minutes later and squinted until her eyes adjusted to the change in light. Seeing Paul's upraised hand, she stepped firmly toward the table, a wide smile lighting her face. She reached the table and started to give him a wifely peck on the cheek, but he quickly turned her face with his hand and kissed her full on the mouth.

"Mmm! I sure didn't expect that," she said, surprise and delight evident in her voice. "I take it you've got good news."

Paul smiled. "Not really. It's just nice to see you in the middle of the day. We so seldom go to lunch together."

They sat down, ordered a half-carafe of white wine, and perused the menu. After the waiter took their order, Helen asked about his meeting with Colonel Wheeler.

"He wants me to consult for the government."

"And you told him no, I take it."

Paul grinned. "I gave him my ritual denial about not wanting to work for the military. The usual bleeding-heart stuff."

"What'd he say to that?"

"Well, to tell you the truth, he caught me off guard. Said it was definitely *not* military, though he wouldn't say exactly what it did involve."

"Did he give you a hint?"

Paul squinted and slowly, theatrically, scanned the room. He lifted the tablecloth and then picked up the salt shaker. "Zere may be sumvun listnink," he said in a mock German accent.

Helen's eyes flashed in merriment. "Paul, really."

He shrugged. "He did hint at the problem, but he did not want to talk about it out loud in my office. In fact, he wrote it down on a piece of paper and handed it to me."

"What did it say?"

He smiled smugly. "Loose lips sink ships."

There was a hint of exasperation in Helen's smile. "I'm surprised that you, of all people, would buy that top-secret hokum. It's a wonder he didn't start reciting from one of Nixon's old speeches about national security."

Paul smiled and sipped his wine. "Well, getting back to national security, the good colonel said he would not have come up here if the matter were not, at least to them, of some importance."

"And who is 'them'?"

"The National Security Council. Wiley Simpson's the director now, you know."

"Of course I know. I also know what you used to say about that right-wing claptrap he writes."

Paul had been looking forward to a pleasant hour at lunch

and was determined to steer it away from controversy. "Darling, you know I would never make an important decision without you. In ten years of marriage, have I ever done that?"

Helen reflected momentarily. "What about those horrible red slacks you bought?" she said sternly.

Just then, the waiter brought their plates: avocado and crab salad smothered with alfalfa sprouts. Later, as they were drinking coffee, Helen resumed their earlier conversation. "Paul, what did Colonel Wheeler want you to do? You said he hinted at it."

Paul nodded.

"What was it, then?" There was an odd, almost plaintive note in her voice.

"He gave me no details. He just said I would be told the entire scope of the problem once I went to Washington and that I could withdraw at any time. He also said I would be paid twelve hundred dollars a day."

Helen's jaw gaped. "Twelve hundred dollars? *A day*?"

"That's what he said."

"That's an awful lot of money for a consultant."

"It sure is. Hell, with just a few days' work, we'd be able to have the plumbers *and* the electricians redo the house in Stowe."

Helen looked at him quizzically. "Paul Sager. I do believe you've already decided to do it."

"I'm considering it. That's why I brought it up. But I've made no decision."

"We don't need the money. All we have to do is sell a few of those 'penny stocks' we own."

Helen's caustic reference to their stock portfolio brought a wry smile to his lips. A number of Paul's colleagues had, over the years, started small companies specializing in microbial cultivation, recombinant DNA, satellite-to-home communications, and other high-tech ventures. With money they had saved from their two paychecks, Paul and Helen had something to invest. Five hundred here, a thousand there. It had been done more as a gesture of goodwill toward his colleagues than as a way to get rich. After all, how high could a fifty-cent share of stock go? Quite high, it turned out. So high that Paul was almost embarrassed to glance at the stock pages. The last time he did, he had found that each of the 2000 shares of their first "penny stock" was now worth twenty-three dollars.

"Paul?"

"What? Oh. I'm sorry, darling, I was just thinking of something."

"Yes. I'm familiar with that glazed look of yours." She was smiling now.

"Then it's settled. I won't do it."

"Have I objected?"

"Not in so many words, but it's obvious you don't want me to."

Helen shook her head. "It's not that I object. It's that I don't understand what it is you'll be doing for twelve hundred dollars a day. That colonel, he wrote something down, you said."

Paul nodded.

"What was it?"

"Three words: 'Banks. Computers. Terrorists.'"

Helen was taken aback. Then she recalled the old woman on the newscast who could not withdraw her Social Security check. "Oh, Paul, this is something different, very different." She paused. "I think you should do it."

"You do?"

She nodded vigorously. "The whole thrust of your book was that we, our society, are in danger of losing our right to privacy. That computers have made it easy to invade our phone conversations and other personal matters that no one, including the government, has a right to know. Maybe you can do something about that."

"My one-woman fan club."

She smiled. "And why not? You're probably the top man in your field. And more important, you're a good man. With all those ultraconservative dodoes in the White House and Cabinet, Washington could use a few good men."

Paul grinned. "You sure you're not recruiting for the Marines?"

CHAPTER 5

The blue Chevrolet van slowly approached the bank, turned, and drove into the parking lot. A yellow light on the dashboard flashed.

"Stop," said Tom. "Pull into that space."

Zed parked the van but did not turn off the engine, which continued to idle at an unusually high speed.

Tom rapped once on the metal behind the high-backed seat. Receiving a single knock in reply, he made a final check of the microphone and wires concealed beneath his windbreaker, got out of the van, and began walking toward the bank.

George and Willard felt the door slam and could hear through their headsets the sound of Tom's shoes scuffing the asphalt and the rustle of his sweater against the microphone. The interior of the van was crammed so full of electronic gear that there was barely enough room for the two men and their backless stools. Though it was a brisk March morning outside, the heat generated by the machinery was already making them sweat. Yet both were indifferent to their discomfort as they stared at the seemingly random groups of symbols that danced across the screen of the cathode ray tube.

They heard Tom partially unzip his jacket as he walked into the bank.

"Good morning, may I help you?" The voice was cheerful, Midwestern, girlish.

"Yes," said Tom. "I'm new in town, and I'd like to open an account."

"Checking or savings?"

"Both."

"Fine," she replied. "My name's Marcia. Welcome to Wausau."

"Thank you. I'm Tom Rice."

"Hi. Well, if you'll just have a seat here, Mr. Rice, I'll get you the forms, and we'll get your account opened in no time."

George reached up and pressed the single earpiece closer to his ear. Willard swiveled on the stool to face a second CRT. Tom methodically read each item on the form as he filled it out; Willard typed the entries, one after another, onto the screen.

"What's this?" Tom asked.

"That's your account number," said Marcia.

Tom read the nine digits and chuckled. "With that many numbers, you could have a billion depositors here."

The woman laughed. "We've got our hands full with nine thousand."

After a minute or so of small talk, Tom said, "I've got several checks I'd like to deposit."

"Fine," she said. "If you'll just fill out a deposit slip. They're in your checkbook behind the checks. Yes. That's it. I'll deposit them when I enter your account on the computer."

"Great," said Tom. "Oh, one other thing. I've been looking at a car I'm thinking of buying, and my dad's going to loan me the money. He told me that his bank could send it electronically to my new account if they knew the, ah . . ."

"Access number?"

"Yeah, that's it."

"I'll write it down for you," she said.

"Thanks. You've been quite a help."

"That's what we're here for," she said cheerfully.

Tom looked up from a full dinner plate and shook his head, smiling. "I still don't understand how you guys do it," he said.

Willard shrugged. "It's easy. Just a matter of getting—"

George cut him off. "Wait a minute, Whiz. You know the rules. As a matter of security, you are permitted to talk about details only with those who have a need to know."

Willard set his fork down deliberately and glared at George. "Details? I was going to talk about the principle of the thing."

George's ruddy face relaxed. "You did well today, Whiz. All of you did. As long as you confine your discussion to general principles, there would be no breach of security."

Willard turned from George to Tom. "Have you ever seen heat waves rising from a highway?"

"Yeah," said Tom.

"Well, computers also give off energy. They call it electromagnetic radiation. You can't see it coming off a CRT, the way you can with heat waves, but with the right sort of antenna, you can pick up the signal just like it was coming from a radio station." He paused. "That's what we've been doing with all that stuff in the van."

Tom cocked his head. "Well, if it's so easy, why don't bank robbers do it?"

Willard speared a piece of meat with his fork and put it in his mouth. "It may be easy," he said between bites. "But it's not *that* easy."

"How's that?"

"Well, when we pick up the signal, it's kind of blurry at first, more like those heat waves than a radio signal." He swallowed hard. "We can pick up the transmission, but unless we have some idea what they're transmitting, it comes out like static. That's where you come in."

"You mean, opening the bank account."

"Right," said Willard. "That gives us a known sequence of symbols—your name, address, account number, that sort of thing—to match against the radiation the antenna's picking up. When the teller types those symbols or deposits money into your account, we know what the radiation from the screen should be telling us at that moment. That gives our computer something to match against the blurry signals the antenna has been picking up. It's like tuning in a radio station. Or putting on a pair of glasses. All of a sudden those blurry things become people or signs, things you can see."

"Then why do we have to intercept the line?"

Willard shoveled in a forkful of mashed potatoes and gulped them down. "That comes later. All we're trying to do now is find out what's going on in the computer. If we could stand around in the bank and watch them all day long, we wouldn't need the van. Obviously, we can't do that."

Willard turned to George. "Can I tell him what we do next?"

George made an open gesture with his hands. "So long as you avoid specifics."

"Okay." Willard turned to Tom. "Now, we know what's going on in the machine. The next thing we need to know is the language and the encryption system the machine uses when it communicates with other banks or branches of the same bank. That's a lot more complicated technically because it involves matching the signal we pick up in the van against the actual communication of that information over phone lines or between microwave relay towers. Sometimes the transaction in the bank is stored in the memory of the bank's own computer and doesn't go out for several minutes or maybe even several hours. That's where the machines in the trailer come in. They match all the intercepted phone communications against the ones we know, the ones the van has picked up. That can take a while. It took me almost three days in Kansas just to figure out their system."

George interrupted. "That was only your first assignment."

Willard acknowledged the implied compliment. "True. And it's gotten a lot easier since then because we're finding many of the banks use similar encryption systems. Not identical, but similar. In fact, I'd be willing to bet the computers will have cracked this bank's code by morning."

Zed, who had been silent throughout the meal, looked up from his plate. "Why?" he asked.

"What do you mean?" asked Willard.

"We don't steal money. So what are we robbing banks for?"

"For practice," Willard replied. "We need to have a better understanding of how computers control commercial banks before we go against the Chicago Switch."

"Stop right there," said George sharply. "Neither Zed nor Tom has any need to know about that."

Willard glowered at George, but the beady blue eyes would not yield.

"Is that understood?" asked George in a quiet but firm voice.

"Yeah," said Willard.

On Saturday, as George was getting ready to leave the farm, he went to the trailer where Willard was working.

"You've done well, Whiz. Very well," said George. "The

director will, I am certain, be as favorably impressed as I am with the rapidity with which you deciphered the bank's working methodology."

Willard grunted.

"The operation is running well ahead of schedule. We are, however, to take no action before next Friday; that timing remains unchanged." He paused. "Because you have performed so commendably here, I hesitate to mention this. Nevertheless, after the incident in Cleveland, I feel it incumbent upon me to reiterate that the director's policy on unauthorized operations remains as firm as ever."

Willard continued to stare at the green glowing screen.

"That is understood, is it not?"

"Yes," said Willard softly.

"Very well," said George. "I have a call to make on the transmitter in the cottage. I'll be on my way after that."

A few minutes later, when George left the cottage for his car, he found Willard standing beside it, hands behind his back.

"George?"

"Yes, Whiz."

Willard extended an arm and handed him a thick envelope. "You'll be at headquarters. That means you'll get to see Marlie. I want you to give her this. Tell her it's from me and that I want to see her."

"We have, I believe, discussed this before."

"I know we have," said Willard plaintively. "But I want to at least communicate with her. You can do that much for me, can't you?"

George hesitated momentarily, and then tucked the envelope inside his jacket. "All right, Whiz, but remember that I cannot promise that the two of you will be able to visit one another. You do understand that, do you not?"

Willard nodded. "I understand. But you have to understand how hard it is on me. I'm lonely. I want to see Marlie."

George changed tack. "We have sought to provide you with the equipment you requested, including gallium arsenide. We have also improved your living conditions." He gestured toward the cottage. "This, certainly, is an improvement over the warehouse in Cleveland."

"Yes, it is. And I appreciate it. I've never been on a farm before. It's nice here." He sighed. "But that doesn't change the way I feel. I still want to see Marlie."

George scrutinized Willard's face and saw his distress was

genuine. Though George much preferred this Willard to the foul-mouthed lout who sometimes challenged him, he also knew that an unhappy operative could undermine the mission. *Maybe Marlie is the key to keeping him docile, contented, working.* In that instant he came to a decision. If Marlie were necessary to keep Willard in line, he would use her.

"I will, of course, deliver your letter to Marlie," said George, "providing it does not contain any information pertaining to the operation. That is the case, is it not?"

"No, I swear, it's strictly personal. And I don't want anyone to open it but her."

"Certainly. Your privacy will be respected."

"I appreciate that, George. I really do."

George glanced at his watch. "I have to be going. The jet leaves at nineteen-thirty hours. It's sixteen-fifty now, and I have a two-hour drive ahead of me." He opened the door. "Again, let me reiterate how very favorably impressed I am with the way in which you have conducted the present operation. You can be assured the director himself will be gratified with my report."

Willard nodded. "Please see that Marlie gets my letter."

"I certainly will," said George, as he got into the car. "And keep up the good work, Whiz."

"Yeah."

CHAPTER 6

Helen had already left for her mother's house in Vermont, which was close to the one she and Paul had bought, when Colonel Wheeler arrived Saturday morning. Ready to go, Paul closed and locked the door and followed Wheeler to the rental car, suitcase in hand.

A graduate of the Air Force Academy, Wheeler had made all the right moves. He realized early in his career that valor and leadership had little to do with success in the modern American military; he'd met far too many gung-ho pilots who were outstanding in the cockpit but would never command more than a squadron. To become a general—and it would have been a ludicrous waste of his time if that were not his goal— one need only appear to possess those warrior virtues. So he went to pilot training and then to the Strategic Air Command, where he quickly became one of the youngest officers ever to command a B-52. Two tours in Vietnam gave him the indispensable combat duty to fill out his ticket.

When he spoke with civilians, he kept his references to the war brief, not out of modesty but simply to avoid explaining the rather insular, nine-to-five existence of a B-52 pilot during that time. The base in Thailand, a short drive from the warm and gentle waters of the Gulf of Siam, was a bit of a country club as so-called remote bases go, and the missions he flew over North Vietnam seemed no different from those he had once flown over North Dakota. A place on a map. A KC-135 tanker refueling his bomber en route. A few switches to flip over target, and a gently banked turn toward home.

Though he grew to dislike his own cynicism, he continued going through the motions, making the right moves. Having flown in combat, he now had to have his ticket punched at the proper schools. His wife—a general's daughter, of course—wanted to live near her parents, who had retired in San Jose, so he managed to get the Air Force to send him to Stanford for a master's degree in business administration. A tour at the Pentagon was followed by a year at the War College. His assignment to the National Security Agency came as something of a shock.

He had been skeptical of getting so far removed from the Air Force. God forbid he should be branded a specialist in intelligence or telecommunications. That, he knew, would have been a one-way road to retirement as a colonel. To get ahead, one needed breadth, or at least the appearance of breadth. You did not have to become an expert in many fields; you simply had to show you were not incompetent. In another business such people would be branded dilettantes. In the Air Force they are called generals.

But the NSA assignment eventually led to a post as military assistant to Dr. Simpson, the director of the National Security Council. Though some of his Air Force friends grumbled about his newly won political influence, he knew them well enough to realize they would have gladly changed places. His colleagues might grouse about politicking, but they all knew how the game was played.

Wheeler revealed little of his inner thoughts and none of his cynicism, cloaking both with tiny barbs of self-deprecation. It was an engaging performance, and Paul found himself liking the man.

After dropping off the car, they checked Paul's bag at the airline counter and made their way to the gate for the flight to

Washington. Soon after they had taken their seats in the first-class cabin, a stewardess approached them. "Colonel Wheeler?"

"Yes."

"Captain Severs would like to see you."

Wheeler turned to Paul. "Neal's a classmate from the Academy. I'll be up in the cockpit for a few minutes."

When Wheeler returned to his seat, he leaned toward Paul and spoke softly. "I don't want to alarm you, but we're going to be leaving the plane."

"What?"

"That's what Neal wanted to see me about. I'll explain later, but we've got to move now, before the Marriott truck finishes loading up the food. Just stand up when I do and follow me to the galley."

It was bizzare, and Paul wanted an explanation. But before he could articulate a question, Wheeler was on his feet, and Paul found himself following. The colonel sidestepped a large plastic case of stacked trays and walked from the plane onto the ramp of the elevated truck. Paul was a step behind.

"What's going on?" whispered Paul.

"Not now," said Wheeler. "We're going to the other side of the field. One of our jets is waiting for us there. I'll explain once we're on board."

A few minutes later, the truck stopped beside a sleek four-engine executive transport jet with U.S. rather than Air Force markings. As Wheeler walked toward the plane's ramp, a man in civilian clothes saluted him.

Wheeler returned the salute. "Good morning, Captain."

"We're ready to go," said the officer.

"Good," said Wheeler. He turned to Paul, who had just caught up with him. "Dr. Sager, I'd like you to meet our pilot, Captain Hall."

"Good morning, sir," said Hall, who then gestured toward the stairs of the C-140. "If you're ready to board, Dr. Sager, we'll be on our way."

The door was secured and the engines began their whining start as Paul and Wheeler took their seats. There were no other passengers.

"I know this is unusual," said Wheeler. "But before I left Washington, our intelligence people informed me they had electronic indications which suggest that I have been under surveillance. Who's been doing it and why, we don't know."

"Good Lord, are you—are we—in danger?"

"That seems unlikely. Washington's thick with intelligence types from all over the world. But because my mission is so sensitive, Dr. Simpson advised me to take precautions: change my routine, make reservations on one flight but take another, things like that."

"And that's what this is all about?"

Wheeler nodded. "We were booked on Pan Am. The switch should throw off anyone who might be looking for us when the plane lands at National Airport."

"But what about my bag?"

"One of my assistants, Captain Cerri, will pick it up and bring it to Fort Meade, which is where we'll be working this weekend."

Wheeler swiveled his chair and leaned toward the small safe that was built into the plane's bulkhead. He entered a number on the small digital keyboard and the safe came open, revealing a single brown folder. Wheeler handed it to Paul. "I think you'll understand why we're concerned about surveillance when you've finished reading this."

Paul began reading the document and was immediately engrossed. He leaned back in his seat, his concentration so complete he was not consciously aware of the roar of the engines as the plane began its takeoff roll. When he finished twenty minutes later and turned in his chair, he found Wheeler looking at him.

"Frightening, isn't it?"

Paul could not put into words the jumble of thoughts going through his mind and simply nodded in reply.

"If they'd just stopped after the bank in Kansas, we would probably not have caught on to what they were up to. But the pattern was repeated in Ohio. But even more important, they, whoever 'they' are, appear to be preparing a challenge to the Federal Reserve's Chicago Switch. We think our telecomm security is pretty good, but you can see the position we're in. We can't afford to take any chances."

"No, we can't," said Paul.

A moment later, he realized the implication of his words. The government was no longer "they"; it had become "we." When he turned toward Wheeler, he found the concerned look on the colonel's face had been replaced by a smile.

"You're absolutely right, Paul," he said. "We can't."

A half hour later, as Paul was rereading the document, he heard the engines change pitch.

Wheeler looked up from his advance copy of *National Report*. "We're beginning our descent to Andrews," he said.

Paul glimpsed the cover of the conservative newsweekly, a quizzical look on his face. "Is that next week's issue?"

Wheeler nodded. "Hot off the press, as they say. They send a batch over to the E.O.B.—that's the Executive Office Building—every Friday night."

"And chalk up a few points, no doubt."

Wheeler chuckled. "That isn't the half of what they do for us. We actually get to edit any interview the administration gives them. Hell, we rewrote most of what Dr. Simpson gave them last month. And if there's a real crunch, I'm told, they'll go even further," said Wheeler, a wry smile on his lips.

"What do you mean?"

"About three or four months after the administration came in, a couple of young hot-shots at State wanted to force the President's hand and dreamed up an elaborate contingency plan for the invasion of Cuba. Not an embargo, not a quarantine, but a flat-out, honest-to-God, send-in-the-Marines invasion." Wheeler started to laugh.

"Of course, it was strictly off the wall," he continued, "put together by an ex-reporter and a right-wing academic, both brand-new to government, who actually believed all that campaign bullshit and figured the President really did want to singe the old bastard's beard."

"Good God," exclaimed Paul.

Wheeler shrugged. "Any idiot can write a contingency plan; I've written a few myself, for that matter. The point is, it never would have gone through, it would have been squelched inside eventually. But *NR*'s State Department guy somehow got wind of it and started asking tough questions. When Dr. Simpson found out, he hit the roof and called the magazine's number-three guy, an unreconstructed cold-warrior if ever there was one. That's all it took. They gave Jay a dog-and-pony show about national security, and he bought it whole. Took the story away from the reporter and wrote it himself. When it finally got into print, the story was so bland it was meaningless. Said that the administration was considering 'new sanctions' against Cuba. Well, that was true in a sense but a far cry from what the real story was: a plan for a balls-out invasion."

"Wow," said Paul. "Can you imagine what the *Post* would have done with that story?"

Wheeler rolled his eyes. "Hell, they would have published the schedule for the invasion fleet."

Paul felt the aircraft lurch slightly and then heard a rush of wind as the landing gear was lowered into the airstream. Through the window he could see the Maryland countryside, the spare budding trees and sprawling subdivisions. A six-lane highway passed beneath them just before the plane touched down.

A dark blue sedan was waiting on the ramp as the C-140 taxied into place. The driver stood beside the car and opened the rear door the instant Wheeler's shoe touched the tarmac. Paul followed him into the car.

"We're a bit ahead of schedule," said Wheeler, "so I thought we might have lunch here at the club. The Army'll take us by chopper to Fort Meade this afternoon."

"Fine," said Paul. "And my suitcase?"

"No problem," said Wheeler. "Captain Cerri will pick it up at National and meet us at Fort Meade."

The officers' club at Andrews was a sprawling nondescript building with lots of glass and no atmosphere; it reminded Paul of one of those large suburban restaurants that specialize in simultaneous wedding receptions. The food proved compatible with the environment.

Wheeler was interrupted during lunch by a phone call informing him that the helicopter had been delayed an hour by a minor maintenance problem. Instead of taking the car to Fort Meade, he decided they would wait the extra hour at the club and relax over dessert and coffee.

An hour later, as they were riding back to the flight line, the car's telephone buzzed.

"Colonel Wheeler," he said into the mouthpiece.

Paul was looking out the window. When he turned to Wheeler, he saw color draining from the colonel's face.

"I see," said Wheeler quietly. "We're en route now to the Eighty-ninth's hangar; I'll call you on the scrambler as soon as we get there." He put down the handset and stared silently ahead.

"What's wrong?" asked Paul.

Wheeler spoke softly. "The car that was carrying your suitcase? It apparently exploded on the Baltimore-Washington Parkway, just north of the Beltway."

"Oh, Jesus. Anyone hurt?"

Wheeler nodded. "They're flying Joe Cerri by chopper to

Baltimore. They've got the best shock trauma unit in the country." His jaw tightened. "But it looks bad."

Paul shook his head.

"The driver's in better shape. He managed to radio the Park Police and the White House Situation Room. Joe was in the back seat. Apparently, it was your suitcase, in the trunk, that exploded."

"Good Lord. How could that be?"

"Think hard," said Wheeler. "Were you carrying anything in there, you know, like a gun, a butane lighter? Anything flammable?"

"No. All I had in there were some clothes and a few papers, academic papers I've been reviewing for one of the journals."

The car stopped at the gate to the 89th Military Airlift Wing, the special unit that maintains Air Force One and other VIP transports. The guard glanced at the White House sticker on the windshield and waved them through. The driver pulled up to the hangar.

"I may be a while," said Wheeler. "There's a lounge inside. You can wait for me there, if you like."

Paul nodded numbly, and they got out of the car.

Wheeler returned fifteen minutes later. "I've been talking to Dr. Simpson, and I need to ask you some questions."

"What?"

"Does Helen know why you've come to Washington?"

"I only told her what you told me."

"Forgive me, Paul, but I have to press you on this. How much did you tell her?"

"Well, pretty much what you told me, I guess. That the work was nonmilitary and that I'd be getting twelve hundred a day."

"Did you tell her what I wrote down?"

Paul hesitated. "You mean about banks, computers, and terrorists?"

"That's exactly what I mean."

"I suppose I did. Why?"

"Where did you tell her?"

"We were having lunch."

"At home?"

"No. We were at a restaurant in Cambridge."

"Damn!" Wheeler exhaled sharply and then forced himself to breathe deeply before speaking. His voice was soft, controlled. "Paul, I wrote down those words for a reason. I didn't want to risk being overheard. It appears that my visit to your office led to someone tailing you."

"What?"

"You didn't discuss it on the phone, did you?"

He shook his head.

"Then that seems the most likely explanation," said Wheeler. "Someone had me under surveillance and began tailing you after our meeting. When they saw you go into the restaurant, they followed you with a parabolic mike. Had you said nothing, they probably would have dropped off. As it is, they've probably had you under surveillance since we met. To see what you would do."

Paul opened and then closed his mouth.

"You represented no threat to them as long as you were on the outside," Wheeler continued. "Inside the government, they'd be faced with a formidable adversary. So they tried to eliminate you."

Dumbfounded at the enormity of what had happened, Paul averted his eyes and remained silent.

"Well, Dr. Simpson wants me to call him back." Wheeler started to leave and then stopped. Touching Paul on the arm, he said, "Can I get you something?"

"No, thanks. I'm all right."

"Help yourself to the coffee," said Wheeler, as he left.

Paul sat in silence holding a cup of coffee. When Wheeler returned, the cup was still full, the coffee cold.

"I'm afraid there's bad news," said Wheeler.

Paul got to his feet.

"Joe Cerri died ten minutes ago."

"Oh, Jesus."

"Army ordnance experts are on the scene. They've confirmed that some form of plastique explosive was used. They've also recovered what appear to be pieces of a remote-controlled mechanism embedded in a fragment of your suitcase. Somebody apparently slipped the device inside your bag."

"But where?"

"There must be at least a dozen places between Logan and National where it could have happened. Someone could have opened your bag, dropping in the device, and closed it in a matter of seconds."

Paul felt his forehead turn cold, damp. The thought was inescapable. *I got that man killed. He'd be alive if I'd kept my mouth shut.*

"We're going to have to come to some conclusions pretty quickly," said Wheeler.

"What do you mean?"

"Let's start with the obvious: someone tried to kill you."

"But why?"

"Most likely, because they fear what you could do working for the government. In a perverse sort of way, it's a compliment. I realize that's a terrible thing to say right now. Let's just say that they, whoever 'they' are, recognize that in the field of cryptography Paul Sager is one of a kind."

"Now what do I do?"

"At this point, we can assume that the enemy knows the bomb detonated. What he may not know at this point is the result. They had no reason to kill Joe Cerri, so we have to assume they were out to get you. If they find out you're still alive, they'll probably try to kill you again."

"No, damn it. No," said Paul, his voice quavering. "I want out. A man died. And for what? I just want to get out of here. I'll get a cab to National and fly back to Boston. Or, better yet, Burlington." He was shaking now. "Helen's at her mother's house in Stowe; she could meet me at the airport. She could pick me up there; it's only an hour away."

"You've got to calm down and try to think clearly," said Wheeler. "If you want to, you can go home this afternoon. I'll even have a staff car take you to National. But I don't think you should. They've already tried to kill you once. Unless they think they can get you to work for them, they'll have no compunction about trying again."

"But what about Helen? She'll think I'm dead. I can't put her through that."

"But what's the alternative? I've been trying to think of one that would not endanger either you or your wife, and I can't. For the life of me, I can't."

Paul lowered himself into a chair. Wheeler sat next to him.

After nearly a minute of silence, Wheeler spoke. "I have a suggestion."

"What is it?"

"With your approval, of course, we'll proceed to Fort Meade by helicopter. Once there, we'll give you a cover: new name, new identity papers, the whole nine yards. Only Simpson and a handful of people at NSA with a need to know will be told who you really are." He paused and then lowered his voice.

"As for the rest of the world: Paul Sager died this afternoon when the car in which he was riding exploded."

"But what about Helen?"

"Dr. Simpson told me he would call the Secretary of the Treasury and request the Secret Service keep her under surveillance until we can be certain she is out of danger. For a while, she'll have to think you're dead. At some point, later on, when we can be absolutely sure she's not being watched, we'll have someone contact her and tell her you're alive."

"No," said Paul. "That's not good enough. You're asking me to put Helen through the horror of my death. And for what? For my country?" He shook his head. "I can't do it. I will not endanger my wife."

Wheeler spoke softly. "We have to assume she's already in danger."

"Look," said Paul, "I'll just go home. I'll tell the press where I was going and that I've decided not to work for the government. Not now. Not ever."

Wheeler nodded. "It might work." He paused. "But suppose it doesn't. Suppose they don't believe you. We may not know who killed Joe Cerri, but we do know one thing: we're up against cold-blooded assassins."

"And?"

"Simply this," said Wheeler. "If they decide you represent a threat to them, the next bomb could get you and Helen."

Paul lowered his head and brought his hands to his face. His voice was shaky. "What is it you want me to do?"

"Go to NSA. The Agency's tighter than a drum; once you're inside, you'll be totally secure."

"Yes, but doing what?"

Wheeler met his eyes. "Helping your government find the bastards who killed Joe Cerri . . . and tried to kill you."

Paul shook his head. "Part of me wants to stay and fight. Get revenge. But another part of me is almost screaming to get the hell out of here. Escape to the Green Mountains with Helen and simply hide there until it all blows over."

There was a rap at the door. An airman entered. "Colonel Wheeler, there's a call for you on the secure line."

Wheeler excused himself and left the room. When he returned a few minutes later, he was smiling.

"That was Dr. Simpson. Treasury has cleared Secret Service surveillance and protection for Helen."

Paul nodded.

Wheeler faced him squarely. "Are you with us, Paul?"

He hesitated an instant and then extended his hand. "Yes."

Wheeler gripped Paul's hand and held it firmly for several seconds. Then, wordlessly, they left the lounge and began walking across the hangar floor, their heels mimicking the rotor beat of the approaching helicopter.

PART II

CHAPTER 7

A bell was ringing, a church bell, its peal reverberating against the Alpine mountainside, the morning breeze scented by new-mown hay. Resisting the drift toward consciousness, Paul curved his body against the arc of Helen's back, trying to dispel the light with her warmth. But the light would not recede. More bells. Bronze bells. Each a different pitch. Some ringing at a stately pace, others jingling, as the brown Tyrolean cows came down the hills to the glacier-fed stream. Paul smiled as he recalled the cattle crossing the road, the Mercedes trucks and yellow Austrian postal bus confronting gridlock in Gerlos. He felt Helen stir and nuzzled the side of her neck. Listen, he whispered. High, melodious, the church bell continued its unbroken toll. He brought his arm across her body and felt her cheek caress his hand. I love you, he whispered. The warmth of tears welled in his eyes.

A pipe banging. The rush of water. He turned away.

They made love, indulging in a luxury denied them most mornings by more worldly considerations. A quick breakfast of freshly baked rolls and dark aromatic coffee. A hike into a narrow canyon that suddenly broadened into a magnificent valley. Images flew past him. The meandering dirt road, hikers and farmers who doffed their hats. *Gruess Gott*. Cattle grazing beside the stream, pigs wallowing in the mud. A huge wheel of cheese being salted and washed down in a storage hut, its long right wall built into the earth. A swiftly flowing stream, its water cold and effervescent on the tongue. The tiny restaurant high in the valley, an omelette in an enormous iron skillet, eight eager hands shoveling out portions with their spoons, the earthy Zillertal beer, the hot July sun on their bare shoulders. The hike home, hands touching. The taste of salt on Helen's lips.

Leather heels clicked purposefully in the distance. Again, he turned away.

They walked along the road, stopping for fruit to balance the heavy load of potatoes, eggs, beer, and *knoedels*. Her face, reddened the day before, now brown and glowing. Her hair, unshackled and lightened by the sun, streaming free beside her face. For a moment he simply looked at her, in awe of her beauty, as if seeing her for the first time. When she saw the way he was staring, she smiled, teeth glistening in the light. Tiny pearls of perspiration shimmered on the fine blond hair above her lip until he flicked them away with his tongue. They laughed. Two old women clad in black, faces stern, lowered their gaze, saw the matching gold bands, and raised their heads, smiling in unison. Paul glanced away, straining for control, but when his eyes met hers, their laughter exploded.

Hand in hand, on the road to Gerlos, they approached the onion-shaped steeple and saw people leaving the little church, black armbands against Tyrolean green. And then he knew. The bell. The church bell. The sound that had so gently roused him from sleep had been someone's death knell. Helen had known instinctively what it meant. Village bells do not sound merely to enchant paying customers. They are witnesses of human events: the birth of a child, the joining of a man and woman, the flight of a soul from earth. And when he asked her why she had not told him, the blue gray eyes sought and held his. To spare you, she replied, to shield you as you shield me. He fought to hold the image, the feeling of that moment, to prolong it past all time, and then felt himself beginning to fall. In desperation he thrust his arm toward her.

A bell was ringing. It stopped and rang again.

Paul's hand grasped the receiver. "Hello?"

"Good morning, Paul. Did I wake you?"

"Oh, uh, no."

"I've got six-thirty," said Wheeler. "I was planning to go over to the club for breakfast around seven. Would you care to join me?"

"Sure."

"Good. See you in half an hour."

Paul eased himself from the bed and fumbled for the light switch, squinting in anticipation of the brightness. The shower jolted him fully awake. He was shaved and nearly dressed when he answered the knock on his door.

Wheeler came into the room wearing his uniform, silver eagles gleaming from his epaulets and on the left side of his overseas cap. He gave the room a quick glance. "Not bad," he said.

Paul shrugged. "It's like a Holiday Inn."

"It may not be the Plaza," said Wheeler. "But it is a two-room suite; the Army normally holds these for visitors of one-star rank or higher."

"Yeah? Well, right now I'd trade it for a place I know in Vermont."

A silence came between them. Wheeler broke it by lightly clapping his hands together. "I have some good news," he said. "The Secret Service team flew into Burlington late yesterday. They've got four people, two men and two women, and they're going into Stowe looking like any other foursome on a skiing vacation. They'll keep their distance, but they'll be watching Helen. And if anyone else is watching her, you can be damn sure they'll pick up on it."

Paul thought momentarily of the Service's record guarding Presidents, but let the reflection pass unvoiced.

"It may be Sunday, but we've got a full day ahead of us," Wheeler continued. "I've been up most of the night, conferring with Dr. Simpson and NSC's liaison officers from the various agencies: State, Defense, Treasury, Transportation, and, of course, the Federal Reserve. You name it, just about everyone has a piece of this one. You'll meet some of them later this morning at NSA headquarters. I'll give you a rundown on who they are and what they do over breakfast."

Paul ran the towel through his wet hair another time and

finished buttoning his shirt. He faced the mirror, quickly combed his hair and did his tie. "I'm ready," he said.

The dining room of the officers' club at Fort Meade was nearly empty, and they were quickly served. Wheeler was drinking his coffee when he noticed Paul staring at the medals on his chest.

"Not all of them, I can assure you, were for looting and pillaging in Vietnam."

"I have so little contact with the military," said Paul. "I was just wondering what they were for."

Wheeler sipped his coffee. "Some of them are automatic, like the one on the bottom for service in Southeast Asia. It didn't matter if you were a Marine fighting to hold Khe Sanh or a clerk handing out jock straps at Ton Son Nhut. If you were there, you got one of these whether you asked for it or not. Naturally, it carries about as much distinction as a bumper sticker from 'South of the Border.'"

"And the rest of them?" asked Paul.

"Many of them did come from the war," Wheeler replied. "Most of them for flying and not getting my ass shot off. It also helped being awards-and-decs officer."

"What?"

"Sorry, I forget you don't know the jargon. That stands for awards and decorations. Every unit has one, and it's his job to see that merit and valor are rewarded through proper channels. I was just a captain back then, and I spent a lot of time filling out forms for majors and colonels. They, of course, returned the favor. I know this will sound horribly cynical, but that was probably the most important job I ever had as far as advancing my career is concerned. I got promoted to major and lieutenant colonel below the zone and picked up a reputation as a fast burner. That got me to colonel."

"What'll it take to get you to general?"

He grinned puckishly. "A well-placed patron."

"Like Dr. Simpson?"

"He'll do," Wheeler replied.

"You're serious, aren't you?"

"Don't get me wrong," said Wheeler. "I love the Air Force, I really do. But if I were going to settle for mediocrity, I'd do it in the civilian world, where the pay is better—and the work a lot safer. Besides, I don't think the service is any better or any worse than business, the professions, or the academic world." He looked up from his cup. "Tell me, Paul. Are all the appointments and promotions at MIT, or any other university that you know of, based entirely on merit, or does it take some political talent to get ahead?"

"You know the answer to that as well as I."

Wheeler grinned. "Q.E.D."

There were few cars in the lot at NSA headquarters where Wheeler parked the brown sedan with government license plates. The colonel reached inside his jacket and produced a steel chain on which were hanging several plastic-laminated identification cards. He showed them to the guard at the gatehouse and signed for Paul's red-and-white striped visitor's badge. Paul looked at the badge, flipped it over, but found nothing that identified the Agency. There were just two words, and he read them aloud: "'One Day.'"

"We'll be getting you a permanent one in the next day or so," said Wheeler.

"One day would be plenty," Paul replied softly.

Wheeler nodded. "That badge is only good if you're accompanied by someone with permanent credentials, such as these," he said, fingering the green badge on the chain.

"Suppose I have to go to the bathroom."

"Then someone will have to go with you. But don't worry," Wheeler added, chuckling, "you'll have a stall to yourself."

They began walking down the corridor, turning left at the huge mosaic of the seal of the National Security Agency and stopping at a bank of six automated elevators. They got off at the ninth floor, and Wheeler led them down "Mahogany Row," the wood-paneled corridor where the director of the NSA and other high-ranking executives had their offices. A guard checked their credentials at the door to the conference room and let them pass.

A stout man in a three-piece gray pinstriped suit came forward with his hand extended.

"Good morning, Harding," said Wheeler, as he shook his hand. "I trust we haven't kept you waiting."

"Not at all, Otis. I had the others get here early." He nodded toward two chairs at the near end of the conference table. "If the two of you will be seated, I'll get started."

Paul glanced along the table before he sat down and saw a dozen or so people, mostly men, dressed in somber colors.

Harding Harrison, special counselor to the President, wheezed as he took his seat in the center of the table. "Before I begin, a few ground rules. The President has taken a direct and personal interest in the subject we are going to be discussing this morning. Though NSA will be the operating agency, it will be directly responsible to the President through the NSC director. I will be working with Dr. Simpson to coordinate policy direction at the White House.

"Now, and this is important, no one in this meeting is to take notes or make any report whatsoever, oral or written, to the cabinet department or agency to which they are attached. This is by presidential direction." He scanned the faces from one end of the table to the other. "Are there any questions?"

A naval officer at the far end of the table raised a hand.

Harrison nodded. "Captain Myers?"

"Thank you, Mr. Harrison," said a dark-haired officer with wire-rim glasses. "I could have a problem with that, in that the Chairman and the C.N.O. are aware of my attendance at this meeting. How should I deal with any questions they may have?"

"The answer, Captain Myers, is quite simple," Harrison replied. "You refer any and all questions concerning Working Group Seven, which is, by the way, our official title, directly to me. Should it become necessary to include Defense in operational planning, we will expand the scope of our operations to include the appropriate departmental elements. Until that time, Captain, neither the Chairman of the J.C.S. nor the Chief of Naval Operations has a need to know."

With meaty hands, Harrison smoothed his amply filled vest. "At this point WG-Seven exists only here"—he tapped his forehead—"and here," he said, gesturing around the table. "It's an informal, ad hoc arrangement. Each of you was chosen because you have specialized knowledge of a particular area of technology or branch of government that could be of substantial value to the President in resolving the problem. We hope it will be resolved promptly, with no need to involve your departments or agencies in a direct operational capacity. At the moment, we are proceeding on the premise that it will be resolved in house, here at NSA." He nodded toward Paul. "With the assistance of some outside scientific advice."

Harrison reached for the controls on the table, dimmed the lights, and turned on the slide projector. "Most of you have only a partial understanding of the nature of the problem. I'll be more explicit." A slide clicked into place. "If you'll look closely at the first chart, you'll grasp the enormity of the potential threat facing the Federal Reserve System. As you can see, the Chicago Switch is now handling more than eighty thousand electronic transactions every working day. In a year's time, the Switch will handle cash transfers in excess of seventy trillion dollars." He drew a deep breath. "Think of it: seventy trillion dollars. That averages out to more than two hundred and fifty *billion* dollars every working day. To give you some perspective, it means that every two to three weeks the Fed's computers will transfer funds that *exceed the entire gross national product of the United States.*"

He paused for additional emphasis. "Now, try to imagine the consequences to our economy if a hostile power were able to compromise that system by either cracking the encryption standard or finding a way to substitute false messages for some of those eighty thousand transactions." He drew a breath. "The result would be chaos. Anarchy. We have not faced a financial emergency of this potential magnitude since 1929. Yet that is precisely the nature of the threat."

Harrison went through several more slides, starting with the bank that had collapsed in Kansas in January. Then he described the electronic sabotage that had forced banks in Ohio and, just two days ago, Wisconsin to close their doors while auditors reconstructed on paper electronic records that had simply vanished. He mentioned the potential threat to the Federal Reserve's electronic banking network, but omitted many of the details Paul had read the day before while flying to Andrews. When the briefing was over, forty minutes later, most of the people wordlessly left the room, each nodding to Harrison on the way out.

Paul and Wheeler stood behind their chairs as the others left. Then, Harrison came forward, followed by a man and woman.

"Dr. Sager. A pleasure to meet you," said Harrison, extending his hand. "I have to return to Washington, and I'll be taking Colonel Wheeler with me. But before I leave, I want to introduce two people you'll be working closely with: Dr. Winchell and Dr. Ho."

Paul vaguely recognized William Winchell from an academic conference on cryptography he had attended in Santa Barbara a few years before, but Nancy Ho was a complete stranger. Indeed, had they met he would almost certainly have remembered her because there were so few women in computer science; she was also very attractive.

Paul guessed her to be about thirty in spite of the lack of visual evidence: unlined face, clear skin, brown eyes unblinking behind large round glasses. She was wearing a gray suit tailored to her small frame; her sleek black hair was pulled straight back and cinched by a simple band. Her expression remained neutral as Paul exchanged pleasantries with her superior, but her face eased naturally into a smile when Winchell introduced her.

"Dr. Sager. This is indeed an honor." The inflections in her voice were American rather than Chinese.

They talked for a minute or so, mentioning academic colleagues they had in common.

Harrison interrupted. "Dr. Sager, because of the peculiar—indeed, tragic—nature of the circumstances under which you arrived at Fort Meade, we will have to establish a cover for you. We want you to be able to blend in with the thousands of other people who work here. That means I.D. cards, parking stickers, that sort of thing. Dr. Winchell will see that you're taken care of. Do you have a name you'd prefer?"

"You mean an alias?"

Harrison smiled. "You could put it that way."

"You mean just pick a name?"

"Sure," said Harrison. "Who were your heroes as a youngster?"

Paul grinned. "How about John Kennedy?" he asked the ultraconservative counselor to the President.

Harrison's smile evaporated. "That might be, uh, too conspicuous."

Paul laughed. "When I was a kid, I didn't like my name, and I once demanded that my parents change it to Hopalong Caddisy."

Harrison's sense of humor returned. "Well, Hopalong might be stretching things a bit, but there's no reason you can't become Dr. Cassidy. Or Caddisy, if you prefer."

"I'll stick with the adult spelling," said Paul.

"We'll also have to change a few details, such as date and place of birth, get you a new Social Security number," said Harrison. "Those are the sorts of items that, as you well know, turn up on lots of computerized files and can be crosschecked.

We'll also create medical, academic, and financial records, even subscriptions to magazines and professional journals, for our new Dr. Cassidy. After all, we wouldn't want someone running a computer check and finding nothing. That, too, would create suspicion."

Wheeler saw Paul's brow tense. "I know it's a lot to swallow all at once, but we have to be thorough," said the colonel.

Paul turned to Harrison. "And who will know who I really am?"

"As few people as possible," he replied. "In addition to the people in this room, there might be half a dozen more who will know your true identity. For obvious security reasons, the fewer the better."

"I see," said Paul.

Harrison stepped to the projector, removed the slide tray, and put it in his attaché case. "As I mentioned, Colonel Wheeler is coming to Washington with me. But he'll be back tomorrow." As the two men reached the door, Harrison turned.

"One last thing," he said. "Don't make any phone calls except on secure lines. Dr. Winchell will explain why."

When the door closed, Paul turned to Winchell.

Tall and skinny, with a prominent Adam's apple, the silver-haired Winchell nodded and puffed several times on his pipe before taking it from his mouth. "Harrison's point is well taken," he said. "We have to assume the adversary has technological capabilities similar to our own until we can conclusively prove otherwise."

"You mean wiretapping?" asked Paul.

Winchell's blue eyes crinkled into a smile. "We seldom use such quaint terms as 'wiretapping' anymore. In point of fact, it's as much a technological anachronism as the term 'aeroplane.' You will find, Dr. Sager—I mean, Dr. Cassidy—that our antennas can simultaneously record and evaluate the signals reflected from every microwave relay tower in the Baltimore-Washington area. If I have someone's voiceprint, that fellow can drive from one pay phone to another within a fifty-mile radius of the Capitol, and I will be able to pick up and identify no less than ninety percent of his long-distance calls as well as some of the local ones."

Paul was flabbergasted. "That's amazing."

Winchell puffed his pipe. "That, I can assure you, is one of the simpler tasks we are capable of performing. Over the next few days you will find that many of the mathematical principles you and your academic colleagues have been discussing in the abstract have already become rather formidable pieces of hardware." He exhaled a huge puff of smoke. "You may also find that you are in for an interesting time."

CHAPTER 8

A swarm of fat, wet snowflakes, defined in the yellow-white beams of the van's headlights, suddenly floated up and enveloped the windshield. Steady as a metronome, the wipers beat a path through the advancing snow. Willard squirmed uncomfortably in the high-backed driver's seat.

George switched on the overhead light and scanned the road map. "We are about forty miles from Sioux Falls. I would assume there must be a truck stop on the periphery."

Willard grunted.

George turned up the volume control on the transmitter and picked up the mike. "How do you work this scrambler device?"

"Christ," Willard hissed. "It's the middle of the night. We're in the middle of a goddamn blizzard in Minnesota, and you want to play with the scrambler. Who the hell do you think's going to be listening in?"

"I just wanted to see if it works."

"Look, it worked when I put it in this morning, and I'm sure it'll work if we need it to."

"Very well," said George. He brought the microphone close to his mouth and squeezed the button. "Van to One. Radio check. Do you copy? Acknowledge."

"One to Van," came Tom's voice. "Copy loud and clear."

"Van to Two. Radio check. Do you copy? Acknowledge."

Zed's voice came over the receiver. "Yep."

"You would think," said George, with evident irritation, "he could at least acknowledge a transmission properly."

"Oh, get off it, George. Zed's a damn good mechanic. He actually *does* something. I don't see you doing much of anything except give orders. But then, Tom and Zed and I aren't executive material, are we, George?"

George ignored the provocation and raised the microphone. "We anticipate a refueling stop within the next twenty to thirty minutes. We will transmit details at the appropriate time." He paused. "Van to One. Do you copy? Acknowledge."

"One to Van. Affirmative."

"Van to Two. Do you copy? Acknowledge."

"Yep."

Twenty minutes later, George saw a truck stop and ordered the caravan—the van, Tom's new pickup truck, and a tractor-trailer with the logo "Kitty's Kreemy Kookies"—to pull into the station. After the vehicles had been filled, the four walked into the restaurant.

Little was said during the meal, except for Tom's repeated observation: "Bitch of a storm, isn't it?"

When they finished their coffee, George got to his feet. No one else stirred.

"You might as well sit down," said Willard.

"We can take a few more minutes," said George. "Then we have to get going."

"I think we should spend the night here," said Willard. "Why don't you see if they've got any of those cabins free?"

George lowered his voice for emphasis. "We cannot leave the vehicles in such an unsecured location."

"Would you rather have them in a ditch in the middle of I-90? 'Cause that's where we're liable to wind up if you push things in weather like this."

"But what about the vehicles?"

"Look, I've already put alarms on all three of them. If you

want, I can rig it so that anybody who touches them gets his nuts fried."

Tom and Zed began laughing. George turned on his heel and left. When he returned, he spread four keys on the table.

"Now you're being reasonable," said Willard. "Just make sure you give everyone a chance to get a decent night's sleep. None of this six A.M. shit."

"Eight o'clock, then?"

"Look, it's already three." He glanced at Tom and Zed and received quick, affirming nods. "Make it nine, and you've got yourself a deal."

The caravan was on the road by ten the next morning. Snowplows had cleared the right lane, and the sun was beginning to nibble at the edges of the snow. George was at the wheel of the van, Tom following in the pickup, with Zed a half-mile to the rear in the truck.

Willard smiled. "Now, admit it, George. It did make sense to spend the night, didn't it?"

"You always underestimate the importance of security."

"Was anything stolen or compromised?"

"Not that we know of."

"Jesus Christ! Can't you ever admit you were wrong?"

"That's not the point."

"Goddamn it. That *is* the point."

George kept his eyes on the road and made no reply.

Willard leaned back in the seat and gazed out the window, letting the snow-covered sameness of the highway numb his consciousness and sense of time. He tried to concentrate on the program he had been developing to find a "trapdoor" into the Chicago Switch, but his thoughts would not stay in focus. He closed his eyes and began to think about Marlie. The scenario he had envisioned so many times was enacted again, the hum of the tires became the hum of his machines, Marlie lying naked across them. A momentary skid jolted him awake, and he suddenly realized he was hard. He shifted position so George would not see the bulge in his pants.

"No problem," said George. "Just a patch of ice."

Willard grunted and closed his eyes, trying to revive his fantasy, but Marlie had disappeared.

They stopped for lunch at another truck stop and were back on the road within an hour, Willard at the wheel.

He sipped the last of his Tab and put the large cup in a holder on the dashboard. "Why didn't you let Marlie come to the farm? She wouldn't have had to stay for very long. You could have brought her, if you wanted to. I know you could."

"You really overestimate what I can and cannot do," said George, in a conciliatory tone. "As long as the director wants her to remain at headquarters, I cannot override his request."

"'Order' is more like it," said Willard.

"If you wish, yes. It is an order."

"But you gave her my letter?"

"Yes, I did."

"And what'd she say?"

"I did not ask, nor did she volunteer, a reaction."

Willard sighed. "You know, I love my machines. I really do." The tone was plaintive. "But I'm having trouble concentrating on the new program. The banks are easy. Some of them don't even encrypt their data. The rest have codes that are bletcherously simple to crack. When I close my eyes, it's like I can see the programs. I can't explain what it is I'm seeing, but I *am* seeing it. But the Switch is going to be something else. I keep trying to concentrate on it, but I can't get Marlie off my mind."

George nodded. "I have nothing but the highest respect for your intellectual capabilities. You are a genius, Whiz. There is no other word for it. I am certain you will crack the Switch."

Willard glanced in the rearview mirror and pulled into the freshly plowed left lane to pass a snow plow; the van swayed slightly as he returned to the right lane. He arched his back and repositioned himself on the seat. "I don't know," he said softly.

"Look," said George, "you have to concentrate on how to break into the Switch. We know the DES has a trapdoor built into it; it has to. The NSA would never have let the Fed develop a code the agency could not break. They want no one's codes but their own to be unbreakable."

Willard stared stonily ahead.

"No one expects the task ahead to be simple," said George. "That is why we are going to Colorado. We have a ranch there, and you will have plenty of time to think and work. You will get the fullest possible support."

"Can I have Marlie there? She could help me."

George glanced out the window, brow knit, eyes narrowed.

"I can make no promises, Whiz, but when I get to headquarters tomorrow evening, I will take the matter up, once again, with the director."

"You will?"

"You have my word on it."

CHAPTER 9

Having arrived at the National Security Agency with just what he was wearing, Paul needed a complete new wardrobe, but Winchell ruled out letting him do his own shopping. Some-one might recognize him from the photos that had appeared that weekend on TV and in the press. So, at Winchell's sug-gestion, Paul wrote down his sizes, and a secretary from the Agency made the purchases for him; the government, of course, picked up the tab. Though the shirts, slacks, and jackets fit reasonably well, Paul felt strange every time he looked in the mirror. It was as if he were wearing the clothes of someone who had died. But by the end of his first week at Fort Meade, he no longer noticed; the clothes had become his.

The days were filled with meetings, reports, and tedium. Paul would work late, learning all he could about the Agency's technological prowess as well as its limitations. Finally, when he was so tired he could no longer hold a coherent thought, he would return to his quarters and try to sleep, hoping fatigue would prove an antidote to the fear and guilt that dominated his mind at night.

Lying awake, thinking about Helen and the grief he had caused her to suffer, he would try to reason out a better course of action—one that would allow him to go home without exposing Helen and himself to a second assassination attempt. It was, he knew, a hopeless quest. Until the people who wanted to kill him had been identified and captured, he and Helen would find no peace. Every time they started the car, walked in the woods, or peered into the dark, they would feel a cold hand at their throats.

Again and again he would go over the events, until he finally forced himself to stop. Then he would begin a litany, saying it over and over until his brain surrendered to sleep. I had to do it. There was no other way. They might have killed Helen. What else could I do? I had to do it. There was no other way. No other way.

"I don't believe it." Paul's voice was trembling. "How could you be so damn shortsighted?"

Winchell took the pipe from his mouth. "Try to put yourself in our place, Paul. I don't wish to be melodramatic, but an important part of the Agency's mission is to protect the nation's most sensitive secrets. It would have been morally unconscionable for us to have permitted civilians to use a code that we can't break."

"Civilians? Is that how you regard the rest of the government? Didn't anyone consider the possible consequences?"

"We realized there'd be risks."

"Such as endangering the Federal Reserve and the entire banking system? Was that a part of your so-called 'risk assessment analysis'?"

"To be quite frank about it, no. Our principal consideration was that a civilian group—an arms merchant, to name one of your own concerns—might use the DES to carry out illicit sales transactions. We were worried about unscrupulous businessmen selling arms to terrorists."

"Like Wilson and Terpil did with the Libyans?"

"Precisely."

"You didn't need a trapdoor in the federal government's Data Encryption Standard to get them. One of their ex-CIA buddies turned them in."

"I can assure you," said Winchell between puffs, "that our successes have been substantial."

"But they're secret, naturally."

Winchell's lips curled into a slight smile. "Naturally."

Paul turned to Nancy Ho. "What do you make of this mess?"

Nancy glanced warily at her superior before answering. "The DES was developed before I came to the Agency. My current responsibilities are programming for SIGINT—that is, signals intelligence. I was not even aware there was a potential threat to the Federal Reserve's data network until recently."

Not wishing to embarrass her in front of Winchell, Paul simply nodded and absently fingered the papers in front of him.

Winchell knocked his pipe against the side of a large glass ashtray and reached inside the gray herringbone-tweed jacket for his tobacco pouch. "I would concede that, with the benefit of hindsight, our input into the design of the DES was probably much too parochial."

"Parochial? Paranoid is more like it," said Paul.

Winchell filled his pipe and began tamping it down. "I do think you're overreacting." He swabbed the table with his finger, picking up the wayward flecks of tobacco, which he carefully brushed into his pipe.

Paul smiled, suddenly aware that Winchell, like many of his academic colleagues, used his pipe the way another man might use a crutch: to make it appear that he was doing something during those awkward moments when events moved too quickly for him.

"We were not unaware, I can assure you, of the potential problems that might arise from a flawed DES," he continued. "We simply concluded that we should reserve the most secure encryptive modalities for our most sensitive communications and not encourage the marketplace to spread the technology to foreign governments—or the multinationals, for that matter."

"And so you developed a federal standard that you *knew* could be broken," said Paul, anger etched in his voice. "Now, of course, someone is trying to do just that." He paused. "And may damn well succeed."

"There is that risk," said Winchell, as he lit his pipe and began slowly puffing.

Paul forced himself to lean back in his chair and relax. "I'm sorry, Bill. I didn't mean to get down on you personally. I just think the NSA did a very stupid thing."

Winchell smiled evenly. "Yes. You did make that rather apparent."

Paul and Nancy returned the smile, and the tension visibly eased.

Winchell drew evenly on his pipe, tilted back his head, and released a huge puff of smoke toward the ceiling. "Let me be candid with you. We run a closed, a tightly closed shop. And you can consider it a measure of our desperation that we brought an outsider, you, into our midst. With the exception of a few people from MATER—"

"You mean the electronics think tank?"

Winchell nodded and continued: "In any event, you can be sure that we are quite aware of how precarious our situation is. Perhaps they will be unable to crack the Switch. As you know, you can't break the code with even the most powerful computers using a brute-force approach. Without the key, they would have to choose from over seventy *quadrillion* possible codes. And, of course, the key is changed quite often."

Paul scribbled the figure on the note pad in front of him: 70,000,000,000,000,000. "That, obviously, is not a workable approach," he said. "What do you think they'll do?"

"Our first inclination was to look for an inside job," said Winchell. "And while we have not entirely ruled out that possibility, it now seems less likely to us."

"Why?"

"First of all," said Winchell, "these people do not appear to be interested in money. We have no indication they took so much as a dollar from any of those banks. Their objective has been disruption. Instead of blowing up these banks with dynamite, the way terrorists might have done some years back, they're doing the same sort of thing, albeit in a bloodless way, with computers. So we're almost certainly dealing with a political group of some sort."

"Anything else that suggests it's not an inside job?" Paul asked.

Winchell nodded to his associate.

"Their approach," said Nancy. "If they had an inside source at the Federal Reserve with access to the key, they probably would not have made those initial challenges to the Chicago Switch. It seems more reasonable to assume that they have been developing their own program methodology and been testing it on small targets."

"Sort of like a pre-Broadway run," quipped Paul.

Winchell smiled. "You could put it that way."

"But to what end? What do they want?"

Winchell slowly puffed his pipe and then took it from his mouth. "That's obviously the big question. If we knew the answer to that, we might be able to stop them. At this point we can do nothing more than speculate."

"Give me an example," said Paul.

"There are the obvious possibilities: the Russians, the Libyans." He arched an eyebrow. "The White House certainly thinks the Soviets are behind it."

"That's nothing new. What's your theory?"

"I wouldn't use a word like 'theory' to describe my thoughts on the subject," said Winchell, taking the pipestem from his lips. "Let's just say I'm willing to consider all the possibilities. In any event, Harding Harrison and the rest of those political types are better versed in such matters than I."

Winchell then began to discuss some of the electronic countermeasures the Agency was considering. A half hour later, he excused himself. "We've got you an office of your own," he said. "If you'd like, Nancy'll show it to you."

Nancy led Paul down a corridor and into a brightly lit, high-ceilinged room filled with a vast assortment of machinery. "My God, it looks like Mission Control at NASA."

"Ours is bigger," said Nancy. "If you add up all the floor space, we've got ten acres of computers at the Agency."

"I'll take your word for it."

"We've also got at least one model of every computer ever built, anywhere."

"Including the Russians'?"

"Oh, yes."

"And are they as backward as everyone says?"

She smiled. "As clunky as Volga sedans."

As they walked through the operations center, Nancy introduced "Dr. Cassidy" to several of the technicians and then used an electronic card to open a door in the rear of the huge room. After a short walk down the inner corridor, Nancy stopped at an unmarked door, unlocked it with her card, and preceded him into a small, empty office lined with blackboards.

"We assumed you would want to have a private place to think and work," she said.

"I had that sort of place at MIT," he said wistfully.

Nancy's voice was soft. "I know you've been through a lot."

"Someone died because of a bomb that was meant for me."

"I know."

"I'm not sure I'm doing the right thing, either." He drew a breath. "When I think of what Helen must be going through, I . . ."

Nancy ended the silence. "You dedicated your book to her."

The remark broke his reverie. "You read it?"

"It was actually a bit of a cult item when I was in graduate school. Not just for the mathematics, but because you showed how important human considerations are in all aspects of science and technology. Some of my friends would tease me about what happens to people who remain in computer science. One of them told me that to get my Ph.D my heart would have to be replaced by a microchip."

Paul chuckled. "I hope you enjoyed the book."

The brown eyes widened. "Oh, yes. Very much."

CHAPTER 10

"I won't! I refuse! I absolutely will not!"

"Calm down, Marlie," said George through clenched teeth.

"Calm down!" she said, voice rising. "Do you know what that skinny creep wants me to do?"

"Yes, I do," said George evenly.

Disbelief, then anger flashed in the blue eyes. "I don't believe it!" she exclaimed. "What the hell do you think I am?"

Heads turned in the passenger cabin of the Denver-bound airliner. George glanced over his shoulder, glaring. The on-lookers immediately turned away.

George spoke deliberately, jaw tense, eyes microdots. "I read the document strictly as a security precaution. I delivered it to you as I said I would. You do not have to answer it nor do you have to see Willard." He drew a breath. "Now, will you please calm down? This is no place to call undue attention to our presence."

Marlie brushed a wayward strand of silver blond hair behind her ear, exposing the exquisite lines of her profile. "You actually read this, this *thing*?"

"I scanned it briefly simply to ascertain that there were no breaches in security. What little I did read, to be frank, I found quite distasteful."

"Distasteful? Disgusting is more like it." She riffled several pages of the computer printout. "Look at this. Just listen to this: 'With your tongue follow the seam of my cock from the head to a point just beneath my balls. Gently take first the right then the left ball in your mouth, exerting slight but firm and even pressure.'" She dropped the papers into her lap. "What sort of creep would write something like that to a woman?"

"I would not pretend to understand what goes on inside Willard's head."

She started to pick up the printout, then decided not to. The anger in her voice surrendered to despair. "Why, why did you even hand me this piece of trash?"

"Believe me, Marlie, I share your sense of revulsion."

"You do? You honestly do?"

"Yes, I do. Who would not?" He paused. "But there are other factors to consider in this instance."

Color rushed to Marlie's face, but George cut her off before she could speak.

"Please try to contain your anger for just a minute and let me explain. Willard is admittedly erratic, but he is also a brilliant computer programmer; that makes him an extremely valuable member of the organization. But in most other ways he is more child than man. Self-assured and arrogant one moment, a little boy on the verge of tears the next. You, of all people, should understand that type and the fantasies they can create for themselves. You used to deal with disturbed personalities, as I recall."

"That was in California," Marlie replied softly. "When I joined the organization, I put those days behind me."

"But you learned something about people in those encounter groups, did you not?"

She nodded.

"Like all novitiates, you voluntarily revealed your entire past when you came to us. I read your entry interview as well as the verity disclosure under sodium thiopental, which you, of course, have not seen. The latter, as you know, is a requirement for anyone who may come into personal contact with the director. The fact that you were accepted for so sensitive a position testifies to your worthiness."

Marlie's eyes swept down, lashes fluttering. "Thank you, George."

He leaned slightly toward her and whispered. "Few members of the organization ever get to see the director, much less meet him. You are among the privileged few who have. That, too, is an honor."

"I know it is," she said softly. "And I want to remain worthy of the director's faith in me."

"Good," said George. "The director is particularly concerned about Willard's mission. It is, in fact, his highest priority; thus, it is my highest priority. I cannot, of course, reveal any details—at least, not at the moment."

"I understand."

"In a different situation, we would never have tolerated the first impertinence from the likes of a Willard, but he is unique, irreplaceable. You and I might be replaced, but there is no one in the organization who could possibly carry out his mission. So we have to tolerate his, uh, erratic personality and eccentricities." He paused. "You cannot imagine the strain this has created, not only for me but for the director as well."

Marlie nodded sympathetically.

"So, within reason, we must try to humor him. All of us."

Marlie stopped nodding. "What do you mean 'all of us'?"

George exhaled. "The director told me to do whatever was necessary to create a working environment conducive to improving his productivity."

"Those are your words, not the director's," Marlie countered. "What did *he* say? What were *his* actual words?"

"He said, and I quote: 'To provide for us, we must provide for him.'"

"That's it?"

"Those were his exact words. They seem quite clear to me. Do they not to you?"

"Well, uh, yes. Certainly."

George glanced at his watch. "We should be starting our descent soon."

As if on cue, the plane gently banked left. George turned toward Marlie, the hint of a smile on his lips. "I have an advantage in that I know quite a lot about you even though we have spoken only on a few occasions. You have seen some of the files. You know how extensive they are."

She nodded.

"In reading yours, I was fascinated by the variety of therapy you used in encounter sessions," said George. "Particularly with those who were sexually dysfunctional."

"I'd rather not talk about that."

"You freely accepted the principle of self-revelation when you became a part of us, did you not?"

"Yes, but—"

"Please, let me continue," said George affably. "There is a point to all this."

"Yes. I'm sure there is."

"As I recall, you permitted—no, encouraged—people to pair off in so-called informal sessions. Men with women, men with men, women with women. Everyone had a partner. Is that not correct?"

Marlie clenched her lower lip in her teeth and nodded.

"And what if some poor soul were left without a partner? Did you consign him to the hot tub to masturbate?"

Tears began to well in her eyes.

"No, of course not. That would have been insensitive. So, you became his partner. Or perhaps, *her* partner. You had a rather quaint, if vulgar, name for that form of therapy. What was that phrase? Oh, yes, now I recall. 'Mercy-fucking.'"

A tear emerged from the corner of an eye and ran down her cheek.

"It seemed like such a wonderful idea at the time. Friendship, respect, hot tubs, and sex. Salvation for the masses at a mere fourteen hundred dollars a week."

Marlie tried to blink back her tears but could not.

"And you were the most popular therapist of all. Everyone wanted Marlie. And what did Marlie want? She was only too eager to service their needs and even some of their fantasies. How many were there? Five hundred? A thousand? Do you remember faces, or just the odd piece of plumbing?"

Marlie turned toward the window, but George grabbed her arm and pulled her toward him.

"No. You are going to listen to me," he said. "You believe in the principle of self-revelation, do you not?"

"Yes," she whispered hoarsely.

"Good, because I want you to recall what happened to Marian. You remember Marian. She said she loved you. And what did you do? You told her that it would be unprofessional for you to see her outside the encounter center. So, she kept coming back. Did you ever wonder where a young secretary got four-teen hundred dollars a week? Did you care? Or were you too busy giving 'therapy'? Of course, when it was over, the center was quite generous and returned the money she had stolen from her family. Only by then it was too late. Even you knew that. Too bad you failed to realize it sooner. Before Marian blew her brains out on your windshield."

Marlie stared straight ahead, white with anger, eyes dry.

"We will be landing within ten minutes," said George. "Your face is a mess. Go to the restroom and wash up."

She hesitated and then pushed her way past him. When she returned five minutes later, she was transformed. Every head looked up as she stepped into the aisle, her firm, slender figure erect, head thrown back, long blond hair brushed and bouncing with each step. When she reached her seat, she leaned over and let her breasts brush against George's shoulder.

"Could you move your legs, please?" The voice was soft, sweet. But when George swung to the side and looked up, the smile dissolved and the blue eyes turned hard. "You bastard," she whispered.

Willard heard the engine pass overhead and looked up, gaping at the strange-looking plane as if he had just seen a pterodactyl.

"I think it's Swiss," said Tom. "They use them a lot in the mountains." He grinned. "The CIA used to fly them on spook missions into Laos back in the bad old days."

The Pilatus Porter, a propeller turning at the tip of its long, pointed nose, banked its boxy wings and began a sudden descent.

Willard clenched his fists and held his breath. It was going to crash. Marlie was going to crash. Die. But he was frozen, unable to make a sound.

The plane leveled off just before touching down on the rough dirt strip and came to a quick stop. The door opened and two people got out. Zed drove up in the red pickup truck and put their baggage in the back. As the truck pulled away, the pilot ran up the engine, which hummed rather than roared. The plane lurched when the brakes were released and bounced slowly down the strip. A few hundred feet later, it was airborne.

Willard's eyes kept flitting from the pickup that held Marlie to the airplane. How could so small an engine lift so large a plane? The odd-looking Porter made a steeply banked turn north. Willard watched it climb into a thick gray cloud, rising into the sky like a homesick angel.

The pickup truck crossed a small wooden bridge over the South Platte River and raised clouds of dust as it bounced across the field toward the cluster of farm buildings where Willard and Tom were standing. Willard could see Marlie sitting between Zed and George, but she did not acknowledge his upraised hand as the truck passed him en route to the house. So he stood there, unsure of what to do, hoping that Marlie would come to him so he would not have to go to her. But when Tom began walking toward the house, he followed, arriving just as Marlie and George went into the house; Zed followed with the bags.

Willard stopped near the truck and simply stared at the house. Zed came out a few moments later, waved, and drove off with Tom. A minute passed. Two. Feeling self-conscious, Willard turned on his heel and went to the barn where the large trailer was parked. He climbed the metal stairs, closed the door, and was immediately bathed in the green glow of the cathode ray tubes. He sat before the console. Nothing had changed in the fifteen minutes since Tom had told him the plane was coming. The cursor was still winking at him from precisely the same spot on the screen. How predictable it all was. How comforting to have something that will do only what you tell it to.

He resumed working on his program and immediately heard the buzzer.

SHIT said the computer.

Willard glanced at the line, found the misplaced symbol, and corrected the instruction.

GO said the computer, its LEDs flashing green.

His hands moved quickly across the keyboard as he immersed himself in the act of creation, the computer clicking generously with applause. All other thoughts vanished as he concentrated on a world of his own making. His singlemindedness kept him from noticing that the trailer door had opened and closed.

A few minutes later, he swiveled to face another keyboard and caught the movement of a silhouette in the periphery of his vision.

"Hello, Whiz." The voice was soft, warm.

He knew immediately it was Marlie, yet could not utter a reply.

"I was watching you," she said. "You're so intent on your

work, so intense. You're really into this stuff, aren't you?"

He mustered a not very firm affirmative.

"Would it bother you if I sat down and watched?"

Willard stumbled to his feet. "Uh, no. Not, uh, at all."

He went to the far end of the trailer, retrieved a small stool, and placed it beside his.

Marlie sat down. "I don't know very much about computers. I mean, there was a word processor in an office where I worked once. But I really don't know much about them." She paused. "I do find them fascinating, though."

"You do?"

"Oh. Yes." Her voice sank into each syllable as if it were a feather bed.

Willard felt his throat constrict; his forehead suddenly turned clammy. A single question transfixed his mind: Now what?

"Would you tell me what you do? I'd like that."

"Really?" His voice almost squeaked.

"Really," she said. She crossed her legs, brushing her thigh against his. "Tell me what you're doing."

"Uh, sure."

She leaned toward the screen, the pressure of her thigh much more firm.

He started out slowly, his voice wobbling, but his confidence grew as he talked about his machines and the program he was developing to intercept the Chicago Switch.

"We know the algorithm," he said. "The government published it in 1977."

"They published a secret code?" she asked incredulously. "Boy, that was dumb."

Willard mustered a nervous laugh. "An algorithm is simply a known mathematical function, like two and two are four. That by itself won't give you an encryptive cipher—a code, that is. To do that, you need a key. In this case, the key is simply a binary number."

"A what?"

"That's a numbering system that uses only zero and one, instead of zero through nine." He cleared the screen of the cathode ray tube and typed zero through nine in a column. "Now, that's the way the numbers look to you. But the machine only knows if it has an electronic pulse, in which case it's a one, or if it doesn't, in which case it's a zero." He typed four zeroes on the screen. "That, in machine language, is zero." Three zeroes and a one appeared. "And that, obviously is one."

"What happens when you get to two?"

He typed "0010" on the screen. "That's two." He then typed "0011."

"And that must be three," she said.

"That's right. And it goes on like that. Inside the machine there are millions of bits arranged in groups of eight. That's called a byte."

She giggled. "What a cute name."

Willard relaxed. "Okay, you remember the algorithm I told you about."

"You mean, two plus two is four."

"It's not that simple, but you've got the idea."

"Go ahead."

"Well, the key is made up of fifty-six bits. When the electronic signal with bank transactions goes into the computer, a tiny microelectronic chip scrambles the information so that only someone who has the key can unscramble it."

"But if there are only fifty-six bits, can't your computer just try fifty-six different codes until one of them works?"

Willard laughed. "Don't I wish it were that easy." He shook his head. "No, it's more like seventy *quadrillion* possible codes."

"How much is that?"

"Can you imagine a million dollars?"

"I'd sure like to," she said throatily.

"Well, a quadrillion is a billion times a million."

"Wow!"

"Hard to imagine, isn't it? Few people can. But that should give you some idea of the problem we're facing."

"You mean, *you're* facing. You're the only computer expert the organization has."

"Well, that's not quite right. We do have twelve mobile units and two electronic intercept teams, one in Chicago, the other in San Francisco."

"What do they do?"

"They've got antennas and other kinds of listening and transmitting devices." He paused. "Of course, I did have a hand in writing the program."

"You're much too modest, Whiz." She turned toward him. "Do you know what the most important part of a man is?"

He felt the warmth of her breath against his cheek. "Uh, no."

"His brain," she said. "And Whiz?"

"Yes?"

"You have a beautiful brain."

He kept his eye on the screen, afraid to turn and meet her face to face. "Thank you," he said.

She put her hand lightly over his. "Why don't you look at me?"

He turned on the stool until their faces were only inches apart. Her head began to tilt, eyes closed, lips slowly parting. At first he was afraid she was going to faint. Then he realized it was, unmistakably, an invitation.

He meant to kiss her lightly, but as soon as their lips touched, her arms shot around his neck, and her tongue invaded his mouth. It was so sudden, so surprising that he felt powerless to respond. It was if he were on a roller coaster—unable to control it, unable to escape.

She loosened her grip and pulled back. "I closed the door," she said. "But I'm not sure it's locked."

Willard fumbled for a switch beneath the console and heard the tumblers click into place. "It's locked."

"You're sure? I'd hate for anyone to come in on us."

"No. Uh, I mean, yes. Yes, I'm sure."

"Good. We wouldn't want that now, would we?" The tone was teasing, suggestive.

Willard replied with a palsied nod.

Marlie stood up, slowly undid the three remaining buttons on her blouse, and shook it from her shoulders. Willard could not move; he just sat there, staring at her, eye to breast.

She closed the inches between them, gently rubbing her breasts against his face. He made a few feeble efforts to kiss them.

Taking a half step back, she reached down and took him beneath his arms, coaxing him to his feet. Quickly, she unbuttoned his shirt and tossed it on the keyboard. Regaining some presence of mind, Willard swept the shirt to the floor behind him.

Marlie let her hand slide from his chest to his crotch and slowly squeezed. "My, my, my. What have we here?"

This was not the way he had imagined it. This was not on the program. But it felt good. Very good. And most important, she was here. Marlie.

She loosened her grasp and deftly unbuckled the too-long belt. Practiced hands rapidly undid the snap and smoothly lowered the zipper. Willard's pants fell to his ankles, revealing a pair of jockey shorts that were as taut as a crossbow.

Marlie looked down and smiled. When her eyes met his, she slowly, sensually, ran her tongue over her upper lip. Then she slid her hands down the sides of his body into his shorts, pulled them over the flagstaff, and let them fall.

"My, my, my," she purred. In a matter of seconds she stepped out of her skirt and kicked it away.

Willard took a step toward her and started to trip on his pants but quickly caught himself. "Uh, my shoes. I, uh, ought to, you know, take them off, I guess."

"No problem," she said, as she knelt before him. Once she had freed him from the tangle of clothes and shoes, she began to nibble on his inner thigh, gradually working her way toward his crotch.

Willard pulled back.

"Is something wrong?"

"No, uh, no. It's the computer. Let me set it."

"Go ahead."

Willard groped toward the keyboard and quickly cleared the screen. He tapped a few keys and suddenly the diodes began to flash bright green. LICK LICK LICK said the computer.

"Wow! That's terrific!" Marlie exclaimed. She immediately began to follow the commands, her tongue flicking rhythmically with the lights.

SUCK SUCK SUCK said the computer.

She began drawing him into her mouth, in synchronization with the flashes.

Willard just stood there in a state of transport, reality and fantasy finally fused into one.

When the lights began to flash FUCK FUCK FUCK, she lifted herself onto the printer, back arched, legs spread. As Willard advanced toward her, a diode in the machine shorted out.

SHIT said the computer.

"Shit!" said Willard.

"NO!" screamed Marlie.

"B-b-b-b-but," Willard shouted.

"I won't! I absolutely refuse!"

"B-b-but you don't understand."

She slid off the printer and began to retreat. "Get away from me! Back off!"

Willard's spirit and his member began to droop. "Please," he pleaded. "It's not what you think it is."

"Yeah? Then what the hell is it?"

"It's just the machine telling me something's wrong inside.

Something could have burned out. Or, maybe there's a mistake in the program."

"Yeah, one hell of a mistake, if you ask me."

"Please, Marlie. I wouldn't . . . I mean, I couldn't have wanted you to do something like . . . well, like that." The panic and distress in his voice were clearly genuine.

Her anger spent, Marlie extended her hand toward Willard, who grasped it eagerly.

He hardened quickly and, in a swirl of action that left his face burning and his heart pounding, found himself on top of her, drawn into her body, deeper and deeper, the heat rising almost to the point of pain, until the sole focus of his physical and mental force suddenly exploded. His knees began to buckle, but Marlie steadied him. And his strength quickly returned.

After remaining in each other's arms for several minutes, Marlie pulled away. Crouching in the dim light, she began to retrieve her clothes from the trailer floor. She dressed herself unhurriedly, ran her hands through her long blond hair and shook it free. Wordlessly, Willard also got dressed.

"We mustn't tell anyone," she said. "We have to go on as if nothing happened between us. You do understand that, don't you?"

"Yes," said Willard, who did not understand.

"Well, I should probably be going."

"Okay."

She drew close to him and kissed him lightly on the mouth. "It's getting late. See you at dinner?"

Willard nodded. "I'd like that."

The sun was now behind the clouds and the Continental Divide, but Marlie's eyes quickly adjusted to the failing light. She walked slowly toward the house, aware that Willard was watching her from the darkened doorway. It had not been as bad as she had feared. The novelty of having the computer flash those dirty—no, naughty—words almost made it fun. She began to smile. Men are so easy to control. Fuck them good *and* make them afraid of losing it, and they'll do damn near anything. Well, most men, that is. The director was different. She owed him, the organization, everything. Had he not found her when he had, she almost certainly would have killed herself. Though her friends at the encounter center argued that she was not to blame for Marian's death, Marlie had not been able to erase the image from her mind. The gunshot, the blood and brain tissue spewed all over the inside of her car.

She shuddered at the thought and crossed her arms as if to ward off a chill. George thought he could control her by exploiting her sense of guilt. Well, let him try. I'll show the director just what that little bastard is. And Willard's going to help me.

She stopped several feet short of the house, ran a hand through her hair, shook it free, and sighed. He's weird, all right, but underneath it all Whiz is just a lost little boy who needs one hell of a lot of work. She smiled. Then again, for a mercy fucking, he's not half bad.

CHAPTER 11

She moved like a dancer, and Paul's eye fixed on her from a distance when all he could see was the outline of a tall brunette walking toward him. There was both grace and precision to her step, elegant symmetry as each foot was splayed and extended forward.

Wheeler, his back to the woman, was talking about that morning's deliberations of the National Security Council. When he realized that Paul's attention was somewhere else, he stopped in mid-sentence and turned his head. A smile of recognition lit his face.

"My God, who is that?" asked Paul.

"You're about to find out," said Wheeler.

She stopped directly in front of them and extended her hand. "Good morning, Colonel."

"Good morning, Miss Ellsworth," he replied, accepting a firm handshake.

Her direct brown eyes moved immediately from Wheeler to Paul. "And you must be Dr. 'Cassidy.'"

Before Wheeler could make an introduction, she gave her hand to Paul. "I'm Natasha Ellsworth," she said. "We're scheduled to meet this afternoon."

Paul recalled the brief entry on the schedule of meetings Nancy had given him that morning: "3:00. Ellsworth, MATER."

"I would stop and talk, but I am due in the deputy director's office," she said. "So, if you will excuse me . . ."

"Certainly," said Paul.

She nodded first to Wheeler and then to Paul. "See you at three."

"At three," echoed Paul.

She smiled and resumed walking down Mahogany Row. Paul and Wheeler followed with their eyes, her long dark hair gently rising and falling with each step, the movement of her lithe limbs accentuated by the closely tailored cream-colored suit, the slit revealing a provocative flash of leg.

"Magnificent, isn't she?" said Wheeler.

"I'll say." As she turned the corner, Paul asked: "What does she do for MATER? Programmer? Analyst?

"That, my friend, is the president of the company."

"Really? How well do you know her?"

"Acquaintances only. Besides, like you, I'm a happily married man—and plan to stay that way."

The remark turned Paul's thoughts back to Helen. Where was she? How had she handled the news of his death? Would they be able to put their lives back together?

"Look," said Paul, "I'm worried about Helen. I want you to have someone, maybe that Secret Service team, contact her, tell her I'm alive and . . . Well, I just don't want to put her through too much. Could we, I mean, could you do something like that for me?"

"I talked to Dr. Simpson about that after the meeting this morning. The Secret Service is keeping their watch on her, and they've spotted no other surveillance teams. At some point we'll find a way to get word to her, but for the time being, we think it best that you not communicate with her. We just can't take the chance: it's too dangerous." He paused. "We may not know *who* the enemy is, but I don't need to tell you what *sort* of enemy we're dealing with."

Paul nodded gravely. "No. You're right."

After an awkward silence, Wheeler picked up the thread of their interrupted conversation and forcefully regained Paul's attention. "You would not believe the pressure Dr. Simpson is under to blame the whole damn thing on the Russians."

"Blame what? Nothing's happened yet. At least nothing's happened to the Fed."

"True," said Wheeler, "but you don't know these guys. Most of them are pimply-faced academics who gained what little knowledge they have about the Soviets from right-wing magazines. I guess I shouldn't be surprised. Ambitious young, and not-so-young, men arrive in Washington with the baggage of each new administration. And all of them have the same thing in mind: get tough with the Russians."

"One day they're going to blunder us into war," said Paul.

Wheeler glanced at his watch. "Well, enough of this cheerful talk. Winchell's expecting us."

The meeting centered on the technology NSA could command if the Chicago Switch were electronically challenged. Paul was amazed at how far the Agency's reach extended. Many of the concepts he and his academic colleagues had only discussed as theoretical possibilities had already become hardware in NSA's technological arsenal. But what form would the threat take? More important, how would *they* respond?

The Agency, Paul soon discovered, was riven by fierce bureaucratic competition, each of its disparate parts concentrating solely on its own narrow tasks. Highly capable when it came to encrypting US military communications or intercepting and decrypting those of foreign governments, the Agency was weak in conceptual matters. And not for lack of brain power. No, these government scientists, many of them defrocked professors surrounded by computer terminals and blackboards, were unquestionably talented when it came to the mathematics of breaking ciphers. What they could not crack were the walls of their own bureaucracy. And while no one had said so explicitly, it became clear to Paul that this was one of the reasons why he, an outsider, had been invited into the inner sanctum.

When Natasha Ellsworth came to his office that afternoon, she confirmed his conclusion in a long and thoughtful conversation. He tried at first to concentrate on what she was saying but soon found himself mesmerized by her physical presence: the flash of her brown eyes, the brows rising for emphasis, lips slightly parted, slender hands conducting an animated counterpoint. Of her beauty and brains, the evidence was considerable.

Except for a muted shade of lip gloss and a light touch of color on the high cheekbones, Natasha wore no makeup. There was obviously no need for it. Her face was flawless: the nose slender and perfectly straight, lashes long and full, skin glowing like alabaster at sunrise. Paul could not remember the last time he had seen, much less met, a woman so beautiful. And he was certain that no woman had ever seemed so eager to listen to him, to draw out his thoughts. So when Natasha suggested that he and the colonel meet her for dinner at the officers' club at seven o'clock, he readily accepted.

At six-thirty Wheeler came to Paul's room. Simpson's secretary had just informed him that he had to return to the West Wing of the White House immediately for a special meeting of the National Security Council.

As he walked to the club, Paul tried to assuage a growing sense of uneasiness. Could he not simply admire a woman, Natasha, for her intellect and beauty? Did there have to be sexual overtones? He tried to recall when he had last, as someone once said, "looked upon another woman with lust in my heart." No example came to mind. Then he smiled, recalling how he often felt during those first warm days of spring when the somber shades of winter were banished to the closet and women began to appear in bright colors, sheer fabrics clinging to curves, gusts of wind revealing firm slender thighs. Helen would laugh as he described his reactions—his head swiveling from one woman to the next, each looking better than the one before. You're just like a little boy in an ice cream parlor, she would say. But at night, alone with Helen, no daylight fantasy entered his mind as he entered her body.

As he passed the parking lot, he saw Natasha just as she was getting out of her Porsche. She had changed into a black dress, which wafted over her knees as she slid off the seat. Paul waited until she caught up with him.

That afternoon they had talked almost exclusively about business. Paul focused on the sorts of individuals he might need to help him on the project, while Natasha described in candid detail the qualities and qualifications of the scientists and engineers at MATER who would be available to assist him. Over dinner, the conversation gradually became more personal.

Paul, feeling a pleasant tingle from the wine, suddenly asked, "How did you get involved in this business?"

She smiled. "You mean, what's a nice girl like me doing et cetera, et cetera?"

"Something like that."

"What do you know about MATER?

"To tell you the truth, not very much. And what I recall from a few years back is not too, well . . ."

"You saw some of those ads, I'll bet."

Paul nodded. "I'm afraid so."

She laughed again. "Imagine how I felt. I was at Smith when those ads started running in the aerospace journals. The anti-war movement was riding high, and like everyone else, I was caught up in it." She stopped and began to smile. "Well, about as caught-up as a Smithie is likely to get."

"You mean you wore white gloves to the peace rally."

"Of course not. It was strictly Villager skirts and Pappagallo shoes."

Paul shook his head. "It's coming back to me: one of the ads, the one with the fighter pilot."

"You mean 'Catch a Killer at Forty Thousand'?"

"Yeah, that one: with the young pilot. All you see between his oxygen mask and helmet are a pair of hard blue eyes. Outside the canopy are big puffy clouds; in the background the silhouette of a Mig. Then at the bottom: 'A killer is stalking Lt. Gavin. Who can find him? We can. We're MATER. And MATER knows best.'"

Natasha threw her head back and shook her long brown hair appreciatively. "Do you remember the one in the jungle?"

Paul nodded. "I forget what it was called, but it had a young infantry officer, face blackened, eyes hollowed by fatigue. And it said something like: 'Somewhere beneath triple-canopied jungle a guerrilla death squad stalks Lt. Rose and his platoon. His mission and their lives depend on their eyes . . . and our ears. Who can find them? We can. We're MATER. And MATER knows best.'"

"I was appalled when my father showed me those," she said. "But he just laughed it off. To him it was just a big put-on—his favorite term in later years. It also turned out to be good for business. We made quite a bit on our ELINT patents."

"But you still haven't told me," Paul continued, "how you got into the business? It's a long way from being a lit major at Smith to classified consulting with the National Security Agency."

"It's a long story, but I'll try to make it short," she said. "Dad was in the O.S.S. during the war and was a bit at loose ends when he got out of the service. He came from an old Connecticut family more distinguished for its ancestry than its credit rating. So, what's an unemployed Yalie to do?

"Fortunately, Dad had a genuine entrepreneurial flare and correctly calculated that there was a niche in the marketplace for someone who could serve as a broker between the sellers of technology and the military men who would lead the Cold War. Originally, our acronym stood for 'Military Applications in Technology, Electronics, and Radar'; at least, that's what he used to tell anybody who asked. But the truth is, Dad had a strange sense of humor and thought it a rather droll name for an outfit that peddles the stuff of war."

"So, Pater had an odd sense of humor."

"Oh, yes. And it didn't stop there. How many God-fearing, anti-Communist patriots in the fifties, do you suppose, named their daughters Nataska?"

Paul began to laugh.

"I've also got an older brother. He got stuck with Vladimir. But unlike me, he has a nice, normal middle name: Richard. So, we've always called him Rick."

"But why didn't *he* wind up in the business?"

She smiled. "It was one of those typical father-son conflicts. Rick denounced Dad's work as immoral—this was during the Vietnam thing, of course—and headed for the mountains of Utah so he could be free of what he called 'the money-grubbers of the military-industrial complex.'"

"I had friends who did the same sort of thing in Vermont and Colorado," said Paul, "but most of them eventually went straight. Did that happen with Rick, too?"

"If you mean, did he come home, the answer is no. Oh, he and Dad reconciled just before he died, but Rick was determined to stay in Utah, and that's what he did."

"What's he doing? I mean, is he some sort of latter-day mountain man?"

She laughed. "Not hardly. Oh, he started out with that in mind, but eventually moved to Park City and joined the ski patrol. He started meeting people that way, and one thing led to another. The next thing you know he was studying for his real estate license and buying and selling little parcels of land. Strictly to help his friends, he would tell us. Pretty soon he was borrowing from banks and putting together larger and larger parcels and holding onto them. The next thing you know, the Deer Valley ski resort hits the drawing board, and big brother decides to chuck flower-power once and for all and go full-time into land sales." She shook her head, smiling. "He's got a net worth now that runs well into seven figures. And you know what? He still thinks of himself as a ski bum. He just can't see how much like Dad he really is. I'm convinced the entrepreneurial thing's genetic."

"And what about his daughter?"

The brown eyes flashed momentarily. "I don't have Dad's flare for salesmanship, but I am very much his daughter."

"In what way?"

She reflected for a second, brow slightly knit, before replying. "I doubt that I could have launched a business like this from scratch the way he did. Perhaps I could have, but there's no real way of knowing. What I *can* do is sustain it and make it grow." A mischievous smile crooked her mouth. "After all, nurturing is supposed to come naturally to women, isn't it?"

Paul shook his head. "I've been married to a feminist for ten years, and if I've learned anything from living with Helen, it's how to avoid booby-trapped questions like that."

Natasha laughed appreciatively and then met his eyes. "Tell me about her," she said softly.

Floating pleasantly on a vinous cloud, Paul smiled. "That's very polite of you to ask, but you don't really want me to talk about my wife, do you?"

Neither her voice nor her eyes were ambiguous. "Yes, I do, Paul; I really do."

He started at the beginning, describing how he met Helen on the ski lift at Stowe, the excitement of their two-year courtship, the danger of the snowy mountain roads he would drive each weekend. Except for an occasional word or gesture of encouragement from Natasha, his monologue continued unbroken through the dregs of the wine and over coffee. When he finished, both sensed the evening was over. After splitting the check, they walked in silence to her car.

"May I give you a lift?" she asked.

"It's just a short walk to my quarters. But thank you, anyway."

When they reached the Porsche, she opened the door and

met his eyes. "Thank you for a very delightful evening." She raised her hand to his cheek and touched it lightly. "I think your Helen is a very lucky woman."

He bade her good night and began walking toward his room, breathing deeply of the mild April night, images of Helen dominating his inchoate thoughts. Thunder in the distance. A wind rising. Suddenly, a bolt of lightning illuminated the sky and the concrete fortress now controlled his life. Though he had no sense of impending danger, he realized in that instant that he had never felt more alone.

PART III

CHAPTER 12

"Look, damn it! You ordered me to do it."

George Anders looked down at his short porcine fingers. "I issued no such order."

"Bullshit!" Color began to rise in Marlie's face. "You know what Willard wanted from me. You read that disgusting program of his. You brought me here, out in the middle of nowhere, and did everything but put a gun to my head to get me into that trailer."

At the mention of the word *gun*, George looked up, the sliver of a smile on his round, ruddy face. "I serve the director. We both do. As it happens, Willard and his machines are vitally important to the organization. My assignment is to facilitate his mission. And that is also why you are here. As for what transpires in the trailer"—he gave a slight shrug—"that is between you and Willard."

"And what did you think we'd be doing in there?"

"I did not think anything."

Marlie's eyes widened. "Oh, come on. You knew damn well what he wanted."

"That may be true," he replied. "What I did not know was what *you* would do. And frankly, I do not want to know."

"Yeah? Well, you'd better think about it, because Willard wants to marry me."

"He *what*?"

"You heard me. He wants the two of us to get married. Maybe go to Wisconsin and live on that farm."

George's eyes hardened into microdots. "That is impossible."

"Well, how about that. We finally agree on something."

George glanced to the side, seemingly lost in thought. A minute passed.

Marlie ran her hands along the front of her jeans. The motion caught his eyes.

"We will have to devise something," he said.

"How about letting me go back to headquarters?"

He gave a quick shake of the head. "We did that after Willard met you in Kansas, and his work product went into decline. Since your return, the, ah, human interface you provide has had its correlation in his productive capacity."

"You mean he works better when he's getting laid."

"I would not put it so crudely."

"No, George, your *language* is never crude." She paused. "But you sure are."

"Your personal opinion of me is unimportant," said George. "We have a mission. And unfortunately, its success hinges on the performance of a very unstable human being."

Marlie ran a hand through her long blond hair. "A loony, is more like it."

"I know you will find this hard to believe," said George, his voice turning soft, "but I deeply appreciate the personal sacrifice you have been making. Indeed, I commended your performance in my most recent communication with the director, just last night."

"You did?"

"I most certainly did," said George. "And, I might add, the director expressed his appreciation and, if I may interpret his remarks, his *admiration* for your effort."

Marlie glanced down and then raised her eyes. "That means a lot to me."

"As well it should." He paused. "But we do have a problem, and we need your cooperation in dealing with it."

"You mean Willard?"

"Indeed."

"Look, it's bad enough having sex with the guy. I'm not going to marry him."

"Nor would you be expected to."

"So, what do we do?"

"To be frank, I do not know. Just try to keep him happy and productive." He met her eyes. "May I speak in confidence?"

"Certainly."

"Our entire operation hinges on Willard perfecting his program. Once that happens, the director is prepared to move swiftly into the next phase. And at that point, we will be transformed immediately from a peacetime garrison, if you will, into an army on the field of battle."

"Really?"

"I assure you, I do not exaggerate."

"And my job is to keep Willard happy, is that it?"

"I realize that is something you would not have chosen to do on your own," said George. "But we, ah, the director is counting on you."

Marlie sighed. "Don't worry. I won't let him down."

"No. I knew we could count on you."

George glanced at the papers on his desk as Marlie started to leave. But as soon as her back was turned, his eyes moved to the seat of her jeans and followed the rhythmic swing of her stride.

Marlie found Willard easy to control. At the breakfast table, it was strictly small talk. The main topic was always the unpredictability of Colorado weather. When Marlie would leave the table, Tom would leer appreciatively, drawing smiles from Zed and Willard and an inevitable scowl from George. Neither Marlie nor Willard gave any outward sign that there was something between them.

Willard would then go to the trailer, begin working on the machines, and immerse himself in his program. At one o'clock, Marlie would bring sandwiches and a thermos of hot spearmint tea. Willard did not care at all for the sprouts that spilled out of the strange-looking pocket bread, but he was not about to say anything that might offend Marlie.

After their first lunch, he made an advance toward her, which she deftly rebuffed.

"Not now, darling. You have work to do. I'll see you here later, sometime tonight."

He carried the word *darling* for the rest of that day as if it were a vase of delicate crystal. Over and over he would say the word and try to imagine the sound of her voice, the way she looked at him when she said it.

He skipped dinner that evening and kept working on the computer, covering the digital clock with a printout so he would not know the time. The hum of the machines hid the sound of the door opening; only when the stale air in the trailer surrendered to a more pleasant scent did he realize she had come.

He turned and found her smiling, lips parted, teeth glowing in the green light of the cathode ray tubes.

"Hello." Her voice was deep, warm.

"Have you been here long?"

She shook her mane. "Just a few minutes. I like watching you work."

"You do?" The second word almost stuck in his throat.

"Yes. It's all so, you know, scientific. Like I imagine a spaceship might be."

In his imagination he immediately pictured the two of them, naked and tumbling weightlessly in a space capsule.

"Did you get a lot done today?" she asked.

"Sure did. Would you like to see what I've been working on?"

"If you'd like to show me. Not that I'd understand it."

"Oh, don't worry. You'll understand it."

He reached for a stool and placed it next to his. A taut denim-clad thigh brushed his arm as she sat beside him.

He typed a command on the console and sat back. "Just watch the screen," he said.

For the next fifteen minutes she sat there dumbfounded as one image after another appeared on the CRT. The first was a needle-nosed airplane, similar to the one that had brought her from Denver to the ranch. It moved slowly across the screen, propeller turning, gathering momentum, the dashed lines of the runway flashing by. When it was airborne, it turned right and headed directly toward them. She had to restrain the impulse to duck as the onrushing image filled the screen.

One electronic specter followed another: a car racing around

an oval track, crashing and exploding into thousands of shooting stars; a farm with barns, cows, and a running brook; a
woman with long hair who was transformed into a wild horse
and back again. The final image began with a small point of
light that slowly blossomed into the shape of a heart containing
their names: Whiz + Marlie.

"Well," he said, "what do you think?"

"I don't know what to say. I really don't."

"Did you like it? I did it for you, you know."

"Of course I liked it. I guess I'm just amazed at how very
creative you are. You're not only a genius; you're an artist as
well."

He grinned. "It's really not all that hard."

"How long did it take you to do that?"

He uncovered the clock. "Well, it's ten-sixteen now, and I
began working on it after lunch. So, all in all, maybe eight,
nine hours."

"What about your program?"

He shrugged. "I'll get back to it tomorrow."

"It was nice of you to do this," she said. "It was like a
valentine." Then, in a cooler voice: "But I don't think you
understand. The only reason headquarters let me come here
was because they think I can help you. If you don't get that
program done, they'll order me back. Don't you understand
that?"

"But I'm right on the verge of finishing it. If it runs, we
could try it on line next week."

"How're you going to do that?"

"We're going to alter a transfer on the Fed's network between San Francisco and New York. We'll intercept the signal
before it gets to the Chicago Switch and change the amount—
but not by very much, maybe a dollar or two, just to prove we
can do it. Then, we'll intercept, and alter, the confirmation
message going back to San Francisco, to make sure it matches
the original amount." He paused. "Did you follow that?"

"I'm not sure."

"Okay," said Willard. "Let's use a simple example: San
Francisco sends a hundred dollars to New York. We intercept
the transfer and alter it to a hundred and one dollars *before* it
gets to New York. But the confirmation message going back
to San Francisco will now show a hundred and one. So, we
have to do a second intercept to change that confirmation signal

from a hundred and one back to the original hundred. If the program works, it could be days, even weeks, before anyone finds out."

"How long does all this take?"

"That depends on how busy the circuits are. If there's not much traffic, both intercepts could be over and done with in a matter of minutes, even seconds."

"That's amazing."

"We haven't done it yet."

"Oh, but I *know* you can do it," she said.

The enthusiasm in her voice broadened the smile on his face.

He turned and found her mouth waiting for him, but the kiss was brief.

"You have to promise me something, though."

"What?"

"You have to work hard on your program. No more valentines. It was sweet of you to do it, and I really liked it, but no more. Okay?"

Willard agreed.

When Marlie closed the trailer door an hour later, she left him weary but smiling. But instead of going to bed, he stayed in the trailer to work on his program. Tom found him passed out on the console the next morning.

CHAPTER 13

Art Hamlin looked nervous as he stood beside Harding Harrison in the Agency's ninth-floor conference room. A bald, heavy-set man with gold-rimmed bifocals, Hamlin felt most comfortable with the machines and technicians of the Chicago Switch. Sensing Hamlin's unease, Harrison took the director of the Federal Reserve's Systems Communication Center around the long table, introducing him to the members of Working Group Seven.

When it was his turn to speak, Hamlin fumbled momentarily with the dimmer switch. When the lights were low, he turned on the projector and began talking about the computer center, using slides to walk the group through the Fed's building at Jackson and LaSalle in Chicago's financial district.

In the machine room, the technicians, tieless, cigarette packs bulging from shirt pockets, had clearly posed for the photograph, because they were looking at the computers rather than working on them. "We're totally automated now," Hamlin acknowledged. "These fellows are here in case one of the machines goes down, but they rarely do." He paused. "At top speed, we can process about forty-eight thousand messages per hour. On the average, we handle about eighty thousand a day among the twelve districts; there are also about the same number of transactions *intra*district."

A closeup of the printer clicked into place. "Here is a typical *inter*district transaction. This particular one is from Dallas to Chicago."

The next slide closed in on the four-line message. Hamlin continued: "What does it take to move several million dollars from one commercial bank account to another? As you can see, the communication is quite brief. This transaction, for instance, originated at one thirty-seven on the afternoon of April tenth, and it was message number 3899 from Dallas to Chicago on that day. The remaining symbols have no significance other than to synchronize the machines.

"Now, just beneath the message-number group is the name and account number of the person initiating the transfer. The amount: Three million, seven hundred and some thousand. Then we have routing information to send it to the Chicago district and, finally, the name and account number of the recipient at Continental Illinois, which happens to be across the street. It could just as well have been a member bank in Peoria or anywhere else in the region served by Chicago."

"That's it?" asked Harrison. "Just four lines?"

Hamlin nodded. "That's all it takes. It doesn't matter if they're transferring several thousand or several million."

"And your error rate?" asked Paul.

"Fairly small," said Hamlin. "It ranges, I suppose, from about one error per hundred thousand bits to one in a million."

"What does that mean in practical terms?" asked Harrison. "How often does a message contain an error?"

"It varies, of course," Hamlin replied. "But as a rule of thumb, we figure there'll be one transmission error in every fifty messages."

"That's machine errors, I take it, not human error," said Paul.

"Correct," said Hamlin. "And it can be caused by any number of things besides glitches in the program. Lightning. Squirrels biting the wire." He paused, a slight smile on his face. "But we rarely get involved in that; the system pretty much corrects itself. It makes cyclic redundancy checks to verify that the message Chicago received was identical to, say, what Dallas sent. The machines do that automatically whenever the verification message we transmit to Dallas fails to match what they sent us. When that happens, the machine simply repeats the initial message."

"And it doesn't set off any sort of alarm?" Harrison asked.

Hamlin shook his head. "No reason to. It's strictly a mechanical problem; the machines handle it."

"And what about operator error?" asked Paul. "How do you handle that?"

"Take the message we were just looking at," said Hamlin. "Suppose the operator had accidentally punched *four* million instead of three. That'd probably be cleared up by the banks themselves, the same as if someone had written a check that was too large or too small. Most wire transactions go through in less than two minutes, and it's not unusual at all for account holders or commercial banks to correct errors like that in a matter of hours."

"But," said Harrison, "suppose the system broke down completely. What's your backup?"

"Our down time on these machines is less than an hour a month," Hamlin replied. "And it's unlikely we'd ever have a complete breakdown. But we do have some redundancy in the system. In fact, we can run the system on just one machine. Not on a real-time basis, mind you, but the system can catch up by the end of the day."

"And if the Chicago Switch were knocked out, say, by an act of sabotage," said Wheeler, "what then?"

"That, too, is built into the system," said Hamlin. "If Chicago goes down completely, Atlanta and Philadelphia could operate the entire system, dividing the twelve districts between them."

"What do you see, then, as your principal security problem?" asked Wheeler.

"The same as it's always been, Colonel: the human problem," said Hamlin. "In the old days, before everything was computerized, no bank would issue a large check unless two officers approved it, one to draw the instrument, the other to countersign it. And when I say large checks, I'm talking about thousands, not millions, of dollars.

"Now, banks routinely conduct transactions in the millions, and they're usually done by young men and women sitting at computer terminals. They're taking home only a few hundred dollars a week, yet they're moving millions of dollars every minute just by tapping a few keys. The temptation, even for a basically honest person, must be tremendous. For a relatively intelligent person with a bit of larceny in his soul, that temptation could be overwhelming."

"But even with a few million dollars," said Paul, "you're talking about limited sums. The fellow who illegally transfers ten million to an accomplice's account in New York is gambling on one big throw of the dice. There may be other people who'll try to do the same thing, but that particular fellow is not going to show up at the bank Monday morning to steal ten million more."

"I'm not sure I follow you," said Hamlin.

"My point is this," said Paul. "Your concern about electronic criminals is understandable. But from a mathematical perspective, crimes such as those are relatively low cost and not very high probability events." He drew a breath. "Working Group Seven is predominantly concerned about something quite different: events of very low probability but extremely high cost."

"In military terms," Wheeler added, "it'd be the difference between terrorist attacks and a nuclear war. However dangerous they may be to individual generals or ambassadors, terrorists by themselves cannot destroy the United States. But a nuclear war could."

Hamlin took off his glasses and rubbed the bridge of his nose. "I understand the analogy, but I'm not sure how it applies to the Switch. I mean, I suppose somebody could try to blow us up." He shook his head. "Is that what you're driving at?"

"Our principal concern," said Harrison, "is that someone or some group—perhaps even some country—might develop a technological rather than physical means of penetrating the Chicago Switch. They might, for example, try to jam your wire and microwave transmissions."

"Or even worse," Paul added, "they might use state-of-the-art electronic equipment that could not only intercept your traffic but also alter its content."

"If they had that sort of capability, they wouldn't have to blow us up," said Hamlin. "We'd be out of business."

"Does that concern you?" Harrison asked.

"If I thought it were a serious possibility, I'd be extremely concerned," Hamlin replied. "But you're talking about someone neutralizing the system on a permanent basis, and I just don't see how that could happen. Do you?"

"I don't know," said Paul. "What we're trying to do is make sure we've correctly anticipated the sort of damage the Switch might suffer if it were subjected to an assault by a team of sophisticated computer and telecommunications experts."

"I see," said Hamlin, who did not.

Winchell took the pipe from his mouth. "We've got electronic experts here who'll do their best to make certain that vital communications links are protected. But suppose the Fed could not operate the Switch, what would that do to the financial system?"

"I, ah, I don't know," said Hamlin. "We move about two hundred and fifty billion dollars a day. The banks, the financial markets—all of them depend on us." He shook his head. "I'd hate to think what might happen if the country suddenly had to go back to paper."

He paused momentarily and then continued. "To give you some historical perspective, Woodrow Wilson signed the legislation that created the Federal Reserve's first telegraph switch in 1913. And a major reason for creating it was to preserve financial liquidity so there'd be no repetition of the Panic of 1907.

"That came about because the government's metallic holdings put a ceiling on the currency available to the banking system. Capital was fixed and had to be moved physically or on paper. When brokers and banks started calling in their notes, there wasn't enough currency to cover them. That started a panic that swept the nation as suddenly as a tidal wave. Banks had to close their doors, and dozens of them, large and small, went under."

"Could that happen again?" Harrison asked.

"Not with government agencies like FDIC backing the financial system and the enormous liquidity of our major institutions," Hamlin replied. "But the system depends on liquidity—on the ability of capital to move swiftly to wherever it's needed. If it can't move . . ." He let the words trail off.

"If it can't move, what?" Harrison asked.

Hamlin drew a breath. "Let me put it this way: people think the banking system's built on money. It's not. It's built on confidence. If everybody walked into their bank tomorrow morning and demanded their money, there'd be no way in the world they'd be able to get it. The money a person puts into his checking or savings account is loaned out to businesses, homeowners, and the like. Cash sitting in a vault doesn't make money; loans do. So, on any one day, a bank may have on hand only a tiny percentage of its assets in cash." He leaned forward. "I'm not telling you, I suppose, anything you didn't already know."

Harrison smiled. "Please continue."

"Well, my point is simply this: confidence is all that keeps us from beating down the doors, demanding our money. Destroy that confidence, and God knows what might happen."

There was an awkward silence, and then Harrison spoke. "Well," he said, smiling, "you could always say, 'The check's in the mail.'"

CHAPER 14

Willard hadn't seen so many men wearing suits since his father's funeral. And at first, he felt as alienated from them as he had from his drunken uncles.

There was a sameness to the men. Precisely tailored pin-striped blue suits with matching vests. Hair neatly trimmed. No beards or mustaches. Small black notebooks open, gold-plated pens at the ready. They even traveled in pairs, Willard observed, like nuns.

In his white shirt and tan cotton slacks, Willard felt out of place; yet he was unmistakably the center of their attention. Their pens would move when he spoke, freezing in mid-air with each pause.

He was explaining how the computer would test the Federal Reserve's communications network the next day, but he could tell from their questions that none of them grasped the technical aspects of his program. One man was so awed that he began calling him "Dr. Zack."

Willard was too surprised to correct him. And soon, everyone was calling him "Dr. Zack," even "Professor Zack." George, standing on the periphery, said nothing to contradict them.

So he accepted the unearned honorific and tried to affect a serious and, he imagined, professorial mien. After nearly an hour of answering questions, he felt so comfortable in the role that the expression on his face did not so much as flicker when the lone German in the group referred to him as *"Herr Doktor Professor."*

Later, alone in the trailer, he began to laugh. Though he had attended three universities, each soon expelled him for failing to complete basic courses. He had managed to get through one full semester at MIT only because a professor had intervened with the administrative office to grant him an extension for freshman mathematics and English. But when he ended the second semester with twice as many "incompletes" on his record, the school dropped him.

Not that it mattered. The only reason he had gone to college in the first place was to gain access to the school's computers. The machines he had used in high school were much too simple; the programs were geared for novices, and the teachers seemed to have less of a feel for the system than he had.

Feel. That was it. He had tried once to explain to his mother why computers fascinated him, but was never able to put it into words. All he could tell her was that he had a *feel* for the machines, a sense of their internal order, their inexorable logic. While others saw only the keyboard and CRT, he saw, or felt that he saw, into the machine's anatomy—indeed, into its very soul. Those microcircuits may have appeared inanimate chips to others, but to Willard they were as alive, as vital, as the organs and appendages of the human body.

Every university left its computer room open around the clock. The rent-a-cops who were supposed to check student I.D. cards rarely gave them more than a cursory glance, and Willard was so familiar a figure there that they usually just nodded him inside. So it often took several months after he had been expelled for someone—usually, a new guard—to catch up with him. When that happened, he would pack his printouts into a couple of suitcases and move on to a new city, a new campus. There was a national network of computer addicts—"hackers"—who were in regular contact with one another, so he never had trouble finding a place to stay. He also found a ready circle of people whose interests were similar to his own, people who did not regard him as a misfit. Indeed, they respected him and sought his advice.

How different they were from most of the people he saw on campus: the jocks who would stride to the center of the walk, forcing him to the edge; the women who would look past him as if he did not exist. Outside of his small circle of acquaintances, Willard was the center of nothing and the occasional target of unpleasant remarks.

But now everything had changed. Today he had been the center of attention among men who might once have laughed at him. "Dr. Zack," he repeated aloud to himself. "*Professor* Zack." He chuckled with pleasure at the sound of it.

He wished Marlie could have been there to see how the men from headquarters had treated him. But the director wanted her to return to the ship, wherever that was, to report to him on the progress of the operation. He had started to protest when she told him of her trip, but she stopped him.

"Look, Whiz," she said, "the only reason we're here and together is because the director wants your operation to succeed in the worst way. But if I cross him, that's it. I'm out. So when I'm ordered to the ship, I go." She paused. "Besides, you're going to be very busy with the sector heads."

"The who?" he asked.

"Your computer program is the heart of the operation, but there's a lot more to it than just you."

"Like what?"

"We have people all over the country, working in banks, in the government, *everywhere*," she said. "The sector heads will be arriving right after I leave. I'm not sure what each sector does or how things are divided up and all that. I'm not supposed to know. Besides, I'm not sure anybody knows the whole thing, except the director."

"What about George?"

"Possibly," said Marlie, "but there's no way of knowing. I mean, we can't just come out and ask the guy. And even if we did, and he gave us an answer, there's no way we could be sure he was telling the truth." She shook her head. "No. There's no way you can ever be sure about George."

Willard had no idea where the eight men stayed. They simply appeared in the morning and parked their rental cars beside the house. But by the time he left the trailer to go to bed at night, the four cars would be gone.

George had introduced the men collectively as "my colleagues" but did not volunteer their names, and Willard did not ask them. They kept to themselves, clustered in small groups around the dining room table or walking outside when it was sunny. The door to the den George used as an office was always closed, the muffled sounds of a one-sided conversation indicating that someone was on the phone. Though the men seemed busy, as far as Willard could tell they did nothing except talk to one another.

When he mentioned that to Tom, he ran a hand through his curls and grinned. "Don't you understand? They don't have to do nothing," said Tom. "They're executives."

But this morning had been different. After breakfast, George asked Willard to stay at the house. After Tom and Zed left, he poured himself more tea and offered the pot to Willard, who declined.

"This is it," said George. "The day all of us have been waiting for."

"You've got the line?"

"Yes," said George. "One of the men—they will be here soon—has a crew that has patched into the line the San Francisco Fed uses to transmit to Chicago. A second has an insider in the wire transfer room at one of the banks. As soon as that person sees a transaction going to New York, we will get a call with the details. At that point, you will take over."

Willard had been through the drill so many times that the actual event now seemed trivial. Indeed, all he had to do was plug in the account number from San Francisco and let the program do the rest. The challenge had been in writing the program. As far as he was concerned, the results were a foregone conclusion.

George continued: "After it has gone through, our people in San Francisco and New York will report to their sectors by phone. That information will pass, in turn, to us. If the two numbers differ by precisely the margin we have grafted onto the transaction, then we will know to a certainty that the program works."

"It works," said Willard.

"I am sure it does," said George. "But the director wants to see proof, and that is precisely what we will give him. Today." The tight line of his mouth had broken into a smile.

Willard was about to ask him about Marlie, how soon she would return, when he heard the cars pull up.

"You can stay here, if you wish, or you can go back to the trailer," said George.

"I think I'll go back to the trailer," said Willard, getting to his feet.

"Fine. When we have the account number, we will bring it down. You are set up with the communications team, are you not?"

"Yes," said Willard. "Everything's on line."

"Good," said George, who walked him to the door.

As Willard opened the screen door, eight voices, singly and in pairs, began to greet him. "Good morning, Dr. Zack." "Good morning, Professor." *"Guten Morgen, Herr Doktor Professor."*

Willard nodded wordlessly and proceeded toward the trailer. When he had closed the door, he sat down and looked at the console. The cursor was winking at the point where he had stopped an hour or so before. He smiled. How reliable, how predictable, how comforting he had made his world.

Two hours later, there was a knock at the trailer door. "It's open," called Willard.

George entered; the eight men followed, crowding into the narrow aisle between the machines.

"Here it is," said George, as he gave Willard a slip of paper.

Willard turned to the keyboard and quickly typed in the number.

George looked at the screen and silently read it. "That is correct," he said.

"And how much do you want to change the transaction?" Willard asked.

"One dollar less."

"Okay," said Willard, as he tapped the keys. "One dollar less going in. One dollar more on the confirmation, going out."

"Is that all that is necessary?" asked George.

Willard nodded. "The intercept and alteration are handled automatically."

"Very well." Then, turning to the group, he made a gesture toward the door. "Gentlemen, if you will."

After the door was closed, Willard cleared the screen and went into the computer's memory for the program Marlie had called her valentine. He had been working on a rocket-firing sequence when he heard someone at the door. He quickly cleared the screen.

It was Tom. "George would like to see you up at the house."

When Willard got to the house, he found George seated at the dining room table, surrounded by the eight men, all of them smiling broadly.

"Congratulations, Whiz," said George. "It went splendidly."

"I told you it'd work," said Willard evenly.

"And so it has. So it has."

Willard shifted uneasily from one foot to the other. "Is there anything else you want me for?"

George got to his feet. "No, but please feel free to join us here," he said, his arm sweeping across the table.

"Oh, that's okay. I mean I've got some things to do in the trailer."

"Whatever suits you," said George, expansively.

All nine men were looking at him, and Willard could see they were not only pleased but somewhat in awe of him. It was an unsettling, though not an unpleasant, feeling. He had learned after many years how to handle anger and disdain when they were directed at him. But admiration and respect were utterly alien to his experience.

Not sure of what he should do, he simply nodded to the group and left.

CHAPER 15

"That's it," said Wheeler, as the car pulled into the driveway.

As the gray sedan came to a stop, Paul could see the windows had an opaque, silver coating; a short aerial protruded from the roof. The driver got out and opened the rear door. Wheeler got in first. As Paul sat down, he reached reflexively for the door handle.

"That's all right, sir," said the driver. "I'll get it."

After a short stretch down the parkway, they turned onto a two-lane blacktop. The red light on the telephone flashed. Wheeler picked it up, spoke briefly, then put the handset back into its cradle.

"That was Winchell," said the colonel. "He's sorry he didn't get to talk to you before you left, but the meeting didn't let out until just a few minutes ago. Anyway, he says you can stay at MATER as long as you wish. Just call the dispatch office when you're ready to leave, and they'll send a car."

"What about you?" asked Paul.

"I'll sit in on the first session this morning, but it'd be a waste of time for me to have to plow through all that technical stuff. Besides, Dr. Simpson's called an NSC meeting for four this afternoon, so I've got to get back."

Wheeler led him into a steel and smoked-glass office building that would have been unremarkable but for the radar dishes and electrified barbed wire surrounding it. At the first meeting, Paul recognized several at the table from past academic conferences.

At first he was reluctant to get into the discussion, but the group seemed intent on drawing him out. When one of them made a disparaging remark about public-key cryptography, Paul immediately sprang to the attack.

"And what would you put in its place?" he asked. "The DES with its quaint little trapdoor? Or do you think everyone should be using one-time pads?" Paul glared at the man who had challenged him and was now retreating behind the logistics of lighting his pipe.

"The idea is so elegant," Paul continued. "Primes are the basic building blocks of numbers; they're also one of the oldest fields of study in mathematics. The earliest algorithms go back some two thousand years. Mathematicians have been trying to factor large numbers into primes for thousands of years. Gauss, who was probably the greatest mathematician who ever lived, failed to solve it."

He drew a breath. "With the machinery you fellows have, you can test a hundred-and-fifty-digit number to determine if it's prime in a matter of microseconds. But you could run every machine in this building and at Fort Meade—every damn one in the country, for that matter—for billions of years and not be able to break a number that long into its prime factors. You don't need couriers; you don't need secure lines to protect the key. With one-way mathematical functions like that, you can publish your key in the newspapers, broadcast it on television, send copies to the Russians if you like. Build a cipher on sufficiently large primes, and I'll bet everything I own that neither you nor they are going to break it."

Paul looked around the table and let his gaze come to rest on the man who had challenged him. The man nervously tamped down the tobacco in the bowl of his pipe and began trying to light it. Paul watched, saying nothing.

Finally, the man spoke. "It's been a few years since I read

your paper in *Transactions*. Clearly, I'm going to have to reread it."

Paul smiled at the man's amiable concession, took a deep breath, and eased back into his chair.

He spent the rest of the morning with individual scientists who were working on contracts for the Agency. At noon, his guide left him in the reception room that led to Natasha's office; her secretary immediately picked up the phone to announce his arrival. Natasha came through the door moments later.

"Paul, how good to see you again," she said, taking his hand in both of hers.

"Good to see you," he replied.

And it was good. His memory of her beauty seemed inadequate with her standing before him, the warmth of her hands around his. An instant later, she released her clasp and preceded him into her office.

Paul glanced around the room as Natasha led him to a soft gray sofa. The office was sparely yet elegantly furnished, the muted colors of the walls and furniture offsetting the sharp lines of the glass tables, the gleam of brass and chrome. The paintings, which reminded Paul of the pourings of Pollock and the rectangles of Rothko, proved on closer inspection to be, in fact, Pollocks and Rothkos.

"Excuse me for a moment," said Natasha.

She passed in front of him, long, dark hair bouncing, her body moving with the grace and precision he remembered. Stopping in the open doorway, she leaned on the doorjamb and spoke briefly with her secretary. Paul's eyes seemed to have a will of their own as they followed the graceful arc of her back and the smooth curve of her buttocks.

When she turned and found him staring, she smiled and closed the door. "I've told Angie to hold my calls," she said as she walked toward him. She sat in a chair adjacent to the sofa. "I thought we'd have lunch here a bit later, if that's all right with you."

"That'd be fine," said Paul.

"I've asked John Scotto to join us," she continued. "We don't have titles and ranks at MATER—everyone here is simply an 'associate'—but if we did, John would probably be our chief scientist. Everyone on staff has their own projects, most of which are funded by Big Brother, but some of them we underwrite."

"Sounds a bit like the university."

She smiled. "It is. And intentionally so. Dad wanted to make money, but he understood that scientists and engineers need room to think and tinker. Other firms buy staffs to match their contracts; MATER has always regarded her people as long-term investments. It's proven to be a wise approach. We still need government contracts to cover the mortgage—we own the building—and pay the light bill. But when you're trying to attract talented scientists, you need to let them use that talent as they see fit. Some of the time, at least. Once they've signed on, their care and feeding become my top priority."

"Your 'maternal nurturing role'?"

Her eyes and voice united in laughter. "I see I'll have to watch what I say around you. You have an excellent memory."

"Not really," said Paul. "It's just that, well, that dinner was a very pleasant, very memorable evening." He had spoken without thinking, and when he realized what he was saying and how she might interpret it, he felt a sudden sense of panic.

Natasha had been looking down. After an awkward pause, she raised her eyes and met his. "Yes," she said softly. "It was."

During the ten years he had been married to Helen, Paul had often looked at other women, admiring their beauty without ever feeling any real desire. He had always assumed that his loyalty to his wife had grown naturally from their love. Now he found himself wondering. Had he been faithful out of loyalty, or merely out of habit?

"Paul?"

"What? Oh, I'm sorry."

Her lips parted in a smile. "I think I remember that, too."

"What?"

"That look you get when your body's here but your brain's somewhere else."

"That obvious?"

She shook her head. "You're too complex a man to be obvious."

He grinned. "Come on."

"No, I'm serious," she continued. "I cannot claim to know you well, but you're no 'linear function.'"

He chuckled. "An 'imaginary number' then?"

"We'd better quit now," she said.

"Why?"

"Because I've just about exhausted my limited knowledge of mathematics."

After discussing the people Paul had met that morning, Natasha said, "You remember my mentioning John Scotto?"

Paul nodded.

"You didn't get to meet him this morning because he was at the Agency," she said. "But I think you'll find him interesting."

"I seem to have heard his name."

"He was at Stanford some years back as an electrical engineer. We brought him here to work on telecommunications. He's our guru on packet-switching and digital data transmission. He's also been working on an analog scrambler for voice, but that's proving the tougher problem."

"I can believe it," said Paul. "Why doesn't he just go to digitized, synthetic speech?"

She shook her head. "I think you just overloaded my circuit again. Remember? I'm the gal who quits at 'linear functions.'"

When John Scotto joined them several minutes later, Natasha led them through a door in the rear of her office to an adjoining room; a small table was set for three.

"A think tank may not travel on its stomach, but I have always abhorred cafeteria fare," said Natasha. "So, we have a caterer in Baltimore who cooks for our dining room downstairs, and we order from the same menu. This being Friday, crabcakes are the entrée. I know John likes them, but I took the liberty of ordering for you."

"That sounds fine," said Paul.

"We also have what I call our 'panic steak,'" she continued, "for those who don't like what's on the menu."

"MATER wouldn't dream of serving her toilers a hamburger," said Scotto.

"*Her*? I notice people here tend to use the feminine when speaking of MATER."

"Force of habit," said Scotto. "Miss Ellsworth's late father always used the feminine pronoun when speaking of MATER. Most of us unconsciously picked up on it."

Paul immediately liked John Scotto. There was something comfortable about the man. His clothes could have been described as campus-rumpled: well-worn herringbone sport coat, button-down shirt, and Irish wool tie, its bulky knot slightly askew. He was just as rumpled physically: short and getting a bit pudgy, curly brown hair turning silver at the tips, facial lines that flowed naturally into a world-weary smile.

The conversation ranged broadly. But after the plates had been cleared, the coffee served, and the waiter dismissed, Natasha took the initiative.

"John has been working on a number of concepts to make digital communications more secure," she said to Paul. "And I wanted the two of you to meet so you would be aware of each other's work."

Scotto needed no additional encouragement. "You're familiar, I assume, with multipath networks and packet-switching."

Paul smiled. "Familiar? Yes. But I'm no expert in such things. I guess I still consider myself to be something of a pure mathematician."

"Stick around here," said Scotto, chuckling, "and you'll wind up an *im*pure mathematician."

After acknowledging their appreciative smiles, Scotto sipped his coffee, leaned back in his chair, and began to speak. "The problem I'm dealing with here is as old as the race. To wit: how can two people be certain that the message that has passed between them was not read by someone else?

"We've got all sorts of ways we can communicate electronically: land lines, microwaves, optics, satellites. And with digital encryption we can protect our transmissions from unsophisticated eavesdroppers. But the opponent who has sophisticated communications is something else. If he has the technology necessary to intercept the message, he may also have sufficient computing power to decipher it."

For nearly an hour, Paul listened, occasionally interjecting a question, as Scotto described the intricate network of computers and multiple paths of communication he was developing to prevent digital messages from being intercepted.

"What it comes down to," said Scotto, "is an intricate sequence of encrypted digital packets. To intercept them, an opponent would have to be monitoring every land line, optical fiber network, microwave repeater, and satellite channel over which those packets could be moving. And he would have to put the packets together—in sequence, mind you—before he would have the complete message. If just one packet were missing, there'd be no way he could decrypt the parts of the message he did have, *even with the key*."

Prompted by several more questions from Paul, Scotto began going into detail. Fifteen minutes later, Natasha rattled her cup and saucer. Both men turned.

"Well, you two seem to have hit it off rather nicely," she said. "And I hate to intrude, but we do have Paul scheduled rather tightly this afternoon."

It was nearly six o'clock when the last meeting ended. As Paul was leaving the room, a secretary handed him a message. It was from Natasha, asking him to stop by her office.

Angie was leaving when Paul arrived. He leaned around the open door and saw Natasha at her desk. She was on the phone but waved him into the room and pointed toward the sofa. He sat down.

Paul listened to her voice, its rich timbre, the almost melodic cadences punctuated every so often by laughter. He paid no attention to what she was saying; he simply listened to the sound. Leaning back against the sofa, he closed his eyes and other senses to everything but her voice. Her laughter rang in the room like a small silver bell.

He opened his eyes when the sound stopped and saw her moving toward him. She took the adjoining chair.

"Tired?" she asked.

Paul shook his head. "Just relaxing a bit."

"It's been a long day for you. I would imagine my associates have given you some things to think about."

"That, I can assure you, is an understatement. You have some excellent people here, individuals who could hold their own anywhere."

A smile lit her face. "Coming from you, that's quite a compliment."

"And I meant it to be," said Paul. "As a personal matter, I prefer the university. But the way scholars go about their work, well, it tends to be haphazard. A department might try to achieve some balance by hiring a professor who specializes in this or that field, but once you've got tenure, you can try something new, move on to something else. You're pretty much free to pursue whatever you want to."

"We've got a little bit of that here, too," said Natasha. "But we're contractors. So, of necessity, much of our work—most of it, to be frank—is tied to a contract."

"A government contract," Paul added.

"At this point, yes. But I think a lot of our project output could eventually spin off into the private sector."

Paul raised a hand. "You're beginning to sound more like a government contractor than an erstwhile English lit major."

"But that's what I am, Paul. I'd like nothing better than to read books or take off for the Rockies." She swept her hands through her hair and shook it free. "By the way, that was my brother Rick on the phone. He called to tell me that Park City got ten inches of snow last night, and it's now sunny and in the high fifties. This is the last weekend for Deer Valley, and he wants me to come out."

"You going?"

"Don't I wish," she said. "No, I've got too much to do here."

"How often do you get to Utah?"

"Not very," she said. "But it is nice to know there's someplace in the mountains that you can call home."

"Yes," Paul said softly. "It is."

As Natasha continued talking, Paul let his mind drift north to Helen and their house in the Green Mountains of Vermont. He was so tempted to call, if only to hear her voice, and had reached for the phone several times. But each time he was frozen by doubts. Would someone be eavesdropping now, more than a month after he'd been "killed" in a car bombing? He doubted that they, whoever "they" were, would still be monitoring her phone. Yet, could he take the chance? He had seen how easy it was for the NSA to intercept microwave transmissions and sort them out by telephone exchange and number. *Until we have identified the adversary,* Winchell had warned him, *we have no choice but to assume that he can, at a minimum, do whatever we can do—and, perhaps, more.*

No, damn it. He couldn't do it. Even if the risk were one in a thousand, he would not risk Helen's safety simply to indulge his loneliness.

"Paul?"

"Uh. Oh, I'm sorry."

"You had that lost-in-space look again."

He sighed. "Something you said started me thinking."

"A pleasant thought, I trust."

"Yes," he said. "It was."

She smiled. "Well, it's nearly seven, and you've been here almost all day. You must be getting hungry."

He patted his stomach. "That, I'm afraid, is a congenital condition with me."

"You look to be in good shape."

"Well, they do have a gym, so I manage to burn off some of the calories I gobble down," he said. "My basic problem is that I like food, although what they serve at NSA could cure me of that."

She leaned forward. "Would you like to have dinner here?"

"You mean, your caterer works evenings, too?"

"No," she replied. "But I do."

He cocked his head quizzically.

"There's a full kitchen adjacent to the room where we ate lunch. We might not be listed in the *Guide Michelin*, but I'm told I do passably well at the range."

"I wouldn't want to impose on you."

"It wouldn't be an imposition, Paul. It'd be a pleasure."

"You're sure?"

"I'm sure. In fact, I do this fairly often."

"What's that? Lure men up to your office for dinner?"

She laughed. "Sometimes, if a meeting runs late, I'll cook for whoever's staying. Besides, you'd be amazed how a home-cooked meal can loosen up a tightfisted banker. The guy usually comes in wound up tight anyway. First he had to sit in a cab in the Midtown Tunnel eating fumes, then he gets packed into the shuttle at LaGuardia with a hundred-and-some other people with identical attaché cases. He leaves National in his Hertz, and then gets lost on the interstate trying to find his way up here." She drew a breath. "That sort of routine would try anyone's impulse toward generosity. It's amazing what a little mothering can do."

"You serious?"

She smiled. "Well, let me put it this way: last month I doubled MATER's line of credit, and you know what it cost me?"

"What?"

She opened her hands as if holding a platter. "About this much Coquilles St. Jacques."

Paul laughed appreciatively.

Natasha moved swiftly in the kitchen. A butcher had already deboned and flattened the chicken breasts, and she deftly stuffed them with fresh tarragon and parsley rolled in butter. Paul was still making the salad when she finished the Chicken Kiev.

At dinner the talk was mostly about business.

"You remember my talking about weaning MATER away from government contracts?" she asked.

"Your spin-offs?"

"That's right. I was starting to explain when you chastised me for using 'Newspeak.'"

Paul sipped his wine and smiled. "Go right ahead."

"When Dad brought me into the business—and that was only five years ago—we focused almost entirely on how the Soviet Union might compromise our computers or telecommunications and what we, meaning the United States, could do to keep our edge in technology. You've seen what they have at NSA and what our people are working with here. And I think you'd concede that we've maintained that technological edge."

Paul nodded. "I had assumed we were ahead of the Russians in practically every department, and what I've seen in the past month at Fort Meade has convinced me that that is in fact the case."

"And I'd agree," she said. "Naturally, we have to maintain that lead, but I'm now convinced that we—and now I mean not just the United States but Western Europe and every other modern country—must become more concerned about threats from within."

"You mean subversion?"

"If by subversion you mean political action, Commies at home and all that stuff, no. Absolutely not. But if you mean private greed and economic disruption, yes."

"I'm not sure I follow."

"Well, let's take those banks that got hit electronically. It sure wasn't the Russians who went into Kansas and Ohio and Wisconsin."

"You know that, and I know that," said Paul. "But Otis tells me there are guys in the White House who're trying like hell to pin it on Moscow or, at the very least, Havana."

"That's to be expected when you're dealing with ideologues, whether they're of the far right, like the current crowd, or of the far left." She paused. "No, I'm convinced that whoever crashed the computers at those three banks did so for their own, private reasons."

"But who?"

She smiled. "If I knew that, Harding could disband WG-Seven tomorrow. We've got a serious problem, no doubt about it. But the problem isn't going to go away when we finally discover the people behind all this. And for one reason: the problem *is* the technology."

"And not the criminals?"

"Look at it this way, Paul: there have always been thieves, but it took railroads to create train robbers. And you could say much the same thing for airplanes and hijackers. Does that make any sense?"

He nodded.

"So the problem, as I see it, is that technology is creating new types of criminals. And it's not simply a new classification. Anyone with a gun can walk into a bank and hand the teller a scribbled note and a paper bag to fill up. But the sort of individual who can penetrate a bank's computer or a company's communications network is a breed apart. He doesn't need a gun, and no one's going to shoot him if he gets caught, so he doesn't even have to be gutsy, in the sense of physical courage. Yet, he can do more damage to a bank with a computer than a thousand bank robbers could do at gunpoint."

"I couldn't agree with you more," said Paul. "In fact, I expressed some very similar ideas in my book."

She met his eyes directly. "I know. It was your book that started me thinking about these things."

Momentarily speechless, Paul finally said, "I'm flattered. No, that's not it. I'm honored. That's the word. Honored."

She drew a breath. "I know how much you value your work at MIT. And I know how very deeply the Agency has drawn you into this crisis. But at some point, this contretemps will pass. The problem will not. We've got the nucleus here of an organization that can make computers serve rather than threaten us. I would like you to be a part of that." She paused. "A part of us."

"Uh, I don't know what—"

"I'm not looking for an answer now," she said. "I just want to lay my cards on the table. When the time's right, we can talk seriously." She stood up. "Now, enough of business, let me clear the table and make some coffee."

Later, the torrent of conversation now at an ebb, they were listening to a Mozart piano concerto on the stereo when the phone rang. Natasha moved across the room to answer it. Paul glanced at his watch. It was nearly 10 P.M.

She answered, spoke briefly into the mouthpiece, and then covered it with her hand. "It's for you, Paul. It's Winchell."

Paul crossed the room and took the handset. He spoke briefly and then hung up. He turned to Natasha.

"Something's come up," he said.

"Did he say what?"

"No. But he's sending the car for me."

"It'll be here in about ten minutes, then."

"Should I go downstairs?"

"No, you might as well wait here. The guard will buzz the office."

Paul was leaning back on the sofa, eyes closed, as the second movement of Mozart's C-major piano concerto began to draw him into its elegiac harmonies. The dissonant buzz of the intercom broke the spell.

Paul found Nancy Ho and William Winchell in the operations center when he returned from MATER.

"Chicago reported an anomaly I thought you'd want to know about immediately," said Winchell, through pipe-clenched teeth. He nodded to Nancy.

"If I can direct your attention to the screen," she said, indicating the large CRT in front of the console. A column of four-line bank transfers appeared. "Now," she continued, "look at message 156 from the San Francisco Fed: A routine transfer of $1,876,932 from a Transamerica account at Crocker to an IBM account at Citibank in Manhattan."

She punched several keys, and the message received by the Federal Reserve Bank of New York appeared alongside the original transfer. "These messages are identical but for one digit," she said. "Citibank is crediting the IBM account with a dollar less than was actually transmitted by San Francisco."

Paul did not immediately grasp the significance. "What's so unusual? As I recall, Art Hamlin said the system experiences about one error in every fifty messages or so."

"That's correct," said Nancy. "But what happened here was quite different: a one-in-a-trillion shot."

"If it was, in fact, a random event," Winchell added.

"As far as San Francisco is concerned, the last three digits of the transaction were 932," said Nancy. "But Chicago and New York are *both* showing 931."

"And there were no other errors on the line?" asked Paul.

"Chicago and San Francisco went over every one of the day's transactions," said Winchell. "And there were several more errors. But all of them—all of them, that is, except this one—were corrected automatically by the system and retransmitted."

"I'm curious," said Paul. "How did we find out about it?"

"It was discovered by someone at IBM in New York who

wondered why Transamerica was underpaying the invoice by a dollar," said Winchell. "She called the fellow in San Francisco to kid him about it, and he called the wire transfer room at Crocker. Then the Fed got into the act. Hamlin called here about an hour ago."

Paul smiled. "You know, Hamlin said transmission errors are sometimes caused by lightning or squirrels biting the wire. Which do you suppose it was this time? Lightning striking twice? Or a matching pair of fried squirrels?"

For the next two weeks, Nancy and Paul worked together monitoring the Chicago Switch. But nothing happened. Every error that turned up proved to be random, mostly garbled names or account numbers.

Once, when the Switch reported a discrepancy in a transaction from the Federal Reserve of San Francisco, Paul felt a sudden rush of adrenaline. After a frenzied hour preparing for a full-scale attack, the error was traced to an electrical storm in Utah.

As the Memorial Day weekend approached, Paul's loneliness acquired a new companion: tedium.

CHAPTER 16

Willard looked at the digital clock, not to read the time but to calculate to the minute how long it had been since he had last seen Marlie. Every day for the past two weeks he had asked George when she was going to return, and each time the answer was the same: he didn't know.

Then, that morning, after Tom and Zed had left the table, George told him what he had been waiting to hear, that Marlie would be returning the next day. Willard immediately wanted to know when she would arrive and whether she would be flying on that funny little plane, but George said he would not know any details until the following morning.

George then steered the conversation to the next phase of the operation: diverting some $80 million or more in transactions over the Chicago Switch to designated accounts in major city banks. It was no longer a matter of simply altering a single digit; Willard's program would have to change the name and the account number going into Chicago and modify the return confirmation to match the original message. The operation was set for the Friday before the Memorial Day weekend, just three days away.

When Willard asked who would be receiving the money, George set his jaw. He would supply the names and account numbers on Friday morning just before the operation. Willard would know only what he needed to know and nothing more.

It was not only a familiar reply, it was final. Whenever George invoked security as the rationale for a decision, Willard knew it would be futile to argue. Not that it mattered. His program was the important thing. If the organization got rich off it, so what? As long as it continued to provide him with top-line equipment, he didn't care. Besides, with Marlie returning, he had more pleasant things to contemplate.

There was so much he wanted to tell her. How much he missed her. How lonely he had been. The pride he felt after the first operation had gone off perfectly. The eight men from headquarters who seemed so open in their admiration for him.

He had so thoroughly immersed himself in perfecting the program that he was not even aware that Mother's Day had come and gone until he glanced at a calendar one evening. He had seen his mother only twice since her remarriage three years before, and though she and her new husband seemed friendly and had invited him to move into their house, he sensed their relief when he declined. He had called her from Cleveland two months ago to tell her that he had found work with a small computer firm, but their conversation had been desultory, filled with nearly as many pauses as words.

How are you? she had asked. How do you feel?

I'm fine, he replied without elaboration.

When she tried to draw him out, he withdrew. He didn't know what to say. In spite of the cheerfulness in her voice, he felt the distance between them increasing. Once a safe harbor from his father's drunken rage, she now seemed beyond reach. She remained his mother in name, but the sense of kinship was gone.

He had never talked about his mother to anyone. Several so-called guidance counselors at school had tried to encourage him to speak about his family, but he had refused. Maybe Marlie would understand. She understood so many things. At least she seemed to. Yet she had said very little about herself. In fact, he knew nothing at all about her life before she joined the organization. Even now, when they spoke it was about the work they were doing, the computer, their mutual disdain for George. And when they weren't talking or eating, they were usually making love.

Willard glanced away from the screen. Yeah, he thought, it'd be nice to have somebody to talk to. He began to grin. But it'd be even nicer getting laid.

After breakfast the next day, George announced that Marlie would be arriving by car early that afternoon. So Willard sat in a chair outside the trailer, pretending to scrutinize the stack of computer printouts in his lap. It was a mild, windless day, and the sun felt good on his face.

He glanced now and then toward the distant highway, and shortly after three o'clock saw a plume of dust. A moment later, a black sedan came over the rise. He was standing beside the ranch house when the car came to a stop.

A man in a dark blue suit got out and opened the rear door. Marlie, who had been stretched out on the back seat, slowly got up. Her face was drawn, her hair stringy. She smoothed her rumpled clothes and managed a wan smile when she saw Willard's upraised hand. The man removed her bags from the trunk of the car, closed the doors, and drove off without so much as a word.

"Are you all right?" Willard asked, as he moved to pick up the two suitcases.

"I'm okay now, but that ship . . . We had rough seas, and I was sick the night I got on it and for most of the last two weeks." She ran her hands through her hair and shook it free. "If you even showed me a picture of a ship, I'd barf on the spot."

"I wouldn't do that to you," said Willard earnestly.

She glanced at him sideways. "No, Whiz. I don't think you would."

She walked ahead of him and stopped at the side door. Willard's arms were straining with the heavy bags, and he let out a sigh as he set them down.

"Can I get you anything? A sandwich or something."

She gritted her teeth. "I don't even want to look at food. I just want to take a bath and go to bed."

After an awkward silence, she reached for the doorknob.

"I, uh, I'm really glad you're back, Marlie."

She nodded and began turning the knob.

"And I was, well, hoping that, you know, you might like to come over to the trailer."

She shook her head.

"No, I don't mean now. I know you're tired and all. But, you know, maybe later?"

Willard followed her into the house with the suitcases.

She stopped at the door to her room. "Thank you, Whiz."

"Sure. Glad I could help."

A nod.

"See you later?"

A shrug. "We'll see," she said softly.

Marlie was not at the dinner table that night nor at breakfast the next morning, but she dominated Willard's thoughts. Indeed, he could think of little else. He tried to work on his program and then on the electronic valentine, but found he could concentrate on neither task. Shortly after noon, the trailer door opened, and he saw her familiar silhouette against the light. She was carrying a tray of sandwiches.

"Oh, it's you. I mean, it's really good to see you," said Willard. "Are you feeling any better?"

Marlie nodded. "After my bath, I climbed into bed and put a pillow over my head. The next thing I knew, it was ten o'clock this morning."

"Wow. You really were tired."

"Yeah, I was. But I feel a lot better now."

Willard smiled. "That's good. I was starting to get worried about you."

"You needn't worry about me. I can take care of myself."

"I know that. It's just that I was, well, concerned about you." He lowered his voice. "You mean a lot to me."

Marlie's face remained a mask.

"Well, uh, what's for lunch?"

"The usual: avocado, string cheese, bean sprouts—"

He finished the sentence: "And wholewheat pita bread."

"You got it."

They ate quietly for several minutes. The food and hot spearmint tea seemed to perk her spirits.

When they finished eating, Willard asked about her trip. She began to describe it but stopped in mid-sentence and turned to him.

"What do you think about our next mission?"

"You mean shifting funds from one account to another?"

"Yes."

"Well, it's a bit harder than diddling with the numbers, but I don't think we'll have any trouble with it. We'll only be hitting transfers over a million dollars. I figure we'll have to hit forty, maybe fifty that day to get us in the eighty-million-dollar range."

"So, you think you can do it?"

Willard grinned. "If we can switch one number, it won't be all that much harder switching a sequence. After all, we're not going to alter the entire message. The money will still be going between the same banks. I'm just going to change the account it's going to. That's all. It'll still be going to the same bank. And the rest of the message will stay the same."

Marlie drew a breath. "But do you feel right about it?"

"Yeah. I think it'll work."

"That's not what I meant," she said. "I'm asking how you *feel* about doing it. How do you feel about stealing eighty million dollars?"

He shrugged. "I don't know. I guess I really hadn't thought about it that way."

"Is it just some sort of game to you?"

"In a way. I mean, it's a lot more of a challenge than playing those idiotic video games."

"And you're doing it with somebody else's quarter. Is that it?"

He chuckled. "Yeah. I guess you could say that."

Marlie refilled her mug and quietly sipped the tea.

Willard broke the silence. "Did I say something wrong? Did I upset you?"

"That's not it."

"Are you okay? I mean, you're not going to get sick again, are you?"

"I'm all right," she replied.

She continued sipping her tea until it was finished. Then she set the mug down and turned to face him.

"If I tell you something, Whiz, will you promise to keep it a secret?"

"Of course," he said earnestly. "I'd never break my word to you."

She nodded. "Well, I tried to argue against this operation on the ship, but when they knew how I felt about it, they wouldn't even let me in to see the director. A few months ago, I could have gotten in to talk to him about practically anything."

"I don't understand. Before you left, you seemed enthusiastic about what I was doing."

"That's true. But that was when we were acting out of principle, striking back at a government that has been brutal to us. We were acting for a reason, out of conviction. Now all we're doing is stealing. Just like real estate swindlers, phony stock peddlers, bank embezzlers, you name it. We're no different from any of them. We're just doing it on a larger scale."

"But you and me, *we're* not stealing. I mean, not a dime of it's coming to me."

"I know. I know," she said softly and then lapsed into silence.

A minute passed before Willard spoke. "I've had a lot of time on my hands since you left. So I made something for you."

"What is it?"

Willard grinned. "You'll see."

He tapped a few keys, and a digital image of the needle-nosed airplane appeared.

"I have a feeling I've seen this before." The tone in her voice was gentle, without a hint of reproach.

"The first part is pretty much the same, but I added a whole lot of new stuff while you were away."

The airplane sequence was followed by the racing cars that crashed and exploded in a shower of stars. Though she remembered the pastoral scene, she found herself fascinated once again by the transformation of the wild horse into a woman with long hair. Though she could easily envision herself as a wild mare, picturing Willard as a mustang on the open range required a lot more imagination.

When a ship appeared on the screen, Marlie let out a groan. "God, I think I'm going to be sick," she said in mock anguish.

Willard immediately stopped the sequence.

Marlie started to laugh. "I was just kidding, Whiz."

"Well, uh, I wasn't sure."

"No, I guess not." She ran her hands through her hair. "Well, are we going to see the rest of it?"

"You want to?"

"Of course. I find it very interesting."

"You do?"

She exhaled audibly. "Let's see the rest of it."

Willard entered a command on the keyboard, and the sequence resumed. The ship metamorphosed from an ocean liner into a destroyer with guns firing broadside, the shells exploding into stars. Then it became a submarine and dove beneath the waves, the periscope receding toward the horizon until only a point of light remained.

"I hope you like this next one," Willard whispered.

The point of light began to grow and took the shape of a spaceship. The rocket roared off the launching pad and shed its first, second, and third stages. The cabin seemed to float in space as the screen began to zero in on the side window.

Two astronauts were tumbling in the weightlessness of space, naked but for their helmets. The computer images emphasized the phallus of one, the mammaries of the other.

"Well, how about that," said Marlie. "A little soft-core space porn."

But after the first sexual episode, she interjected: "Better make that hard-core."

When the two figures were finally fused together, there was the ritual explosion and shower of stars. "Whiz + Marlie" once again appeared in a heart.

"Not bad," said Marlie. "Not bad at all."

"Does that mean you like it?"

"Of course." She paused. "I'm more amazed than anything. I had no idea you could do such things with a computer."

"It's not that much different from those video games."

"I suppose you're right," she said. "I just haven't had much experience with computers. They really are fascinating." She turned to him. "And it takes a real genius to do what you can do with them."

Willard gulped in reply.

"God, I bet there are all sorts of things you could do with a machine like this."

Willard nodded. "They're everywhere. Banks, all sorts of businesses use them. You can even use them to send letters."

"Letters?"

"Yeah. There are networks, just like the phone company— electronic billboards, that's what some people call them."

"How does it work?"

"First, you start off by making a local call. Then, you punch in your own special identification code on the computer; that connects you into a nationwide network. People can leave messages for you, and you can send them messages. I used to use it all the time."

"What for?"

"Well, when I was leaving one school and looking for another, I used to put a message on the board to find out what schools had computer departments that were easy to get into. I'd get a bunch of replies back and the names of the computer jocks at each school. By the time I got there, I'd already have the names of people to contact and several places to stay."

Marlie's eyes suddenly lit up. "If I wanted to write something, send a message, could I do it on your machine?"

"Sure. It'd be easy."

"Would you help me?"

"You know I would. What do you want to write?"

"A story," she said. "And I'd like you to help me write it."

"What kind of story?"

"I want the two of us to write down everything we know about the organization. Who's in it. What we've done and what we're planning to do." She paused. "But no one must know we're doing this. You've got to be able to hide it on your computer so that no one but you will know where to find it. Can you do that?"

"That's no problem. I can even code the information so that, even if somebody did find it, they wouldn't be able to make any sense out of it."

"And you're sure of that?"

"It's really simple. I swear it is."

"I'll take your word for it, then."

"But I don't understand why you'd want to write anything down. George'd be pissed if he found out."

"So what? If you don't tell him and I don't tell him, how'll the little shit even know it exists?"

Willard grinned. "I guess 'the little shit' won't."

"Good."

"You know, we could start right now if you want to."

"I can't. George wants me to tell him what happened on the ship. And I know him. He'll want every little detail: who said what, the tone of voice, everything."

"I see."

"Fact is, I'd better be going."

Willard stood silently as she gathered the plates and cups on the tray.

"I'll see you tonight," she said as she turned to leave.

"Okay," he said quietly.

She caught the edge of sadness in his voice and stopped. "Something wrong?"

"No. It's just that I, uh, missed you. A lot."

She glanced from his face to the bulge in his slacks and immediately understood. Setting the tray on the floor, she deftly unzipped him as she knelt down. Rapidly working him in her mouth, she brought him to a climax as if the world's record for fellatio hung in the balance. Willard fell back against the console, eyes closed, each spasmodic explosion bursting into thousands of stars.

That night they began writing what they knew about the organization. When Willard asked what they should call their effort, Marlie thought for a moment and dubbed it "the bomb." They made no effort to organize their report chronologically; they just concentrated on writing down everything they knew.

On Friday, George gave Willard a long list of names and account numbers for banks in New York, San Francisco, and Los Angeles.

Willard glanced at the list and mentally reckoned its length. "I thought we were just going to hit forty to fifty accounts. It looks like you've got more than a hundred here."

"There are one hundred and fifty-five names and account numbers, to be exact," said George.

"Why so many?"

The reason, quite simply, is that it will make it more difficult for the Federal Reserve to discern a pattern."

"Why not just scramble all the messages and crash the system?"

George shook his head. "We will save that tactic for another day, when our objective is the creation of chaos. The director has a different objective today."

"You mean he wants to steal, don't you?"

"I would, if I were you, take particular care whenever you speak of the director. You have been informed of the potential consequences of such invidious characterizations."

Willard had heard the same chilling tone in George's voice once before, in Cleveland, and decided not to press the matter. "Sorry I asked," he said.

"Consider your apology accepted," said George.

When Marlie came to the trailer, he told her what had transpired.

"That was really stupid," she said sharply. "The last thing in the world we want to do is get George angry or suspicious.

Don't you ever, directly or indirectly, let him on to what you're thinking."

"I'm sorry, I didn't mean to—"

She cut him off. "Enough. Just don't let it happen again."

Willard lowered his head like a schoolboy being scolded.

"Anyway, what you told me is very interesting."

He looked up.

"From what I could gather on the ship, the organization has dummy accounts at a number of major banks, like Citibank, Chase, Bank of America. They've been doing this for several years now just to make it easy to move around big sums of money."

"What do you mean by 'big'?"

"In the millions," she replied. "Each of the accounts, as I understand it, is supposedly connected to a business, but the business exists on paper only. Over the past couple of years, they've been using those accounts as temporary holding points for large sums of money. I mean, several million dollars a day can move through each of them. They're all under different names, so if a couple of million is deposited and withdrawn from each of them just before a holiday weekend, there's a good chance no one'll notice."

"But what's going to happen when the Fed or the company that was expecting the money doesn't get it?" Willard asked.

"Obviously, we're gambling that we can get the money out of the bank before anyone's the wiser. Besides, even if they do block some of the transactions, we'll probably get away — with most of it."

Willard chuckled. "You keep saying 'we,' like the two of us were going to rob a bank or something."

"What the hell do you think we're doing? We may not be wearing ski masks and carrying pistols, but we're sure as hell stealing."

Willard shrugged. "If you put it that way, yeah, I guess we are. But I'm still not sure how they're going to get away with it."

Marlie smiled. "That's the easy part. They'll simply transfer the money by wire to offshore banks in places like the Netherlands Antilles, where the laws protect customers from Uncle Sam's prying eyes. Considering the billions in drug money that gets hidden like that, laundering eighty million won't be any big deal."

"I hadn't thought of that."

"Why should you? You're responsible for the computer. As long as you keep it running and do what you're told, George will tolerate you. Start poking your nose into those pieces of the operation that are none of your business, and you'll get George suspicious for sure. Hell, if he thought you were an infiltrator"—she drew a finger across her throat—"that'd be it for you."

Willard gulped.

Marlie laughed. "Hell, you don't have anything to worry about. If it weren't for you, there wouldn't be an operation."

"Yeah, but what if George finds out about the bomb?"

"Is it safe in your computer here?"

Willard nodded.

"Then, he won't find out unless one of us tells him. And I'm not going to tell the little shit."

"That makes two of us."

"There, then, it's settled."

Willard had little to do but wait. He had already copied his computer program and randomly divided the one hundred fifty-five names and account numbers among the three mobile units. It was a sunny day throughout the Rockies, and the microwave antennas in the three vans had been monitoring transmissions to and from the Chicago Switch since early morning. Indistinguishable from dozens of hikers and campers, the mobile teams now had nothing to do but enjoy the brisk mountain air and sunshine while their computers shunted millions of dollars to the organization's accounts. By mid-afternoon, the teams had doused their charcoal fires, put up their folding chairs, and were rolling down the interstate toward the arid basin between Colorado's Front Range and the Continental Divide.

The first van arrived at the ranch in South Park that evening; the couple parked beside the barn and left immediately in one of the rental cars. The two other vans would arrive during the night and make the same sort of switch.

At dinner that evening George was ecstatic. Again and again, he kept saying: "Can you believe it? Eighty-nine point four million dollars!"

Shortly after eight o'clock, the phone rang. George went into the study to answer it, closing the door behind him. When he emerged a few minutes later, he was beaming.

"All sector reports are in, and there were *no* inquiries—*not one*! And by now, everyone is gone for the weekend. It will be Tuesday before even a penny is missed." He shook his head. "Can you believe it? Eighty-nine point four million dollars!"

PART IV

CHAPTER 17

On Memorial Day, Winchell's division had a picnic. Men and women who dealt daily with electronic intercepts, encrypting devices, and some of the nation's most sensitive secrets, were playing softball, grilling hot dogs, and slurping beer from paper cups. To Paul, the utter normality of the day was unsettling.

Sitting on a wooden bench and watching an assortment of kids and dogs chasing balls and frisbees, he felt more alone than he had since leaving Cambridge. Lost in reverie, he did not immediately notice Nancy standing beside him with a plate. When he did, she met his eyes with a smile.

"I thought you might like to try some of these."

Paul looked at the assortment of pastries. "Did you make these?"

"What do I look like? The Peking Dough-Boy?"

Paul chuckled. "They're dim sum, right?"

"Is there anything you don't know?"

"I've had them a time or two."

"Truth to tell, I didn't make these. There's a restaurant in Wheaton, the Tung Bor, that specializes in dim sum. I stopped by this morning to get some for the picnic."

"Mmm," said Paul, as he bit into a sticky pork bun. "I'm glad you did."

Nancy glanced at the half-full pitcher of beer beside him. "Can you spare a drop?"

"Sure," said Paul. He put down the bun and filled their cups.

They made small talk about the weather and how strange some of their colleagues looked in mufti, swinging a bat or attending to a child's scraped knee. Then Nancy turned to him.

"How are you doing?"

"It's a bright and beautiful day. Good food and"—he nodded to her—"pleasant company."

"Thanks," she said. "But how are you *really* doing?"

"In a word? Rotten."

"I thought so. You've been so quiet of late."

He gestured toward the other tables. "I don't begrudge anybody a good time, but . . ." He shrugged his shoulders and left the phrase unfinished.

"And things aren't going all that well with WG-Seven."

"That may have something to do with it, too," he said. "I came down here in the first place because I thought we, meaning the country, faced imminent danger. Well, the danger may still be there, but after two months, it no longer seems imminent."

"Thinking of calling it quits?"

"At least once an hour."

"Why haven't you?"

"Because every time I do, I think about Joe Cerri. I never even met the fellow. But that bomb was in my suitcase; it was meant for me." He drew a breath. "I *want* those bastards."

Nearly a minute passed before Paul spoke again. "I'm sorry. I shouldn't be letting my mood darken so nice a day."

Nancy reached for his hand and touched it lightly. "That's all right, Paul. I want to help, if I can."

He turned to face her. "You've been at the Agency for a while. Is it always like this? People spending all their time in meetings talking about contingency plans and countermeasures? Is most of the real work just so much routine?"

"Like everything else in government, there's a lot of routine at NSA," she replied. "Sometimes we get a juicy bit of signals intelligence to pass along, but as you know, so much of what we call work is done by machines. We've still got photo experts and other specialists who interpret raw data, but a lot of what we do could be described as bureaucratic wheel-turning."

"Wheel-*spinning*, you mean."

"In fact, WG-Seven is the most exciting thing that I've been involved with since coming to the Agency."

"And you're not frustrated by the delay?"

"A little—but not nearly as much as you. When this thing is over, I'll still be here doing SIGINT. With you, it's strictly a one-time thing."

"True," he said. "But it's still frustrating. Most of the time all we really do is sit around and talk and try to figure out what we're going to do if they—whoever 'they' are—make this move or that. And it's not that it isn't interesting. It is. But in the end it's *only* talk. It doesn't lead to anything."

Nancy nodded.

A wry smile crooked his mouth. "I've developed my own term for all that stuff."

She cocked her head. "What is it?"

"I call it 'mental masturbation.'"

She began to laugh.

"Think about it," he said. "It fills up the time. It feels good while you're doing it. But in the end you're left with damn little to show for it."

"Except perhaps," said Nancy, eyebrows rising, "a misconception."

Paul laughed loudly and reached for the beer.

The first indications that anything was wrong began to trickle in just before noon on Tuesday as corporate executives on the East Coast began calling the Federal Reserve Bank of New York to inquire about wire transfers they should have received before the holiday weekend. Paul was working at the blackboard in his office adjacent to the operations center when Nancy came in.

"Something's up," she said.

Paul turned from the board to face her.

"Art Hamlin just called from Chicago. The New York Fed

has been getting queries from some of its constituent banks about transactions that should have cleared on Friday, but didn't."

"Is there a pattern?"

"If you mean altered numbers and stuff like that, no," she replied. "Art also says that it's not all that unusual, especially after a holiday weekend." She paused. "Except for one thing. All of the expected transfers originated in California."

"The same link where we had our one-in-a-trillion shot?"

"Exactly."

Paul set down the chalk and brushed the dust from his hands. "What do you think? Is this it?"

"Could be," she said. "Hamlin said it's not unusual to get one or two inquiries from a branch like New York after a long weekend. But Chicago had four inquiries as of ten o'clock . . ."

"Let's get going, then."

As they were walking to the operations center, Paul added: "You know it just occurred to me how things have changed over the years."

"What do you mean?"

"Well, in 1941, the Japanese attacked Pearl Harbor on Sunday morning because they thought that was the time Americans would be least prepared to defend themselves," he said. "Now, I think, if we're ever attacked again, it'll be the Friday before a long weekend."

"You may be right," said Nancy, as they took their places at the console. "That blinking light—number three—is a secure and open line to Hamlin's office at Chicago."

Paul punched the button and picked up the receiver. "This is Dr. Cassidy. Mr. Hamlin, please."

Hamlin came on the line. "Good morning, Paul. It's been rather hectic here this morning."

"I can imagine."

"The Board of Governors have called an emergency meeting in Washington for five o'clock. We're doing our best at this end to sort things out." He paused. "It doesn't look good."

"Nancy says you've had four inquiries from the New York branch."

"Make that eight," said Hamlin. "We alerted our people in San Francisco at home and told them to get to the office early. We've turned up some problems at that end of the line, too."

"Anywhere else?"

"Individual queries from Dallas and Atlanta, but they appear to be random. The problem's on the San Francisco wire."

"Is there a pattern?"

"I don't know that I'd call it a pattern, but we tracked down the first inquiry. It was a transfer from one of Security Pacific's L.A. branches to Irving Trust in Manhattan. At some point between San Francisco and Chicago, the name and account number at Irving were altered in transmission to New York. But, get this, the confirmation we flashed back to San Francisco was apparently intercepted and altered en route to match the original."

"Good Lord."

"Everything's okay on that one. No one tried to withdraw or transfer the funds, and Irving moved it to the proper account this morning. So that one's been cleared."

"And the others?"

"It's going to take a while," said Hamlin. "Friday was a heavy day: we handled nearly ninety thousand transactions. About nine thousand involved the San Francisco branch. We just don't have the circuitry to recheck all those transactions and still handle today's traffic. As you might imagine, the day after a holiday is also quite busy. We'll probably top ninety thousand today."

"And how do you know those transfers aren't being altered?"

"To be honest, we don't."

"Why don't you shut down, then?"

"Believe me, Paul, if it were up to me, that's exactly what I'd do, but Washington says no. The way they figure it, if there were intercepts on Friday, the people responsible will be long gone; they're not going to sit around waiting to let us catch them."

"And if they're wrong?"

Silence.

"Are you there, Art?"

"I'm here, Paul. I was just trying to think of an answer, and I'm afraid I don't have one. We'll handle over three hundred billion dollars today. That's nearly a tenth of the gross national product." He paused again. "God only knows what'll happen if we have to shut down."

"Someone had better be thinking about it," said Paul.

"I agree," said Hamlin. "And I presume the Board of Governors will be getting into that sort of thing later today."

"Will you be there?"

"I'm booked out of O'Hare on a noon flight."

"You'll keep me posted?"

"We'll be leaving the line open. And someone from my staff will be here to keep you up to date."

Details from Chicago continued to arrive, but by one o'clock the pattern was clear: someone had altered transmissions between the Federal Reserve of San Francisco and the Chicago Switch. Though most of the false transfers had been corrected, it looked as if one of every three had either been withdrawn or moved Friday afternoon to overseas accounts. FBI squads in New York and California were investigating the companies whose accounts had been been drained and were turning up mail drops, "desk offices," and answering services instead of corporate suites.

At four o'clock, Hamlin called Paul from the Federal Reserve's headquarters in Washington. "We're flying in Friday's tapes from San Francisco. They'll get here this evening, and we'll be working all night checking each of the transactions against our tapes. That will give us the exact magnitude of the embezzlement. The Board of Governors have already committed the Fed to covering the loss."

"What should we be working on?"

"That will have to wait until the Board comes to a decision. We know *what* was done; what we don't know is *how* it was done."

"It's clear they've cracked the DES," said Paul. "So, we've got an encryption problem as well as a transmission security problem. And it'll probably take a while to figure out how to deal with both of them. If worst comes to worst, you may need to shut down the Switch."

"God, I hope not," said Hamlin. "The last thing we need is a liquidity crunch. You remember what I told you about the Panic of 1907?"

"I do," said Paul.

"Well, it went off like a chain reaction. Major institutions were suddenly strapped for currency. The brokerage houses responded with calls on margin accounts, and that got people selling like mad. Prices on Wall Street sank right through the floor, so that dried up as a source of funds. The banks tried to raise cash by calling in their notes, and that set off a chain of credit liquidations. In a matter of hours—not days or weeks but *hours*—the United States was brought to a standstill." He paused. "I know that may seem like ancient history to you, but I've been with the Fed for twenty-two years now, and I can tell you that liquidity is a matter of Holy Writ throughout the system."

"I understand what you're saying," said Paul. "But you've shut down before for short periods."

"We've had our computer downs like everyone else, but people could adjust to those because they were temporary," said Hamlin. "This is something else. You're talking about shutting down a system that's averaging two hundred and fifty billion dollars a day in EFTs. To make matters worse, we'd be shutting it down for an unspecified period because the whole damn banking system isn't safe."

"But that's the whole point," said Paul. "What happened Friday *proves* it isn't safe. If it happened last Friday, it could happen again next Friday or maybe next month, just before the Fourth of July weekend."

"I'm not disagreeing with you," said Hamlin. "I'm just trying to give you what I think will be the Board's perspective on this thing." He paused. "Well, I've got a meeting to go to. I'll get back to you, probably this evening."

Paul sighed. "I have a feeling we're going to be here quite late tonight."

The President's counselor, Harding Harrison, called a meeting of Working Group Seven that evening. Paul felt his stomach tighten as he got off on the ninth floor. When he entered the conference room, Harrison waved him over to the seat on his right in the middle of the long table.

"It looks like you've finally gotten yourself into the center of things," he said.

"Looks that way," said Paul, as he took his seat. He glanced around the room, returning the nods of those who caught his eye.

After Otis Wheeler and John Scotto came in a minute later, Harrison began the meeting. "To start off, let me reiterate the ground rules. You are not to take notes or make any record, oral or written, for the agencies you represent. You are here solely in an advisory capacity to help the NSA, which, at the direction of the President, is the lead agency in this matter. Any questions on the ground rules?"

When no one spoke up, he gave them a quick rundown of what had happened.

While Paul disliked Harrison's politics, he had no doubts about the man's competence. Though freshman physics was the beginning and end of his technical background, he seemed comfortable describing what had happened to the electronic fund transfers that had passed between San Francisco and New York four days before. Not only was the man well briefed, he knew the limits of his knowledge. When he had finished, he asked Paul if he had left anything out.

"No," he replied. "You've hit all the high points."

After fielding several questions, he resumed. "What I'd like to do now is discuss, in a general way, the nature of the problems we are facing. Now, I know this may be difficult because we don't know who our adversary is or what his objectives may be. Nevertheless, some decisions will have to be made soon, and they will probably have to be made with only limited information. I'm told that we have essentially two problems: data security and transmission security. Let's start with data. Dr. Cassidy?"

"As I see it," said Paul, "the federal Data Encryption Standard was mathematically weak from the start. To put it simply, a fifty-six-bit key is much too short; doubling the length would have made it considerably stronger. To make matters worse, the DES has apparently been compromised. It's possible, of course, that someone gained access to the key for last Friday's transmissions, but I think we have to operate on the assumption that they cracked the algorithmic function on which the DES is based. If that proves the case, then the DES can no longer be relied upon to protect sensitive data. We will have to use something better."

"Any ideas?" Harrison asked.

"For absolute security, we could use one-time pads," said Paul. "Those are simple one-for-one transformations that are never repeated. The only way you can crack it is to have the pad itself. I'm informed that most of our nuclear command and control circuits are one-time pads."

A bald man at the end of the table raised his hand and was acknowledged by Harrison. "Bill?"

"I can't speak for the Secretary of Defense, but the logistical complications involved in establishing data security for one-time pads in the Strategic Air Command are formidable. It would take you quite a while to set up a working system. Not only do you have the problem of generating and distributing long and unique keys; you can have horrendous synchronization problems."

Harrison turned to Paul. "Dr. Cassidy?"

"Those points are well-taken," said Paul. "And I'm not saying that there are no other alternatives. What I am suggesting is that if we need *absolute* security we may have to consider 'borrowing' the Pentagon's system for a time."

"Out of the question," said the man from Defense. "As important as the Federal Reserve System is, the nuclear command and control network cannot be compromised. Until we know who our adversary is, the Soviets must rank high on our list of suspects. We have to consider the possibility that they could be trying to compromise our C-and-C network as a prelude to a nuclear first strike."

"Good God," said Paul, "you don't actually think—"

Harrison cut him off. "Bill's point is well taken. Even if the possibility of the Soviets' being behind this is small, the consequences could be immense if they were. So, I think we'll have to rule out any use of nuclear command and control circuits to do the nation's banking. *Period*. Any other suggestions?"

"We know that the DES can be cracked and that one-time pads cannot be," said Paul. "That does not mean there are no options in-between that could provide the Chicago Switch with an acceptable level of security. I think public-key cryptography, an area in which I have done some work, is one possibility. But these are rather technical matters. I'd be happy to get into them, if you wish, but you may want to get on with a more general discussion of some of the other problems first."

Harrison nodded. "Okay. Let's take up the dimensions of the transmission problem. Dr. Cassidy?"

"On that question, I would defer to John Scotto of MATER," said Paul. "That's more his field than mine."

Scotto's eyes crinkled into a smile. "So far, we know they've been able to intercept microwave as well as land-line transmissions. But that's no surprise—at least, not in the technological sense. Everything you need for such a system can be purchased openly and off the shelf. The Agency," he said, nodding to Winchell, "has been doing TEMPEST intercepts since at least the early seventies, and I can recall one mission when we took a tractor-trailer jammed to the gunwales with gear to Foggy Bottom to see if we could pick up emanations from a new computer system at the State Department."

Scotto paused and glanced toward the Foreign Service officer at the end of the table. "We couldn't pick up that particular terminal, but we did manage to record and decrypt a lot of other signals coming out of the building."

"A deficiency we promptly corrected," said the woman from State.

"Indeed," said Scotto. "But I cite that example to show how rapidly the exclusive—and, I might add, *expensive*—intercept technology of the seventies has become cheap and commonplace in the eighties. The electronic gear in that tractor-trailer must have cost the Agency several million dollars; today, you can get much more sophisticated machinery for less than fifty thousand dollars and tuck it all neatly into a small truck."

"In other words," said Harrison, "the technology is out there for anyone who's got the money."

"Not exactly," said Scotto. "You still need individuals who can program imaginatively. The technology may be off the shelf, but it's not so easy putting it all together. Intercepting signals from a microwave repeater is strictly a passive operation. But *changing* those signals—on a real-time basis, no less—that's one hell of an accomplishment."

"And who do you suppose might be capable of that sort of, as you put it, 'accomplishment'?" asked Harrison.

Scotto shrugged. "That calls for conjecture. As an engineer, I'd just as soon let someone else field that one."

Paul glanced at Wheeler and caught an approving nod. The colonel had warned him over the phone to stick to science and avoid the political questions that would inevitably arise. "Unless you're willing to have your political beliefs dissected before Harrison and his friends," he had said, "you'll be a lot better off sticking to your own field. They can't touch you there, but they can cut your balls off if you venture into their domain."

Harrison accepted Scotto's reply and returned to his earlier line of inquiry.

"If they can intercept microwave and land lines, what alternatives do we have? Satellites?"

"That's a possibility," said Scotto. "The footprint from a satellite can be hundreds of square miles in size, so it's easy to intercept. Whether they could alter those signals is another matter. I just don't know what their capabilities are. But based on what they've done so far, I wouldn't underestimate them."

"Nor," said Harrison, "would I."

CHAPTER 18

Though George kept his distance, Marlie sensed that he was interested, attracted to her. Face to face, he appeared indifferent; the microdot eyes, so often focused on an imaginary horizon, seldom met hers directly. She had never liked him and had assumed until recently that the only thing they had in common was their disdain for one another. Yet, she felt he was watching her, following her with his eyes, whenever her back was turned to him. When covert glances at his reflection in the window proved that he was indeed looking at her, it gave her an enormous sense of satisfaction. George was not so different after all. That would make him vulnerable.

It was a hot June day, but not so hot that Marlie really needed to wear cutoffs and a tank top to be comfortable. But after Tom and Zed left for Denver to get electronic parts for the vans, she changed from the jeans and shirt she had worn at breakfast. George affected not to notice, but Willard practically drooled at the sight when she brought him lunch and "dessert." Willard hated the heat and always remained in the trailer until the sun had gone behind the Continental Divide. That meant that she and George would have the house to themselves.

Marlie had no explicit plan to entice George; she simply intended to test him to see how far he wanted to go. If he responded, she would go through with it; if he did not, she would let the matter drop. Sex was not the objective; Marlie wanted control. And she intended to acquire it so gradually, so subtly, that George would not even realize he was losing it.

George, as usual, was in the study, and Marlie made it a point to walk by the window or open door every so often to get a soda or another magazine, before returning to the lounge chair in front of the house. Then she would sit down, pull off the tank top, and slowly rub coconut-scented suntan oil on her body, starting at her feet and gradually working her way up each leg. She took particular care rubbing the oil into her breasts.

A few minutes after the fourth such slathering, George called her from the porch.

"Be right there," she said, as she stood up and unself-consciously put on the tank top.

"We have a call from headquarters," said George, as she approached the house. "It will be in code."

"Okay," said Marlie.

In addition to keeping Willard happy, Marlie was responsible for coding and decoding communications with headquarters. Only the most sensitive messages were delivered by couriers; the rest went over the telephone. Radio transmitters were rarely used because they left a trail of power surges that the NSA or FBI could track by hooking up their computers to local power grids. Most communications between headquarters and the field were "hidden" in the words of ordinary telephone conversations.

At the mention of a key phrase, Marlie would switch on the tape recorder. The caller could be talking about the weather in California or a wedding he was about to attend; the subject was unimportant so long as the conversation was made to sound normal to potential eavesdroppers. After hanging up, Marlie would transcribe the conversation and bring it to George. Sometimes he would do the decoding himself, but more often she would do it.

When Marlie came into the study, she found George had already unlocked the drawer and was holding the coded phrase book.

"Is it very long?" he asked.

"Only three lines this time. It should be easy."

"Fine."

After starting toward the door, she turned suddenly and found George's eyes focused at hip level.

"Would you like some iced tea?" she asked. "I'm going to make some."

"Yes. Thank you."

After boiling the water, she sat at the kitchen table and began the laborious task of looking up each word in the coded sentences. The herbs were steeping when George came into the kitchen.

"How are you doing?"

"Fine. Just a few more minutes."

He lifted the lid on the teapot. "Is it ready?"

"Oh, I'll get that," she said and started to rise.

George put his hand on her shoulder. He had meant to touch her briefly and lightly, a restraining gesture, but his hand remained on her skin as if it had a will of its own. Marlie sat back down.

"Do you want lemon?" he asked.

"Yes, please."

He stood behind her and took his time, putting ice in the glasses and cutting the lemon into wedges. He studied her back, the lithe arms, the elegant curve of her neck, the upswept hair, the tiny blond strands, like some impossibly fine down, swirling about her nape. He leaned over to set her glass on the table and drew in the scent of coconut on suntanned skin.

She turned in his direction. "Thank you."

He felt the heat of her breath brush his face.

"I'm almost done," she said.

He put his hand on the table and pretended to be reading what she was writing. Though his face was mere inches from hers, she continued to leaf through the code book, writing down the key words in the final sentence as if there was nothing unusual about his presence. He tried to concentrate on the decoded message, but his eyes drifted uncontrollably to the distinct outline of her breasts and nipples straining against the tank top. The warmth of her body rose about him.

"One more," she said in a conversational tone and began turning the pages again.

George was unaware that he was breathing heavily. Indeed, he was aware of nothing but her body, its scent, the rise and fall of her breasts, and how much he wanted her.

"There. That's it," she said.

No reply.

When she turned, their lips touched, seemingly by accident. But there was no hesitation on her part, so he pressed his mouth against hers, tentatively at first, then with increasing ferocity, until his teeth were digging into her flesh.

"Not so hard," she said.

He lifted her from the chair, coiled his arms around her body, a hand embedded in each buttock, and pulled her against him. "I want you," he said.

Wordlessly, they left the kitchen and walked toward his room. He neither held her hand nor made any other gesture of affection. When the door was closed, he began to undress her, pulling off the tank top, unzipping and lowering her cutoffs. She stood naked beside the bed as he took off his clothes and put them on hangers. He pulled back the covers and followed her beneath them.

There was no foreplay, no touching of any kind. They connected with almost brutal efficiency.

Except for a grunt when he reached orgasm, George remained silent the entire time. When Marlie brought her arm around him, she felt him shrink from her touch. She had not expected much from him, but that did not lessen the revulsion and rage she now felt.

After a minute or so, George got up, grabbed the hangers that held his clothes, and went to the bathroom. The water ran for almost ten minutes before George emerged, fully dressed.

"I will be in the study," he said from outside the door.

Marlie went to the bathroom to clean herself. As she put on a shirt and jeans, she remembered the smug, twisted look on George's face as his short, fat fingers pulled down her cutoffs.

When she returned to the kitchen, she found the message she had decoded was no longer on the table. She picked up another magazine and was walking outside when George called her into the study.

"You realize the importance of this," he said, gesturing to the message in his hand.

She nodded.

"We've got just three weeks to prepare for the next mission," he said. "Willard will have to adapt his program to work on all three media: wire, microwave, and satellite. We will be going from three mobile units to six, and expanding our operational coverage from one Federal Reserve district to six."

George continued speaking until he realized that Marlie was looking at him but apparently not listening. "Is something wrong?"

After containing the impulse to give vent to her anger, she replied simply: "No."

"I see," said George. "In that case, let me say that, with regard to what transpired between us this afternoon, I trust you will handle the matter with discretion."

"I've already forgotten it."

"Do I detect a note of sarcasm in your voice?"

"It certainly wasn't intended," she said breezily.

"Good," he said, "because, correct me if I am mistaken, but you did freely offer yourself, did you not?"

Marlie remained motionless.

"And I freely accepted," he continued. "Though the director might not be pleased with the turn of events, I doubt he would judge it anathema. So, I trust it will remain a matter that is strictly between the two of us."

"You needn't worry, George," she said, and turned to go.

"One more thing."

She spun around to face him.

"You are an attractive and desirable woman, Marlie. But I hope you are also wise enough to realize that, unlike Willard, I cannot be manipulated by you and your body. Is that understood?"

She clenched her teeth and nodded.

"If, in the future," he continued, "you wish to offer yourself, I would, at an appropriate time, be prepared to accept."

After several awkward moments staring at one another, she said, "Thanks, George. I'll keep that in mind."

Tom and Zed remained overnight in Denver, so there were just three at the dinner table that evening. When Marlie went to the trailer afterwards, she put off Willard's sexual advances but told him to come to her room that night after George went to sleep.

It was after midnight when Willard slowly edged his way down the hall and noiselessly turned the doorknob. A single candle glimmered on the night stand.

She was lying on her side, breasts bared, a smile on her face. "Make sure you lock it," she whispered.

Willard slowly slid the latch into place. As he reached the bed, she sat up and immediately began undressing him. When he was completely nude, she began touching him, first with her hands and then with her tongue, letting the excitement and tension slowly build within him.

Guiding him onto the bed, she climbed on top of him and began moving with almost glacial slowness, tightening around his penis as she rose, hovering loosely on the tip, almost losing it, and then plunging down hard and fast. The rhythm began to build, and Willard lost all sense of time and place.

Her voice began as a whisper. "Fuck me. Fuck me. Fuck me." The tempo increased, and her words became louder, more insistent.

In spite of her voice and the incessant creak of the bed, Willard soon lost contact with everything but the nerve endings at the tip of his penis. When he finally exploded in orgasm and the shuddering stopped, he felt as if he were floating amid total silence, a traveler in the black void of space.

Marlie lay on her side. George, she knew, would be awake and would have heard everything.

The thought brought a smile to her lips.

CHAPTER 19

Paul had not been more than a few miles from Fort Meade since that fateful weekend in March. So, he was content to lean back against the seat and enjoy the rich green of the Maryland countryside and the warm June sun as Wheeler drove down the Baltimore-Washington Parkway.

As they approached the Capital Beltway, Wheeler tapped his arm. "It was over there," he said, pointing to the left.

Paul knew immediately what he meant. Indeed, the explosion that killed Joe Cerri was never far from his mind.

After Joe was killed, Paul had recalled an incident that occurred in Vermont during the first year of his marriage. One of Helen's uncles needed some help digging a hole to set a dynamite charge beneath the stump of a huge oak that had been downed by lightning. New to the family and eager to ingratiate himself, Paul volunteered to dig the hole and then stood at a safe distance, fingers plugging his ears, to watch the charge explode.

The sight of the deeply rooted oak being ripped from the earth startled him. But even more startling was the stump itself: severed roots; bone-white shards of wood, shattered and scorched. It lay there dismembered. "Dismembered." The word kept going through his mind. The explosion had turned solid oak to splinters.

Paul had forgotten the incident until Joe Cerri was murdered. Now, he could not erase the image from his mind.

"Paul?" Wheeler touched his arm. "Paul?"

"Oh, uh, sorry. Guess I'm preoccupied."

"I know," he said. "I can't drive past here either without thinking about Joe."

Paul nodded.

"Look, we're going to be downtown in about twenty minutes, so it might be worthwhile going over the way Simpson runs these NSC staff meetings."

"Sure."

"I gather you didn't know Dr. Simpson all that well at Cambridge, but he runs the meetings rather like a seminar. Or maybe I should say he lets the meetings run themselves."

"Yes. I know the style."

"Everyone there, in theory, is free to speak his mind. In practice, it's another matter entirely. As an outsider, your function will be to give the staff expert advice—*factual* advice. If you can, stick to your field and avoid being drawn into political debate."

"Like I did with Harrison yesterday?"

"Precisely. You and I—and Harrison, too, for that matter— know that there's not a shred of evidence linking the Soviet Union to our problems at Chicago. Unfortunately, there are a lot of people in this administration, including some on the NSC staff, who are professional anti-Communists. It's like membership in one of those extreme religious cults. They've got the answer, *one answer*, for everything."

"You serious?"

"Oh, they may not actually blame our domestic problems on Communism, but that's what some of them think," said Wheeler. "I should add, by the way, that I am not among their favorite people."

"Why's that?"

"I don't want to get into that now," he replied. "But keep your ears open at the meeting. I try to stay out of the usual run of arguments, but sometimes I can't resist challenging the more ludicrous scenarios some of those weenies come up with. I know these guys, and sure as hell, they're going to divine the 'covert hand of the Kremlin' in last Friday's incident at Chicago."

Paul had had little more than a nodding acquaintance with Wiley Simpson when he taught political science at MIT. Not only were they in different departments, they were different in political outlook. Though Paul favored liberals, he considered himself an agnostic where politics was concerned. And except for occasional checks to the campaigns of liberal legislators and biennial trips to the polls, he devoted very little thought to politics.

For Simpson, politics was everything. A leading theoretician of the neoconservative movement, he positioned himself to the right of the academic herd early on. With monographs and articles, he developed a dedicated audience among the far right who, not satisfied by money and the power of elective office, longed for a patina of academic respectability on their most deeply held prejudices. It was a yearning Simpson was only too eager to fulfill.

So when the ultraright finally put one of their own in the White House, Simpson was superbly positioned to emigrate from Cambridge to Georgetown. Short, slender, his brown horn-rimmed glasses the only distinguishing feature on an otherwise blank face, Simpson enjoyed the cachet of his position but, oddly, found he did not truly savor the exercise of power. Though his distaste for Soviet Communism was genuine, he would never have dreamed of being photographed at the Khyber Pass aiming a rifle toward Soviet-occupied Afghanistan. He was a political scientist and serious about the logic and order science could bring to public affairs. In short, he lacked the skills and bloodlust of the true politician.

So under him, the National Security Council had become more a clearinghouse for ideas than a source, and Simpson found himself the honest broker of other men's scenarios.

After showing their credentials to the guard on Seventeenth Street, Wheeler drove the sedan down the ramp into the basement garage of the old Executive Office Building.

"Just to give you an idea of how things have changed," he said to Paul, "at the start of World War II, this one building housed the departments of State, War, and Navy."

"You're kidding."

"Not at all. It was big enough for three departments then, but you couldn't fit the Pentagon's PR officers in it today."

Another guard checked their badges at the elevator, which they rode in silence to the third floor. After a brief wait in the anteroom, Simpson, in shirt sleeves, came ambling through the door.

"Paul. Good to see you," said Simpson, clasping Paul's right hand in both of his. After the obligatory coffee was offered and accepted, they went into his office and sat down on brown leather chairs, setting their cups on a low brass table. Paul could see the white marble of the West Wing of the White House through the window.

Simpson took off his glasses and rubbed the bridge of his nose. The skin, once ruddy, had taken on a gray pallor since his days at Cambridge; deep, dark pouches swelled beneath pale brown eyes.

"Paul, let me start by saying how very much I appreciate the sacrifice you are making for your country. I might also add that the President himself wishes me to express his gratitude for your sacrifice. He considers you a true patriot. And that, I can assure you, is not a compliment the President renders lightly."

"Thank you," said Paul.

"Having said that," Simpson continued, "let me be the first to admit that we really botched things up after the, uh, accident that took Captain Cerri's life. I'm convinced now that we made a grave error in reporting you had also died in the bombing. We should have handled things straight. Put both you and Helen in protective custody, if need be. But I'm afraid that option has been closed to us."

"Dr. Simpson," said Wheeler, "I have talked to Paul about this, but I think it's important for him to hear from you the rationale for keeping him under cover."

"Yes. Well, we certainly owe you that much, don't we, Paul?"

Simpson began by describing the situation he was facing the afternoon of the bombing. The President had called a meeting of the full National Security Council to deal with a deteriorating situation in the Middle East. The chain of events involving Paul, Wheeler, and Cerri began unfolding at the same time Simpson was caught in the middle of a bitter dispute between State and Defense. Things had gotten so bad that the Secretary of Defense seemed on the verge of resigning, and the President was counting on Simpson to find a compromise that would keep both men in the cabinet. He was able to leave the room for only a few minutes at a time, so the decisions he made in his conversations with Wheeler that led to the contrived report of Paul's death were made instantaneously. It was impossible for him to consult more widely.

"I feared that once the word was out that only Captain Cerri was dead the killers would come after you or, perhaps, after Helen," said Simpson. "I felt we had to move quickly, and I'm afraid we've been trying to make up for that haste, *my* haste, ever since."

"And what about now?" Paul asked. "This thing has gone on nearly three months, and we don't know when it'll end. My wife thinks I'm dead. The longer this goes on, the less chance Helen and I are going to have to put things back together again."

Simpson sighed. "I don't know what else I can tell you, Paul. We don't know who our enemy is, although I wouldn't be surprised if some of the boys spice up the meeting this afternoon with a few ideas of their own. If you were to leave now—and you still can, if you so decide—you and Helen may be able to put things back together as if nothing had happened.

"What happens to your country is another matter. We may not know who the enemy is, but we know *what* he is. He's a killer, and a cold-blooded professional, at that. He's also bent on disrupting the American economy and clearly has the technological means to do it.

"Now, if we come clean in public about what happened with you, we could suffer a tremendous loss of credibility. We can't afford to do that because we will amost certainly need the public's confidence when we ultimately have to fight these terrorists in the open. Finally, and this is hardly a small point, we need your brains working actively on our side."

The points Simpson raised were not new; Wheeler had gone over them with Paul several times before. Secret Service agents continued to watch Helen, and their reports suggested that she was handling her grief by plunging more deeply into her work. On weekends she went to Vermont to be with her mother, who was recuperating from a stroke she had suffered in April. Because that stroke had come two weeks after his reported death, Paul felt he was at least partially to blame for it.

He was sure Helen would ultimately understand why he took the course he did. Yet, he knew that he could not continue to live under cover indefinitely. Helen was still a young woman, a beautiful woman, and—he could not suppress a smile—a very sexy, very physical woman. In time, new men would enter her life, and he was not at all sure what he would do if that were to happen before his work at NSA was finished.

Simpson stood up. "Well, gentlemen, I think it's time we head for the conference room." He turned to Wheeler. "Did you give Paul a rundown on the format of these meetings?"

"Briefly," said Wheeler. "But I thought the best way would be for him simply to be there and observe it firsthand."

Simpson turned to Paul as they walked down the corridor. "I like to have an open exchange of ideas at these meetings. We don't take formal notes, and everyone knows they can float an idea even if it hasn't been fully staffed out. Feel free to speak up. Don't feel you have to limit your role to that of expert witness."

As they turned the corner, Wheeler smiled and gave Paul a covert wink.

The staff was standing around the conference table when Simpson entered the room. After introducing them to "Dr. Cassidy, a cryptographic expert from NSA," he had them take their seats and turned the meeting over to his chief of staff, who gave them an abbreviated report of potential trouble spots in each of the world's geographical regions. Then Simpson called on Wheeler to brief the staff on what he called "the Chicago caper." From the expressions on their faces, it was clear to Paul that this was the first any of them had heard about it.

Though he often shared his observations with Paul about what had transpired at meetings they had attended, Wheeler seldom spoke unless asked to, so Paul was surprised as well as impressed with how smoothly Wheeler made his presentation. Like Harding Harrison the day before, Wheeler covered the essential points, including just enough detail to anticipate the more obvious questions but not swamping them with the sort of data that would interest only a specialist.

When Simpson asked Paul to explain the technological implications of "the Chicago caper," he repeated what he had told Working Group Seven about the weakness of the federal Data Encryption Standard and the sophistication of the adversary's computer program and telecommunications.

"And you don't have a clue who's behind this?" The speaker was a slender man at the end of the table.

"None whatever," Wheeler replied.

The man resumed. "But let's examine what he has done. It seems to me his objective is disruption rather than theft. True, he appears to have stolen almost ninety million dollars. Yet, he didn't take so much as a penny from those banks in Kansas, Ohio, and Wisconsin. That suggests to me that his goal is political rather than economic. And if that is in fact the case, it seems to me that our short list of suspects should include governments which possess the sort of electronics that could successfully penetrate and compromise something as technically complex as the Chicago Switch."

"Meaning?" Wheeler asked.

"Meaning, of course, the Soviet," said the man. "Anything that weakens the United States, militarily, politically, *or* economically, naturally strengthens the appearance of the Soviet system in the eyes of the world. If they can create a financial panic here, our free-world allies and some of our friends in the third world could lose confidence in the vitality of democratic capitalism."

Simpson interrupted. "Let's follow your hypothesis and see where it leads. Assuming for the moment that the Soviet hand is cleverly cloaked in this instance, what policy options and contingency plans might be indicated?"

An intense, dark-haired man across from Wheeler began to speak. "Clearly, we need an effective means of leverage. A bargaining chip, if you will."

"Such as?" Simpson asked.

The man then went through a rather detailed scenario of escalating economic, political, and, ultimately, military pressure against Cuba. Paul found the man's arguments incoherent and gave up trying to follow them, but Wheeler listened carefully, staring intently across the table.

When the man finished, Simpson removed his glasses and began cleaning them on his tie. "What you have suggested is a rather energetic course of action. But before proceeding further, perhaps you would elucidate why you would direct such actions against Cuba if, as you posit, the Soviet is responsible for the Chicago caper."

"Because if you can sever the cat's paw, you may not need to attack the cat itself." The man smiled. "Moreover, insofar as one is concerned about matters of practicum, the Cuba option has the virtue of being a series of limitable, supportable, and sustainable actions which carry none of the escalatory risk factors associated with a confrontational mode vis-à-vis the Soviet."

Wheeler spoke evenly. "I am not certain what you mean by 'limitable, supportable, and sustainable actions.' Perhaps you might expand on that."

"I'd be happy to, Colonel." The man reached beneath the table and retrieved a case, which contained briefing charts and a portable stand. He deftly unfolded its contents on the table, extended a telescoping pointer, and started with the first chart, "Naval Quarantine of Cuban Archipelago." The next was labeled "Surgical Air Strikes"; several more followed before the final chart, "Popular Uprising Against Cuban Dictatorship."

Good God, Paul thought, it's the Bay of Pigs, Round Two.

Wheeler's voice remained dispassionate. "What sort of casualties do you anticipate?"

The man smiled again. "Ours or theirs?"

"Ours."

"If we can attain our objectives at the lower end of the escalatory spectrum, I would anticipate only the routine casualties normally associated with a fully mobilized naval operaton. Perhaps six, maybe as high as ten, KIA."

"And at the high end?"

"Then one would have to anticipate dozens, perhaps hundreds, in the full array of casualty modes."

Wheeler's voice remained cool. "It looks as if you've put a considerable amount of effort into your presentation. It certainly bears the mark of professionalism."

"Why, thank you, Colonel." The man was beaming.

"It sounds as if you've had some experience with this sort of thing. Navy? Marines? You must have seen action in Southeast Asia."

The man's face suddenly went pale.

Wheeler's voice became warm, friendly. "You weren't Air Force, were you?"

"N-no," the man sputtered.

"Well, then, which service were you in?" The voice remained cordial, but the eyes had turned hard.

"I, uh, actually did not get to, you know, have the opportunity to serve. I was not, uh, medically qualified."

"Oh. That's too bad."

And with that, all discussion of Cuba came to an end.

* * *

In the car, on the way back to Fort Meade, Paul complimented Wheeler. "I've got to hand it to you, Otis. You really put it to him. When he got up there and started going through all those flip charts, I wanted to start yelling: 'You idiot! It's the Bay of Pigs all over again.'"

"That's the problem," said Wheeler. "They *do* want the Bay of Pigs all over again. I can't tell you how many times this so-called Cuba option has come up. It doesn't matter if it's a revolution in Central America or Soviet support for one of its African clients, these guys inevitably come up with the same all-purpose solution: 'Bomb Cuba. Bomb Cuba.'"

"Did you see that guy's face? I thought he was going to throw up on the spot. Were you just stringing him along, or did you know he'd never been in the service?"

"Oh, I knew all right," said Wheeler. "I've read the background investigations on most of these guys. And the thing that really stuck out was how few of them were veterans, even though most of them were old enough to have served in Vietnam. Some of them pyramided student deferments, one on top of the other. When that route was cut off, a lot of them applied to divinity school." He started to laugh.

"What's so funny?"

"It just occurred to me that if you checked the academic credentials on most of the ultrarightists in this administration, you'll find a lot more of them went to Harvard Divinity School than all three service academies combined."

Paul laughed.

"You think I'm kidding," said Wheeler. "I'm not. I'm also not the least bit surprised."

"Why's that?"

"As I think I told you, I know damn few combat veterans who are war-lovers. The most warlike people I've run across are politicians who have been civilians all their lives and probably feel guilty as hell that they were making money in their law practices or as investment bankers while other men were getting their asses shot off in Korea or Vietnam. If you want real proof, take a look at Congress. The senators and congressmen who talk the most about fighting are those who know the least about it. They kept their sweet asses out of action any way they could when they were young, and those who did go in signed up for short stints in the Guard or Reserves."

"And that guy across the table?"

"He was disqualified from the draft after his family doctor certified he had had childhood asthma," said Wheeler. "Now, he brags about his time running marathons."

"You're kidding?"

"It all fits, doesn't it? Marathons, invading Cuba: the guy's still trying to prove his manhood. Well, I could care less if he gets calcified knee joints, but when he starts talking casually about 'limitable, supportable, and sustainable actions' that are going to get people killed, that's it. He gets no mercy from me."

"The guy was obviously waiting for a chance to unveil his Cuba charts," said Paul.

Wheeler nodded. "And he won't give up. There'll be memos, contingency option papers, you name it. These guys know only one thing, and they aren't about to give up on it."

"That's not a very comforting thought."

"No," said Wheeler, "but then this whole situation is not very comforting."

CHAPTER 20

The men began arriving in pairs shortly after nine o'clock. By nine-thirty, four rental cars were parked beside the house, and eight men were sitting around the table with George. Marlie, open notebook in her lap, sat in an armchair behind the table.

When Willard walked into the room, the men stood up. Some simply nodded. Others greeted him by name. "Good morning, Dr. Zack." "Good morning, Professor." *"Guten morgen, Herr Doktor Professor."*

Willard recognized the men from their previous visit and smiled as he returned their greetings. But, again, none of them volunteered their names, nor did George introduce them. As Willard took his seat, he glanced toward Marlie and winked. An eyebrow rose in acknowledgment.

George got straight to business. "As you know, phase three of the operation goes into effect two days hence. Mobile teams are currently positioning themselves to intercept transmissions between Chicago and six of the Federal Reserve's twelve branch banks. Thus positioned, we will be capable of interposing our signals on approximately half the transactions conducted each day by the Chicago Switch.

"But unlike phase two, in which diversion of funds was the objective, our goal this time is disruption. On Friday, we will prove conclusively that we can compromise the integrity of the Federal Reserve System. We shall prove to the government that it has no choice but to end its policy of harassment and to do so on our terms."

George paused, his eyes briefly taking in each man at the table. "If the government refuses to respond in good faith," he said evenly, "it shall bring upon itself the untoward circumstances of phase four."

George unfurled a national map on the table and indicated where each of the vans should be positioned. He then asked Willard to talk about the technical aspects of the modified computer programs that would be used. The eight men listened carefully, scribbling in their small black notebooks.

"A final point," said George. "Thus far, this has been a centralized operation. With phase three, your sectors become the front line. On Friday, you will operate to a maximum of four hours, withdrawing if there is even the slightest risk of detection. We shall communicate our offer to the government through one of the sectors next week. The director will designate which sector, and I will communicate that choice to the appropriate sector head."

"And those of us who are not designated?" asked one man.

"You will await further instructions," said George. "Safeguard the field equipment and perform whatever maintenance may be necessary."

"With regard to maintenance," said another man, "the vans returned here after each previous phase. There have been no operational problems thus far, thanks to Dr. Zack's estimable work. But suppose a sector experiences problems with the field equipment, either hardware or software. What is the line of authority for correcting it?"

"If you cannot correct the malfunction through utilization of your own resources, contact field headquarters," said George. "We have installed a telephone line to the trailer. We are developing a program to perform remote diagnostic maintenance on your equipment. If that proves insufficient, we shall see to it that someone is dispatched to your sector to perform the necessary maintenance."

"And the programs for phase four?"

"Those will be dispatched by courier at the appropriate time. Sector heads will, of course, receive advance notification."

That night, Marlie was typing at one of the keyboards in the trailer. Willard was sitting at the main console, methodically checking each line of code in his program to diagnose problems in each sector's computer. It was boring work, and Willard finally stopped and swiveled on the stool to read what she was writing on the adjacent screen.

"You know, Marlie," he started to say.

But at the sound of his voice, she jumped, pulling her hands back as if the keyboard were a hot stove.

"I'm sorry," he said. "I didn't mean to frighten you."

She sighed. "That's okay, Whiz. I'm just nervous about this."

"Yeah, I don't blame you. George'd really be pissed if he knew what you were doing."

"What'd you say?"

"Just that George'd be pissed if he knew you were writing this thing."

She shook her head. "I don't think you understand. This isn't a game. We're not kids trying to sneak a smoke behind the house, worrying that Daddy's going to catch us. This is for real. If George finds out, there's no telling what he'll do."

"What do you mean?"

"Just what I said: 'There's no telling what he'll do.' In the extreme, I don't think he'd hesitate at murder."

"You're not serious, are you?"

"Oh, yes," she replied.

"Then, I don't understand. Why are we writing this thing? 'The bomb,' as you call it. If it really is a bomb, what's to keep it from going off in our faces?"

"Look, as long as George doesn't find out, we've got nothing to worry about," said Marlie. "If I don't tell him and you don't tell him, how's he going to find out? You've encoded the thing and hidden it, right?"

"Yeah. But I still don't understand why you're doing this. I mean, if we weren't writing anything down, there'd be nothing for us to worry about; there'd be nothing for George to find."

"True," she said. "But suppose we need something to buy our way out of here."

"'Buy our way out'?"

"Look, let's think ahead. Suppose the operation goes bad, or the director orders George to stop it and get rid of the evidence."

"Yeah, but it's working. I've written a program that works. I've been doing exactly what they want."

"But what if they change their minds and don't want you or your program anymore?"

"I wouldn't tell anybody," said Willard.

Marlie tapped him on the forehead. "God, you're dense. I'm not saying it's going to happen. This is an insurance policy. It gives you and me something to hold over George if we ever need to. They're not going to do away with you and me if they know it'll result in their exposure. Don't you understand?"

"Yeah," said Willard, "except for one thing."

"What's that?"

"What good's it going to do if we have the bomb stored in the computer? All anyone would have to do is destroy the discs."

Marlie smiled. "You've got a point, a good point."

"Well?"

The question hung there, unanswered.

"Well," said Willard, "got any ideas?"

"At the moment?" Marlie exhaled. "No. But I'm thinking about it."

"Well, something just occurred to me."

"What?"

"You remember when I told you about networks and electronic bulletin boards and all that stuff?"

"Sure."

"Well, now that we've got a phone in here, I can hook this thing up and send messages to anyone on the network. I've got my own special password. That lets people send me messages that only I can read. I could put your stuff in my file—coded, of course—and keep it there as long as you want me to. Nobody else'd ever see it."

Marlie nodded. "That might just do it."

"If you'd like, I'll show you how it works."

"Sure."

He picked up the receiver and started dialing.

"Who are you calling?"

"Denver," he replied. "That's the nearest access number."

"No," she said sharply, bringing her hand down on the button. "That's long distance. George looks at the phone bill. He'll wonder who you're calling and why. We don't want to do anything that attracts suspicion."

"Well, I can't get on the network if I can't dial the access number." He paused. "Wait a second. I've got a blue box. I can bypass long-distance billing that way and make the call for nothing."

Willard rummaged through a canvas sack and came up with a packet that resembled the front of a push-button telephone.

"Are you sure the phone company won't be able to trace it back to here?"

"Not a chance," said Willard.

A minute later, after the connection was made, he put the handset in the cradle and tapped in his password on the keyboard. The CRT was suddenly filled with writing.

"Those are messages for me," he said. "I haven't been on the network since January, so they've kind of piled up."

"Sort of like letters in the mailbox," said Marlie.

"Yeah," said Willard, "except these don't pile up for other people to see. They're addressed specifically to me: they go into my 'read file.' No one can see them but me."

"And you could put the bomb in your file, and no one else would be able to read it?"

"That's right."

He began scrolling through the electronic messages in his file, stopping occasionally to read one, deleting most of them.

"How long would it take you to put the bomb in your file?"

"The modem here puts out about twelve hundred baud."

"The *what* does *what*?"

"Modem. That's an abbreviation for modulator-demodulator. The data in my computer is digital, but the telephone circuit is analog. A modem converts from one to the other. And baud— that's a means of measuring how fast the data is transmitted. At twelve hundred, we'd be sending the equivalent of a type-written page every fifteen seconds. So, it'll take a couple of minutes to transfer the bomb from the computer into my read file on the network."

"And no one else would be able to read it?"

"Right."

"You're sure?"

"Of course, I'm sure. In fact, if you want to, I'll go ahead right now and put what you have in the file."

"No," she said quickly. "I don't want that thing out of our hands unless we absolutely have to use it."

"Okay," said Willard, as he signed off the network. The screen glowed green once again.

"In fact, I don't want to talk about computers, phase three, and all the rest of that horseshit," said Marlie. "I've had it for tonight."

"So have I. What do you want to talk about?"

"I don't know," she said. "Maybe I'll just go inside and go to bed."

"Oh, do you have to? I mean, it's only a little after ten. Don't you, uh, want to, you know, stay around and, uh . . ."

"And, *uh*, what?"

"You know," he said.

She sighed. "All right, Whiz. Roll out the bag."

Willard retrieved the down-filled sleeping bag from the corner and rolled it out in the narrow aisle. Marlie methodically took off her clothes and lay down; Willard undressed quickly, almost tripping over the stool, and stretched out beside her.

Marlie moved expertly but without enthusiasm, bringing him to orgasm in a matter of minutes.

"God, that was good," he said. "Uh, was it good for you?"

Marlie stifled a yawn. "It's always good," she replied.

Willard shifted to his side and propped himself up on an elbow. Marlie continued to lie on her back, eyes closed.

"Don't you think it's, well, kind of funny?" he asked.

"What?"

"You and me together. Here."

Marlie opened her eyes, glanced briefly at the eerie green glow on Willard's face, and closed them again. "Yeah. I guess it is," she said.

Willard missed the irony in her voice. "These last two months have been really great." He paused, anticipating a response but receiving none. "I mean," he continued, "it's really been great having you here. I don't think I could have gotten everything done if you hadn't been here."

"Sure you would have. I haven't been any help on the machine."

"That's not what I mean," said Willard. "I've got all the time I need to work on the machines. More than enough. But if it was just me here, I'd probably be messing around with them."

"Doing what?"

"Lots of things. Seeing if I could get into a company's computer, reprogramming it, crashing it maybe."

"Crashing it?"

"You know, shutting it down."

"I see."

"So, I probably got a lot more done with you here than I would have just on my own. I mean, I knew you'd be asking me what I did every day so I figured I'd better get on with it." A long pause. "Besides, I was worried George'd send you away if I didn't."

"I see."

"I'd have walked out if he'd done that. I really would have. I'd have snuck out at night and hitched a ride on 285 to Denver. There're some guys in Boulder I could have stayed with."

She nodded, eyes closed.

"But George said you'd be back; he promised. That's why I stayed." He took a breath. "And I'm really glad I did. I mean, it's been wonderful."

Again, she nodded.

Willard lay back on the sleeping bag and stretched out beside Marlie, his thigh against hers.

"I don't think I've ever been as happy," he said softly. "I guess you've probably been happy a lot. I mean, you're so beautiful you must have always had lots of friends, somebody always calling you, people telling you how nice you are. That sort of thing.

"I guess I'm maybe what you'd call a late bloomer. When I was a kid, I felt I was always on the outside. You know how kids always seem to have somebody to pick on. Well, I guess I was it. I never had anybody like a best friend. Not for long, anyway. Sometimes, a new kid'd move in during the summer, and we'd get to play a lot before school started. But then we'd go to school, and the kids'd start in again. They'd be calling me 'Weird Willard' or say over and over again: 'Willard has cooties. Willard has cooties.'"

"I see," said Marlie.

"That was when I was real young," he said. "By the time I got to high school, things got better. I never did that good with most subjects, but I got along with computers right from the start. A lot of kids'd be having trouble and would ask me to help them with their homework. Most of the time it was so easy I did it myself. It was kind of hard sometimes explaining to them what to do. It's still kind of hard for me putting things into words.

"But that really kind of changed things. It was like I was on a team and, you know, the star player. We even called ourselves 'computer jocks.' And when other guys'd be out practicing football or in the gym shooting baskets, we'd be in the computer room doing our homework or running programs. The teacher would stay after school a lot of times, and when I was a senior he gave me a key to the room. I was president of the computer club then, and he'd let me lock it up at night on my own. There'd be some nights I'd be there until real late, you know, like two or three in the morning.

"It was mostly guys in the club. We had a couple of girls, but they weren't very smart; I don't think girls understand computers like guys do. Anyway, I was spending so much time on the machines that I never had time to go out on dates. Besides, the ones that would've gone out with me were not the real pretty ones. Those were the ones I wanted."

Marlie was breathing deeply, steadily. Willard assumed she was still listening.

"I don't know why I'm telling you all these things," Willard continued. "I haven't thought about this stuff for years. I guess I just want you to get to know me better." He paused. "I also want to get to know *you* better."

When Marlie did not respond, he turned on his side, stirring her awake.

"Oh," she said.

"Were you sleeping?"

"Not really," she replied. "I just had my eyes closed."

"That's okay," he said. "I was just wondering what you were like when you were growing up, what sort of things you liked to do. You know, that sort of thing."

"Uh, maybe some other time," she said. "You were talking, uh, about computers. You're obviously brilliant in that field. How'd you get involved with them?"

"Well, you know the computer club I was telling you about?"

"Uh, sure," she said, closing her eyes again.

"Well, that was, like I told you, the start. I guess it was mostly because I like the machines the way some people like dogs. I was never allowed to have a dog. My old man said all they do is shit and piss all over the floor. Of course, he used to throw up all over the house when he was drunk, but that was different, I guess.

"Anyway, the thing I liked right off was the way computers listen to you. They don't care what time it is, day or night. You can leave them late at night and come back the next morning and pick up right where you left off; it's like they've been waiting for you. They treat you kind of like a good friend. You tell him to meet you at the corner, and sure enough he'll be there whenever you show up. It wouldn't matter if you were right on time or four hours late. He's your friend, and he'll always be there.

"They're also smart. They can crunch numbers faster than you can even write them down. But it's you that's in control because you tell them what numbers to crunch and when to do it. So, in a way you're really the smart one. They do only what you tell them to do. And when you give them the right instructions, they work perfectly. If you mess up and don't tell them the right way to do something, they won't work. They're kind of like kids that way because you've really got to show them exactly what you want or they'll get it all wrong. But they're also patient. They'll wait as long as you want until you get it right. And one thing for sure, they don't laugh at you. They never make fun of you."

Marlie suddenly sat up on the bed roll. "It's getting late."

"Do you really have to go?"

"I'm tired," she said. "I'm going to have to get up early to send those messages George is writing to the sector heads."

Willard expelled a heavy sigh. "You mean a lot to me, Marlie."

"I know," she said softly.

"And one day, I want the two of us to get away from here."

"I don't know, Whiz."

"But I love you. I want to marry you."

She shook her head. "No. Don't talk like that."

"But that's how I feel. I want you to know that. I mean, if it wasn't for you, I wouldn't be here. I'd have split months ago."

"You wouldn't do that, would you?"

"Yeah, I would've. I mean, there really hasn't been a whole lot for me to do. They're using basically the same program I wrote three months ago. Besides, I don't like George. If you weren't here, I'd have split just to be rid of that asshole."

"You can't leave, Whiz. Everybody's counting on you. I'm counting on you."

"You know I'd never walk out on you," he said earnestly. "You're the reason I'm here. Don't you understand that?"

"Yes," she said, getting to her knees. Then she put her arms about his neck and drew him toward her.

Willard buried his face in the crevice between her breasts and began nuzzling them. "God, you're getting me excited again."

"I know," she said. "And I'm going to take care of it in a minute. Just promise me one thing."

"Okay."

"No more talk about leaving. I want you to stay. Will you do that?"

He was breathing more heavily. "You know I will."

"Good," she said, as her hand began sliding down his chest.

CHAPTER 21

Paul sat at his desk staring at the sandwich he had just pulled from a cellophane wrapper. He peeled back a limp slice of bread and peered at gray flecks of tuna and green specks of celery imbedded in a viscous yellow substance. He let the slice flop back into place, reached for the apple, and took a bite. It was mushy.

Involuntarily he balled his hands into fists, but then caught himself, consciously reining the urge to knock the food from his desk into the trash can. Quick, sharp clicks came from the hallway. He turned in his chair in time to see Nancy walk through the door.

"Chicago just called," she said breathlessly. "It looks like they're getting hit again."

Paul got to his feet and followed Nancy into the operations center. Hamlin was on the line when Paul took his place at the console and lifted the handset. Nancy slipped on a lightweight headset with a built-in microphone.

"This is Paul. What's going on?"

"At exactly twelve-thirty EDT," said Hamlin, "the system began to generate transactional errors on six of our lines: San Francisco, Kansas City, St. Louis, Minneapolis, Dallas, and Cleveland."

"Are they showing up on the confirmation messages?"

"Negative. It's strictly on the transmission end. The error check is catching them on the confirmation and resending them. But there's an error every time, so nothing's coming through right. We're already backlogged ten to twenty minutes."

Paul glanced at Nancy and nodded.

"Art, this is Nancy. How long can you keep the system up?"

"We've already called the six branches and told them not to send any new transmissions until we've cleared things up. The ones we've got in the system now could stay in the loop indefinitely."

"Standby, one," said Nancy, as she finished tapping commands on the keyboard. The cathode ray tube in front of her promptly produced a status report. "Okay, Art, we're on line with you here. And we're prepared to conduct airborne sweeps on your San Francisco and Minneapolis circuits. If you have to shut down any of the links, could you leave them until last?"

"Affirmative. We'll keep SF and MPLS up until advised to the contrary."

"Good," she said. "I'm giving you back to Paul."

Nancy switched to another circuit and began speaking quietly into the mouthpiece while Paul finished his conversation with Hamlin. He put the handset on the receiver and turned to Nancy.

"The Defense command post has been alerted," she said. "The Air Force is scrambling an SR-71 from Beale in California. It'll sweep the microwave path from SF to Chicago and then fly back over the Minneapolis link. They'll be doing photo as well as ELINT reconnaissance."

Winchell joined them moments later and took the seat next to Nancy. While she was briefing him, Paul called John Scotto.

After an exchange of pleasantries, Paul said, "We've got a big one today."

"You want me to get back to you on the scrambler?"

"That won't be necessary," said Paul. "But we'll probably need to get together this evening or, more likely, tomorrow morning."

"Oh."

"Is something wrong?"

"Not really," said Scotto. "But it *is* the Saturday before the Fourth of July weekend, and I was planning to get away. Don't get me wrong. I'll stick around as long as you want."

"How about early in the morning?"

"Where?"

"If you have something to show me, I'll come over there."

"I do have something."

"Good," said Paul. "Is eight o'clock too early?"

"No, that'll be fine."

"Good. I'll have more complete information for you, then."

"Okay," said Scotto. "See you at eight."

John Scotto was waiting at the entrance of the MATER building when the car pulled up. Paul emerged from the rear seat with a briefcase locked to his wrist.

"Wearing government-issue jewelry now, I see," said Scotto.

Paul grinned sheepishly. "Winchell gave me a choice. It was either this damn thing or a courier dogging my heels."

Scotto led him into the building. After Paul showed his I.D. card to the guard and signed in at the main desk, they took the elevator to Scotto's office.

"What have you got?"

"No one's quite sure," said Paul, as he opened the briefcase and began spreading its contents on the table. "The photo experts at the Agency are just starting to go over the pictures. But the ELINT people think they may have something on the electronic stuff."

Scotto riffled the papers in the first pile. "It looks like you turned up a couple of anomalies."

"The SR-71 picked up these emanations," said Paul, indicating two graphs. "One in Utah, the other in Wisconsin."

"Have they identified the source?"

"No. There aren't any known transmitters there. In fact, both areas are in or near parks."

"It's not going to be easy to pin down," said Scotto. "Microwave repeaters are usually about forty kilometers apart, and you can be ten clicks off the center line—maybe more, depending on your equipment—and still make an intercept."

"Wouldn't it take a lot of equipment to do that? And wouldn't it be conspicuous?"

"Yes, it would take a lot of equipment, but, no, I don't

think it'd have to be very conspicuous," he replied. "It wouldn't be that hard to hide a fair-sized parabolic reflector. Bell System TD-2 receivers are easy enough to come by, but they've got crystal oscillators, and that limits them to fixed frequencies. So, my guess is they'd go for something with continuous tuning capability, like a Gunn oscillator with some YIG waveguide filters. With that for a nucleus and a suitable microprocessor plus an off-the-shelf transmitter, they'd have a package capable of hitting every government microwave circuit from one to fifteen gigahertz."

"How much space would it take?"

"Not much. Like I said at the meeting, you could probably stuff the whole thing into a small truck."

"Or a camper, maybe?"

"I don't see why not." A smile crinkled his eyes. "I think I see what you're getting at."

"Well, it does stand to reason that we're dealing with some sort of mobile operation. And the fact that the SR-71 detected those anomalies near park areas tends to strengthen the possibility."

"That's a step in the right direction," said Scotto, "but it's not going to be easy pinning down the exact source. There are probably more than a hundred microwave towers between San Francisco and Chicago. The first thing you'd have to do is locate the interval where you're being intercepted.

"Once you've determined the interval, you have to find the transmitter. And that'll really be tough. Not only could it be hidden from view in a camper or truck, you've got over one hundred and fifty square miles between each microwave tower where the system could be operating, and the transmitter could be anywhere in that zone. All he has to do is shut down and drive away, and you're left with nothing. There'd be no trail to follow."

"You don't make it sound very promising."

"It isn't," he said. "This isn't high tech; we're talking about stuff that just about anybody can get his hands on. He can steal it from a warehouse or buy it off the shelf. A skilled amateur can put together a system that'll intercept microwave transmissions anywhere in the country. True, the challenge of altering those transmissions is an order of magnitude higher, but it's by no means impossible." He grinned. "Hell, the Agency's been doing that kind of stuff since the fifties."

"So, where does that leave us?"

"From a communications standpoint, we have two broad choices: go after the causes, or deal with the symptoms. It could take a while to find out who or what is behind all this, so I think the first order of business is to deal with the symptoms."

"You've got some ideas, I hope."

"They've shown they can tap into land lines, microwave, and satellite transmissions. But most of the traffic goes microwave. And the problem there is that the signal can be taken, literally, out of the air."

"So the problem is with the transmission media?"

Scotto chuckled. "I'm a communications man. What the hell'd you expect me to say? Cryptography?"

Paul smiled. "No. That's my line."

"As I see it," Scotto continued, "we have to deal with the problem in two stages. First, we have to be able to detect immediately any microwave link that's been compromised. Second, we have to reroute that segment."

"But doesn't the system automatically do that already?"

Scotto nodded. "Depending on the load, the system can switch to a different microwave route or land line. That may complicate things for the enemy, but remember all he's got to do is break one link in a very long chain. We've got to defend *every* link in that chain. In a way, it's like the classic air defense problem. What good does it do to protect, say, Philadelphia from an air attack only to have the bombs fall on Wilmington?"

"A lot," jibed Paul, "if you live in Philadelphia."

Scotto laughed. "Well, you know what I mean."

Paul nodded. "So, what media would you use?"

"The most readily available choices are laser and optical," he replied. "And both have their limitations. On a clear day you could substitute laser repeaters, one for one, with the microwave repeaters. But it's a line-of-sight network, and on a cloudy day you've got a penetration problem with lasers that you don't have with microwaves.

"With optical it's simply the lack of infrastructure. You can't exactly go stringing optical wire between microwave towers. You'd have to find a way to reroute the traffic over existing optical systems, but most of them are in the DC-Boston corridor. That wouldn't have done us much good yesterday in those two parks."

"So lasers would be the best bet?"

"For dealing with the immediate problem? Yes," said Scotto.

"And I suppose you have some ideas about how to do this."

"So happens I do," he said, smiling. He walked to his file cabinet, tapped in the digital combination, and unlocked it. He returned to the table and spread out his notes.

For the next hour, they discussed Scotto's idea of deploying helicopter teams that would be on alert to counter any disruption of microwave communications. Positioned throughout the country, the teams would respond immediately whenever transmissions to Chicago were disrupted and rig line-of-sight laser transmitters on the microwave towers over the segment that was being intercepted. Though both men knew weather would limit its effectiveness, the idea seemed worth a try.

After Scotto locked his notes in the file, he came back to the table. Paul was gathering his papers and putting them in his briefcase.

"You've got an invitation to lunch," said Scotto.

"Oh," said Paul. "I thought you were going away for the weekend."

"I am," said Scotto, brown eyes crinkling in a smile. "It's an invitation from the boss lady. She said you should just mosey on up to her office whenever we finished."

"Does she usually come in on weekends?"

"I don't know. I've got a computer terminal at the house, so I do a lot of work there rather than come in on weekends. But other people tell me she really does put in the hours." He paused, grinning. "She just makes it *look* like it's one big dinner party."

As they got into the elevator, Scotto asked, "Any luck talking them into giving public-key cryptography a try?"

Paul shook his head. "Not yet, but I'm working on it."

"What's the problem?"

"It's not clear. Winchell says WG-Seven is studying the idea, but I suspect it's more a political thing. If they go with a different cryptographic system, they'd be admitting, in effect, that the federal Data Encryption Standard has been compromised."

"You may be right," said Scotto. "But in a way, it's also a compliment."

Paul cocked his head.

"I mean that," said Scotto. "The Agency knows they can crack the DES. Why else would they be so insistent about keeping it? But I suspect public-key has them stymied." The elevator opened, and the two men stepped out. "They've probably got their Crays working overtime, crunching away on hundred-digit primes, to see if they can crack your public-key system."

"And I had the impression we were all working on the same side," said Paul with obvious sarcasm.

"Welcome to the wonderful world of the NSA," said Scotto.

They were laughing as they opened the outer door to Natasha's office.

On hearing them, Natasha got up from her desk and began walking toward the door. "Hello, Paul. John." Though she greeted both men, her eyes remained fixed on Paul.

"Delivered him safe and sound," said Scotto, clapping Paul lightly on the shoulder.

"Off to the beach?" she asked.

He nodded.

"I'm going to make lunch. You're welcome to stay."

"Thank you," he said, "but I think I'll hit the road. I've given Paul the number at the cottage in case he needs to call me."

After Scotto left, Natasha led the way to the dining room behind her office. "I picked up some basil and fresh pasta at an Italian deli on the way over. I thought I'd make pesto and toss it over fettucine."

"Sounds wonderful. Can I help?"

"You can do the salad, if you like."

Standing at an adjacent counter, he spent almost as much time looking at her as he did washing, drying, and tearing the greens. He could not keep his eyes off her body.

At the table, Paul spoke about some of his frustrations. The NSA had been resisting his suggestion that the Federal Reserve drop the DES in favor of public-key cryptography, and though he liked Scotto's suggestion for helicopter teams using laser links to restore any break in the circuits, he now found himself trying to anticipate the bureaucratic obstacles he would have to overcome.

Natasha was sympathetic. "We're always encountering problems of one sort or another at the Agency. The only difference is that we've got the meter running. No matter what they do—or don't do, for that matter—we continue to get paid on a cost-plus basis."

"What I don't understand is how people on the inside put up with it. I know I couldn't."

"That's because you're a scientist, a mathematician," she

said. "Take a good look around you at Fort Meade. Count the number of top-notch mathematicians or engineers you've run into. You won't even need most of your fingers to do it." She sipped her wine. "The reason is simple: most really good scientists have no patience with bureaucracy. The sort of people who thrive in places like that are two-bit power-players. It doesn't matter how many letters they can string after their names; they're courtiers, different in dress from their counterparts in ancient Rome or medieval Europe, but no different in what they do. Their game is, and always has been, politics. You'd be making a big mistake if you expect them to be anything else."

"I know what you're saying," said Paul. "I guess I just expected something different, given the gravity of the situation."

"Even in war, allies can be as frustrating as enemies," she said. "You remember what Churchill said of the French?"

Paul shook his head.

"'The greatest cross I've had to bear is The Cross of Lorraine.'"

Paul chuckled. "No wonder DeGaulle hated '*les Anglais*.'"

Natasha smiled and stood up. Paul followed her with his eyes as she went to the refrigerator for a second bottle of Chardonnay.

The conversation shifted from politics. Paul talked about the country house he had near Stowe. Natasha told him about the Maryland farm her father had bought a few years before his death. After she inherited the place, her first impulse had been to sell it, but after a love affair turned sour, she began to go there on weekends and found the seclusion very much to her liking. A city creature, she returned most evenings to her circa-1830 townhouse in Georgetown. Still, she told him, it was comforting to know that she could always head for the rolling hills of Maryland when things went wrong, either at the office or in her personal life.

A pleasant vinous cloud had descended over them. When Natasha rose to get a third bottle of wine, Paul followed unsteadily, brushing her body as they went into the kitchen. She giggled as she fumbled with the corkscrew, and Paul covered her hand with his and held it there for a moment before taking the bottle.

She turned and met his eyes, smiling. "Would you like to

hear some music? We could listen to the radio here or the stereo in the office."

"Either would be fine."

"Okay," she said. "Let's go to the office. I've got some Mozart tapes you might like."

Paul rummaged through a cabinet to get a wine bucket, surrounded the bottle with ice, and was walking toward her office when he heard the opening bars of Mozart's Fortieth Symphony. Natasha had just locked the door to her outer office and was heading toward the sofa.

"Over here," she said, indicating the end table.

Paul set the wine bucket down. Natasha kicked off her shoes, lowered herself to the floor, and leaned against the sofa. Paul filled their glasses before joining her on the thick ivory rug.

He closed his eyes and tried to concentrate on the music, but found he could not. She was close to him, so close he could feel the warmth of her body, the subtle scent of her perfume wafting about him.

After the first movement, he said softly, "I really love this next movement."

"So do I," she whispered.

He tried to think of Helen, the times they had listened to this music together, but his mind would yield no image, no face, no feeling. It was as if she had passed into memory and become an idea, an abstraction. It must be the wine, he thought. But when he tried to summon her presence, to *feel* the love they had shared, he could not.

His head started to spin, slowly at first, then he felt himself being drawn down, down, down into the vortex. Without thinking, he reached out to steady himself and found his hand on top of hers. An instant later, she was leaning against him, her head against his chest.

He was hard now. When he stirred to reach for his glass, she lifted her head. He started to take a sip, decided not to, and set the glass to the side. When he turned, he found himself looking into her eyes.

"It's all right, Paul," she said softly. Her gaze was direct, her breath warm against his cheek.

All right? he thought. What's all right? All right if I do? All right if I don't? What do you mean?

An instant later he found himself kissing her. But when he

tried to ease away, he found he could not or, maybe, would not.

Her arms came around his neck. He put his hands on her shoulders, perhaps to restrain her, perhaps to hold her. But the gesture, like the man, was tentative and incapable of restraining either of them. A moment later he enveloped her in his arms.

Paul could feel the weight of the alcohol across his brow; his fingers seemed made of lead as he fumbled with the belt at her waist.

"I'll get that," she said and got to her feet. She undid the belt and then slowly slipped the dress over her head. Now wearing only a bra and red bikini panties, she looked down and smiled.

Paul's eyes began taking inventory. Her ankles were slender, the calves lean and lightly muscled, the thighs hard. Her ass looked firm and nicely rounded; her waist was the narrow end of a long taper that began with her shoulders.

He stood up. When they kissed, Paul reached around her back and undid her bra. As he unbuttoned his shirt, he looked admiringly at her breasts, two small but perfect hemispheres. A minute later, both were nude. Natasha stretched out on the floor. Paul lay alongside and began stroking her, his hands gently, tentatively, roaming her body. At first her reactions seemed cool, but as he became more assured in his touch, she began to respond, her breath quickening, nipples hard. A deep moan reverberated in her throat as his hand slowly moved along her inner thigh, then came a sharp gasp as he lightly brushed her clitoris. Arching her back, she began to thrust against his hand, the pace increasing, his touch becoming more firm. She began to move rhythmically, eyes closed, face taut with concentration, thrusting harder and harder until, finally, she reached climax, the aftershocks sending wave after tingling wave the length of her body.

"Don't stop," she whispered. "Please don't stop."

Paul continued to touch her, letting her come again and again. Finally Natasha, silvery beads of perspiration glistening on her forehead, skin deeply flushed, pulled away from his hand.

"Lie down. It's your turn," she said softly.

Paul put his arms behind his head and watched as Natasha began to touch him with her hands, her mouth, and her tongue. It had been so long since a woman, since Helen, had touched him that the pleasure was sweet, so excruciatingly sweet that he came quickly.

Natasha reached for her glass and cleared her throat with a long pull of the wine. Then she straddled him, drew him into her, and began what seemed to him an exquisite dance, now lifting, now turning, now tightening around him. All sense of time was extinguished as the tension once again began to build. When he came the second time, it sent a shudder through his body, the release so thorough that he promptly fell asleep.

A ringing phone awakened him, and at first he was disoriented, not sure of where he was, his eyes squinting against the afternoon sunlight. Then he saw Natasha, fully clothed, take the phone in hand. He looked down; a crocheted Afghan was covering his body. He reached to the left but found the jumbled pile of clothes were gone. Natasha raised a hand and gestured toward the open closet where his suit now hung.

"And how are you, Bill?" she said into the mouthpiece. "I see," she said. "Well, if it's urgent, I can have him call you." A pause. "Okay, I'll tell him." Another pause. "Fine. Oh, and regards to Elizabeth. Bye."

"Winchell, I take it?"

"Yes," she replied.

"Is it urgent?"

She shook her head. "He just wanted to know if you were still here. I told him you were. He said he'd be at the office until six-thirty and to give him a call if you were getting back to the post after that time."

"What time is it?"

"Almost five."

"You're kidding."

"Not at all. You've been out like a light for nearly two hours."

"Oh. Must have been the wine," he said, grinning.

"Yes," she said, eyes flashing. "Must have been."

PART V

CHAPTER 22

To the President of the United States:
1. Through intimidation and criminal acts of repression, agencies of the U.S. Government have selectively and systematically attempted to suppress free speech, the practice of religion, and other freedoms explicitly guaranteed by the First Amendment to the U.S. Constitution. These freedoms must be restored.
2. The Federal Bureau of Investigation and the Internal Revenue Service are the principal engines of this despotism. They must immediately cease their unconstitutional activities.
3. Our demands are unconditional. All prisoners of conscience must be released. Indictments against all men and women of principle must be quashed. Harassment under the guise of investigatory activities must be terminated.

4. If corrective actions do not commence within 48 hours, chaos shall follow.

5. Reply by message from Chicago to all branches of the Federal Reserve at 0900 hours EDT, Friday.

Willard read and reread the typewritten page. He turned to George. "You really want me to send this?"

"Yes."

"Should I do it from here or through one of the mobile units?"

"It cannot be traced back to here, correct?"

Willard sighed. "For the millionth time, *no*. Electrons leave no tracks."

"Do it directly, then."

"Okay."

"What about the reply?" George asked. "You will be able to monitor it from here, will you not?"

"No problem."

"Good." George turned to leave.

"One question," said Willard.

George looked over his shoulder. "What is it?"

"Aren't you going to sign it?"

"No."

"But who are they going to reply to? I mean, I can sit in front of the screen all day waiting to see if a message comes across. But that's really a waste of time. Besides, I might miss it."

"We cannot let them know who we are."

"Give me a little credit, will you? I know you don't want to let on who we are. But if there's a name, any name, someone who's supposed to be getting the message, I could program the machine to record and store it automatically. It doesn't have to be a real name. Make one up. But give me something."

George sat down on a stool. "Go ahead and type in the message. I will come up with something by the time you finish."

Willard typed the message, slowly reading each line before typing the next. When it was done, he raised his hands from the keyboard with a flourish, as if he had just finished a piano concerto.

"Very well," said George. "On line five, make that 'Reply to CPJ' and leave the rest of the message the way it is."

"What's CPJ stand for?"

"The Council for Peace and Justice," said George. "Do you think you can program your computer to pick that out?"

Willard laughed. "You've got it."

After breakfast on Friday, George followed Willard to the trailer.

"It is almost nine o'clock in the East. I do not want to miss this," he said.

"The machines are automatically recording everything that goes out of Chicago to San Francisco. If it gets sent, we'll have it."

The two men sat down in front of the main console. Symbols began crossing the screen.

"What is that?" George asked.

"That's a synchronization signal. You'll see them go across the CRT every so often. It's on a real-time basis. What you're seeing is being sent by the Chicago Switch this very instant."

"What if Chicago has already sent its reply?"

"It'll be in the memory." Willard turned and faced the screen on the adjacent console. He entered a command on the keyboard. CHARACTER STRINGS A–F NEGATIVE said the computer.

"What does that mean?" George asked.

"I simply asked the computer to audit all messages transmitted from Chicago this morning for certain character strings, like 'CPJ' or ''Council.' If those appear in any of the transmissions, the machine will display the message. As you can see, nothing like that's come through."

The digital clock flashed 7:00.

"It should be coming through now," said George.

But no message came. George stared intently at the green glowing screen for five, then ten minutes. A string of letters and numbers flashed across the cathode ray tube.

"Synchronization strings," said Willard.

At seven-twenty, George began lightly drumming his fingers on the metal ledge in front of the screen. Shortly after seven-thirty, he stood up.

"I can accomplish nothing here," said George. "Let me know if anything comes through."

"Sure."

George came back to the trailer periodically throughout the day, opened the door, and asked if anything had come across the wire. Each time, the answer was the same. After dinner that evening, George led Willard to the study, closing the door behind them.

"I had anticipated any number of reactions," said George, "but to be frank, the one I thought least likely was no response."

Willard shrugged. "I don't see what difference it makes. I mean, we're all set for the blitz."

"Good," said George, "because that is precisely what we are going to give them."

"When?"

"That depends. I would prefer to strike with all twelve of the field units, but two of them are down. I intend to give the sectors several days to see if they and you can get them working."

"I thought all of them were working."

George shook his head. "The Boston and Atlanta sector heads called during the day. It sounds as if each of them has the same problem."

"Hardware or software?"

"The latter."

"Bullshit," said Willard. "There's nothing wrong with my program. Somebody's probably been frobbing around with it and crashed the damn thing."

"Their technicians are working on the system. If they fail to clear up the difficulty by morning, they have been instructed to phone the trailer for remote diagnostic action."

"Why not tonight? I've got the time. I can handle it."

"Your dedication is commendable, Whiz. But I want the sector technicians to become more familiar with the system. This will give them an opportunity."

"Shit. They'll probably gronk it for good."

George gave a slight shrug. "If possible, I would like to go with all twelve field units, but I am willing to settle for ten."

"Why not some backup units?"

"We gave that some thought and, for reasons of security, decided against it. By remaining small and elite, we can effectively preclude detection and capture." He raised his head and looked hard into Willard's eyes. "Also, putting more people into the field compounds the danger of disloyalty. All it takes is one defector."

He knows, thought Willard. No, he can't. He's just trying to scare me, test me.

After what seemed to Willard an uncomfortably long silence, George resumed. "Marlie's decoding messages from the

Atlanta and Boston sectors describing the nature of the problem. She will bring them to you when she has finished."

"Okay. Anything else? I mean, I'll be glad to contact them and try to diagnose the problem."

"As I said, if it is not cleared up by morning, I will ask you to use remote diagnostics. In the meantime, you might want to run your program one more time."

"Sure," said Willard. "Anything else?"

George shook his head.

"Okay, I'll be in the trailer."

When Marlie came in, she found him staring at a nearly blank screen. "What are you doing?"

"Nothing."

"Yeah. I can see that."

He forced a small laugh.

"Something bothering you?"

"No. Not really."

"What is it?"

"Oh, just something George said."

"What was it?"

"Well, we were talking about how some of the other guys were having trouble with their computers, and then for no reason at all he starts talking about 'disloyalty' and how 'all it takes is one defector.'"

"That's just the way he is. He's always been concerned about disloyalty. Before he got this project, he ran the director's anti-subversives program."

"'Anti-subversives'?"

She nodded.

"What did he do when he found one?"

"Probably killed him."

The color drained from his face.

"Now, I don't know that for a fact," she said. "But that's what some people say."

"Oh, Jesus. What if he finds your bomb?"

She smiled. "Oh, it's *my* bomb now, is it?"

"N-no. I didn't mean it that way. We're in this thing together."

"And don't you forget it."

"How can you be so calm?"

"You asked me a question, and I told you what I'd heard. But I'm not really sure it's true. George may be a nasty little shit and all that, but I don't think he'd actually kill somebody."

Willard exhaled. "That's nice to know."

"Of course, he could have had somebody else do the actual killing," she said in a relaxed, almost breezy tone.

Willard shook his head. "I don't get you. You're talking about a guy who may have killed people he thinks were subversives. And here we are putting into the computer a history of everything we know about the operation and the organization, things that would bring down George and the whole fucking thing. Now, if that isn't subversive, what the hell is?"

"You're right."

"That does it," he said. "I'm deleting the whole thing from the memory."

Her tone was sharp. "Like hell you are. You leave that damn thing in there. You understand?"

"Yeah, I mean, Jeez, don't get mad."

"Look, Whiz, you're just going to have to trust me on this," she said, her voice more gentle. "I know these people. I know the way they think, the way they operate. We may never have to use it, but that bomb could save your ass as well as mine if we ever have to bargain our way out of here. Think of it as an insurance policy—one *they* can't cancel."

He swallowed hard. "Yeah. Okay."

"Look, I think George was just sort of fishing. He wanted to see how you'd react."

"You mean he was testing me?"

"I don't think he suspects you of anything. I think he was just trying to keep you in line, maybe shake you up a bit."

"I see."

She smiled. "Looks like he did."

Willard grunted.

"Oh, I almost forgot," she said, raising the papers she held in her hand. "These messages came in about an hour ago."

Willard tilted the papers so they would catch the light from the cathode ray tubes.

"Can you make them out? There were some words in there I wasn't too sure of."

"Yeah," said Willard. "It looks like they were frobbing with the run and crufted some of the code. It'll be an easy win decrocking it."

Marlie looked at him sideways. "Huh?"

"Oh, sorry," said Willard. "I was just saying that they were trying to modify my program and apparently wrote in some faulty logic. I should be able to straighten it out in no time."

"Good."

He set the papers on the metal ledge in front of the screen and reached for her with his arms. She stood there stiffly, not responding.

"Is something the matter?" he asked.

"I'm just tired. I need to get to bed."

"Can't you stay, you know, just for a little while?"

"Not tonight, Whiz." She kissed him lightly on the lips and backed away. "See you at breakfast."

His arms, now empty, seemed to freeze momentarily in midair. "Yeah," he said softly, "see you in the morning."

CHAPTER 23

"Of course it's a Soviet front. What else in God's name could it be?"

Paul turned away from the intense young man he remembered from the earlier meeting and looked toward the head of the table, where the Director of the National Security Council was sitting. "Perhaps," said Wiley Simpson, in his most relaxed professorial manner, "you would care to elucidate your reasons."

The man continued. "We can begin with the rhetoric. Take the first point. That opening phrase, 'Through intimidation and criminal acts of repression,' is standard Marxist-Leninist cant. And in spite of what might initially appear to be domestic references, the rest of the rhetoric is laced with similar phraseology. 'Engines of despotism.' 'Unconstitutional activities.' 'Unconditional demands.' 'Prisoners of conscience.' 'Men and women of principle.'

"These, I submit, suggest the Soviet hand or, at the very

least, a crude third-world imitation. But the true stigmata may be found in the name: 'The Council for Peace and Justice.' 'Peace'? 'Justice'? Who but a Communist would use words like that?"

Wheeler's voice was even. "If, as you suggest, the Soviet Union is ultimately responsible for this ultimatum, why the subterfuge, the obviously phony name?"

The man smiled charitably, as if a child had just asked why the sky was up and not down. "Clearly, the risks of a direct confrontation with the United States would be far too grave. The subterfuge allows them to have their borscht and eat it too. In sum, what I am suggesting is that the ultimatum was drafted by someone so thoroughly indoctrinated by Marxist-Leninist rhetoric as to make even his simplest statement veritably reek of its influence."

It was only the third such session Paul had attended, but already it was as familiar as a faculty meeting. The same people, the same ideas, the same arguments, and, of course, the same indecision. Though Simpson professed to run an open meeting, Wheeler's skepticism had been right on the mark. Except for Wheeler, a Navy captain, and an Army colonel, the rest of the staff, all civilians, all handpicked by Simpson himself, were hawks of the most irrational sort. In the insular world of the university, it had been easy, too easy, to blame militarism on the military. Now, Paul could see the greater danger posed by pin-striped militarists whose dreams of victory would be purchased with other men's lives.

"What do you think, Dr. Cassidy?" Simpson asked.

"As far as who sent the ultimatum," said Paul with a slight shrug, "I'd just be guessing."

"Aren't we all?" Simpson asked.

Paul smiled and continued. "But in terms of the technology and what it might cost, we are talking about an investment on the order of a million or two. So, governments are a logical possibility, but I hasten to add that we are not talking about high-order, top-secret technology. We're talking about stuff anyone with enough money can buy off the shelf. The hardware, in fact, is quite cheap—perhaps fifty, maybe sixty thousand for a small truck with communications intercept equipment and a modest computer. The tough part is the software. That's where the real investment would have to be made in terms of time, money, and, most of all, brain power."

"And who, in your opinion, would be capable of making that sort of an investment?" asked Simpson.

"I could only speculate on that."

"That's exactly what we would like you to do," said Simpson.

"In addition to governments," said Paul, "we would have to consider any number of private concerns. Computer companies, here as well as abroad, are obvious possibilities, but programming technology is so widespread that it could be the work of a small group of experts practically anywhere you find computers. Some of my better students might even be able to pull off something like this."

Simpson and his staff laughed heartily.

"In short," Paul continued, "we have a very large universe to consider. After all, you can find computers practically everywhere: businesses, schools, even churches use them."

Simpson chuckled. "Surely you don't suspect a church might be behind all this?"

Paul laughed with everyone else in the room. "I don't know who's behind it. What I am suggesting is that computer programming is no longer an arcane science; it's commonplace. Church organizations routinely use it to raise money; the Mormons in Utah have extensive genealogical files stored on computer tapes.

"So I don't think you're going to track down the people behind the Chicago caper by focusing on the technology. Any number of groups or individuals could possess the money and the machinery to do it. The real question, as I see it, is one of motivation. We need to figure out who would *want* to do it."

The last item on Simpson's agenda was the most important: How should the government reply to the ultimatum?

Paul thought, but did not say, that it would be worthwhile to answer it, if only to open a dialogue and, perhaps, find out who or what was behind the Council for Peace and Justice. But the opinions suggested by the staff ranged from silence to a declaration of war. The moderates won out, and when the meeting was adjourned, Simpson went to the Oval Office to recommend that the government simply ignore the ultimatum. The President agreed.

Paul found that he did not mind the waiting game, not when he had Natasha to help pass the time. His movements were no longer so tightly controlled by the NSA, and he traveled almost daily between Fort Meade and MATER. As long as the operations center had a number where he could be reached, he was free to call a car from the motor pool and go where he wished.

And he wished most to be with Natasha. In spite of the Agency's top-secret missions, the pace at Fort Meade tended to be quite routine, the scientists as eager as everyone else in the bureaucracy to leave the office precisely at 5:30. A week after the ultimatum, the crisis atmosphere had dissipated. So no one took particular notice that Paul's afternoons at MATER had a way of extending into the evening.

Natasha would make dinner, and they would talk, much as they had before they became lovers, only now there was something more between them, indefinable but as palpable as an arc of lightning. They talked ostensibly about politics, the Chicago Switch, and commercial applications of cryptography, but the real, unspoken exchange involved thoughts, feelings, impulses. An inflection in the voice, a flash of the eyes, a tongue moistening a lower lip. Everything she said, everything she did, seemed to intensify his desire.

The furtive, illicit nature of their affair added to the excitement. The locked doors, the wine glasses on the office floor, the soft carpet gently cushioning the weight of their bodies.

One Thursday in mid-July, she suggested they go to her farm for the weekend.

"That'd be great," Paul replied. "But I'm not sure it'd be okay with the Agency. I mean, I've never done that."

"Well, if you want, I could ask Bill Winchell to clear it."

"Umm," he said, shaking his head. "I don't know."

"Except for that ultimatum, it's been two weeks since anything happened."

"Yeah, but tomorrow's Friday. That's the day they usually hit us."

"And if nothing happens tomorrow?"

He grinned. "Are you trying to tempt me?"

Her fingertips traced a path along his inner thigh. "What do you think?"

He made a deep, throaty growl. "I think you're succeeding."

"Should I talk to Bill, then?"

"No," he said. "I will."

When the Chicago Switch closed without incident Friday evening, Paul went to Winchell's office and, trying to put the best face on things, said he had been invited to spend the weekend at "the Ellsworth farm."

"A lovely, lovely place," Winchell replied. "Elizabeth and I have been there a number of times over the years. You'll enjoy it. Just leave the number with the Ops Center and, just to play it safe, no trips into Baltimore or Washington. We should still be cautious about your being seen in public."

Paul was pleased that Winchell had so readily agreed. Was the man being tactful, or was he simply naive? Paul gave the question no further thought once he was on the road with Natasha.

It was the first time in four months that Paul had been in a car without government markings. Though the July heat and humidity had lingered into the evening, the air that spilled over the windscreen of the Porsche was cool and only slightly humid as Natasha navigated the narrow two-lane roads and rolling hills of Howard County.

The sight of Natasha at the wheel, her hair flowing in the wind, her skirt billowing around her thighs, excited his mind no less than his body. If the crisis that had created Working Group Seven and brought him to the National Security Agency ended tomorrow, would he go home? Two weeks ago, the question would not have crossed his mind. Now, he was uncertain of the answer.

He leaned back in the soft leather seat and drew deeply of the fragrant evening air. If the government could take his old life, it could also give him a new one, as well as a new identity. If Mafia stool pigeons and Soviet KGB turncoats could get new names and new faces, why couldn't he? It would be embarrassing for the government to admit it had staged Paul's death; Wiley Simpson had said as much. How easy it would be for everyone, then, if he could simply remain Paul Cassidy when WG-Seven's mission was over.

Natasha downshifted, braked, and took a quick turn to the right. A minute later they stopped in front of a gate. She took a plastic card from the sun visor and put it into the electronic box. The gate swung open, and they drove slowly up the gravel driveway.

A small house sat on the left, its front window illuminated by the silver-blue glow of a television.

"Jess and Mary are home as usual," she said. "They manage the place and keep an eye on the big house when I'm not here."

"What do you have here?"

"About five hundred acres, but most of it's across the road. We grow corn for silage, some soybeans, a few milk cows and the horses." She glanced at him and smiled. "If it was up to me, we'd just have the horses, but Maryland law says horses alone are not enough to qualify the place as a farm."

"So the cows and the corn are just for tax purposes?"

"My tax attorney insisted on it," she said. "By the way, do you ride?"

"Poorly."

"I was afraid of that." She stopped the car beside the house and turned toward him. "But then, you do everything else so well."

From the outside, it appeared to be a large, typical farmhouse, but as soon as they were inside, Paul could see at a glance that the furnishings were as modern as those in Natasha's office. And a glance was all he got. As soon as the door was closed, she led him up the stairs to her bedroom. She was in his arms an instant after their suitcases hit the floor.

After several long and deep kisses, he began to unbutton her blouse.

She touched his hand and took half a step back. "We'll waste less time if we undress ourselves," she said.

While Paul was taking off his clothes and tossing them on a chair, he heard her flip a switch. There was a distant but deep rumble.

"What's that?" he asked.

"The hot tub."

In a farmhouse? he thought. "Oh," he said, "I've never been in one."

"You're in for a treat." She paused and added in a low voice: "The whole weekend."

After making love, they lay silently in each other's arms for several minutes.

"Are you hungry?" she asked.

"I really hadn't been thinking of food. But now that you mention it, I guess I am."

"Okay, how does this sound? There's a quiche in the freezer. I'll heat it in the microwave, open some wine, and meet you in the hot tub."

His brows raised. "I don't have a whole lot of experience being sybaritic, you know."

She was walking to the closet. "Well, darling, you're going to spend the whole weekend learning how."

She returned in a blue jersey robe. "It might get a bit cool outside," she said, handing him a matching robe.

"Well prepared, aren't you?"

The question hung between them like a curtain. It was the wrong thing to say, and Paul realized it the instant the words escaped his lips. She pretended to ignore it.

"Just open that sliding door and take the stairs down from the deck," she said. "But be careful with the lid; it's quite heavy."

Paul removed the lid and slowly entered the tub, bending his knees when his feet touched bottom until the warm water gently lapped at his chin. Natasha came out carrying a tray, which she set beside the tub, then shucked her robe and lowered herself into the water.

In silence, eyes closed, hands touching, heads resting against the rim, they let their bodies drink in the warmth. Then Natasha came alongside and gave him a playful nip on the ear.

Paul opened his eyes. "Ready for dinner, I take it."

They greedily devoured the quiche and fruit between sips of a crisp Colombard. Paul was not sure whether it was the time and place or the meal, but food had never tasted so good.

They slept late the next morning and, following a quick breakfast of café au lait and brioche, walked across the road, and toured the farm. After a leisurely lunch, they went into the living room. Paul perused the records on the shelf until he found what he was looking for.

Natasha came into the room as Mozart's Fortieth Symphony began. A smile blossomed on her lips.

"Remember the first time we heard this together?" he asked.

"Why do you think I'm smiling?"

They lay side by side on the floor, huge pillows behind their heads, and listened to the music, saying little, their hands intertwined. When the symphony ended, neither stirred.

"I don't know what it is about Mozart, but every time I listen to him it does something to me," she said. "Like a lot of people, I guess, I sometimes turn on the stereo and don't really pay attention to the music. It takes a moment like this, when I'm relaxed and with someone who can share those feelings, that it really touches me." She sighed. "I wish I could articulate what I feel, but I'm really not sure what to call those feelings; I just know they're there."

"I think I know what you mean," he said. "But while there's

a part of me that can *feel* the music, Mozart also makes me think."

"The mathematician in you," she said teasingly.

"Perhaps," he said. "There is, of course, something characteristic about Mozart; it's fairly easy to recognize a piece of his even if you've never heard it before. Yet, he's never entirely predictable. Quite the contrary. A couple of times, when I heard something of his for the first time, I'd listen to the first few bars and try to guess the next. And every time, time after time, I'd be wrong. So I don't try to second-guess him anymore. I just listen."

"I have a lot of Mozart, as you probably noticed. But you picked the Fortieth, Why that?"

"The simple answer is that I love it, particularly the second movement."

She smiled. "As a music-lover or a mathematician?"

"Both."

"I'm intrigued. How does a mathematician listen to Mozart?"

"I wouldn't even try to analyze Mozart mathematically." A wry grin crossed his face. "But if you'll settle for something less than scientific rigor, I'll be happy to give you a less than scholarly impression."

A brow raised. "We certainly wouldn't want rigor to set in now, would we?"

He smiled. "It's not that we're lazy, but mathematicians tend to look first for simplicity. Failing that we look for elegance. That could mean any number of things. Subtlety. Insight. Delicacy, perhaps.

"Take the second movement. The basic melody is simple. Someone sitting at the piano might be able to tap out something just as nice. But Mozart's genius transcends those simple notes. It's what he does with them, how he transforms them.

"When you first hear it, you don't realize how inventive he is. But the more you listen, the more you begin to sense his subtlety. He never repeats himself. Something in the music is always different. So what might first seem perfectly symmetrical becomes, when you listen more closely, something else. 'A delicate asymmetry,' someone called it. But then, those are just words. Only Mozart can speak for Mozart, and he did quite eloquently, in a language all his own."

Had the stereo not had an automatic changer, they would

not have heard much music that weekend, but the machinery took care of the records, freeing them to do other things with their hands. It rained all day on Sunday, scotching their plans for a picnic, so they stayed indoors, listening to Mozart amid scattered sections of the newspaper, wine bottles, and what seemed an assembly line of food and fruit.

They awoke with the light on Monday. A northwesterly had cleared the sky of clouds and driven out the humidity as well. Paul wanted to savor the last moments of their time together, but Natasha was a whirlwind of activity, closing the house and getting ready for the office, alighting in the kitchen only long enough to nibble at an omelet before herding the two of them out the door.

They exchanged glances and smiles but few words as she navigated her Porsche among the country roads. Though she was not unfriendly, Paul sensed a distance coming between them.

She went through the gate at Fort Meade and took him to his quarters. He got his case and hangup bag from the back and stood beside her open door, feeling awkward. He looked down and saw the breeze lift the dress above her knees; her hand immediately slammed it into place. Yesterday, he mused, she would have laughed and let her legs show.

She raised her eyes. "It was a lovely, lovely weekend, Paul."

"Yes, it was." He leaned down and kissed her. "You're leaving tonight?"

She nodded. "First to New York to see some bankers. Then it's off to London to see about opening an affiliate there."

"Will I see you next weekend?"

"I'm afraid not. I have friends in Britain who've invited me for a weekend in the country."

He felt his stomach sink. "I see."

They kissed lightly again. As she drove off, she raised her hand through the open sun roof and waved.

Paul went to his room feeling slightly dazed, his steps leaden, a hollow feeling in his gut. He dropped his case on the chair and draped his hangup bag across the bed.

Why, he thought, do I feel so bad? Something's wrong. What the hell is it? You spend two days making love, sharing your thoughts with a woman, and then, all of a sudden, she's gone. You share all of your body and a part of your soul, and it's as if it didn't happen. You start as strangers, and you part as strangers.

As he walked toward the entry gate, he let go of Natasha and began thinking about the ultimatum the Council for Peace and Justice had issued five days before. The Agency and Working Group Seven had scheduled meetings for most of the day to approve contingency plans for an alternative means of communication for the Federal Reserve. He showed his card at the gate and was cleared through. Here we go, he thought, another week of mental masturbation.

CHAPTER 24

On Sunday, George had Willard transfer the final computerized instructions to each of the mobile units. Monday, the blitz began.

Willard remained in the trailer all that day. At one o'clock Marlie brought lunch and told him that the first news reports of delays in electronic banking transactions were coming over the radio, but Willard showed no emotion, asked no questions.

With his program running perfectly, Willard had nothing to do. He resumed work on a computer problem he had been given by one of his professors during his year at MIT. Can a computer be programmed to break down very large numbers into their prime components? Determining if a number was prime, even if it had more than a hundred digits, was easy. Why, then, was it so damn hard to break down large numbers into their prime factors?

Damn it, he thought. God damn it. There's got to be a way.

All it is is a computation, finding numbers that can be divided only by themselves or one—prime numbers—that make up a composite number. It's just a math problem, damn it. God damn it. There's got to be a way.

But as the hours wore on, he realized why he had set the problem aside for so long. Try as he might, he could make no headway. There were no shortcuts. The machine had to test each number against every known prime. Against six-, seven-, or eight-digit numbers, the answers came almost instantaneously, but as the numbers increased in length, the responses took longer, the machinery's innards churning in search of that unique string of primes that lies hidden in every composite number.

"Damn it," he said aloud. "There's just no way. No way."

Marlie opened the door as he spoke. "'No way'? What are you talking about?"

Willard was momentarily disoriented. Then he realized where he was and who had spoken. "Oh, it's just an old math problem I've been working on. I'm having a hell of a time with it."

"I thought your computers could do anything."

"Don't I wish."

"They got me to do plenty."

Willard turned on the stool, looked at her, and smiled at what was unmistakably a sexual reference.

"The evening news will be on in a few minutes," she said. "George said you should come in and watch it unless, of course, you have something you need to do on the computer."

"No," he said, "I've about had it with this thing."

The failure of the Chicago Switch was mentioned on each of the network broadcasts that Monday evening, but each spot ran barely a minute and consisted of the anchorman repeating the official explanation: a computer down.

But as the week wore on, the reports became longer, more detailed. On Tuesday, there were interviews with people waiting in line to withdraw their money. On Wednesday, banks were locking their doors, leaving long but orderly lines outside. On Thursday, the sense of order began to dissipate, and there were filmed reports of sporadic violence. On Friday, the President declared a state of national emergency, called up the reserves, and ordered the armed forces to maintain the peace.

George was exultant, bounding out of his chair to change channels, replaying videotapes of the newscasts late into the night. Willard watched in silence, accepting with no more than a nod or a muttered word the praise that poured from George's mouth. George smiled and even complimented Willard on his modesty.

Something was wrong, terribly wrong. To Willard, it had all been a game, a marvelously exciting and challenging game: one man taking on the Federal Reserve; a college dropout, a computer hacker outsmarting the entire government of the United States. But as the camera began to dwell on people lined up in front of their banks, he could see the fear etched in their faces. His stomach suddenly felt hollow.

That Friday night on the news, a correspondent was describing the scene in front of a bank near Boston. People were yelling and pushing one another. A window was smashed, and troops with upraised clubs began to charge. When the crowd pressed forward, the soldiers panicked and began to flail wildly, trying to force them back. The human wave ebbed for a moment and then surged again with increased strength. The camera zeroed in on a woman, her eyes wide with fright, as a soldier lifted his club.

No, thought Willard. He opened his mouth and screamed voicelessly as the club came down on the woman's head. Her face shuddered and then went slack, the eyes rolling back into her head as she slumped to the ground.

Willard's fists were clenched, his arms shaking.

CHAPTER 25

It was the second meeting on Monday, and Paul was already tired and starting to get angry. The Army colonel was threatening to withhold the helicopters until the National Security Agency agreed to be billed for them. The Air Force major was being equally sticky about who would pay for the laser communication links and the technicians needed to install them.

Jesus, thought Paul, billions of dollars and the economic stability of the nation are at stake, and these clowns are fighting over nickles and dimes. And for what? It's all coming out of the same Treasury Department.

The Air Force man was holding out for hazardous duty pay for the technicians when the light flashed on Winchell's phone. He spoke briefly into the mouthpiece and set it down.

"I'm sorry, but we're going to have to adjourn," he said, as he got to his feet. He looked at the two officers. "Gentlemen, we've run out of time to haggle. We'll arrange the interagency billing from this end just as you wish."

He beckoned to Paul and Nancy and headed with them toward the door, nodding a curt good-bye to the smugly smiling officers. Wordlessly, they walked to the Operations Center and took their places in front of the main console. Nancy tapped the keyboard, and the Chicago status report promptly appeared.

"Good God," said Paul. "All twelve districts have been jammed." He picked up the handset and punched in the code for a secure circuit to Chicago. Hamlin came on the line a few moments later.

"Good morning, Art. It's Paul."

"I'm getting tired of hearing 'good morning.' There's not much good about it at this end."

"What the hell's going on? The status report shows all twelve circuits down."

"It's the same thing as before, only they're blocking *all* the circuits this time, not just six. Every transaction that reaches us has some kind of error in it. A digit changed. An extra bit that garbles the message. The branches are picking up these errors on the confirmation and retransmitting, so we're not losing any money. But the error's different each time. Not one of the transmissions is coming through correctly."

"Nothing?"

"Zilch."

"What are you going to do?"

"Well, first and *most* important," he said, sarcasm evident in his voice, "we're going to have a meeting of the Board of Governors. That's set for five this afternoon in Washington."

"You going?"

"They'll want someone's head, so, yeah, I guess I am going."

"You're just going to wait it out, then?"

"Not much else we can do," said Hamlin. "We could have handled six down. We've got enough extra capacity on the Atlanta and Philly wires to have carried the whole system if we ran it twenty-four hours. But this one's beyond us. There's just not enough backup." He paused. "Barring divine intervention—and God knows I've been praying all morning for just that—it's going to be up to you guys."

"I just got out of a meeting with the Army and Air Force on the mobile teams."

"Are they set to go?"

"Not exactly. All we talked about was intragovernmental billing procedures."

"Christ Almighty, you're not serious, are you?"

"Unfortunately, I am. I think we've got things straightened out now. But I don't see how we're going to be able to get them into the field before Wednesday. And that's at the earliest."

"Isn't it wonderful working for the government?"

"I just don't understand the way these people operate. We're dealing with a situation that's going to require some imagination, and all we're getting is the usual run of the bureaucratic mill. I'm sorry you're getting hit so hard, but I'm afraid it's going to take a full-fledged crisis to wake these people up."

"Well, it looks to me like we're about to get one," said Hamlin. "We can be down for a day or two, and the banks will adjust. The private wires can handle some of the intercity transactions. But after that, we're on borrowed time. How much is anybody's guess.

"The third day will probably be critical. If we're not clear by then, the smaller institutions are going to get caught in a liquidity crunch. The major banks will feel it next, along with Wall Street and every business that relies on cash flow. If the thing keeps up, we'll be in a financial panic by week's end."

Wheeler tried to put the mobile teams into action, but the Defense Department was slow getting its men, equipment, and paperwork in the same place at the same time. SR-71 reconnaissance planes flew over the microwave relay networks and managed to pinpoint some of the electronic anomalies. The first mobile team opened the Philadelphia line with laser links on Thursday, but heavy clouds in the Southeast kept a second team from opening the Atlanta wire.

To make matters worse, the broken link changed each day. By the time the SR-71 would locate an area and have the mobile team move into place, it was often late afternoon or early evening. Though the Federal Reserve kept open whatever lines it could and ran all night, Chicago was now carrying only a tenth of its normal traffic.

The week passed in a blur. Though Paul had rarely watched television since coming to Fort Meade, he made a point of looking at the network news each evening. The Thursday telecasts worried him; the Friday broadcasts left him shaken. Not since the 1970s, when college students led campus riots against the Vietnam war, had he seen American military troops wade into an unarmed civilian crowd with clubs and rifle butts. And like millions of other Americans that night, he found himself riveted in horror as the camera closed in on a nondescript middle-aged woman whose face seemed to dissolve beneath a soldier's billy club.

In that moment, the frustration that had been building in him since March coalesced into rage. He knew now, to a certainty, that he had made the right decision when he chose to work with the Agency. Whatever price he might have to pay would be worth it as long as he destroyed the men behind this plot. And if he had the chance, he would exact that vengeance himself.

CHAPTER 26

Willard skipped breakfast on Saturday and went straight to the trailer. He said little to Marlie when she brought him lunch, feigning deep involvement in his program. Though he grew hungry later in the day, he did not return to the house for dinner. When Marlie commented at the table that Willard seemed immersed in his work, George evinced no surprise.

Willard spent most of the day staring at a blank screen, unsure of what to do. Problems, tricks, games. Computers no longer filled him with a sense of joy. He understood them now as machines, sometimes fascinating, sometimes *fun*, but always machines. Tracking down an error in computer logic, creating visual images to please Marlie, altering some banking transactions—each was a challenge, one greater the other, but that was all they were.

The image played again and again. The crowd surging, the soldier preparing to strike, the woman's face dissolving as the club came down.

He had been watching the Friday news telecast with his customary detachment. Though it might present itself as reality, he knew that everything on television was entertainment. The news was no different. Its carefully coifed correspondents were indistinguishable from game-show hosts; the newscast, with its hand-held cameras bobbing amid waves of war and violence, seemed no more authentic than the movie of the week glimpsed between commercial exhortations. One moment someone is bleeding to death in living color. An instant later the victim vanishes, replaced by a woman bemoaning the painful swell and itch of hemorrhoidal tissue.

At first Willard could not believe that what he was seeing had actually happened. The sight of the woman crumpling beneath the trooper's blow—because of something he, Willard, had done—had rendered him numb, so numb that he could not give voice to the scream that rushed to his lips. When the scene was replayed, he averted his eyes. He had seen enough. A lubricous commercial deadened him into silence.

He slept fitfully that night. Though he would never have raised a hand to this or any other woman, he felt as if he had struck her. That he had not held the club meant nothing; it was he who set in motion the events which culminated in that blow.

He tried to console himself. The anchorman said the woman had been treated at the hospital and released; her injuries were not serious. Yet he knew he was responsible for what happened to the people in that line; they would not have been there, no one would have been beaten, but for his program. He had known all along what it would do to the nation's banks; what had made him so blind to its flesh-and-blood consequences? Did he think the men and women who were being pushed and clubbed were mere actors? Did he expect to see them next week amid twisted bedsheets playfully tussling with their live-in lovers for *People* magazine?

He sat in the cold airless room, the machines emitting their monotonous hum, their steady green glow. The screen was blank, ready to become whatever he made of it. And yes, he thought, it is what I make it, what I *choose* to make it. It can be a calculator; it can be a toy. And it can also be a weapon. As deadly accurate as a sniper's rifle. Or as deadly careless as a maniac's pipe bomb.

He knew now that he would have to decide. The mobile teams had his program. So, even if he left that night, the chaos would continue. And then, there was Marlie to consider. He could not simply leave her behind. She knew the organization far better than he and would not have had him put together so incriminating a record of its operations had she not had good reason to fear for their safety.

Still, he would have to act. He knew that much. And in those long hours alone in the trailer, the elements of a plan slowly began to cohere.

Willard spent most of Sunday sitting in the shade of the barn, flipping through a pile of computer printouts. When George passed by that afternoon, Willard motioned for him to come over.

George squatted rather than sit on the dusty ground. "You look quite busy today."

"I've been going through some of my notes on cryptography. There's an excellent program that uses prime numbers as the basis for encoding computer-to-computer data streams. I was thinking we might be able to use it for communications with the field."

"How does it work?"

"You're familiar with prime numbers?"

George nodded. "A number that can be divided only by itself and one. One, two, three, five, seven, eleven, thirteen, and so on."

"Right. Well, it so happens that it's fairly easy for computers to test a large number—and by large, I mean over a hundred digits or so—to see if it's prime. On a powerful machine that might take a second or two.

"But if you were to take, say, a two-hundred-digit number that was not prime and try to break it down into its prime components, you'd have quite a different problem on your hands. We're not talking about a few seconds here; we're talking about millions, maybe billions of *years* to run out the calculation."

"I find that amazing," said George. "Why is one calculation so easy and the other so hard?"

Willard wrote down an equation: $y = 4x^3 + 3x^2 + 2x + 1$.

"If I asked you to figure out what y is when x is two, you could do that pretty easily. You don't have to know the first thing about factoring. You just plug in two, run out the numbers in your head, and come up with the answer." He mentally calculated. "Which in this case comes out to forty-nine."

"Okay."

"Now, let's turn the thing around. Suppose I tell you that y equals two and ask you to calculate x. That'd be much harder. Well, there are a whole bunch of mathematical problems that are a lot easier to do in one direction than the other. It's that way with primes. You can write down a long number, and a computer can tell you right away if it's prime. But multiply that number times another long prime and give it to someone else, and his computer will be unable to calculate the original prime factors." He looked up from the printouts. "Are you following me?"

"Yes. But what does this have to do with cryptography?"

"In a word, everything. With a single stroke, you eliminate what has always been the weakest link in cryptography: the secret key. You don't have to worry about someone breaking your code or getting a copy of your phrase book. In fact, you can even publish the damn thing."

"Are you serious?"

"Absolutely. Remember what I told you about one-way functions?"

George nodded.

"Well, because your encryption key is based on the product of two primes, you can publish the damn thing without worrying about anybody being able to break it down into its prime components. So, if someone wants to send you a secret message, all he has to do is encode it with the published key.

"And here's the good part: no one but you will be able to decode it. That's because the decryption key is based on those two large primes that you've calculated and, of course, have kept secret."

George shook his head. "That is quite ingenious."

"And if you're worried that someone may have compromised the key, there's nothing to keep you from changing it as often as you'd like. It's pretty easy to test any large number to see if it's prime. And all you have to do is come up with two large primes. You have to keep those numbers secret, of course, but you can send the product number over an open wire to whoever wants to contact you, and instantly, you've got a brand-new key."

"If this is as good as you say it is, why is the government not using it?"

"I'm not sure," said Willard. "Maybe what you said was

true: the NSA wanted everyone to be using the DES because they wrote the damn thing and secretly left a trapdoor in it."

"Which you ingeniously figured out," said George.

Willard acknowledged the compliment with a quick smile. "Anyway, seeing as I don't have all that much to do right now, I thought I'd work up something like that. Okay with you?"

"Absolutely," said George. "How long will it take you to devise the system?"

"It depends on how fast you want it."

"There is, in truth, no need to rush things. Of course, the sooner we could put such a system into operation, the better."

Willard reflected for a few moments before speaking. "Barring any unforeseen bugs, I should have it ready for transmission to the mobile units by the weekend." He paused. "Now, there's something I want to ask of you."

George's eyes narrowed. "What is it?"

"It concerns Marlie. Two things. First of all, I don't want this new code to be used as an excuse to have her leave just because she won't have as many messages to handle."

George gave a slight shrug. "If the director wants her to travel somewhere, I would have to obey. You know that, Whiz. However, I can promise you that I would argue strongly against any permanent move."

"I'll take your word on that . . . for now. There's one other thing."

"What is it?"

"I want to get out of here for a few days, maybe a week. I want to go somewhere in the mountains with Marlie, one of the towns maybe, like Aspen or Vail. I've heard a lot about those places."

"I don't know, Whiz."

"Look," he said, voice rising, "I've worked my ass off for you and the organization for the last six months without a letup. Besides, we won't be more than a two- or three-hour drive away."

"I'll think about it and let you know."

"I want an answer by tonight. And," he said, grinning, "there's one more thing."

"Yes?"

"I want two thousand dollars for Marlie and me to spend."

"What?"

"You and I both know you've got the cash. I mean, my

program's made the organization eighty-nine point four million richer."

"Again, I will have to think about it."

"Okay, but I still want an answer tonight."

That evening, after dinner, George approved Willard's request.

Willard worked quickly, creating and perfecting his new program in just two days. The sector heads came in Thursday night to pick up their copies of the program and to learn how to use it. By Sunday, every mobile team had communicated with the headquarters trailer using public-key cryptography. George verged on ecstasy.

The team intercepting the San Francisco wire was in Utah. After the bank sent its initial synchronization signals to Chicago on Monday morning, Willard followed it with a message of his own that the Utah team was in no position to pick up.

Not that they or anyone else could have deciphered it. The message was the incriminating document Marlie had called "the bomb," encrypted by Willard with a prime-number cipher of his own devising. As long as he kept the two numbers secret, no one would be able to read the message. But should he ever need them, those numbers might provide the key for his and Marlie's freedom.

CHAPTER 27

"I can't believe they actually print this crap," said Paul, tossing the copy of *National Report* on the table. "Who feeds them this kind of stuff?"

"Your guess is as good as mine," said Wheeler. "But you've seen some of the right-wing crazies on Simpson's staff. I imagine *National Report* will eat just about anything they care to shovel out concerning the Soviet Union."

"But there's no evidence connecting the Russians with any of this," said Paul.

"I know." Wheeler paused. "Did I tell you I'm acquainted with one of the editors?"

"You did. On the plane that day."

"Oh, yes. *That* day."

"What about him?" Paul asked.

"He gave me a call on this one, told me what he was going to do. So I invited him to the office, figured I might be able to straighten him out. But he had a big lunch on at the Cosmos Club; so he sent over a reporter instead. A bright guy, straightforward. And I told him we honestly didn't know who or what was behind it."

"Did he believe you?"

"I'm sure he did, but when the interview was over, I asked him how they were going to play the thing. He told me he didn't know, that it was Jay's call. That's the editor. So I laid it on the line, asked him if they were looking to play a foreign angle."

"What'd he say to that?"

Wheeler shook his head. "You're not going to like this."

"I'm sure I won't, but go ahead."

"Well, the guy told me straight out that Jay was looking for 'a Soviet hook to the story.' So I asked him: 'What if there isn't one? What if it's strictly a domestic thing?'" Wheeler shook his head. "You know what he said? 'It doesn't matter. Jay'll find a Commie hook. He always does.'"

"Yeah," said Paul, nodding toward the magazine. "I can believe it after reading this crap."

"You know that old saying that anyone who wants good sausage or good government shouldn't look too closely at how they're made? Well, this guy told me the same thing applies to *National Report*. He says every time they give him an assignment, the magazine's library sends him all the stories they've ever done on the subject. They keep repeating themselves. It's a bit of a joke there. They do two big covers a year on the Soviet Union. Every spring, they write about the relentless march of Soviet power; in the fall, it's the impending collapse of Moscow's restive empire. They update the things, of course, but they've been doing the same basic stories since the fifties, year in and year out; they never change."

"You'd think their readers would catch on."

"Apparently they like it. After all, they pay for it. Anyway, the editorial credo over there, according to this guy, is: 'Don't shake up the readers.' But if you talk to the editors, they'll swear up and down they're running a straight newsmagazine."

"Well, it reads like right-wing propaganda to me," said Paul. "I assume this is the issue coming out tomorrow."

Wheeler nodded. "This is an advance copy. It gets to the stands on Monday. But I wouldn't worry about it."

"You wouldn't?"

"To be honest, hardly anyone in Washington reads the damn

thing. I mean, if it were in *Time* or *Newsweek*, that story would create a big flap. But *National Report*? Forget it. They've got two or three million subscribers, but most of them are out in the hinterlands. They may score a few points with the right wing, but no one else will pay much attention to them."

"I hope you're right."

Wheeler grinned. "I'll bet you dinner that not one of the networks or major papers picks up on the story tomorrow."

"Not one?"

Wheeler nodded.

"You're on."

Paul lost. So, on Monday evening, Wheeler drove them to Baltimore's Fells Point for seafood at Bertha's Restaurant. Wheeler grinned as Paul picked up the check.

On Tuesday morning, they went to Washington for a meeting of Working Group Seven in the Old Executive Office Building. Art Hamlin buttonholed them just after they entered the room.

"I hear you're the main speaker today," said Wheeler.

Hamlin rolled his eyes. "Unfortunately, I seem to be in great demand these days." He turned to Paul. "I brought something for you. We're not sure what it is, but it came over the San Francisco wire yesterday morning." He handed Paul a large brown envelope. "If you get a chance, take a look at it before we leave."

After everyone was seated, Harding Harrison opened the meeting. "The fact that WG-Seven is now sitting next door to the White House instead of at Fort Meade is of symbolic as well as substantive importance. I left the Oval Office a few minutes ago, and the President asked me, once again, to tell you how very important the work of this body is to the security of the United States.

"He, like all of you, has been watching the newscasts and is gravely concerned about the human costs of this financial panic. People are afraid—and justly so—that if they put whatever money they have in a bank or savings and loan they may not be able to get it out. As a practical matter, the equity and commodity markets have ceased to exist. Without liquidity, traders cannot be certain which of their customers will be able to pay, just as customers cannot be sure that their transactions will go through.

"Having represented a few banks when I was a private

attorney, I am not unfamiliar with their operations and perspectives. We used to joke about little old ladies who put their money in a sock or a five-and-a-half percent savings account, which is just about the same thing. And quite frankly, I never thought I'd see the day when cash on the proverbial barrelhead would once again dominate commercial affairs. But as you know—and you can see it in all the stores—cash is once again king, with barter its queen.

"We remain the wealthiest nation on earth, in terms of our resources and the abilities of our people, but without the various instruments of credit—bank drafts, electronic fund transfers, plastic credit cards—we might as well be back in the nineteenth century."

He raised his hands to smooth down his vest. "Art Hamlin of the Chicago Federal Reserve is on hand to give you the perspective of the central bank. As you may recall from his briefing at Fort Meade, he has the unenviable responsibility of managing the Chicago Switch."

Hamlin, who had been nervously kneading his hands, stood up. "I don't know how many of you have been outside the Washington area these last two weeks, but I stayed with my in-laws in Charlottesville last night and drove up this morning just to see what sort of effect, outwardly at least, this financial crisis is having in Virginia.

"Along the rural stretches of 29 and 211, it looks like a normal day in late July. The corn's about chest-high; the Holsteins look well fed. The fruit stands by the roadside are well stocked.

"But it's those stands that give you the first clue that something's not right. All of them have signs, saying: 'Cash or Barter,' 'Cash or Swap.' And even in the early morning, it looks a bit like an Arabian *soukh*. Live poultry, chairs, tables, air conditioners—you name it; they've probably got it.

"And if you slow down going through the towns, you'll see signs in almost every store window, saying 'Cash Only' or 'Cash and Carry.'

"Now, I guess you'd expect to see that sort of thing in the cities where merchants don't know their customers. But in these small Virginia towns, everyone knows everyone else. It's not that they don't trust their neighbors; they do. And if it's a matter of arranging a barter of goods and services, they'll take each other's word on it. But they're not fools. They know the banks don't have the cash to cover all their checks. It doesn't matter if a man put three thousand dollars in his account last month. They know if he goes in today and asks for it, he'll be lucky to get a few hundred."

Hamlin drew a breath and looked down at his notes. "There's an old saying about the banking system being built on two lies: the first: that your money's safe; the second: that it'll be there when you ask for it.

"Much as I hate to admit it, there's an element of truth in that old saying. If bankers unwisely invest their depositors' money, it will, indeed, be unsafe. And if the Fed, the FDIC, and other federal and state institutions cannot maintain liquidity, your money will not be there when you come to withdraw it.

"I guess what I'm trying to say is that the banking system, at the local level as well as throughout the nation, is based on one and only one thing: confidence.

"In the early days, there was no liquidity. Payrolls were a matter of hard cash, stagecoaches, and rail cars. You had to move gold and silver across the country to maintain support of the currency. When our present system works, we in Chicago are the hub of an electronic network that transfers about two hundred and fifty billion dollars a day, among all the states in the Union. Today, we're handling only a tenth of our normal traffic, and we're barely doing that."

The rest of the presentation centered on technical and statistical details. While Hamlin was finishing up, Paul opened the envelope Hamlin had given him just before the meeting began. Inside, he found a computer printout. He recognized the synchronization signals from San Francisco at the top, but the rest was a solid mass of numbers. He slowly scanned each page before flipping to the next, finding nothing but row after row of numbers. It was either a cipher or computerized garbage. Paul was pretty sure it was the latter until he got to the end. There, he found two numbers. The first was just five digits long, but the second ran to four rows. But what caught his eye and brought a smile to his lips was the single word that separated those two numbers: "modulo."

Good God, he thought, it's an encryption key. A *public* key.

It was their first break, and Paul could barely contain his excitement as he stood up to speak. But he pulled the note cards from his inside pocket and dutifully gave the group a quick rundown on several technological moves NSA might make. Wheeler used his time to prod his military colleagues to cooperate more fully with the Agency.

When the meeting was adjourned, Hamlin came over. "I saw you looking at the printout. Does that stuff mean anything to you?"

"It may," said Paul. "But I'm going to have to check out a few things at the Agency before I know for sure. If you get any more messages like this, I want you to flag them immediately for me or Dr. Ho at the Ops Center."

"Be happy to."

"And look, Art, we're trying. I know we haven't been able to do all that much for you, but believe me, we *are* trying."

"I know you are, Paul."

During the drive back to Fort Meade, Paul described the message to Wheeler.

"And what the hell's a modulo?" he asked.

"That's just a mathematical term, meaning the remainder after you've divided by a certain number. Let me give you an example. If I asked you to calculate two to the fifth power, modulo five, the answer would be . . ." A short pause. "Two."

"How's that again?"

"I just multiplied two to the fifth power; that's thirty-two. I divided it by five and took the remainder. Five into thirty-two goes six times. That's thirty. Subtract thirty from thirty-two, and you're left with two."

"But what does that have to do with a cipher?"

"With public-key cryptography, that's all you need. You convert all the letters to numbers, from A equals one to Z equals twenty-six. You use a computer to raise them to a very high power and then divide them by your published key, which is the product of two primes."

"Okay. But what do you think is in the message?"

"I don't know," said Paul. "In fact, I have a feeling that he—whoever 'he' is—has given us only the *encryption* key, not the one we'd need to decrypt the message."

"You mean he's given us a way to communicate with him?"

"I think so," said Paul.

After they arrived at the National Security Agency, Paul showed Nancy the message. She understood its implication immediately. At the Operations Center, she entered the number into the computer to determine whether it was a prime or composite number. It proved, as Paul had hoped, to be the latter.

"Now what?" she asked.

"First of all, only you, Otis, and I know about it. I'd like to keep it that way. At least for a while."

She furrowed her brow. "I don't know, Paul. That's not the way we do things at the Agency."

"I'm aware of that. But suppose we do let Winchell know, and he passes it up the chain of command." He shook his head. "God knows what the White House would do with it. You haven't had to sit through those meetings with Simpson's staff; you don't know how off the wall some of those guys can be. Besides, if they lock onto this, it may take away from what we've been working on."

Nancy nodded. The plan they had developed was nearly ready to be put into action. "You have a point," she said.

"Of course, if anything does come of it, we'll pass it up the proper channels. I'm not doing this just to play Lone Ranger."

Her brown eyes crinkled behind the round glasses. "Okay. What's the next move?"

"First off, we write a short message, encrypt it with the key he sent to Chicago, and put it on the San Francisco wire every morning following the synchronization check. Also, we include a public key of our own so he can communicate with us."

"That shouldn't be too hard to do."

"After that," said Paul with a shrug, "we wait to see what sort of response we get."

Nancy quickly got the computer to generate two long prime numbers to establish their own public key. Then, Paul drafted a message: "If you wish to communicate with us, use the Rivest-Shamir-Adleman public-key format. Precede message with the word, notice, and any number or letter designation. Our replies will use the key you sent Monday. Our encryption key follows."

"How does that look?" he asked.

"Not exactly deathless prose, but it'll do." She took the paper in hand. "Shouldn't it be signed? I don't mean with your name or the Agency. But shouldn't there be something personal at the end?"

"Good point. It may also encourage him to do the same."

So at the end of the message, Paul put his new initials: PC.

On Wednesday morning, Paul asked Hamlin for permission to use the San Francisco wire to send a test message, and got his approval. He sent the same message on Thursday and Friday, but received no reply.

Wheeler called early Friday morning and asked Paul to meet him for lunch at the officers' club. When the colonel arrived, Paul could see something was troubling him.

Wheeler got straight to the point. "It's about Helen."

The blood drained from Paul's face, but before he could speak, Wheeler raised his hand.

"She's fine. I'm sorry; I didn't mean to alarm you."

Paul could hear his voice shaking. "What is it?"

"Two things. Simpson's under pressure from Treasury to pull back the Secret Service detail that's been watching her. It's been nearly four months, and they've detected no hostile surveillance. So the Secretary wants to pull them out at the end of July."

"Well," said Paul angrily, "maybe I'll pull out, too."

"I know how you feel, and believe me, Simpson's going to bat for you on this one. But as a practical matter, the detail will almost certainly have to come out."

Paul gritted his teeth.

"There's one other thing," said Wheeler.

"What?"

He exhaled deeply. "I feel very awkward about this, Paul."

"Go ahead. What is it?"

"I'm afraid there's no easy way to say this." He paused to draw a breath. "Helen has begun seeing someone, a man. And it looks like a, well, something serious."

Paul felt his stomach sink. A waitress came to the table; he waved her away.

"I'm sorry, Paul. But I thought you should know."

Several seconds passed. "Who is it?" he asked softly.

Wheeler hesitated.

Paul met his eyes. "I *do* have a right to know."

"His name is Michael Callas," said Wheeler. "He's a physician in private practice in Quincy."

Paul instantly recalled the tall, dark-haired man. They had met a couple of times at parties; he was newly divorced and noticeably attracted to Helen.

The waitress returned. Paul had lost his appetite but ordered a sandwich and a beer anyway. Each tried to make small talk but finally gave up. Paul ate very little of his sandwich, but drank all of the beer.

Over coffee, Paul finally asked the question that had been gnawing at him. "You said it was serious. I assume by that you mean she's been sleeping with him."

Wheeler's face flushed. "The report says nothing about that. Nothing directly, that is."

"Look, Otis, I appreciate the delicacy of your situation, telling me this. But I must know."

Wheeler nodded. "The report indicates they spent the night at his place twice. At her house, once."

Her house, he thought. It's *our* house, God damn it. *Ours*.

Wheeler continued. "It contains no details beyond that."

After lunch, instead of walking back to the office, Paul went to his room, called Nancy, and said he had an upset stomach, which was true. Then he closed the drapes, stripped to his shorts, and lay on the bed. He needed to think, and think clearly, but his thoughts remained jumbled.

The affair with Natasha had been a mistake. Worse than that, it was wrong, and no amount of mental gymnastics would ever make it right. What did he think he was doing? Whatever future lay ahead, it would not be with Natasha. No, when he could imagine a future at all, it was with Helen.

He was willing to give up his comfort, even risk his life, for his country; he had made that decision after Joe Cerri's death. What he would not do was surrender his wife and his marriage. Yet, he was now in danger of losing both. And if it meant walking out of Fort Meade that very afternoon and taking the next plane to Boston, he would do it.

Still, he wanted vengeance: vengeance for the bomb that was meant for him and, most of all, vengeance for Joe Cerri. As he lay there, he thought again about packing his bags and leaving. A week ago, a month ago, perhaps, that might have made sense. But now, with the first apparent breakthrough, the first opportunity to find out who or what was behind the crisis, he felt duty-bound—no, damn it, he *wanted* to see it through to the end.

There were also practical matters to consider. Had Helen and "the world" been told that Paul Sager was only missing, he might be able to exit a plane at Logan Airport, claim amnesia, and pick up where he left off. But "the world" believed Paul Sager dead, the victim of a car bombing. The government could hardly turn around and announce tomorrow that he was alive and call it a computer error.

But a dead man reappearing on the streets of Boston and Cambridge? He shook his head. No, it simply wouldn't work. Reporters and TV crews would stake out his house and stalk him everywhere. Editorialists would denounce the government for its public lie and demand an accounting. The anonymity, the peace, the chance he wanted so desperately for Helen and himself to put their lives in order, would be destroyed.

Before he could openly return, the government would have to win its war; that much was clear. But there would be nothing for him to go home to if he lost Helen to another man. So, there was no escaping it: he would have to act—and quickly.

But how? One by one, he went over the possibilities: a letter, a tape recording, an emissary. And one by one, he rejected them. Suppose she thought the letter or tape a forgery or, worse, a Nixon-style cover-up. He smiled. Given Helen's feelings about the present administration, he could imagine her immediately calling their attorney, their congressmen from Massachusetts as well as Vermont, and all four senators.

No, he thought. If someone's going to contact Helen, it'll have to be me. No one else could possibly hope to control the way she might react.

Paul returned to the Operations Center at three o'clock, called John Scotto and arranged to see him at MATER at 5:30. Natasha was still in London so he did not have to worry about confronting her. He went over the contingency plans with Nancy a final time and then rang up the motor pool.

It was nearly 4:30 when he got into the sedan; Helen's last counseling session would normally end at 4:45. Although it was Friday, he knew she would not leave the office before filling out her daily log. Such was her Vermonter's sense of rectitude, he thought, a smile on his face.

As the driver turned south on the parkway, Paul told him they would be making a brief stop at a shopping mall en route. The driver stayed with the car, and Paul walked across the steaming asphalt to a clothing store. He headed for the men's department and pawed through the knit shirts. He bought two, paying cash, and carried the bag into the enclosed mall. He glanced at his watch; it was almost 4:50.

Homogenized music blared from the ceiling; a refrigerated breeze rustled the plastic palms. It took a minute or so to find a pair of phones that were free. He put a handwritten out-of-order note on the first phone and let the receiver dangle, so no one would be in a position to overhear him. He went to the second phone and dialed a special access code used by MATER employees for long-distance calls. Then, he dialed Helen's office.

"Counseling center." Her tone brisk.

Paul had given a lot of thought to what he would say, but when he heard Helen's voice, the words stuck in his throat.

"Counseling center. May I help you?" The tone was warmer, more patient this time. She often received calls from people in trouble.

"It's important that you listen and listen carefully," said Paul. "I can't talk for long. Do you understand?"

"Oh my God." Her words were barely audible.

"It's important, very important, that you ask no questions and say no names. Do you understand?"

"No. I mean, yes. Yes."

"You know who this is?"

There was a catch in her throat and then a sudden rush of sound. "Yes. Oh, yes!"

"Say nothing! No names. Give nothing away. Please!"

"Yes."

"Listen carefully. Find the glove before lunch. Say it back to me."

"The glove. What glove? What are you talking—"

He cut her off. "Please! It's important. 'Find the glove before lunch.' Now, say it back to me."

"'Find the glove before lunch'?"

"That's right. Do you understand?"

"No." It was a single note, distilled with fright.

"Listen. You will find the glove with Susan B. Anthony, Carrie Nation, and Bella Abzug. Now, do you understand?"

Suddenly, there was triumph in her voice. "Yes! I do. Yes!"

"Good. I have to go. I will contact you soon. Good-bye."

He stood there in silence, the phone still against his ear.

"Good-bye." And then, in a whisper: "I love you."

Paul felt his throat constrict; tears welled in his eyes; he hung up both phones and moved slowly, somewhat dazedly, back into the stream of bustling shoppers. He looked down and saw that he was clutching the shopping bag so tightly that his knuckles were white. He eased his grip and began to walk more purposefully. A few minutes later, he was in the car and on his way.

The Yankee reserve, the composure Helen had fought to maintain, suddenly dissolved. Now, the tears would not be staunched. She could feel their warmth on her cheeks and brought her hands to her face, smearing her glasses. Then she began to laugh and cry at the same time, feeling utterly foolish but not caring.

"Helen? Are you all right?" It was Anne, another counselor at the center.

Helen removed her glasses and began wiping her eyes. "I, I'm all right."

"Are you sure? I mean, if you want to, we can talk about it."

"No, really, Anne, it's okay."

"You need to get out of here, you know?"

"I'm going to do just that."

"Going to the Cape again with Mike?"

She shook her head. "Vermont."

"It's not your mother again, is it?"

"No, she's better."

"Well, if you want to, if you *need* to, don't hesitate to give me a call. Anytime. Night or day."

"Thank you, Anne."

"I mean it."

"I know you do. I'm all right. Believe me."

She raised her hand. "See you Monday, then?"

"Monday," she replied.

As soon as Anne was gone, Helen phoned Mike Callas's office and left word that she had to go to Vermont on "a family matter" and would speak with him next week. Five minutes later, she was in the car, threading her way through Friday afternoon traffic, trying to make sense of what had just happened.

The coffin had been sealed, of course. Perhaps that was why it had been so hard for her to believe that Paul had been killed. It didn't seem possible. They had made love that morning, and that night he was dead. But when she stood beside the coffin with the mortician and expressed her doubts, asking if she should examine the remains, his words were measured but telling: "Please, Mrs. Sager. It was, after all, a bomb."

If a client had come to her after burying a husband and had said she did not believe him dead, Helen would have entered a single word in her log: "Denial." The first stage of the familiar grief cycle. And while she was rational enough to understand that she was not immune from that cycle, the closed coffin had not only left her with doubt; it had also created an irrational sense of hope. Perhaps there had been a mistake. Perhaps someone else had been in the car with Captain Cerri. Perhaps Paul was injured and had wandered off in a daze. Perhaps, perhaps. It was such a slender hope, and such a large coffin.

The traffic was not very heavy on the toll road across New Hampshire. Her mind was clear now. Paul was alive; there was no mistaking his voice. But why the secrecy? The government had come to Paul and asked him to work for the National Security Agency; then, the same government announced that he was dead in a car bombing. Now, he calls but cannot talk freely. Is he a prisoner? And if he is, who's holding him? The government?

She reached into the glove compartment, pulled out several cassettes, and spread them on the seat beside her until she found what she was looking for: Judith Blegen singing Mozart arias. It had always been their favorite, but after that Saturday in March, the thought of listening to it again, alone, had been too much to bear.

"L'amerò, sarò costante; fido sposo, e fido amante." Helen spoke the words softly as Blegen's voice carried them aloft, each note so clear, the tone as precise, as pure, as a silver bell.

At first she tried to blink back the tears; then she let them flow. She played the aria again and again. By the time she crossed into Vermont, her eyes were dry . . . and smiling.

When Jim Guanti left Brooklyn for Vermont, he lost none of his accent and only some of his cynicsim. A huge, gregarious man, he had made a fortune in advertising, he liked to brag, "without once ever crossing the East River."

His biggest coup, he told Paul and Helen on their first meeting, was a media blitz for a client's new toilet paper. "They said that everything there was to say about toilet paper had been said. Right?

"Well, they were wrong. I mean, you and me, we know what toilet paper's for. Right? It's to wipe your tush. And let's face it, if it's too soft, it's gonna shred and lump up. If it's too hard, it's gonna cut the bejesus out of you. Right?

"So, what do I do? I get a demographic cross-section of America. I mean, it's perfect. Grandmas, babies, blacks, whites, Orientals. You name it; I got them. And what do I have them say? Just two words. That's it. No more, no less. Two words. 'It's cuddly.'

"I mean, you'd think people'd be smart enough to know that no toilet paper's gonna be cuddly. Right? So, what they do? They buy the stuff. That jacks up sales; the next thing you know, I'm into seven figures.

"And that got it going. I mean, it's like everybody wants a piece of Jim Guanti. Laxatives, denture glue, that greasy stuff you use if you got piles. I mean, everybody that's got a product with an image problem starts coming over to Brooklyn.

"The next thing you know, my accountant's all over me to get some shelter. 'What kinda shelter?' I ask. He says, 'Get yourself a farm.' I say, 'What do I know from farming?' He says, 'It don't matter. You just gotta buy it and lose money.'

"So, he gets a real estate guy in Stowe looking for farms up here and comes up with this place. It's losing money; the guy's got three kids in college. And on top of that, he wants to ditch his old lady for this bimbo and move to St. Croix. So, I buy the place.

"Only it turns out that I like it; I *really* like it. And then the Agriculture Extension guy up here tells me the government'll buy all the milk I can't sell. I mean, can you believe it? So, I figure if Uncle Sam's gonna be that good to me, the least I can do is name my cows after famous American women."

It was late in the afternoon when Guanti told them this story, and they could hear cow bells in the distance as the herd returned to the milking barn. He raised his large frame out of the chair and beckoned them to the porch to watch the bovine procession.

"I got names for all of them," he said and began pointing to each. "That's Betsy Ross. The one just ahead of her is Molly Pitcher. Then there's Susan B. Anthony. Carrie Nation.

"And there," he said, nodding toward the lead cow, "she's my favorite. She's the best."

"What's her name?" Helen asked.

"You tell me," said Guanti. "She's big and bellows like a fog horn. She's got the best damn set of mammaries—thirty thousand pounds of milk a year—and she'll push anybody who gets in her way." He grinned. "Now, what would you name her?"

Helen shook her head.

Guanti's eyes took on a manic gleam. "BELLA ABZUG!" he thundered.

Helen smiled as she recalled the day. She also remembered Paul's telling her the name "Guanti" means "gloves" in Italian. Had he been a gunman rather than an ad man, Paul joked, they would probably have called him "Jim the Glove."

On Saturday morning, Helen left her mother's house and drove up the gravel road that led to Jim's farm. She glanced at the clock. It was nearly noon.

She would, indeed, "find the glove before lunch."

CHAPTER 28

It was another world. Though few places on the planet were beyond the reach of his computer, Willard was barely aware of his immediate surroundings. Each day he walked the same seventy-six steps from the house to the trailer, head down, eyes staring blankly at the beaten dirt path. Though surrounded by mountains, he never really saw them until Marlie led him up the spine of the Rockies.

Now, Marlie raised a hand from the wheel and pointed out the Continental Divide. Willard slouched in the seat and followed the sweep of her hand as they turned from the highway toward the mountains. They passed an abandoned mining dredge, a mummified steel-and-wood dinosaur trailing a snakeline skein of spent shale and dirt, and sped through the relics of an erstwhile boom town. A stone building, its wooden roof long since lost to fire; a dingy gas station and cafe with neither cars nor customers; row after row of cracker-box cabins bracketed by decrepit automobiles. A flag hung limply in front of the tiny brick post office.

As they started up the mountain road, Willard looked to his left into a narrow green valley and saw several A-frame houses. Then the left side of the road vanished into a sheer dropoff. He glanced at the flimsy guardrail and gulped. "How far down is it?"

"Here? Maybe two, three hundred feet." She turned to him, smiling. "It'll get a lot higher before we hit the top of the pass."

The engine was straining against gravity; she pressed harder on the accelerator. Willard glanced nervously toward the edge.

"The road on this side is pretty much a straight shot," she said. "The other side's a lot more fun. Switchbacks, hairpins, that sort of thing."

Willard closed his eyes and did not open them until he heard the motor winding down. They had reached the summit of Hoosier Pass. Marlie pulled to a stop in front of a large wooden sign. Both got out of the car.

"We've been on the eastern side of the divide," she said. "When we cross the line, we'll be on the western side."

Willard read the sign. "You mean, if it rains, the water on the right goes to the Pacific, and on the left to the Atlantic?"

She nodded. "That's what they mean by continental divide."

After several minutes, they returned to the car. Marlie turned onto the highway and began the descent. At the first curve, she hit the brakes, swung the wheel hard, and brought them through the long arc.

Willard clawed the space above his right shoulder until he found the seat belt.

"There's such peace, such serenity up here," she said and began pumping the brakes.

Willard clicked the belt into place as the rear end floated around the curve.

"We've been cooped up in that damn house for so long." A truck loomed in the windshield. "I can't thank you enough for getting us out of there." All four wheels spat gravel as they took the switchback.

Willard braced his feet against the floor.

"Think of it," she said, as she swung the car to the left. "This is where the waters begin." She hit the brakes hard and dropped into low, cut to the right and tromped the pedal. "The waters! Our source of life!"

Willard's hands burrowed into the padded dashboard.

"Creation! Think about it, Whiz. This is where it all begins."
The curve seemed to disappear to the left. "They say life began
in the sea." She edged to the right and hit the brakes. "But I
say it began *here*!" She punctuated with a hard left. "Here! In
the mountains!" The tires began screaming. "Life!"

The car careened back and forth as the rear end fishtailed
first right, then left, then right again, before straightening out.

She talked without stopping until they reached the last curve.
A large house loomed in the arc. Willard closed his eyes and
braced himself so hard that his elbows and knees were shaking.
The car angrily protested through the switchback, filling the
air with the stench of smoked rubber.

When Willard opened his eyes and saw the straight road
ahead, he relaxed and audibly drew a deep breath.

"Mmm," she purred, "smell those pines."

"Yeah."

She turned to him and smiled. "I really love the mountains."

"Yeah," said Willard. "I could tell."

With the most terrifying stretch of road behind them, Willard
began to enjoy the scenery. He had been sleeping the night
they drove into Colorado and in the past three months had
scarcely glanced at the peaks surrounding the basin where the
ranch was situated. Now that he was in the mountains, he began
to feel differently, see differently. George, the organization,
the computer, the program—all seemed so alien now, so distant. He had passed from one world into another.

He pulled out the road map and marked the route that Marlie
was following: Breckenridge, Lake Dillon, Copper Mountain,
Vail, Glenwood Canyon, Glenwood Springs, Aspen. And as
the names took on form and dimension, he found himself taking
more pleasure in the sheer beauty of the mountains than he
could have imagined an hour before.

When they made the left turn onto Aspen's Main Street,
Marlie became ecstatic. Willard could not understand why she
was making such a fuss over the simple frame buildings that
lined the street, but kept his skepticism to himself.

She pulled to a stop across the street from the Hotel Jerome.
"Let's get out and walk around a little. It'll give you a feel for
the town." But after several minutes of peering into the windows of various shops, she said, "This is strange."

"What is?"

"This is usually the height of the summer season, and there's
hardly anyone around. It's afternoon; some of the shops aren't

even open, and there aren't many customers in those that are."
She paused. "And they've all got those signs. I guess I didn't
expect that. Not here."

At first, the press had called it "the Chicago caper" and
played it as a typical computer-run-amok story. After the human
consequences became more apparent, the anchormen traded in
their smiles for sterner looks and began calling it "the Chicago
crisis."

Its impact was being felt everywhere. Because money no
longer moved electronically from one place to another, it had
to be transferred physically and on paper. Banks would no
longer guarantee payment on checks, and those that did honor
them were charging discounts of fifteen to twenty percent and
not crediting the deposits until the cash was actually delivered.
Those merchants who did not flatly refuse to accept credit cards
routinely tacked on surcharges of twenty or more percent. Customers who paid cash could, of course, almost set their own
price, sometimes as much as fifty percent less.

"CA$H and $AVE." "BIG DI$COUNT$ FOR CA$H."
"CA$H OR $WAP." Marlie had seen those signs on the news
broadcasts and in some of the store windows when they passed
through Glenwood Springs, but she was surprised to find them
in Aspen. Only one thing was different: the signs in Aspen
were more discreet, some bearing the unmistakable flourishes
of professional calligraphy.

They walked into a restaurant. A man, his face red with
anger, was waving his gold-colored credit card at a waiter.

"This is an outrage!" he yelled. "Thirty percent! You have
a nerve adding a thirty-percent surcharge onto my bill!"

"I'm sorry, sir," said the waiter. "But that is our policy.
It's that way all over town."

"But I paid over twenty percent a few days ago."

"I'm sorry, sir. But the companies just aren't paying the
slips we turn in. The only way we'll get any money out of
this," he said, nodding disdainfully toward the man's card, "is
to sell the slips at a discount to a broker in Denver. And there's
no telling what they'll bring. The rate fluctuates just like any
other commodity."

"Well, I still think this whole situation is outrageous," said
the man in a milder voice.

"I couldn't agree with you more, sir."

The hostess came up to Willard and Marlie. "Two?"

They nodded and followed her to a table.

When they were seated, the hostess said, "Your waiter will be with you presently to tell you the specials of the day, along with the current financials."

Marlie and Willard exchanged quizzical looks.

A moment later, the same waiter came up to their table.

"Good afternoon, I'm Todd. The house specials today are crabmeat-and-avocado quiche, lamb cassoulet, and Veal Oscar. We require a thirty-percent surcharge on credit cards, fifteen percent on travelers' cheques. For cash, we offer a twenty-percent discount. No personal checks." He paused. "Something from the bar?"

Marlie ordered a glass of white wine; Willard asked for a beer. The waiter left.

"Is it like this everywhere?" Willard asked.

Marlie shrugged. "I guess so."

"Well, it's a good thing we brought cash."

"Don't say that too loud. And don't flash it around."

"Wasn't planning to."

When the waiter returned with their drinks, Marlie asked, "When we came in, we saw that man arguing with you. Does that happen often?"

"All the time," he replied. "I told the gentleman and his wife right after they sat down what the financials of the day were. I assumed he heard me. His bill came to only ninety dollars, and that was with the surcharge."

"Some people can be just so unreasonable," said Marlie.

"Isn't it the truth?" the waiter replied.

"But if it's all that bad, why are you giving only a twenty-percent discount for cash? The signs we saw on Cooper and Hyman were all thirty, forty percent."

"Well, that was what the manager told us this morning."

Marlie looked him in the eye and smiled. "We had been thinking of using one of our cards, but if you could raise the discount to thirty percent, we'd be willing to pay cash."

"I'll check with the manager." He returned a minute later. "That'll be fine," he said and took their order.

After he left, Willard asked, "How did you know they'd cut the price even more?"

"I figured if they could vary the rate for credit cards from one day to the next, they might be willing to haggle over the size of the discount for cash."

"That was pretty smart of you."

"I bet we'll be able to do that all over town." She smiled. "You know something? I think this is going to be fun."

After lunch, they began walking. Marlie was interested in seeing what was in the stores, but Willard's eyes were busy following the women, who were mostly long-haired, slender, and tanned. Marlie clearly fit in, but when he glanced in a mirror, it made him wince to realize how much he did not.

Later, as they were walking, he said, "You know, I really don't think any of the clothes I brought with me are, well, right for this place. I thought that, maybe, I'd get a few things."

Marlie stopped. Cool blue eyes quickly appraised him. "That sounds like a good idea." She resumed walking. "As a matter of fact, why don't we do this thing right?"

"What do you mean?"

A smile spread broadly across her face. "You'll see."

Their first stop was a hair salon. The proprieter's upper lip curled ever so slightly when he saw Willard. Then Marlie described the cut and permanent she wanted him to perform on Willard's head, negotiated a price, and left.

When she returned an hour later, she was stunned by the transformation. The dark straggly locks were gone; in their place was a neatly trimmed pile of tight curls.

Dubious at first, Willard could not help but smile at his reflection in the mirror. Even the hairdresser seemed pleased with the result.

The next stop was a Western store. When Willard emerged a half hour later, he was wearing jeans and a Western shirt open at the throat. He tapped the pearl-gray Stetson on his head and wobbled from the store in a pair of stacked-heel cowboy boots.

After they had walked several blocks, Marlie took his hand. "Did you notice the women looking at you?"

"God, do I look that strange?"

"Not at all. You look good." She stopped, looked him up and down. Her eyes flashed. "Good enough to eat."

The time passed blissfully: hiking or swimming during the day, concerts and restaurants at night, and, of course, sex day and night. There were times when they'd made love in the trailer that Willard had sensed she was preoccupied, that her body was doing one thing while her mind was somewhere else. Maybe they both needed to be away from the ranch, away from George, to enjoy one another fully.

Before he met Marlie, he had felt confident of himself only when he was at the computer. At Aspen, he began to grow assured of himself as a man. It was a small incident, but one that pleased him. Willard had gone to the pool while Marlie was putting on her makeup. He found an empty chaise and stretched out. A few minutes later, a shadow blocked the sun; he opened his eyes and saw a tall, leggy blonde standing over him, smiling. They had been talking for several minutes when Marlie came out; even from across the pool Willard could see the angry glare in her eyes. Shortly after Marlie joined them and was introduced by Willard, the other woman made her exit, saying, "Have a nice day."

"Have a nice day yourself," said Marlie, with cyanide sweetness.

She turned to Willard. "And what was that all about? You were making moves on her while I was in the room, weren't you?"

"No, I wasn't," he said. "I didn't even see her until she came over and started talking to me. I couldn't exactly run away."

Marlie reflected for a moment and said, "Yeah, I forgot. This is Aspen, and a woman here is as likely to make the first move as a man." She smiled. "I'm going to have to keep a much closer eye on you."

Marlie lay on an adjacent chaise for a while and then tapped him on the arm. "I'm getting bored out here."

"Well, what do you want to do?"

She met his eyes directly. "What do you think?"

Later that afternoon, Marlie turned on the TV. It was the first time either of them had seen the news since leaving the ranch at South Park. The lead story was, of course, the Chicago crisis.

In spite of the government's efforts, the Chicago Switch remained jammed. The lead story was followed by a series of short reports showing how people around the country were adjusting to what the anchorman called "our new checkless, chargeless society." A rancher in Montana traded a prize bull for a new pickup truck; a vacant lot in downtown Detroit became a tent-covered bazaar where people exchanged home-grown produce and household junk; a grocer in Tennessee gave twenty-percent bonuses to employees who would accept their pay in frozen meat and canned foods.

"Look at those people," Willard exclaimed.

The grocery's employees had driven to the local high school and were using the athletic fields to sell or barter their goods from the back of their cars and pickup trucks. The trading was brisk, the voices loud and raucous, but the men and women who were caught by the camera seemed to be enjoying themselves.

A man walking away with a carton filled with cans and frozen beef was stopped by a reporter. "Did you buy those?" she asked.

"Nope," he replied. "I swapped for them."

"And what did you exchange for it, sir?"

"Well, I'm a roofer, you see, and the guy that was selling said he needed some shingles replaced. I told him I'd do it Friday."

"And did he pay you in advance?"

"He gave me half. I'll get the other half when I've done the job."

Marlie was beaming. "Isn't that great?"

"What?"

"Don't you see what's going on?" she said, enthusiasm in her voice. "People are working with one another. A man with food exchanges some of it for another man's labor. You don't have any corporations, any banks jacking up prices, ripping off wages, sticking them with high interest rates. They're not getting screwed over by the middlemen: the big companies, the lawyers, the brokers, all those people who make their money off of somebody else's work."

"Yeah, some of those people did look pretty happy. But a lot of others are being hurt by all this."

"For a while, perhaps, but they're going to be a lot better off in the long run. You'll see."

"Perhaps," he said.

"You don't understand, do you?"

Willard shook his head.

"With credit," she said, "the farmer borrows money to plant his crops and harvest them; the grain elevator borrows money to store the grain; the railroad borrows money to get cars to move it; the bakery and the grocery borrow money to build stores. And at each step along the way, they add in the costs of the money they borrowed. People want bread and what happens? They wind up paying for everybody else's money."

"Okay," said Willard. "But so what?"

Marlie's eyes hardened. "You're such a fool sometimes."

The tension between them did not dissolve until the evening, with the dinner and wine they shared on the lawn outside the music tent. Both knew it would be their last night in Aspen, and neither wanted to spoil what had been a very pleasant week.

They returned to the ranch by a different route, taking the dirt road over Independence Pass. Willard was surprised to see piles of snow at the summit, but Marlie told him it was not unusual.

A few minutes passed, and then he said, "I wonder what's happened since we left."

"Not a whole lot."

"Did you call?"

"Uh huh."

"You called *George*?"

"Yes."

"And you didn't tell me?"

"What for? All he wanted was a phone call. I'd rather give him that than have him all over our backs. What was wrong with that?"

"Well, you could have at least told me."

"Sorry." The tone was sharp.

While they rode in silence, Willard began thinking of the message he had sent to Chicago just before they left the ranch. He had intended to tell Marlie but somehow never found the time while they were at Aspen. Of course, he had encrypted the bomb so there was no danger of its being deciphered by the government. But he had meant to tell her about the key and how to transmit it to the Chicago Switch in an emergency. After all, it was her idea. She had a right to know how to use it.

But the conversation they had had while watching the news left him troubled. He had always thought of Marlie as an independent sort. He knew she believed in the organization and, indeed, was important enough to have worked closely with the director; yet it seemed not to have tainted her the way it had George. Now, he wasn't sure. It wasn't that she had much in common with George. She seemed to dislike him nearly as much as Willard did. Still, she and George shared a common loyalty to the organization and, most of all, to the director. And in spite of what had transpired between them, particularly over the past week, Willard realized that he wanted no part of the organization and could never swear loyalty to the director. When the time came, he would leave—with her, preferably, but without her if necessary.

George greeted them perfunctorily when they got back to the ranch. After unpacking, Willard went to the trailer. He scanned the memory for messages and was shocked when he found an encrypted, public-key transmission from Chicago.

He retrieved the key from the machine's memory and deciphered the message: "If you wish to communicate with us, use the Rivest-Shamir-Adleman public-key format. Precede encrypted message with the word, notice, and any number or letter designation. Our encryption key follows. Our replies will use the key you sent Monday." It was followed by the initials PC and several rows of number.

Willard entered PC's encryption key into his computer's memory. He stared at the screen for several minutes trying to decide what, if anything, he would write.

Then, with a huge grin on his face, he tapped out a single word, "Hello," and put his initials, WZ, below it. After encrypting them, he transmitted "Notice 1" to Chicago.

He left the trailer for dinner a few minutes later, the grin still on his face.

CHAPTER 29

Paul's eyes kept darting from the screen to the digital time display. It was Saturday, and there were few people working at MATER. He had been on the computer since nine in the morning, using John Scotto's office. Out of the jumble of the last four months, he had composed a long letter to Helen on the computer. She deserved an explanation, even if he could not divulge the details of his work. Though the risk of interception seemed slight, he remembered their conversation in the restaurant and her prodding him to explain why he was going to Washington. Obviously, someone had followed him, overheard them at lunch, and planted a bomb in his suitcase. He would take no chances this time.

There was so much he wanted to say to Helen. He would not, of course, tell her about Natasha. That affair was over, and if Natasha were indiscreet enough to ask why, he would tell her when she returned from London.

He checked the time again: 11:50. He was ready.

Paul and Helen had immediately liked Jim Guanti, largely for his sense of humor. But there was more to the man than his comic bulk and Brooklyn accent. He was intelligent and, unlike Paul's more narrow academic colleagues, curious about matters beyond his own specialties.

Jim had become familiar with computers in advertising, and found a way to use them when he bought his farm. He had an office built at the rear of his farmhouse and kept the computer running constantly. There were "dumb switches" to turn lights on and off and start his coffeemaker in the morning, and "smart switches" to warm the milking shed when the temperature fell below freezing and to maintain the refrigerator at a constant level. He also used the machine to keep his financial records and to get instantaneous quotations from the stock and commodity exchanges.

When Paul told him about his work in public-key cryptography, Jim immediately expressed interest. Paul gave him a copy of the program and an encryption key, and thought no more about it. But a few days later, when he checked the computer network, Jim's encrypted message was in his communications file. Paul plugged in the two prime numbers of his decryption key, and a message slowly marched across the screen: "If you can read this, Paul, then the least you can do is give me a key of my own. Jim."

Paul looked at the clock again. It was nearly noon. If Jim still had his key, Paul would soon be able to "talk" to Helen.

Paul picked up the phone and dialed the computer network Jim used. After transmitting the encrypted message, he signed off.

A half hour later, he phoned Jim. "Got it?" he asked.

"Every word," Jim replied.

"Good," said Paul. "Make no copies. Read it on the machine and then purge the memory."

"No problem."

"Thanks."

"Take care, my friend."

"I will." He paused. "And please, take care of *my* friend."

Wheeler came to his room early Monday morning, excitement lighting his face. "We got the clearance," he said. "And it's straight from the top."

"You mean Simpson?"

"No," said Wheeler, grinning. "I mean the man Simpson works for."

It took a moment for Paul's sleep-fogged brain to react. "You mean the President?"

"None other," said Wheeler. "And he's pulling all the stops. He's issuing a top-secret executive order this morning to all cabinet and agency heads to—and I quote—'make available to WG-Seven such personnel and material as its director may request.'"

"You mean we can get anything we want?"

"The one exception is nuclear."

Paul chuckled. "I wasn't figuring we'd bomb anything."

"What I mean," said Wheeler, "is that we cannot use nuclear command and control circuitry."

"That's it? No other restrictions?"

"None. It's about the clearest directive I've seen in ten years in Washington. And it's all on one page."

Paul caught the gleam in Wheeler's eye. "You didn't by chance have a hand in drafting it, did you?"

The corners of his mouth turned up slightly.

"You did, didn't you?" said Paul.

"A passion for anonymity forbids me to comment."

"Perhaps I should start calling you General."

Wheeler gave a quick shake of the head.

"Why not?" said Paul. "If we succeed, you're certain to get one star, if not two."

"At this point, that's a very big if," said Wheeler. "Besides, you have no idea how many generals' toes had to be stepped on to push this thing through. Success or not, they won't forget."

"Sorry to hear that."

Wheeler shrugged. "At the moment, we've got more important things to worry about. I've called a meeting of WG-Seven for ten o'clock this morning."

"*You've* called the meeting?"

"I've been appointed director. Harrison's our liaison to the President."

"Well, congratulations."

"I'm not so sure."

"Why not?"

"Because it'll be my head on the pike if things don't work."

The conference room on the ninth floor of the Agency was filled. At the table were the departmental representatives; behind them, their assistants and technical experts. When Paul and Wheeler entered the room, everyone got to their feet, including several generals and an admiral.

Wheeler, in a gray suit, nodded greetings as he walked toward to his place at the center of the long table. He wasted no time.

"As you know, this morning the President by executive order placed the resources of your departments at the disposal of WG-Seven. Our needs will, for the most part, entail communications and logistical support, and those requirements will be quite modest relative to the full range of resources each of your agencies possess.

"However, I must stress that time is, and will continue to be, of the essence. When the President appointed me director last night, he gave me explicit orders to report any inordinate delay or lack of compliance directly to the Oval Office through Mr. Harrison. I told the President that I did not think that would be necessary, that I was certain the departments and agencies would be fully cooperative. He agreed but reiterated his remarks about noncompliance.

"Enough said. I would now like to call on Dr. Cassidy, who will outline Operation Doppelgänger."

Paul rose from his chair and stood beside the podium. "'Doppelgänger,' as many of you no doubt know, is the German word for double—to be more specific, a ghostly double. As you will see, our choice of name was not accidental.

"Two days from now, on Wednesday, beginning at oh eight hundred hours, there will be a second Chicago Switch. Only it will not be in Chicago; it will be here, at Fort Meade. The Federal Reserve will continue to operate its facility which will, no doubt, continue to be jammed. Our electronic Doppelgänger will not be.

"In short, what we are going to do is switch the Switch. And no one but the people in this room and a very select group of individuals elsewhere in the government will be aware of it. Understandably, absolute secrecy is required.

"From the perspective of the twelve Federal Reserve districts, nothing will have changed. Their wire transfer rooms will operate as before. If our adversary has people on the inside—and we suspect that that is a possibility—they will see nothing unusual.

"What happens *after* the transmission leaves those rooms is another matter. There will, in fact, be two transmissions: the normal one to Chicago, and a second, ghostly double that will be received here and routed to the proper branch of the Fed. We will have essentially unlimited access to the communications facilities of the National Military Command Center at the Pentagon. They will use commercial lines as well as their own networks."

Paul drew a breath. "The transmissions will, of course, be encrypted, but we will not be using the federal Data Encryption Standard. The algorithm on which the DES was based has been compromised. We will be using a mix of systems or, I should say, we will have a wide range of systems to choose from, including military ciphers.

"However, we will begin with public-key systems. A team directly responsible to WG-Seven will be assigned to each of the twelve districts; each will generate its own public key and transmit the numbers here. Transmissions *to* Fort Meade will be encrypted using our public key; the confirmation messages *from* Fort Meade will be encrypted using each region's key. And most important, each message will be authenticated by the reverse procedure; that is, the region will sign each transaction with an alphanumeric that has been encrypted with its own decryption key."

Paul paused and glanced around the table. "I see some puzzled looks. If you're worried about the technical aspects, don't be. All of these functions—generating the keys, encryption, decryption, authentication—will be done by preprogrammed chips. You won't have to get your hands dirty, so to speak, unless you accidentally blow a chip. And if you do, we'll have backup parts on hand and aircraft on standby. You'll get them in a matter of hours.

"But let me take a minute or so to explain something. As the name implies, public-key cryptography involves keys that are, in fact, public. If, say, you and I have public keys, we can send enciphered messages back and forth that no one else can read, because the encryption and decryption keys are completely different. You could liken it to a strongbox that requires one key to lock it but a second, different key to open it.

"By publishing my encryption key, I can receive secret messages from anyone, including you. But how can I be sure that a message with your name on it was, in fact, sent by you? That's where the authentication procedure comes in. All you need to do is sign it and encode it with your decryption key. Because your encryption key has been published, if I can decipher your authenticating message—your signature, if you will—using that key, then I will know for sure it could have come only from you."

Paul met some of the faces around the room and smiled. "Again, the actual coding and decoding will be done automatically by the computer." He turned to Wheeler and said aloud, "I can see I need to polish up my lecture." He sat down to light laughter.

Wheeler stood up. "As Dr. Cassidy indicated, the technological purpose of Operation Doppelgänger is to create a second, secret Chicago Switch. That should allow the Federal Reserve a secure network for electronic funds transfers. But the operation has a military purpose as well: it is to search out and neutralize the individuals or groups responsible for the crisis. That is why we will leave the Chicago Switch intact. We want them to think they're still jamming us. At some point, when it becomes evident that the financial crisis has begun to ease, they will almost certainly figure out that we've done something to bypass Chicago. But by then, perhaps, we'll have located them and put them out of business."

His planned remarks over, Wheeler began to call on the people who were sitting at the table. An officer from each of the armed services described the forces he was prepared to put into the field. Representatives from the FBI, Treasury, State, and the U.S. Marshal's Service gave quick rundowns on their preparations.

When they were finished, Wheeler said, "One final point. This is, as I'm sure must be obvious, a strictly ad hoc operation. There's no detailed ops plan because, quite frankly, there wasn't time to write one. So, although we'll be calling on you to do certain things to assist the overall effort, we'll leave to you the actual execution. You know your personnel, your resources, and your capabilities far better than we do."

After the meeting adjourned, Wheeler left by helicopter for the Pentagon. When Paul and Nancy returned to the Operations Center, they found three dozen carefully packaged computer chips on the desk.

"Boy, that was fast," said Paul.

"It's all a matter of priorities," said Nancy. "We're presidential now; there's nothing higher. If we ask for something, they're going to put in a max effort."

Monday passed quickly. Paul and Nancy were in the center of a whirl of activity; when they were not on the phone or transmitting over the computer network, they were talking quietly with individuals from the Agency who had been pulled into the operation. Paul knew conceptually what he wanted, but it took Nancy and her considerable knowledge of the Agency's machinery to translate those ideas into action.

It was after six when the direct line from Chicago lit up; Paul was speaking to someone else, so Nancy took the call. When Paul was finished, she leaned over.

"That was Art," she said. "It looks like we finally got a reply to that message you sent last week."

Paul looked at the numbers on the screen. Nancy tapped in the command to decrypt them. A few moments later, the word "Hello" appeared, followed by the initials "WZ."

"That's it?" asked Paul.

"Apparently."

Paul picked up the direct line to Chicago to make sure the entire message had been transmitted. When Hamlin satisfied him that it had, he put the handset down.

"Now what?" Nancy asked.

"Damn good question," Paul replied. "I guess we try again."

That evening Paul thought about what he would say. Who was he dealing with? Why would someone who had caused the worst financial panic in modern history want to communicate *now* with the government? Was it his way of mocking an opponent? Was it a game? Or was he in trouble? Was he looking for a way out?

Paul drafted a short reply and stored it in the computer for transmission on Tuesday; then he left for his quarters. That night, lying in bed, his thoughts drifted to Helen. A moment later, he realized he was smiling. For the first time in four months, he felt at peace with himself.

PART VI

CHAPTER 30

When Zed was not at the dinner table on Monday after Willard and Marlie returned from Aspen, it did not occur to Willard that something might be wrong.

Unlike Tom, who was outgoing and talkative, Zed moved darkly, rarely speaking, his vocabulary in Willard's presence seldom more than an odd assortment of grunts and nods. Sometimes Willard could hear murmurs of conversation wafted on a cannabis breeze as Zed and Tom shared a smoke. But most of the time Zed was so silent that he became almost invisible. He kept the cars and trucks running, cleaned the house and the inevitable mess in the kitchen after Tom cooked dinner. In the six months since they had first met, Willard and Zed hadn't exchanged more than a few dozen words.

After breakfast on Tuesday, Tom came to the trailer, his face taut. "I'm worried," he said. "It's not like him to take off without telling me."

"Maybe he hitched to Denver or something."

Tom shook his head. "Hey, like I've known the guy four years. It's just not like him."

"When was the last time you saw him?" Willard asked.

"I don't know," said Tom. "Two, three o'clock yesterday. About an hour before you and Marlie got back."

"You sure he didn't just split?"

"No. He'd have told me."

Willard scratched his head. "You talked to George?"

"Yeah."

"What'd he say?"

"Nothing."

"That's strange, the way he is about security and all."

"Yeah. That's what I thought."

"What exactly did he say?"

"George?"

"Yeah."

"Something about him just wandering off and that he'd probably be back."

"What are you going to do?" Willard asked.

"Well, I figured on driving around the ranch and..." He paused, toying nervously with the curls over his right ear. "He could've fallen into one of those dry creeks, you know; maybe broke his leg or something."

"You want me to come with you?"

There was relief in his voice. "Yeah, I'd like that. I really would."

A half-hour later they found Zed lying face down, motionless, at the bottom of a steep-sided arroyo.

As Tom stepped close to the edge, the parched soil began to crumble.

"Look out!" Willard yelled.

Tom jumped back.

"Jesus," said Willard. "It looks like he must've fallen down there. Or something."

Tom drew a deep breath. "We gotta get him outta there."

"I don't know," said Willard.

"We can't just leave him there."

Willard brought his arms across his chest and clutched his sides. "I mean, it's steep. How're we going to lift him?"

Tom stood silently, head bowed, fist against his mouth. "I got an idea," he said and went to the pickup.

He put the truck in reverse and backed up, stopping several

feet short of the edge. Taking a rope from the cargo bed, he tied one end to the bumper and tossed the rest of the coil into the arroyo.

"I'm gonna go down there and tie the thing around his chest. Then, I want you to get in and drive forward, real slow like. I'll keep him steady until he's over the top."

Willard was trembling. His mouth opened, but no sound came out.

"You can drive one of these things, can't you?"

"I-I don't know. I guess so."

"Okay, maybe I better do it," said Tom. "Tell you what. I'll go down and tie the rope around him and then climb back up and pull the truck up. All you gotta do is make sure the line don't snag."

"I-I don't know, Tom. Don't you think we should, you know, call the police or something?"

Tom stared at him for several seconds. "Hey, man. *Think!*"

"Yeah. Yeah, you're right. I wasn't thinking."

Tom pulled the rope to make certain it was secure and then let himself down the steep bank. Without turning Zed over, he slipped the rope under his body, beneath the arms, and knotted it tightly. He dragged the body to the side, uncovering a large rock; its quartz crystals glistened in the slanting sunlight.

Using the rope, he climbed back up, scattering dirt from the dry and crusty bank. "It looks like he hit that rock." He paused to catch his breath and wipe the sweat from his forehead. "You can't see it from here, but there's a real jagged chunk sticking up."

Willard nodded.

Tom slapped his hands against his jeans to knock off the dust. "Okay. I'll pull up real slow. All you've got to do is tell me when to stop."

After the slack played out, the rope began slicing into the bank, raising a small cloud of dust and spewing dirt into the arroyo. Willard stepped back and averted his eyes. When the body flopped over the side, Willard opened his mouth, but the scream remained trapped in his throat. The truck dragged the body several feet before Tom, realizing what had happened, shut off the engine and got out.

Zed's forehead had caved in; blood mixed with dirt had clotted in streaks across his face. Tom and Willard stood there, staring.

"What are we going to do?" Willard asked.

"I don't know. I guess we'll have to tell George."

"Yeah. I guess so."

Both men looked away and focused on the distant line of mountains. Then Tom spoke. "We can't just leave him here."

Willard glanced at the cluttered cargo bed. "We can't put him in the truck. I mean, there's no room back there."

Tom walked to the pickup, climbed up the fender, and began sorting through the junk. He emerged a minute later with a paint-splattered canvas and spread it over Zed's body. Then they drove to the house. George was in his study, the door open.

Willard stayed outside but could hear Tom's voice, agitated, trembling. George said little, but when he did speak, his voice was calm, even. Then the two men joined Willard on the porch.

George's eyes were sharp blue points. Willard could not meet his gaze and focused instead on the thick forearms, the curls of reddish-gold hair swirling amid prominent veins and muscles.

"This is our battlefield," said George. "So contacting the authorities, the enemy, is out of the question. But as I suggested to Tom, we can, and we shall, conduct a service and interment here with full honors. Zed was one of us; he believed in our work. He would have wanted it that way."

Marlie joined them on the porch. The blood immediately drained from her face when George told her what had happened.

"Tom and I are going to look for a suitable place for the interment," George continued. "We will come back for you once the grave has been dug." He turned to Willard. "We will need an extra hand."

"Okay," said Willard.

The three men quickly cleared the cargo bed of its junk. Tom put a pick and three shovels in the back and drove them to Zed's body.

George walked to the edge of the arroyo where the rope had cut into the bank. "What happened here?" he asked.

"We pulled him up with a rope," said Tom.

"It dug deeply," said George. He took several steps along the bank, probing it with his toe. Clumps broke and fell away. "It appears rather dry, does it not?"

Tom and Willard bobbed in unison.

"If Zed was walking here and did not see the edge, or failed to realize how weak it was, it could have given way on him."

"Yeah," said Tom. "That's probably what happened."

He looked directly at Willard. "Where did you find the body?"

"Over there," he said, pointing.

"Come here and show me."

Willard moved nervously toward the edge.

George met his eyes. "Where, exactly?"

Willard looked into the arroyo. "There," he said.

"By that rock?" George asked.

Willard nodded.

"It looked like he hit his head on it," said Tom.

George bent over the canvas, raised it, and examined the wound. "It certainly looks that way," he said coolly. He picked up the rope, which was still attached to the body. "Is there any more?"

Tom nodded. "In the shed."

"Very well," said George. "We will use this piece to wrap the canvas around his body and put it on the truck. When we go back for Marlie, we can get another length to lower him into the grave."

Willard looked away as Tom and George wound the rope around the canvas. When it was wrapped, George motioned to Willard.

"Give us a hand," he said. The three lifted the body and laid it on the bed of the truck.

Tom closed the gate. "Where to?" he asked.

"We will have to do the digging," said George. "So, as a practical matter, we should choose a place with some shade."

Tom pointed toward a stand of cottonwoods. "How about there?"

"We will take a look," said George.

Tom drove them to the trees and stopped. The soil was dessicated and bare of any cover. George tested the ground with a shovel; it broke easily.

"This will do," he said.

The three men removed their shirts. Using the pick, George scratched a rectangle three by seven feet in the dirt. With short, rapid strokes, he worked his way around the perimeter, breaking the ground. Tom and Willard began shoveling. When they finished an hour later, their pants were caked with dirt and perspiration, their arms and chests rouged by laterite dust.

"We should go back to the house and get clean before the service," said George.

As the truck came to a stop, Willard saw Marlie walk onto the porch. Accustomed to seeing her in jeans or shorts, he was surprised to find her wearing a dark blue skirt that extended below her knees, and a white blouse, buttoned at the neck and wrists.

"You guys look beat," she said. "I've made some sandwiches. They're on the table. Help yourself."

Willard sat on the stoop. "Why don't you two go first? I'm going to sit here and rest a few minutes."

As Tom and George were leaving, Marlie asked Willard, "Can I get you anything, Whiz? A sandwich, a drink, or something?"

"I don't feel very hungry, but I'd sure like something cold."

"Iced tea?"

"Yeah, that sounds good."

After Willard gulped the spearmint tea, Marlie went into the house, returning with the pitcher. She quickly refilled his glass.

He patted the porch. "Why don't you sit down?"

"The skirt," she said. "It'll get dirty."

After an awkward silence, Marlie said, "Pretty rough, huh?"

Willard nodded.

"George was saying he fell."

"Yeah." He turned toward the bathrooms and heard water running through the pipes. "That's what George says, all right."

She caught the skepticism in his voice. "What do you mean?"

"I don't know. I mean, he could have fallen. The way the land is, flat and all, you can't really see the creek until you're almost on top of it."

"He was in a creek?"

"Yeah. A dry one."

"You know he and Tom do a lot of grass?"

"Yeah, I know."

"He could've just walked out there and fallen."

"The dirt's real dry, real crumbly out there. So, yeah, it could've happened just like George says it did."

"But you don't think so?"

Willard hunched his shoulders and stared at the ground. "I don't know. Something's just not right."

"What are you talking about?"

He slammed his fist on the porch. "Damn it! I don't know!"

Marlie turned and walked into the house.

A few minutes later, Tom came to the door, a towel wrapped around him. "It's all yours, Whiz."

Willard could hear the pump from the well straining to build the water pressure in the tank. A weak, tepid stream emerged from the nozzle. He slowly turned beneath the shower to get wet, then shut it off and worked up a good lather. The pressure and temperature were a bit higher when he turned the shower on again. He closed his eyes and raised his face into the stream. What is it? he thought. Something doesn't fit.

But he could not focus his thoughts. He finished rinsing himself and got out of the shower.

Willard went to his closet, ran his fingers over the colorful western shirts he had bought in Aspen, but finally settled on a white shirt and khaki pants.

George stood at the head of the open grave, looking every bit the small-town minister in his dark blue suit, white shirt, and blue tie. Tom, Marlie, and Willard lined up to his right, along the length of the grave, opposite Zed's canvas-wrapped body. The scattered dirt made their footing uneven. Willard, feeling dizzy, took a step back.

"You okay?" Marlie whispered.

"Yeah," he replied.

George opened the black leather book and began to read. "From the void to the void, we begin as spirit energy and return to spirit energy. So it is with all matter."

"So it is," said Tom and Marlie in unison.

Willard began rocking back and forth, aware of his unsteadiness, yet feeling strangely detached from his body. Numbness was slowly spreading down his legs, and his field of vision was beginning to narrow and darken at the periphery. Distant voices rose and fell.

"In the beginning was the electron."

"So it is."

"From purest energy came purest light."

"So it is."

"Matter and energy are one and interchangeable."

"So it is."

"The flesh is matter, the spirit energy."

"So it is."

"Deity of Deity, Light of Light, Energy of Energy."

"So it is. So it is. So it is. So it is."

Willard felt something cool on his forehead.

"Are you all right now?"

He opened his eyes and saw Marlie, her hand massaging his brow.

"What happened?"

"You passed out."

Willard turned his head and realized he was lying down inside the truck. "How long have I been here?"

"A minute, maybe two."

"That all?"

She nodded. "Look, why don't you just close your eyes and rest for a while? We have to finish the service."

He closed his eyes and immediately fell asleep. He awoke several hours later, momentarily disoriented. Then he realized he was in his bedroom at the house. Slowly, he swung his legs to the floor, stretched, and drew in a deep breath. Was it his imagination or was someone grilling steaks? His stomach was hollow with hunger.

After washing his face and rinsing the bitter metallic taste from his mouth, he went to the dining room.

Tom had just set a platter of steaks on the table. He forced a smile. "Good timing."

Willard smiled wanly and sat down.

"How are you feeling?" Marlie asked.

"I'm all right."

"You shouldn't have gone out there on an empty stomach."

"Yeah. I guess not."

"Besides, you missed a wonderful service."

Willard gave a slight nod.

Marlie turned to George. "It was beautiful, George. It really was."

"Thank you," he said.

Willard added little to the conversation. He kept his head down and devoured a steak, a baked potato, and two ears of corn. When he finished, he left the table.

He walked past the barn to the fence, leaned against the rough-hewn rails, and looked toward the retreating light. The sun had dropped behind the Continental Divide; the sky, so vibrantly blue and gold that afternoon, was fast fading. Gusts of cool air, scented with sage, gently shook the curtain of radiant heat that hung above the sere landscape. He focused on the distant line of peaks and watched the day being drained of color.

Like blood, he thought. And in an instant he understood.

The quartz rock, its crystals glinting in the light.

Zed's face streaked with blood and dirt.

It was clean, he thought. The rock was clean. There was nothing on it. No blood. Nothing. George killed him. He bashed in his skull.

"Whiz?"

He jumped at the sound of his name.

"I'm sorry," said Marlie. "I didn't mean to startle you. I just wanted to see how you were doing."

"Huh? Oh. I'm all right. I'm all right."

"You sure?"

He nodded.

"It's been a terrible day. What a horrible accident."

Willard hesitated a moment and then asked: "Are you sure?"

"What else could it've been?" Her mouth fell open; instantly she raised her hands to cover it. "Jesus, you don't . . . I mean, really, Whiz, you don't think George had anything to do with it."

"You didn't see Zed's body. You didn't see his face."

"Please," she said, shaking her head. "I don't want to talk about it."

"His forehead was bashed in. There was blood and dirt—"

She cut him off. "Damn it! I don't want to talk about it!"

"No. You've got to understand."

She grabbed his arms, clamping them hard, and looked directly into his eyes. "Maybe I don't want to understand."

"But don't you see? If he did that to Zed, he could do it to you. To me. Don't you see?"

She eased her grasp. "Maybe I don't want to."

Willard shook his head. "What do you mean?"

"Suppose you're right. I don't think you are because it doesn't make any sense, but suppose he did kill Zed. What can we do about it?"

"We can get the fuck out of here, that's what!"

"And go where?"

"Anywhere."

"Do you have any money?"

"Five, no, six hundred left from Aspen."

"How far do you think we'd get?"

"A lot of truckers go down 24 and 285. We could hitch to

Denver or Colorado Springs. Or we could head west. Arizona. California. I could walk in tomorrow just about anywhere and get a job programming."

"And do we go to the cops about Zed?"

"I-I don't know."

"And what if George tracks us down? We've got more than a million of people, and they're all over the country. How long do you think it'd be before somebody turned us in?"

"I-I hadn't..." He paused. "They wouldn't come after us...would they?"

"With what we know about the organization, what do you think?"

"Yeah," he said, his voice now small. "I see what you mean."

An awkward silence came between them.

"You can't leave," she said. "You do know that, don't you?"

"What do you mean?"

"What do you think would happen to me if you left?"

"Oh, no, Marlie. I wouldn't leave without you."

"That's good."

"I want us both to leave."

"Didn't you listen to me? Didn't I just tell you why we can't leave?"

He nodded.

"Good. Then I don't want to hear any more about it."

Willard turned from Marlie and looked to the west. The mountains had become an indistinct line in the dark glowing sky; hard, diamond points of light were beginning to emerge.

A shiver passed through her. "Boy, it sure is cold out here." She leaned against his shoulder and began nuzzling his neck.

When he put his arms around her back, she moved against him, slowly thrusting her pelvis against his. An instant later, he could feel himself getting hard.

"Why don't you get the sleeping bags from the trailer?" she whispered, letting the warmth of her breath caress his ear.

He leaned down and kissed her, letting his hands slide down her back until they were firmly wrapped around her buttocks.

She pulled away, giggling. "Hurry up," she said, "before I freeze my ass off."

The session was brief but intense. She stayed in the sleeping bag for a couple of minutes while she put her clothes on. After a quick kiss, she walked briskly to the house. Willard went to the trailer, opened the door, and stood there for several moments. Then, something caught his eye.

A small piece of paper was protruding from the stack of computer printouts beside the door. He leaned over, pulled it out, and began to unfold it. When he saw it was a note from Zed, he quickly closed the door.

Tilting it to catch the light from the cathode ray tubes, he read the penciled message: "Whiz, This is wrong. I told that to George & he got angry, real angry. I'm going to Denver. There's some people there that can set things to right. I can't tell Tom. He's scared of George. If I don't get back Tuesday, you should get out & take Marlie & Tom with you. Z."

Willard could feel his pulse pounding as he read and reread the note. He forced himself to breathe slowly and deeply until he felt more calm. He would have to do something but what?

As he was thinking, he absently fingered the keyboard, tapping in the code to search for messages. Suddenly, the screen was filled with numbers. He quickly entered the command to decrypt the message and watched the numbers turn into words.

HELLO. IF YOU ARE IN TROUBLE, THERE IS A WAY OUT. WE CAN HELP. DO YOU WANT HELP? PC.

CHAPTER 31

"It's a war, all right," said Wheeler. "But not like any we've ever fought before."

"But to what end?" Paul asked. "What can they possibly hope to accomplish?"

Wheeler sipped his coffee and set the Styrofoam cup on Paul's desk. "It goes back to what we military types call 'the will to resist.' Typically, you try to break it by prolonged bombing or with siege tactics of some sort, like surrounding the city and starving them out." He picked up his cup and looked across the desk. "Not a very pleasant subject, I'm afraid."

"No, it isn't," said Paul, "but go on."

"For all we know," Wheeler continued, "this could be the first war of a new type. No one's being bombed or gassed, so I guess we could classify it as technological. Bloodless." He was raising the cup to his lips but stopped abruptly. "No, with Joe's death, we can't call it bloodless."

Paul nodded grimly.

Wheeler continued. "The battleground is also unlike any other. We're not contesting one another over the high ground or for choke points at sea. When you get down to it, what we're really fighting over is a few square centimeters of silicon.

"But those silicon chips are to our modern economy what the factories of the Ruhr were to Nazi Germany. Money and data are controlled and contained by those chips; our telephone lines and microwave circuits are as much a logistical network as railroad tracks and shipping lanes were in World War II.

"All that's really different is the method of attack. We don't have to fly armadas of B-17s to destroy ball-bearing plants or launch massive invasions to win beachheads the way we did at Normandy. But if an adversary can control those silicon chips and interdict our communications network, he can, in effect, destroy the industrial base of our economy. And he can do it without risking the life of a single soldier or, conceivably, without even revealing his identity."

"We've certainly had no luck on that score."

"You mean detection?"

Paul nodded and tilted his chair until it came to rest against the blackboard.

"No luck so far, but I've just received clearance from the White House to try a new tack."

"Which is?"

"We're going to concentrate our forces instead of spreading them out. Operation Doppelgänger seems to be taking the pressure off our field teams. They're spending a lot more time waiting around than they are choppering from tower to tower keeping circuits open. We're also getting an airmobile battalion assigned to us."

"To do what?"

"They're going into Ohio on a search and destroy mission."

"Against who?"

"Against . . ." A grin slowly spread across his face. "Against raccoons."

Paul almost fell out of his chair. "What? You're putting me on."

"No, I'm not. They've got a serious rabies problem in Ohio; it's practically an epidemic."

"So?"

"We're using that as a cover to put several thousand men

on the ground. We're targeting every state park, national park, private campground; any place where a van, truck, or camper might be parked and intercepting microwave signals. Harrison flew to Columbus the day before yesterday. The governor agreed to help. He'll call up the National Guard and ask the President to declare a state of emergency. Before the ink is dry, we'll have our troops in place, starting the search phase. We've already got two SR-71s sweeping the state for ELINT along the microwave routes; another squadron's doing photo and infrared recon on an hourly basis. If anybody's transmitting down there, we're damned well going to find him."

"What do you think our chances are?"

"If we can do it without scaring him off, I'd say they're damn good. We'll be checking anyone who goes in or out. We'll ask if they have any pets; we'll ask if anyone's been bitten or come into contact with a raccoon or wild dog, alive or dead. And while we're going through the motions, we'll be checking each vehicle for anything suspicious.

"They'll have to have a dish antenna and something covering it; you can't cram that sort of gear into a station wagon. We'll let people in small vehicles pass through quickly. The bigger ones will get close scrutiny. We'll be putting license numbers into the FBI's computer, making sure things check out, looking for anything out of line."

"That sounds a lot more interesting than what I've been doing," said Paul, indicating the blackboard.

"I was looking at those equations, trying to figure out what they mean," Wheeler smiled. "By the way, what the hell do they mean?"

"Damned if I know."

Wheeler chuckled. "Really."

"I'm testing a number of algorithms that might provide a shortcut to breaking an RSA cipher."

"Such as the one WZ sent us?"

"Exactly."

"Any luck?"

Paul shook his head. "The problem of factoring primes goes back a long way. Gauss couldn't crack it, and to be honest about it, my chances of pulling it off are on the slim side."

"Even with ten acres of computers in the basement?"

"We're running now with a lot of parallel processing, but it's essentially a brute-force approach. The machine picks a prime number, tries it against the modulus; when that doesn't work, it goes to the next one. And on and on and on."

"Like the Maryland lottery?"

"Damn close. And our chances of hitting the million-dollar payoff are about as great."

"Two million to one?"

Paul shrugged. "I don't know; it could even be higher. But I figured it's at least worth a try."

"Well," said Wheeler, getting to his feet. "Thanks for the coffee."

"Off to the Pentagon?"

Wheeler dropped the cup in the wastebasket. "I'm briefing the Joint Chiefs. I did my best to put them off, but this Ohio thing will require a max coordinating effort on their part. Harrison set up the briefing and told me to be there."

"Sounds like a command performance."

"Something like that," said Wheeler, pausing at the door.

"Good luck."

"Thanks. See you tomorrow."

Paul stood facing the blackboard, arms folded across his chest, head bowed. Nancy stopped in the doorway, not certain she should interrupt yet not wanting to leave. He seemed to her frozen. No, not frozen, suspended. And in that moment she tried to imagine his mind free of his body, his brain scaling mathematical abstractions as inaccessible to other intellects as Everest is to pedestrians. She felt herself an intruder and turned to go; the click of a heel betrayed her presence. He turned.

"I'm sorry," she said. "You seemed so lost in thought. I didn't mean to disturb you."

"You did nothing of the sort."

She eyed the blackboard. "I know you theoreticians need a lot of room to think, to deal with things conceptually. I didn't want to intrude."

Paul smiled. "Want to know what I was thinking?"

"Sure."

"I was thinking about dinner."

"Come on," said Nancy. "You're not serious."

"Oh, I was trying to make some sense of all this stuff," he said, sweeping his hand toward the blackboard. "But for some reason my thoughts never got much higher than right here." He patted his stomach.

"No wonder. You skipped lunch, as I recall."

"I did?" He paused. "Come to think of it, I did. Just as well. I've about had my fill of the food here and at the club, too, for that matter."

"Understandably."

"You know what I'd really like?"

"What?"

"Moo Shu Pork. Pan-fried duck in lemon sauce. Shrimp in black bean sauce."

"That's great," she said, her eyes crinkling into a smile. "You look at me and think Chinese food. Talk about ethnic stereotypes."

"Know any good restaurants?"

"Dozens."

"Pick one and we'll go. If you're not busy, that is."

"You still have travel restrictions, don't you?"

"I do and I don't. Bill says I can go pretty much where I need to."

"On official business, though."

Paul shrugged. "Again, it's nothing explicit. Otis and I went to dinner at Bertha's in Fells Point one evening. As long as the Ops Center knows where I'm going, it should be okay."

"You sure?"

"Don't worry about it." He edged toward her. "Now, do we have a date or don't we?"

She was smiling. "Okay, round eye. We go chop-chop Chinatown."

They stepped from the air-conditioned building into air as hot and humid as a steam bath. The asphalt gave with each step as they walked across the parking lot.

Nancy slipped off her jacket and draped it across her arm. "You won't be needing that," she said, indicating his tie. "This place is very casual."

Paul tossed his tie as well as his jacket into the back seat of Nancy's BMW. A few minutes later, with cold air pouring from the vents, they were driving south on the Baltimore-Washington Parkway, Nancy deftly switching from lane to lane.

"A typical BMW driver, I see."

"And just what do you mean by that?"

"Fast, aggressive, and oh-so-certain you're in control."

She raised an eyebrow. "Am I going too fast for you?"

"For me, no. But for that guy ahead of you who had a fight with his wife and just downed a pint of whiskey..."

"What guy?"

Paul shrugged. "He may not be out here right now, or maybe he's only had a beer this time. But the statistical probability of his vehicle attempting to occupy the same space at the same moment as your car in the next week, month, or year is damn close to unity."

Her tone was teasing. "You are arguing, I take it, for a strategy of risk minimalization."

"I'd hate to see Uncle Sam lose one of his most capable mathematicians." He paused. "And without question, his most charming."

She eased the accelerator and glanced in his direction, smiling. "Thank you."

A pleasant silence settled over them. Paul tilted the seat, stretched, and drew a slow deep breath. Nancy stayed in the flow of traffic. A half hour later, she pulled into a lot on H Street.

As they were walking, she said, "D.C. doesn't have a Chinatown on the mega-scale of New York or San Francisco. From where we are, it runs several blocks in each direction. Some stores, a lot of restaurants. And the usual social organizations."

"With Peking on one side of the street, Taiwan on the other?"

"It used to be like that. You'd get a visit from the Taiwan consul if he heard you were carrying beer from the mainland or selling Bee-and-Flower soap. A lot of it went back to the civil war. Of course, that generation is very old now—those that are still alive. The younger ones could care less about it. In fact, my sister and her husband went to Peking a few years back and managed to find some cousins we didn't even know we had."

"Have you been to China?"

"With my job?" She shook her head. "There's no way the Agency would let me visit the mainland. Not as a tourist, anyway."

"What about on an official basis?"

She arched a brow. "That's an area we'd best not talk about."

"Okay." He paused. "Tell me about the restaurant."

"It's a nice place, fairly large but reasonably priced. The owner, Mr. Chen, is from Peking by way of Taiwan. He was an infantry officer in the Kuomintang; fought the Japanese during the war and then the Communists. It took him a while to get used to things after we recognized Peking, but like most Chinese in this country, he's come to accept it. I don't think he likes it, though."

"He's lived in what you would call 'interesting times.'"

"Ah, yes. 'May you live in interesting times.' Say that to an American, and he'll think you're wishing him well. But to a Chinese, that's a curse."

"A few months ago, I'd have agreed with the American view. But now?" He shrugged. "I wouldn't mind at all if the next few decades turn out to be very uninteresting."

When they got to the restaurant, Chen warmly greeted Nancy and shook hands with Paul after she introduced them. The main room was oddly shaped, with several smaller rooms appended to it. Chen led them through the maze to a table near the rear of the room, where the walls met at a broad angle. Paul started to take the chair opposite the wall, but Chen motioned for him to sit on the banquette beside Nancy.

"Much traffic here," he said, indicating the aisle that led to the kitchen door. A moment later, a waiter came through the door, carrying a fully laden tray trailing the sound and fragrance of sizzling rice.

Paul took a deep breath and smiled appreciatively. "I think I'm going to like it here."

Chen nodded and leaned across the table. "Have Peking duck tonight. Not on menu. You ask. It very good."

Ten minutes later, the duck landed on their table, the first of three courses they had ordered. With the strong Chinese beer fomenting a mild revolution in their heads, they exchanged more smiles than words as their chopsticks clicked into the shrimp course. Then, suddenly, silence swept across the room. Nancy stopped with her chopsticks in mid-air and turned her head toward the front. Chen, the waiters, everyone seemed frozen: no motion, no sound. Then she saw the two men and their guns.

Even as her brain was trying to articulate the word *robbery*, she knew they were not after money. They had come to kill.

Paul turned his head, and he, too, froze. Then everything seemed to slow down. It was like watching a movie in slow motion; it did not seem real to him.

Backs to the door, the men swept the room with their pistols, their motions as mechanical as tank turrets. From where he was sitting, Paul could see that both men were white, bearded, and of medium height. What he could not understand was why neither man had made a move toward the cash register, where Chen, hands rigid at his side, was standing.

One of the men said something to Chen. The proprietor spoke aloud, first in English, then in Chinese, and people started to stand. The other gunman began motioning with his weapon for everyone to get up.

When the people in front of them were on their feet, Paul and Nancy stood up. Though much shorter than Paul, Nancy tried to block the gunmen's view of him. The man closest to them began to move forward, ignoring the Chinese but scrutinizing the face of each Occidental man. Sensing they were after Paul, Nancy raised herself on her toes, stretching as high as she could.

The man was only twenty feet away, his eyes moving methodically from one face to the next. Then, he stopped; his eyes narrowed as he looked at Paul. He leveled the pistol at Nancy and motioned her to stand aside. Still on her toes, the muscles in her legs trembling, Nancy focused on the gun; it was so close she could see where the silencer had been screwed onto the muzzle.

"Move." The voice was low, guttural.

Suddenly, Chen barked out a command in Chinese. The man turned, and in that instant the door to the kitchen flew open. There was a blur of white as the chef passed in front of them, a huge cleaver in his hand. In a single fluid motion, his arm swept down, the full force of his wiry body behind it, and the cleaver sailed toward the gunman. In the stillness Paul could hear the blade turning through the air, like the final whoosh of a helicopter winding down. In the second it took for the gunman to realize what had happened, the cleaver slammed into his forehead. The gun went off with a muffled crack, the slug striking the ceiling, as the man toppled backwards.

Chen, standing ramrod straight and motionless not ten feet from the second man, issued another command in Chinese. A moment later, his Chinese patrons were dropping to the floor. The gunman seemed confused, hesitant. Chen went into a crouch and quickly closed the distance between them. At first he seemed to be diving toward the floor, but an instant later he was pivoting on the ball of his right foot, his left leg swinging toward the gunman in a wide arc. Chen's foot connected with the man's forearm with an audible crack. The pistol fell to the floor.

As one waiter went for the gun, another pinned the man against the wall. Chen went behind the desk and picked up the phone.

A moment later, he spoke aloud in Chinese; people began standing up. "Please get up," he said in English. "Have called police. They come soon."

Nancy let out a breath. "We'd better get out of here."

"Shouldn't we wait for the police?"

"He was after you, Paul. Don't you understand? He was trying to kill you."

"What? No, you—"

"There's no time to argue. We can go out through the kitchen. I know the alleys around here."

"Look, I—"

"Don't argue. You've got to trust me. You can't talk to the police; they'll want to question you. The reporters at the *Post* listen to the police radio; they'll be here talking to people and taking pictures. You can't be exposed."

"All right," said Paul.

Nancy went to the chef and whispered something. He motioned for them to follow as he went into the kitchen.

Outside, she looked up and down the alley. "We can't go back to the car; there might be others waiting for us." She met his eyes. "It could also be rigged with a bomb."

The stench of Oriental garbage hung heavily in the humid air. Nancy moved quickly, unerringly, through the maze of alleys and narrow passageways. They crossed two streets and then began walking on a sidewalk that was aswarm with people.

"Where are we going?" he asked.

"There's a subway station a block from here. We'll take the Metro to Silver Spring."

"Then what?"

"A friend of mind went out of town yesterday and gave me the key to her apartment so I could water her plants. If there were others involved, they could know where I live; they're also likely to be watching for us to return to Meade. Nobody could possibly know about Betty. We'll stay there until we can figure out our next move."

Few people were left on the subway by the time it reached Silver Spring. As they walked up the hill from the station, Paul kept glancing over his shoulder; no one seemed to be following. A few minutes later, they stopped at the glass entrance doors of a huge apartment building. Using an electronic card, Nancy opened the door to the lobby. When the elevator door closed, Nancy pushed 11.

As the car started up, she said, "Actually, she lives on the ninth floor, but I just don't want to take any chances that someone might see the indicator light downstairs."

"What are you? A professionally trained spy?"

She laughed and shook her head. "Oh, we learned all sorts of stuff at Mata Hari College."

He looked at her quizzically.

"Not really. I just read a lot of spy novels. Just about everybody does at the Agency."

Paul nodded, a forced smile on his face.

From the eleventh floor, they walked down two flights. Nancy led him to an apartment and opened the door.

With the door bolted behind them, Nancy began watering the plants. Paul went to the bathroom, doffed his shirt, and cooled his face and upper body with a cold washcloth. He left his sweat-soaked shirt hanging on a hook behind the door. "I hope you don't mind," he said. "My shirt's drenched, and I couldn't bear the thought of putting it back on. In fact, I'm tempted to take a shower."

"Go ahead. In fact, while you're in there, I could toss your clothes—mine, too, for that matter—in the washer down the hall."

"Really, you don't have to."

"Ho's Chinese Laundry. Very fast. No starch."

Paul laughed. "Okay, but what do I wear in the meantime?"

"Betty's boyfriend is over here a lot; I'll bet he's got a robe or something in the closet."

She went to the bedroom and returned a minute later with a tan raincoat. "This should do."

Paul stood under the shower for a long time, gradually lowering the setting until it was in the full cold position. After drying himself, he slipped on the raincoat and went into the living room. He found a Beethoven piano sonata on the radio, a bottle of wine in a pewter bucket, and Nancy on the sofa in a flimsy red robe.

"Finished?" she asked.

"It's all yours."

"Good. Our clothes are in the washer. Everything of mine's washable. Working woman's wardrobe, you know."

Expecting her to get up and head for the bathroom, Paul hovered awkwardly beside the sofa before sitting down.

"I thought maybe we could relax over some wine. Or would you rather have a beer?"

"No, this looks fine."

She handed him the corkscrew. "Care to do the honors?"

The wine, a domestic Chenin Blanc, was cold and almost effervescent on his tongue.

"The wash cycle's almost over," she said. "I'll put our clothes in the drier before I take a bath."

"I can do that."

"Okay. But there's no hurry."

"What do we do now?" he asked.

"It doesn't look like we've been followed. And even if someone were looking for me, they wouldn't be able to connect me with this place. We're safe here."

"Shouldn't we call security at Meade?"

"We could," she said without enthusiasm.

"Why don't we, then?"

"We know they can intercept microwave, and any call from here would be over an unsecured circuit. So, there's a chance— granted, a small one—they could track us back to here."

Paul nodded.

"On the other hand, it's a big city. No one knows we're here, and there's no way they're going to find us. There's a Holiday Inn across the street; in the morning we could take a cab from there or a limo to BWI. The Agency has an annex right next to the airport."

"I see."

She stood up. "Well, I'm getting into the tub. The laundry room's down the hall just before you get to the elevator."

"Want some wine to take with you?"

"Good idea."

He refilled her glass.

"Maybe I'm being overly cautious. I don't know. What I do know is that somebody was trying to kill you." She forced a smile to her face. "Well, we can talk about it after I've cleaned up."

Paul glanced at the clock. They had left the restaurant just over an hour ago, and in that time he had done all he could to avoid thinking about what had happened. Now, he was doing laundry, drinking wine, and waiting for Nancy to get out of the tub. He was fussing over a sweaty shirt instead of focusing on the one inescapable fact that Nancy, at least, had not forgotten: "Somebody was trying to kill you."

It was no holdup. The men had been looking for someone: *him*. Had Nancy not blocked the gunman's view, had the chef not come charging out of the kitchen . . . Paul felt his stomach drop, his forehead turn clammy. He tried to shake the thought from his mind, but it had taken hold.

A few seconds. That had been the margin. Had the chef not been so quick and so deadly accurate, a bullet would have gone into his chest or maybe his brain.

He refilled his glass and took a long pull of the wine. But who were they after? Paul Sager or Paul Cassidy?

There were enough electronic traces of Paul Cassidy in the phone calls he received every day from Chicago, the White House, and MATER. Though he had been careful not to discuss technical details except on secure lines, someone listening to his calls over open lines could, conceivably, have pieced together what he was doing.

But whether their target was Paul Cassidy or Paul Sager, he was still in considerable danger. It seemed unlikely the gunmen were acting alone. Someone could be lying in wait for him. On the parkway. At the entrance to Fort Meade.

Then, it hit him. Oh, God, what if they go after Helen?

When Nancy left the bathroom, she found Paul on the sofa, fully dressed; her blouse and skirt were on hangers.

"We have to go," he said.

"Now?"

He explained. Ten minutes later they were in a cab on their way to Fort Meade.

CHAPTER 32

When Marlie asked Willard to describe the inside of a computer, to explain how so much information could be stored in so little space, he fumbled with his words at first, looking for an analogy. Then, it came to him. "It's like a castle," he said.

He told her to imagine a fortress with hundreds of rooms connected by a maze of corridors and stairways. When the king wanted something, he simply ordered a servant to move it from one place in the castle to another. The moat and drawbridge prevented anyone from entering without the king's permission.

It was not, he later realized, the most brilliant analogy—arrows, catapults, and cannon were sources of data input quite beyond a king's control—but it seemed to satisfy Marlie's inquisitiveness.

A week after Zed's death, the idea of a castle came to mind again, only this time he saw himself as a prisoner. Or was he? In addition to its rooms and corridors, a castle also had secret chambers and passageways. Messages could be hidden behind loose stones or beneath old floorboards. In a structure as large as a castle, no one, not even the king, could possibly know every one of its secret places.

And with computers, no one, not even the designers and programmers who created the system, could possibly know its entire architecture. Just as a castle might have ancient rooms that were sealed shut centuries ago, every machine has its unknown or forgotten places. Willard knew the computers at the Chicago Switch had to have their secret chambers; it was up to him to find the trapdoors.

Willard had never been to Chicago, yet he knew the interior of the Switch more intimately than any room he had ever lived in. He had already found some of its trapdoors and could easily have set a logic bomb inside any of them. He was on line with the Federal Reserve's wire from San Francisco and had used this access to send his first hello to Chicago. Enciphering and sending Marlie's bomb had been equally easy. It was also exciting, knowing that your adversary had all the information necessary to destroy the organization but could not decipher it; only he had the key.

The thought brought a smile to his lips. He leaned back and stretched. 11:45. He had been on the machine nearly five hours.

Sending those messages had been easy. What he now had to do was difficult, extremely difficult. He had to find a way to hide his secret key on the Chicago Switch so that no one there would find it as long as he deactivated it once a day. That way, if George threatened him or Marlie, he would have something to exchange for their freedom—or even their lives.

It *is* like a castle, he thought. Swim the moat; climb the wall; go in through a trapdoor; light a long candle beside the powder keg. And if I don't get back in time to put it out, *boom*! The king and his whole fucking castle go up. He began to laugh.

"What's so funny?"

The voice startled him. His hands jerked across the keyboard.

SHIT said the computer.

Marlie laughed. "You and that damn computer."

"You surprised me."

"That's obvious. It's lunchtime," she said, nodding toward the basket.

"Thanks."

When they finished eating, Marlie said, "You've been spending a lot of time in here the last few days. You got something hot you're working on?"

The enthusiasm in her voice pleased him, but after a moment's reflection, he decided against telling her about the trapdoors and time bombs he was looking for. He spoke instead about electronic countermeasures, swamping her with computer jargon until she stifled a yawn. Then he changed the subject.

"How are things back at the ranch?"

"Busy," she replied. "The sector heads will be coming in late this afternoon and tonight. Something's up. I'm not sure what, but it looks big."

"You sure?"

"Sure of what?"

"That it's something big?"

"There's usually a lot of advance planning on meetings like this. But George just closed the door and was on the phone all morning. When he came out a little while ago, he told me. Tom and I are taking the pickup into Buena Vista this afternoon and stocking up on groceries. George gave me four hundred dollars."

"Sounds like he's expecting a lot of people."

"That, or they're going to be staying awhile."

Willard realized something was wrong when he returned to the house that evening. George was sitting at the table with several of the sector heads, but when Willard came into the room, they abruptly stopped talking. He said hello and walked past the table toward the kitchen. They followed him with their eyes. The same men who had once been so effusive in praising his program now returned his greeting with silent stares.

Marlie and Tom were in the kitchen, preparing dinner.

"What's with those guys?" Willard asked.

Tom shrugged. "Like they're having a big meeting."

Willard turned to Marlie. "Is something wrong?"

She turned away. "We're going to have at least fifteen, maybe twenty for dinner."

"Okay," said Willard, exasperation in his voice. "Just asking."

"Later," she said.

Willard went to his room, leaving the door partially open, and stretched out on the bed. The conversation at the table had resumed. He could not hear what they were saying, but the voices were low, somber.

He had found several trapdoors at Chicago, but none were exactly right. Some were so far removed from the operating program that any message he hid there might wind up permanently buried. Others were too closely linked to daily operations; someone might find the data inadvertently. What he needed was a loop no one would find so long as he swept it out once a day. If he failed to deactivate the bomb, he wanted the world to know immediately.

He bolted upright. That's it, he thought, the daily report. I can hide the key in the daily report. If I don't deactivate it before the Switch shuts down for the night, it'll print out in the morning.

He got to his feet and went to the bathroom to wash up. As he was drying his face, he looked in the mirror and began smiling. I've got those fuckers. They don't know it, but I've got them.

Wearing suits and ties, George and the sector heads looked as if they had just returned from a dozen separate funerals and had nothing in common, not even the deceased, to talk about. Willard sat on the sofa balancing a plate in his lap, eating his food as quickly as he could. When he finished, he carried his plate to the kitchen and left quietly through the back door.

The air was cool, and when he got to the trailer, he immediately put on a jacket. He went back outside, walked around the barn, and sat on the fence rails. The last traces of sunlight were fading from the sky.

He would have to leave. That much was clear. But would Marlie go with him? And if she wouldn't, what then? His life had been so empty before they became lovers. How much more empty it would be if he just walked away from her. Never seeing her, never touching her, never being inside her . . . He could not sustain the thought. She had to leave with him. There was no other way.

The screen door slammed closed. Willard turned and saw Marlie silhouetted against the house lights, walking toward the barn. He waited until she was near and then called out: "Over here."

She stopped five feet from him. It was a distance he recognized: close enough to talk, not close enough to touch.

"George wants you up at the house."

"What for?"

"He didn't say."

"Yeah, but what do you think he wants?"

"I think something's gone wrong."

"I figured as much, but what? You must have heard what they were talking about."

"Bits and pieces."

Willard moved toward her and lightly clasped her arms. "What is it? Please tell me."

"Well, I'm not completely sure, but it sounds like one of the field units is missing. And some of the sector heads are convinced the program isn't working, that the Fed's found a way to get around it or something."

"What'd they say about me? Anything?"

"Not from what I could tell."

They started walking toward the house.

"Look, Marlie, this is important. We may have to leave here."

"What do you mean?"

"I mean, it may not be safe to stay here anymore. You know George. You trust him?"

"No."

"Then, we're going to have to work up a plan just in case we have to get out of here."

She stopped. "I don't know."

"What do you mean, you 'don't know'?"

"Just that. I don't know." She looked into his eyes. "I don't know that I *want* to leave."

"Look, I only stayed here because of you. Hell, I was ready to leave after Wisconsin. If George hadn't promised me he'd let you come, I'd have split."

Her voice was soft, small. "I know. I'm sorry."

"Sorry? What do you mean, 'sorry'? I love you."

"I know you do."

"And you don't love me, is that it?"

She shook her head and began to cry softly.

"All these months have meant nothing to you?"

"You don't understand. At first, I came to you because they told me to."

"They did?"

"Of course they did. You had them over a barrel. You wanted me, and they wanted your program. They considered it a fair trade."

"Look, I didn't—"

She cut him off. "Yes you did. Remember what you sent me? That so-called program of yours?"

"Look, I didn't know what else to do. I just wanted you. I wanted to be with you."

She raised her hand. "I understand now; I didn't then. But I don't think you understand me. You don't understand how important the organization is to me. I was nothing before the director took me in. I was ready to kill myself. He gave me back my life. And something more. Faith. A vision of the future. A place where I belong. Don't you understand? It's not that I don't care for you. I just can't leave."

They walked in silence the rest of the way to the house. At the door, he took her hand.

"Look, I need to talk to you. Will you meet me in the trailer later on?"

She nodded.

He leaned over and kissed her. The salt of her tears was bitter on his tongue. "I'll see you later."

When he opened the door, everyone turned to face him. George motioned to the foot of the table. The empty chair, the stern faces. For a moment, Willard felt he was once again facing an academic board: the faculty on one side, the administrators on the other, his case about to be heard, his ass about to be had. He looked at George and smiled.

Though his face was flushed, the vessels bulging on his forehead, George betrayed no anger in his voice. "To get immediately to the point, we have a problem. To be specific, two problems. Both of which relate to our field units.

"In the first instance, it appears as if our unit in Ohio was taken on Wednesday. We are not sure how, but we suspect the government used the rabies epidemic as a cover to move in regular army troops. The team is, we believe, being held incommunicado.

"Second, and more to the point, there are indications your program has been compromised."

"Compromised?" said Willard. "You mean, somebody gave it to the other side?"

"At the moment, we do not know. What we do know is that transactions seem to be going through the Chicago Switch. We have tested it ourselves by moving funds across the country through a number of Federal Reserve branches. Every one of the transactions went through."

"On a real-time basis?"

"About half of them. Others were delayed as much as an hour. In one case, two. What matters is that they *are* going through. Your program is no longer working."

"Is that what your field units are reporting?"

"Quite the contrary," said George. "They report that everything is working and working smoothly. They are altering both the incoming and outgoing signals."

"Well, then," said Willard, "the program's doing exactly what it was designed to do. If you've got a problem, it's something other than my program."

"Very well."

"Is that it?"

"For now."

Willard got to his feet.

"One more thing," said George. "Does the name 'Paul Sager' mean anything to you?"

Willard paused a moment, hand against chin. "It does sound familiar, but I don't know why."

"You were at MIT, were you not?"

"That's it," said Willard. "He's a professor in the computer science department. A mathematician. A cryptologist."

Every head in the room snapped toward him at once. So, he thought, that's what they're looking for.

"What can you tell us about Professor Sager?"

Willard reflected for a moment. "That was a couple of years ago. He was really smart, I remember that. Wrote a book, I think, though I'm not real sure about that. I was on the machines most of the time. I didn't read very much." He grinned. "Which was one of the reasons I got booted out."

He glanced the length of the table, anticipating smiles. There were none. He looked at George. "Why do you ask? Do you think he's behind this?"

"That is a possibility," said George. "Does the name 'Paul Cassidy' mean anything to you?"

"Cassidy?" Willard shook his head slowly. "I don't think so. Was he also at MIT?"

"In a manner of speaking, yes," George replied. "We think Paul Sager and Paul Cassidy are one and the same person. Moreover, we have reason to believe he is at the National Security Agency working to counter our operation." His eyes narrowed. "And succeeding."

When Willard stepped outside the house, his nostrils were assailed by pungent smoke. He looked to his left and saw Tom leaning against the pickup, a glowing joint in his mouth. He raised a hand and started toward the barn.

Tom came over to him, smiling blissfully. "You should try this stuff. It's the best. Strictly sacramental quality."

"Yeah, I'll bet it is," said Willard a bit nervously.

"Sure you don't want to try it?"

"No, thanks. I need a clear head for what I've got to do."

"Gotcha."

"Good night, Tom."

"Night, Whiz."

When he got to the barn, he found Marlie sitting on the stairs to the trailer, the down-filled sleeping bag zipped open and draped over her shoulders.

"Is it always so cool this late in August?"

She nodded. "They've probably had their first frosts up in the mountains. Soon the aspen will start changing. This used to be my favorite time up there. The tourists were gone. You had time to yourself. Time to think. Maybe hike up in the mountains."

"You miss that, don't you?"

"It's been a while. But yeah, I guess I do."

"Great. Let's move to Aspen. Tonight!"

A slight smile flickered on her lips and then vanished. "No. I don't think so."

Willard let out a sigh, sat down on the stair just below her, and leaned back. She nestled him between her legs and ran her hand aimlessly through his hair. For several minutes, neither spoke.

Then, almost in a whisper, she asked: "What did they want?"

"Oh, it was like you said. A field unit in Ohio is missing, and they think the Fed's figured a way to get around my program."

"You say that so casually. It doesn't bother you?"

"Nah. In a way, I'm kind of glad. It'll give me something to do. Since the field units went out with copies of the program, I've just been messing around on the machine. Playing, really."

"And that was it. Nothing else?"

"There was one other thing. They asked me about one of the professors I had at MIT. A guy named Paul Sager."

"What did they say?"

"Oh, just that they think he's at NSA working to counter the program. He's apparently using a false name: 'Paul Cassidy.'"

"Oh."

"Is something the matter?"

"What? No. It's just that it's cold out here, and I'm getting tired. I'm going in."

"Can't you stay? Just for a while?"

She shook her head. "Not tonight."

"Tomorrow then?"

"We'll see. Good night, Whiz."

"Good night," he said and watched her walk to the house, his hand poised in the air, hoping she would turn and wave. Not once did she glance back.

Willard felt drained, tired. He took the sleeping bag into the trailer and rolled it out on the floor. After stripping to his shorts, he climbed into the bag and zipped it up.

A blinding light jarred him awake. Through half-opened eyes, he saw George standing over him, aiming a gun at his head.

As George's hand slowly came into focus, the muzzle metamorphosed into a pointing finger. Willard let out a breath.

"Did I startle you?"

"Uh, oh, that's okay. I was just taking a nap. What time is it?"

"Nearly midnight," said George. "I have an urgent message for the Boston sector."

"Okay. Let me get dressed, and I'll send it out right away."

George shook his head. "This one is very sensitive, Whiz. I have to send it myself."

"Yeah, uh, sure. Give me a minute to get dressed, and I'll show you how to do it."

"It has to be encrypted using their public-key cipher."

"No problem."

George left the trailer door open and went down the steps. Willard retrieved his clothes and quickly dressed. He tapped a command on the keyboard; the machine whirred and clicked.

"Are you ready?" George called.

"Yeah. Come on up."

"What do I have to do?"

Willard explained how to encipher and send the message. George nodded and then called Boston. When the phone was in the modem, he asked, "How do I delete this message from memory?"

Willard described the procedure and then headed for the house. He fixed himself a cup of tea and ate two slices of toast slathered with grape jelly. George returned ten minutes later, went to his study without a word, and closed the door.

When he returned to the trailer, Willard locked the door and went straight to the console. In spite of what he had told George, Willard knew the machine had automatically recorded and stored the transmission.

He smiled, anticipating the prospect of peeking at George's message the way a child enjoys sneaking a look in his parents' private drawers. Then the message appeared.

URGENT. IMMEDIATE ACTION MUST BE TAKEN TO DETAIN HELEN SAGER. ACTION MUST BE SWIFT AND LEAVE NO TRACES. SUBJECT MUST IN NO WAY BE HARMED. USE OF VERMONT REFUGE NUMBER TWO IS ADVISED. SURVEILLANCE INDICATES SUBJECT LIKELY TO TRAVEL VERMONT ON WEEK-ENDS. USE DISCRETION AS TO TIME AND PLACE OF ACTION. REPORT HERE WHEN ACTION COMPLETE. G.

Using his own public key, Willard immediately encrypted the message and stored it in his secret file.

He unlocked the door and went outside. The air was cold, the sky a deep blue, the Milky Way a starry cloud. A shiver went through him.

It was no longer a game. The challenge, the fun, had started to disappear months before. The week in Aspen with Marlie had made him forget that. But then came Zed's death. No, God damn it, Zed's murder. And now this: kidnapping an innocent woman. And for what?

Willard had never met Helen Sager, but he had known her husband far better than he admitted to George. Paul Sager had been one of two professors who had honestly seemed to care about him—and the only one who had had any respect for his intelligence.

But why is he at NSA and calling himself Paul Cassidy? He did not seem the sort of guy who'd work for the government, much less the NSA. That made no sense at all. Paul Cassidy. Then, it hit him. P.C. He's P.C.! But why?

Willard returned to the trailer and telephoned a computerized news and research network in Denver. Using a false billing number to gain access to the files, he ordered the system to search for newspaper articles about Paul Sager. A few seconds later, seven entries appeared. He read only the first: NOTED MATHEMATICIAN, CODE EXPERT, KILLED BY CAR BOMB.

Willard made it to the stairs before vomiting, clinging hard to the flimsy railing to keep from losing his balance. When the nausea had passed, he went inside and signed off the network. There was no need to read the story. He knew who had killed Sager.

Then he realized that George had implied that Paul Sager was alive and at Fort Meade operating under a different name. He shook his head. What's going on? What the hell is going on?

Things were no longer so clear. Sager might be alive, he might be dead. But if he's dead, why would they kidnap his wife?

Willard shook his head. No, the answer was not clear. But he knew now what he had to do: he had to cross over. He would become a secret ally of the person he knew only as P.C. Whether it was Paul Sager, Paul Cassidy, or someone else no longer mattered. What did matter was stopping George from having Helen Sager kidnapped, possibly even killed. Stopping him, the director, and everyone else in their so-called church from doing anything ever again.

CHAPTER 33

Wheeler was elated. "It was incredible. Absolutely magnificent."

The stress of the past five months had etched the furrows on the colonel's brow more deeply. Now, the lines seemed softer; he was smiling, his blue eyes as merry as a Santa's. Wheeler sat opposite Winchell in his office, Paul and Nancy on either side.

Winchell took the omnipresent pipe from his mouth. "How did it happen?"

"It was a textbook case," said Wheeler. "First, our ELINT bird made contact. We followed that up with an SR-71 doing photo recon on a two-square-mile area that overlapped a state park and private campground. There were several hundred people mostly in vans and campers. We choppered in a company and had the squads close off the entrances and exits. We had another squad airborne to make sure nobody found a way out on a back road. Then, it was just a process of elimination."

"What'd you find?"

"This is the best part," said Wheeler. "We had the soldiers go from one camper or van to the next. No rifles, no helmets, strictly fatigues and baseball caps. We had them in two-man teams, one handing out material on the rabies epidemic, the other asking questions. It was mostly couples with kids. Some of them said no when the boys asked if they could look inside their trailers, but we had search warrants to get around that.

"A few of them had marijuana inside and were worried they'd get arrested. They were plainly relieved when the soldiers went in and out without saying a word.

"We hit pay dirt in the private campground. It was a young couple, clean-cut types in their mid-twenties; no kids. They had a van and were grilling hamburgers when the troops went in. The guy even had the ballgame on the radio. But the windows were covered with these opaque mountain scenes, and the troops couldn't see anything behind the front seats. When they asked if they could go inside, the guy said no. When they whipped out the search warrant, the guy got really angry; so did his wife.

"Our guys signaled in another team. That pretty much clinched it. When they went inside, it was wall-to-wall electronics. All they had to do was drive out into the boondocks within a few miles of a microwave tower, start the program, and take off at five o'clock.

"It was funny. The guy swore up and down he was just a stereo dealer. When that didn't fly, he got real quiet and said he wanted to call his lawyer."

"Where are they now?" Winchell asked.

"We've got them in custody at Wright-Pat."

"Where's that?" Paul asked.

"Wright-Patterson Air Force Base. Near Dayton."

"What crime are they charged with?" Paul asked.

"We've got a lengthy list of violations of FCC laws, but that's strictly for show. They're being interrogated now."

"Without their attorney, I take it," said Winchell.

Wheeler nodded. "We're not trying to build a court case. We're quite willing to blow a conviction if we can find out who the hell's behind all this."

"Any luck?" Winchell asked.

Wheeler shook his head. "Not yet. I'll be flying up there this afternoon. Harrison says we can hold them twenty-four hours max. We're cleared to impound the van, but we'll have to let them go by noon Thursday no matter what we turn up."

"And have them alert their confederates?" Winchell asked.

"The A.G. didn't give us much choice," Wheeler replied. "We're stretching things as it is, holding them without letting them contact a lawyer."

"And if you don't get the information?" Paul asked.

"We'll keep them under maximum surveillance. If they so much as go to the bathroom, we'll know whether they washed their hands."

When Wheeler walked into Paul's office Thursday morning, his suit was as rumpled as the bags beneath his eyes.

"Did you get any sleep at all?" Paul asked.

"Maybe an hour on the plane." He managed a weary smile. "But it was worth it. It was worth it."

Paul and Nancy leaned forward, but Wheeler, visibly enjoying their suspense, said nothing.

"Well?" said the two in unison.

"Are either one of you churchgoers?"

Paul shook his head.

"Nancy?"

The brown eyes crinkled. "I guess you could call me a lapsed Buddhist."

Wheeler shook his head, chuckling.

"What are you driving at?" Paul asked.

"Have either of you heard of the Church of the Electro-Deity?"

"That California cult," said Nancy.

"It's gone far beyond the cult stage," said Wheeler. "They claim they've got a million members in this country and another million in Europe. The real number's probably closer to a hundred thousand."

"And they're behind all this?" Nancy asked.

"It looks that way," said Wheeler. "The couple we arrested had no police records. But under sodium thiopental, they revealed that they're CED members.

"We questioned them separately. But when we asked what they had been doing, each of them said, 'I serve the director. I serve him, that I might be served.'

"After we found their connection with CED, we ran a computer retrieval on newspaper articles. The FBI's running through its files now to see if CED's been connected with any reported crimes.

"But from the articles I've been reading, it looks like it was started six years ago in California by a man who called himself 'the leader.' The articles weren't very clear on what they believe in, but it looks like a real mixed bag: right-wing evangelism minus Jesus plus electronic gadgetry that's supposed to cleanse the spirit. But what really makes it go is their followers. They've got kids in their late teens or early twenties who proselytize on street corners and airports. They've also got followers all over the country who lead outwardly normal lives but apparently turn over their income to the church. Their local organizations appear to be small and self-contained. But taken altogether, they've apparently put together a nationwide network of cells."

"That couple called him 'the director,' but you said 'the leader,'" Nancy remarked.

"At first," said Wheeler, "he called himself 'the leader.' That was before the cult spread to Europe. Someone must have told him that '*der Fuehrer*' was still a no-no on the Continent."

"Who is he?" Paul asked.

"No one's quite sure," said Wheeler. "He was indicted on income-tax evasion charges four years ago and left the country. They say he spends most of his time on a ship in the Pacific well beyond the two-hundred-mile limit. He's also reputed to have a land base in the Brazilian interior, but that's unconfirmed. Twice a week, he broadcasts to his followers on the short-wave band."

"Where did he come from?" Paul asked. "What's his background?"

"That, too, is part of the mystery," said Wheeler. "In one article the writer claimed he's an ex−Jesuit seminarian. Another says he's and ex−used car salesman. He's Jewish according to some accounts, Protestant in others."

"Thank God he's not Buddhist," said Nancy.

"Well, whatever he is," said Wheeler, "it's damn near certain he and his church are behind this."

"But why?" asked Paul.

Wheeler shrugged. "Any number of reasons. The IRS went after him pretty hard. Confiscated some of the church's property when the director left the country. We've got our people going through some tapes of his broadcasts to see if there are any clues in there."

"That might explain that declaration we got over the Switch from the Council for Peace and Justice," said Paul.

Wheeler nodded. "That had crossed my mind."

"If CED is behind it," said Nancy, "that message would make a lot of sense. Remember all that stuff about suppression of free speech and the practice of religion?"

"They also mentioned the FBI, the IRS, and 'prisoners of conscience,'" said Paul. He looked at Wheeler. "Are there any CED members in prison?"

"The FBI's running a computer search now. But the agent who was with me on the flight said he recalled some church members were jailed about six months ago for stealing IRS files. They had gotten jobs as clerks and were caught taking documents about the church. They were convicted. Ten-year terms, the guy told me."

Paul shook his head. "This is really strange. Why would a church get involved in something like this? It makes no sense."

"Since when has religion had to make sense?" Wheeler asked. "Jim Jones and Jonestown—did that make sense? Catholics and Protestants in northern Ireland—does that make sense? You've got Jews and Moslems killing one another, and Sunnis and Shiites slaughtering each other over the true descendant of the Prophet. None of that makes a damn bit of sense to me. Where I grew up, religion meant going to church, singing hymns and Christmas carols, giving baskets of canned goods to the poor."

"But you went to war," said Paul. "God knows, Vietnam was never a threat to this country, yet you were willing to fight."

"Not with all that much conviction," said Wheeler, "but yes, I was more than willing, I was eager to fight."

"So, you went because your government ordered you; another goes because his God commands him," said Paul. "In most countries, orders to march are usually issued from the pulpit."

"But they don't have a chance," said Wheeler. "As soon as they come into the open, bam! We've got them."

"But what if they don't come into the open?" said Paul.

"What if they remain hidden but continue using their electonic weapons against us? They could influence—perhaps even control—the government without ever setting foot in the Oval Office."

"That's a good point," said Nancy, "especially when you consider what they've been able to do over the past few months."

"You may be right," said Wheeler. "But put yourself in my place. I'm the guy who's going to walk into the Oval Office in a few hours and say: 'Mr. President, we've uncovered a plot to overthrow the lawfully constituted government of the United States.' Naturally, he's going to ask me which Communist government is behind it. And I'm going to have to say: 'It ain't the Commies, sir. It's the Church of the ElectroDeity.'" Wheeler shook his head.

"Yeah," said Paul. "I see what you mean."

On Friday, a security agent met with Paul and Nancy to discuss the restaurant incident. They repeated essentially the same story they had given the agent who'd interviewed them on Wednesday. As the man was leaving, Paul asked if he had any additional information on the gunmen. The agent shook his head. As far as the FBI and Washington police were concerned, it was a bungled robbery. Neither Paul nor Nancy were included on the list of witnesses the police had compiled after the incident, and a chemical analysis of Nancy's car had turned up no evidence of a bomb or any other tampering. It was now strictly a local matter; the Agency was no longer involved.

Paul went back to his office and spent the rest of the afternoon staring at the equations on his blackboard. He was tempted to pick up the phone and call Helen's office just to hear her voice again, to know she was safe. He had been sitting next to Wheeler when the colonel had called Harrison to demand renewed Secret Service surveillance and protection for Helen, but it still had to go through channels. The Secretary of the Treasury was airborne, returning from a round of secret meetings in Europe to assure bankers that the Clearing House Interbank Payment System was once again doing business as normal, that they could continue to rely on CHIPS for Eurodollar transactions, that the liquidity crisis was over. When the Secretary returned that evening, Harrison assured Wheeler, the request would be on his desk.

Paul glanced at his watch; it was nearly five o'clock. He

leaned back in his chair, closed his eyes, and tried to picture Helen. She would be in the office, the little white-noise machine whirring by the door, listening earnestly as her last client of the week was detailing the latest reversal or gain. He had always been amazed at Helen's ability to listen to sad stories eight hours a day, five days a week. Abstractions were so much more comfortable to deal with. There was always the prospect of something new, something that could be solved. Perhaps he would find an algorithm to factor large numbers into their prime components. But even if he fell short and made only a minor contribution to mathematics, it would be unique; it would add in some way, large or small, to the work of Pythagoras, Newton, Gauss. There would, at last, be a resolution.

"Paul?"

No reply.

"Paul," said Nancy, raising her voice a bit.

"What? Oh, I didn't see you," said Paul.

"Lost in thought," she said, adding with a smile, "as usual."

Paul mustered a smile in return.

"Chicago's relaying some cipher-text it received a little while ago," she said. "It's being decrypted now with your RSA key."

Paul got to his feet and followed her to the Operations Center. Sitting in front of his console, the color draining from his face, Paul read the message from "G" to the Boston sector.

"Oh, God," he muttered. "They're going after Helen."

"Where is she?" Nancy asked.

Paul glanced at the time display. It was 5:20.

"She's probably on her way to Vermont." He picked up the phone and immediately dialed Helen's office; a recording clicked on after the second ring announcing that the counseling center was closed until Monday. He called the house. Again, no answer.

"She's already gone," he whispered. "And there's nothing I can do. Nothing."

Wheeler telephoned with the news 7:30 Saturday morning. The police had found Helen's car just north of Waterbury, less than ten miles from the house. The door on the driver's side was unlocked, the trunk empty. The FBI and Secret Service had lifted some fingerprints from the metal and were going to transmit them to FBI headquarters for a computer search of the bureau's criminal records.

Paul was at his console in the Operations Center when the gray phone rang. He picked up the secure line. It was Wheeler again.

"I just talked to the FBI," said the colonel. "No match on the prints."

"What's their next move?"

"They took plaster casts of some tire tracks near Helen's car. There are lots of summer homes around there, as you know, and the police will be going house to house with photos of Helen and the car. They're hoping they can at least pin down the time she was kidnapped."

"Are you sure it's just that? Kidnapped?"

"That's the assumption."

"But what if they've done something to her? I mean, Jesus, they could have . . ." He did not finish the sentence.

"Look, Paul, I realize what you must be going through. But it'd make no sense for them to harm Helen. Remember, the message WZ passed on to Chicago indicated she was not to be harmed. It's you they're after."

"Okay, okay," he said softly. "But what am I supposed to do?"

"Just stay put," said Wheeler. "And let me know as soon as they get in touch with you."

"I was going over to MATER at noon. Is that all right?"

"Sure. As long as you have a staff car take you."

"Okay."

"And please, Paul, don't do anything rash. They've tried twice now to kill you. I don't want anything to happen to you. Or to Helen."

There was no sign of Natasha's Porsche in the nearly empty lot of MATER. After signing in at the guard's desk, Paul went to Scotto's office, unlocked the door, and turned on the computer. He telephoned Jim Guanti, who immediately recognized Paul's voice. They did the rest of their talking over the machines, using encrypted transmissions.

After Paul told him about the kidnapping, Jim asked what he should do. Paul stared at the screen at a loss for a reply.

Again, the letters slowly marched across the screen. RE-PEAT: WHAT SHOULD I DO?

Paul replied that he had no plan. When Jim asked if he knew anything at all about the kidnappers, Paul gave him a quick rundown on the Church of the ElectroDeity.

WE HAVE A CELL HERE, came Jim's reply. I KNOW, BE-
CAUSE A COUPLE OF DAIRY FARMERS OUT NEAR HARDWICK
HAVE BEEN ACTIVE TRYING TO GET ME AND OTHERS TO COME
TO THEIR MEETINGS. NEVER DID GO. THEY ARE ALSO ACTIVE
ON THE NETWORK. EVERY ONE OF THEM HAS A MACHINE.
WE'RE IN TOUCH ON TANK TRUCK PICKUP TIMES, CO-OP MAT-
TERS, AND THE LIKE. DO YOU WANT ME TO CHECK IT OUT?

Paul typed his reply. YES. BUT PLEASE BE CAREFUL.

CHAPTER 34

When Willard came to breakfast Monday morning, he found George waiting for him.

"I have a message that has to go out immediately."

"Okay, I'll send it," said Willard.

"No," said George. "This is too sensitive. I have to do it."

Willard opened his hands and shrugged. "Suit yourself."

"Are you set up to transmit?"

"Not yet. But it won't take me long. Do I have time for a cup of tea?"

"No. You can have breakfast after the machine is set up."

Willard did as he was told and went back to the house. He was on his second cup of tea when George returned and went straight to his study without a word. A few minutes later, with the trailer door locked behind him, Willard retrieved the message from the computer's memory and read it carefully.

Then he patched into the Federal Reserve's wire to Chicago

and sent an encrypted message, asking P.C. to come on line. Several minutes later, a jumbled mixture of letters and numbers began to cross the CRT. He tapped in the command to decipher the transmission, and words began to move across the screen. A sudden tingle coursed his spine. This was not simply a message that had been stored and mechanically transmitted; the unknown individual who had been his technological adversary was at that very moment talking to him.

When it was time to respond, Willard typed slowly.

P.C. I WANT TO HELP YOU. I BELIEVE I KNOW YOU. I WILL NOT TELL YOU HOW. BUT I BELIEVE YOU ARE PAUL SAGER. I WISH YOU NO HARM AND WILL TRY TO HELP YOU FIND YOUR WIFE. A MAN NAMED GEORGE ANDERS IS IN COMMAND HERE AND I WILL HAVE TO BREAK OFF IMMEDIATELY IF HE RETURNS. HE TRANSMITTED A MESSAGE TO THE NORTHEAST SECTOR WITHIN THE PAST HALF HOUR. HELEN SAGER IS SAFE AND IS TO REMAIN UNHARMED AT VERMONT REFUGE NUMBER TWO. I DO NOT KNOW WHERE THAT IS LOCATED PHYSICALLY. I BELIEVE IT MAY BE A FARM. MANY OF OUR LOCATIONS ARE FARMS AND RANCHES. I WILL ATTEMPT TO KEEP YOU INFORMED ABOUT HELEN SAGER, ABOUT YOUR WIFE, BUT I DO NOT KNOW HOW MUCH LONGER I CAN STAY HERE. W.Z.

Willard let out a breath and stretched, trying to relieve the tension that had built in his back. He did not have long to wait.

A minute later, a reply began to appear on the screen.

W.Z. YOUR MESSAGE FRIDAY ARRIVED TOO LATE TO PREVENT HELEN SAGER, YES, MY WIFE, IT CAME TOO LATE TO STOP THEM. I BELIEVE YOU AND THAT YOU WANT TO HELP. WE WOULD ALSO LIKE TO HELP YOU. YOUR ORIGINAL MESSAGE REMAINS ENCRYPTED. WE CANNOT HELP YOU IF WE DO NOT KNOW WHERE YOU ARE. IF WE ARE TO SAVE HELEN, IF WE ARE TO SAVE YOU, YOU MUST TELL US WHERE YOU ARE. WILL YOU? P.S.

Willard cleared the screen and stared at the blinking cursor. Though he had anticipated the question, he still was not sure how to answer it.

Slowly, he typed his response.

P.S. I WILL FOLLOW THIS TRANSMISSION WITH A MESSAGE DETAILING EVERYTHING I KNOW ABOUT THE ORGANIZATION. IT WILL BE ENCRYPTED WITH MY RSA CIPHER. WHEN THE TIME IS RIGHT, I WILL FIND A WAY TO TRANSMIT THE KEY. BUT I MAY NEED YOUR HELP. I WILL TELL YOU APPROXIMATELY

WHERE I AM IN EXCHANGE FOR NAMES AND PHONE NUM-
BERS OF PEOPLE IN THIS AREA WHO MAY BE ABLE TO HELP
ME IN AN EMERGENCY. I WILL NOT GO TO THE POLICE UNDER
ANY CIRCUMSTANCES. THESE MUST BE PEOPLE WHO WILL
BE WILLING TO HIDE ME AND ONE MAYBE TWO MORE PER-
SONS FOR A FEW DAYS UNTIL IT IS SAFE TO LEAVE. IF THIS
IS ACCEPTABLE, I WILL TELL YOU MY APPROXIMATE LOCA-
TION IN THE NEXT TRANSMISSION. THE ENCRYPTED MES-
SAGE FOLLOWS. W.Z.

While the message was being transmitted, Willard went to
the door and cracked it open. Seeing no one, he locked the
door and returned to the console.

A new message was being written on the screen.

W.Z. WE WILL AGREE TO SUPPLY YOU WITH THE NAMES
AND NUMBERS OF PEOPLE WHO WILL PROVIDE YOU WITH SAFE
HOUSES. HOWEVER, IT WILL TAKE A NUMBER OF HOURS TO
COMPILE THIS INFORMATION ONCE WE KNOW YOUR AP-
PROXIMATE LOCATION. WE WILL BE STANDING BY AT FOUR
P.M. EASTERN DAYLIGHT TIME AND WILL TRANSMIT THAT IN-
FORMATION WHEN YOU RESUME CONTACT. P.S.

Willard replied immediately.

P.S. YOU HAVE A DEAL. WE ARE LOCATED IN PARK COUNTY
IN CENTRAL COLORADO. I WILL NEED CONTACTS BOTH TO
THE EAST OF HERE IN COLORADO SPRINGS AND DENVER AS
WELL AS TO THE WEST IN SOME OF THE MOUNTAIN TOWNS.
IF POSSIBLE, I WILL RESUME CONTACT AT FOUR YOUR TIME.
I WANT TO HELP YOU. DON'T BETRAY ME. W.Z.

After signing off, Willard patched into the Federal Reserve's
San Francisco wire and tapped some commands on the keyboard; the current transactions that were going over the circuit
disappeared. In their place was the daily report, still in em-
bryonic stage. He typed another command; an instant later, he
saw the prime numbers that were the basis of his cipher surge
across the screen, crowding out the shorter transaction reports.

"Damn!" he cried. "I did it! I fucking did it!"

He looked at the time display. It was nearly noon. That
meant he had six hours to deactivate the fuse of the time bomb
he had just set. If he did not, his secret decryption key and the
encoded messages he had sent to Paul Sager would be automatically printed out that night with the daily report for Monday. He typed another command and put his decryption key at
the top of the Tuesday report. If anything happened that night

after he had deactivated the Monday report, P.S. would still get the information.

He grabbed a pile of computer printouts, left the trailer, and sat in the shade just inside the barn. Though the sun was hot, a cool breeze stirred the air. It was just after one o'clock when he saw Marlie emerge from the house with a large picnic basket. She had on a pair of skimpy cutoffs and a tank top. Even from a distance he could tell she was not wearing a bra.

Marlie was smiling, and when Willard leaned over to kiss her, she met him full on the mouth, her tongue teasing his.

"Why don't we skip lunch?" Willard asked.

Her smile broadened. "Aren't you hungry?"

He was grinning now. "What I'd like to eat is not in that basket."

She ran her tongue provocatively over her upper lip. "Sounds good."

"Hold it right there." Willard bounded up the stairs and returned a moment later with the sleeping bag. She followed him to the rear of the barn and helped him push aside some bales of hay.

"How about that?" she said. "A real roll in the hay."

Later, after they had dressed and had lunch, Willard rolled up the sleeping bag and suggested they walk. Marlie agreed, and they set off across a field. The land rose slightly before them, and as they passed below its crest, Willard glanced over his shoulder and saw the ranch house pass from view.

He took her hand. "That was so good. I mean, it was too good. I couldn't even begin to describe how good it was."

"Yes, it was," she said softly.

"I've been doing a lot of thinking, Marlie. About us."

"Me too."

"You have?" There was elation in his voice.

Marlie nodded. "There's something I want to share with you."

"Oh, Marlie. That's wonderful. Wonderful!"

She clasped his hand more tightly. "I want you to share the faith with me. I want you to join the church."

Willard's stomach fell.

Marlie continued. "You only see George. He's a politician, no different from thousands of other politicians who call themselves bishops, rabbies, bonzes, mullahs. Has any religion ever been free of politics? We're a minority. We're constantly being persecuted by the government. Don't you see? We have to fight back. If we don't, they'll destroy us."

Willard continued to walk in silence, holding her hand much more loosely now.

Enthusiasm sparked her voice. "We want to build a good society, a just society. We want to get people back to the land. We want to live in peace. The director has a beautiful vision of the future. You could be a part of that. You could share that with me."

"And George? Is he part of that future, too?"

"Forget him, Whiz. He's not what we're all about. He's just another politician."

"Then the director should get rid of him," said Willard. "If he's not what the church is all about, why does he hold so much power?"

"What more can I tell you?" Her voice was plaintive. "I've been at headquarters. I've seen George in action. He knows how to manipulate people. But he's just one man. He's not the faith. He's not what the church is all about."

"And what about Zed? I saw his body, his face. That was no accident. George killed him."

"You don't know that," she said.

"You didn't see him. I did. His forehead completely caved in. Blood and dirt all over his face. But the rock he supposedly fell on was clean. It was so clean you could stand on the bank and see the crystals sparkle in the sun."

"I don't believe it. George had no reason to hurt Zed. He was a believer."

Willard reached into his pocket and pulled out Zed's note. "I found this in the trailer after he was buried."

Marlie's hands began to tremble as she unfolded the paper and read it. "Oh, God," she said softly.

"And that's not all," said Willard. "George sent an urgent message to the Northeast sector head on Friday morning, ordering them to kidnap Helen Sager. You know why? Because they think her husband's working for the government against our program. She has nothing to do with it. In fact, she thinks her husband's dead—blown up in a car bomb."

Marlie stopped and looked away.

He grabbed her arms and turned her to face him. "Look, for all I know the director may be God himself. But George isn't. What he's doing to an innocent woman is wrong."

"And you can prove it?" Her voice was barely a whisper.

"You're damn right I can." He turned around, took her hand, and began striding toward the barn.

With the trailer door locked behind them, Marlie slowly read the two messages George had sent. Then she closed her eyes. "I've seen enough," she said.

"Will you leave with me?"

She hesitated a moment, and then nodded.

"It'll have to be tonight," he said. "I've transmitted the bomb to Chicago."

"You what?"

"It's encoded. They won't be able to read it without the key. They'll be getting that tonight."

"I-I don't understand."

"It's too complicated to explain, but I found a way to hide the key on the Chicago Switch. If it's not deactivated every day, it'll print out that night. We'll be gone by then." He began to smile. "I figure we can slip out of here after dark. Come to the trailer, like you usually do. Then we'll walk to the road and hitch a ride."

"Where will we go?"

"I'll have the names and numbers of people who can put us up. I've also got that six hundred dollars left over from Aspen. We'll have to travel light. Don't do anything unusual tonight. Jeans and a shirt, just like always. But pack a small suitcase—remember, you're going to have to carry it—and just before you leave the house, put it outside your bedroom window."

"What about Tom? We can't just leave him here."

"I've thought about that. He gets up early. I mean, he's usually got the truck running before I'm even out of bed most days. I'll write him a note and put it on the seat with Zed's note just before we leave, telling him to get the hell out of here, to just get in the truck and start driving."

"Okay," she said. "What do you want me to do?"

"The same as every day. Don't do anything that might make George suspicious." He kissed her, opened the door, and then watched her walk to the house.

It was nearly three o'clock when he established contact again with Paul.

The response was immediate.

W. Z. WE WERE WORRIED WHEN YOU DID NOT TRANSMIT AT FOUR EDT. GLAD YOU ARE THERE. WE HAVE SIX CONTACTS FOR YOU IN COLORADO. THEY HAVE BEEN TOLD THEY

MAY RECEIVE A CALL FROM SOMEONE WHOSE NAME COR-
RESPONDS TO THE INITIALS W. Z. THE LIST FOLLOWS THIS
TRANSMISSION. PLEASE ACKNOWLEDGE. P.S.

Willard copied the names and numbers on a slip of paper,
took off his shoe and put the paper in it. Then, he typed on
the keyboard.

P.S. MESSAGE RECEIVED. WE LEAVE TONIGHT LATE. THE
KEY WILL BE TRANSMITTED TO CHICAGO AT THAT TIME. AL-
LOW US TIME TO GET AWAY. W.Z.

The response followed promptly.

W.Z. AGREED. GODSPEED. P.S.

After dinner, Willard began deleting everything in the computer's memory that could be of use to George, including the
ciphers he would need to send encrypted messages to the eight
sectors. Shortly after nine, Marlie came to the trailer; the two
walked to the highway and stuck out their thumbs. A trucker
picked them up not five minutes later and gave Marlie an
appreciative leer as she climbed into the cab. She quickly turned
the ring on her hand so the stone was in her palm; it now looked
like a gold band. She told the driver that their van had broken
down in Salida while they were driving to Denver, where her
husband's folks lived. The driver glanced at her ring and then
at Willard and shook his head. For the next two hours, the
three of them sang country and western songs along with the
radio. The driver let them off in Denver, said good-bye to
Marlie, and gave Willard a long sidewise shake of the head.

"You one lucky sombitch, fella."

Willard smiled. "Yeah" he said. "I know."

CHAPTER 35

At nine P.M. on Monday evening, Wheeler walked into the Operations Center. He stood between Paul and Nancy.

"The JCS just cleared it," said Wheeler. "We'll have the complete resources of an airmobile company when we move against CED headquarters on Wednesday morning. We'll be launching out of Fort Carson, just south of Colorado Springs."

"Airmobile?" Paul asked. "We need helicopters?"

"To be frank, I don't know how much we're actually going to need. I'll be going to a meeting at the Pentagon at eight tomorrow morning. They don't have any current contingency plans for this sort of thing. But I assume we'll come up with some form of nonlethal attack—tear gas, riot control, that sort of thing."

"Riot control? Good God, Otis, it's only a handful of people with a computer."

"Take it easy, Paul. We're not going to bomb the place.

It's going to be minimum force and, as I said, nonlethal. We want to capture these people, not kill them."

Paul nodded.

"Any word on Helen?" Wheeler asked.

"No. They're continuing to circulate handbills with her picture and going house to house. A few people said they saw the car, but none of those leads panned out."

Wheeler shook his head grimly and then turned to Nancy. "You're set up on SIGINT, I take it."

"Yes," said Nancy. "As soon as we found out they were in Colorado, we started sweeping the microwave circuits. Anything going out from Colorado with an 802 digital header is being recorded automatically. We're zeroing in on exchanges in Central Vermont and using voice recognition of key words and phrases. We're also pulling all data transmissions."

"How's it going?"

"The way it usually does: slow."

Wheeler turned to Paul. "Look, if it makes you feel any better, Harrison told the President what happened, and he's pledged the full resources of the government to find Helen."

Paul nodded.

"And by full, he means the Army, the Air Force, Secret Service—whatever it takes to find her and get her back safely."

Paul looked up. "All it takes is one bullet."

Wheeler put his hand on Paul's shoulder. "They're not out to harm her. The transmission W.Z. sent us made that very clear. It's you they're after."

"But where's the ransom demand? It's been three days, and nothing. Not a word."

"I know how hard it must be for you. But we don't have any choice; we have to be patient. We've got thousands of people in New England looking for Helen. The press has picked up on it. If anyone's seen her . . ." He did not finish the thought.

After Wheeler left, Paul and Nancy spent most of the next hour silently staring at the console, waiting, hoping W.Z. would transmit the key. It was nearly eleven when Art Hamlin called from Chicago, excitement in his voice.

"I think we've got something." he said.

"What is it?" Paul asked.

"An anomaly on the daily report. In the San Francisco section."

"What is it?"

"Two *very* long numbers."

Paul felt a shiver pass through his body. "How long?"

"At least a hundred and fifty digits."

"Both of them?"

"Looks to be."

"This could be it," said Paul. "I want you to transmit those numbers immediately."

"Consider it done," said Hamlin.

Paul turned to Nancy. "Art's sending up some numbers." He glanced at his screen. "There they are." He faced her again. "See if they'll decrypt that cipher-text we got from W.Z."

She nodded and began tapping the keyboard in front of her. Too nervous to watch, Paul stared at the ceiling. A minute later, he felt her hand on his shoulder. The broad smile on her face answered his question.

While they were reading the message on the screen, high-speed laser printers were making copies for couriers to carry to Winchell and Wheeler at home. It was all there: names, dates, locations, computer programs. But when Paul saw the long list of public-key ciphers for each of the organization's sectors, he began to smile.

In an instant, he knew exactly how he would free Helen. He wouldn't need an airmobile company nor thousands of men combing the Green Mountains. No shots would be fired; no one would be hurt. Without moving anything other than his fingers, he would order her released the same way a man named George had ordered her kidnapped: by computer. He began laughing.

"What is it?" Nancy asked.

"We've got the bastards. We've got them!"

He cleared the screen and drafted a message.

URGENT. IMMEDIATE ACTION MUST BE TAKEN TO RELEASE HELEN SAGER. SUBJECT MUST IN NO WAY BE HARMED. RELEASE IN RURAL AREA. COMPLETE ACTION NO LATER THAN NINE TUESDAY MORNING. PROCEED THEREAFTER TO VERMONT REFUGE NUMBER ONE TO AWAIT FURTHER INSTRUCTIONS. G.

Paul compared his message to those "G" had sent. Satisfied that it looked authentic, he encrypted the order, using the northeast sector's public-key cipher, and transmitted it. That night he slept soundly for the first time in four days.

The light on the gray phone flashed shortly after ten the next morning. It was Harding Harrison.

"Good news, Dr. Cassidy."

"I know. Helen's been released."

"Good Lord, how'd you know? I just found out not two minutes ago."

"Let's just call it intuition," said Paul. "How is she?"

"Apparently just fine," said Harrison. "She was walking on a road near Barton. Flagged down a motorist and got a ride into town. Called her mother from there. We've had an agent in Stowe since Friday night; he relayed the word to Treasury. The Secretary just phoned me."

"And she's okay?"

"As far as we know, yes. She'll be seeing her doctor later this afternoon, but that's strictly routine."

When he finished talking to Harrison, he wrote Helen a letter on his machine and transmitted it over the network in code to Jim Guanti's electronic address. Then he called Guanti by phone.

"There's a message in your mailbox for my friend. Can you see it gets delivered this afternoon?"

"She's okay?" asked Guanti.

"Absolutely."

"Wonderful. I'll get that letter right now."

A few minutes later, the gray phone flashed again. It was Wheeler.

"Just got out of my meeting. Harrison told me the good news."

"Yeah. It is good news. How're things on the western front?"

"It's set for tomorrow. I'll be flying out of Andrews for Peterson Field about three. We'll be staging out of Fort Carson in the morning."

"What about me?"

"Aren't you going home?"

Paul thought about the five months he had spent in his quest for vengeance. Joe Cerri's murder. The attempt on his life. Helen's kidnapping. It took him barely a second to decide.

"I want to be there," he said.

"Okay," Wheeler replied. "Meet me in the V.I.P. Lounge at Andrews no later than two this afternoon."

The rotors beat a steady tattoo, the helmeted heads of every man in the cabin bobbing in rhythm, young faces mostly, jaunty smiles, gas masks unsnapped and dangling. Paul looked out the window at the deep green of the pine forests below, and then gazed north. A thin morning haze was poised over Colorado Springs; a tuft of snow at the summit of Pikes Peak shimmered in the sunlight. He turned his head; a young soldier who had been staring at him broke into an embarrassed grin. Paul nodded. Yeah, he thought, what the hell am I doing here?

At the briefing the night before, Wheeler had not introduced Paul by name; he referred to him only as a senior intelligence official from Washington. The word had obviously traveled through the company that a super-spy was in their midst, and that morning Paul could see some of the men giving him sidelong glances. At first he enjoyed the cachet. Now, as the helicopters were gaining altitude to cross the Front Range of the Rockies, he felt as if an anvil had been dropped into the pit of his stomach. He slipped his hands beneath the flak jacket and began rubbing his stomach, trying to relieve the pressure. At that moment, he would gladly have exchanged all his worldly goods for the warmth, serenity, and seclusion of a flush toilet.

Wheeler tapped him on the arm and motioned for him to look at the map he had unfolded on his lap. Paul leaned over and watched as Wheeler wordlessly marked where they were and where they were headed. Then he pointed to the top of his watch and tapped his gas mask. It was 7:35. At 8:00 A.M. the attack would begin.

Familiar with terrain maps from hiking with Helen in Vermont, Paul found himself tracing imaginary paths through the mountains, following ridge lines, looking for saddles. His thoughts inexorably turned to Helen.

It would be nearly ten in Vermont. She would be at her mother's house, breakfast long since finished, perhaps sitting at the kitchen table her father had made in the first winter of his marriage. Fashioned from green wood, the planks had warped before Helen was born, and no leg was the same length. Her father had repeatedly threatened to reduce the shaky old piece to kindling but, knowing his wife's sentimental attachment to it, never did. After he died, it became a hallowed memento, and there were times when Helen and her mother would dawdle over coffee at the table, its top worn smooth by four decades of platters and glasses, her mother staring out the window toward the empty milking shed, absently fingering the familiar planks her young groom had sawed and planed, tracking an odd groove with her fingernail, the ministration of her hands an act of worship.

Three sharp blasts from the buzzer jolted Paul from his

reverie. Everyone in the cabin began snapping their masks into place. Fumbling with the rubbery mask, Paul tried to pull it across his face, but the gear had been twisted. Wheeler leaned over, straightened it, and guided the snap into place. When Paul looked up, he saw the soldiers had been watching. Yeah, he thought, some super-spy.

The helicopters hovered east of the ranch. Paul recognized the house and barn from the reconnaissance photos, but they had not prepared him for such utter desolation. The only signs of life amid the sere terrain and dessicated creeks were clumps of yellow grass and a stand of cottonwoods. No crops, no animals grazing, no trace of a human presence except for the pickup truck beside the house.

There was a sudden blur as three helicopters in a perfect V-formation passed below his ship, skimming the ground, casting long shadows across the land. Moments before reaching the barn, they began emitting a fine gray mist that hung momentarily in the air and then wafted down as gently as a silk scarf, enveloping the house and barn. The ships pulled up, their green and tan camouflage stark against the blue sky, wheeled 180 degrees, and made a second pass, blanketing the buildings again. They flew well past the barn, climbed straight up, turned, and hovered above the field.

Wheeler nudged Paul and gave him an upraised thumb. When he returned to the window, he saw three more choppers heading toward the buildings, but they stopped a few hundred yards short, hovering just above the ground. One by one, barely more than second apart, the troops hit the ground, quickly fanned out, and began advancing toward the buildings in a semicircle from the east. Wheeler tapped Paul's arm and made a diving gesture with his hand. Seconds later, their ship banked and dropped as suddenly as a roller coaster.

Paul felt uncomfortably hot, the edge of the flak jacket chafing his neck and gut, the gas mask slithering on a film of sweat, grit grinding into his face, hard rubber pressing on the bridge of his nose. He was breathing heavily, the pulse pounding in his forehead, the arteries constricted by the helmet's tight webbing. It could have been an hour or no more than a minute; but suddenly the ship nosed up, the sergeant slid the door open, and the men began moving out, jumping the last foot or so to the ground and running to the side. Wheeler tapped Paul, who strained to get up but couldn't. The colonel eased him back into his seat with a hand on his shoulder and tapped the seat-belt buckle. Paul quickly undid the catch and headed for the door, Wheeler following. The ship immediately pulled up, the rotor kicking up a swirl of dust, and hovered two hundred feet above and behind them, machine guns silently trained on the buildings.

The squad strung out in a line and began moving at a trot toward the barn, with Wheeler and Paul behind them. Then a soldier from the first contingent came through the rear door of the barn, his rifle at a relaxed position, muzzle toward the ground, and signaled thumbs-up. The squad stopped running and began to walk.

The barn was empty. All that was left of the trailer were tire tracks in the dirt-covered cement floor. There was no trace of the electronic brain that had created the nation's worst financial crisis since the Crash of 1929.

The house, too, was empty. Though there was food in the refrigerator and sheets and blankets on the unmade beds, there was not a scrap of paper in the trash cans—no trace at all of the people who had inhabited the rooms only a day or two before.

Outside, the red pickup truck had been stripped of its license plates. There was nothing in the glove compartment nor in the cargo bed to identify an owner or driver.

The sole human trace was in the cottonwood grove. A platoon leader reported what appeared to be a grave.

Wheeler used his radio to relay a message to the Colorado State Patrol and Park County Sheriff's Office. Then, he ordered the helicopters to land and the troops to form into ranks in a field two hundred yards from the house. The air clear, they doffed their masks. When the sheriff and the state police arrived, Wheeler had the platoon leader show them the unmarked grave. It was now strictly a local matter; the Government of the United States was no longer interested.

Ten minutes later, the troops boarded the helicopters for the flight back to Fort Carson. Wheeler, the impression of the mask still etched in red on his face, sat slumped in his seat, eyes closed but not asleep. Along with the rest of the troops, Paul had shed his helmet and flak jacket, stowing them beneath the seat. Cool air filled the cabin; the men were relaxed now, occasionally talking in half-shouts above the din of the rotor blades.

While Wheeler was talking on a secure line to Harding Harrison at the White House, Paul placed a collect call to Vermont from a pay phone in the hall. Before the operator could finish asking if the charges would be accepted, Helen blurted out: Oh God, yes! He had not heard that much excitement in her voice since the first time he phoned her nearly twelve years ago. At first, both of them tried to talk at once; then both were silent. Soon, they were laughing. He told her where he was. When will you be coming home? she asked. As soon as I can, he told her.

An Air Force executive jet was waiting for Paul and Wheeler at Peterson Field; lunch was served with a California Colombard. Famished, exhausted, yet exhilarated, Paul savored every bite, every sip of wine. No meal had ever tasted better.

Wheeler refilled their glasses. Paul took a long pull of the wine, settled back in his seat, and gazed at the checkerboard fields passing beneath them.

"Tastes good, doesn't it?"

Paul held the glass by the stem and watched the sunlight play with the pale straw-colored liquid. "Very good," he replied.

Wheeler chuckled. "Oh, the wine's good enough, but I had something else in mind. The taste of victory."

"Victory? No," said Paul. "I'm just glad it's over."

Wheeler sipped his wine and set down the glass. "It isn't, you know."

"What isn't?"

"The war," said Wheeler. "Oh, we won a skirmish, all right. To put it in classic terms, we forced the enemy to retire from the field."

"And that isn't enough?"

"It sure beats losing." He paused. "But no, I don't think it's enough. There are too many other fields where he could suddenly strike us again."

"We had them beaten technologically," said Paul. "Every transaction was going through. It might not have been very convenient for NSA, having some of their best equipment tied up with bank transactions, but it worked."

"You're right," said Wheeler. "And it's not as if the CED is going to get away scot-free. The FBI, Internal Revenue, and a lot of other agencies are going to be hot on their ass."

"What is it, then?"

Again, he sipped his wine. "What bothers me is the nature of these shadow wars. We've been able to prevent terrorists from getting nuclear weapons, and though the trade in conventional arms is enormous, it presents no direct threat to this country.

"But high technology is another matter. We can't control that, because we can't stop people from thinking. And if we've learned anything in the past few months, it is how very dependent we are on computers and telecommunications. We can't live without them."

"Agreed," said Paul. "But I don't see any reason for pessimism. If nothing else, maybe this whole thing will serve to wake a few people up."

"I certainly hope so. But I don't think we've seen the last of these shadow wars. Or phantom enemies."

Paul nodded.

Wheeler turned to face his companion. "I was talking with Dr. Simpson yesterday just before we left. He told me that, after the crisis was over, he would appoint me to head a special task force on technological security."

"Well, congratulations." Paul glanced at the silver eagles on his epaulets. "Looks like you're in for a star."

"Perhaps," said Wheeler. "But this task force is not the sort of thing one man can do alone. I'll need the best brains this country has to offer. Engineers. Scientists." He paused. "Mathematicians."

"Oh, no," said Paul. "Are you thinking what I think you're thinking?"

Wheeler was grinning.

"No," said Paul, voice rising. "Absolutely not!"

"I don't want you to make up your mind now," said Wheeler. "I just want you to consider it."

"No offense, Otis," said Paul. "But the next time you need a mathematician, a computer type . . ."

"Yeah?"

"For God's sake, call somebody else."